They entered a larger room lit intermittently by the emergency light. Lines of piping and wiring on each side led to a focal point at the far end of the small room: a makeshift unit covered with bottled liquids, meters, wiring, and tubing, all converging at the center. The hidden travel pod.

It sat heavily on a low base, black and sinister, and at its feet Goren observed through yellow flashes the body of a young woman.

Tannor reached her first. She kneeled down, Goren panting over her shoulder, and rolled the woman gingerly onto her back. Fil took the other side, feeling for a pulse, watching for breathing. Dark blood covered the woman's torso in streaks, distracting at first from the realization that she was naked. Goren shifted uncomfortably, unsure how to help.

"She's breathing. She has a pulse," Fil said.

Tannor swept thick dark hair away from the woman's face.

And they recognized her.

Fil whispered, *"Gods in stars—"* just as Goren yelped.

Relai Mora Aydor. The queen of Arden.

Goren followed instinct and looked away, sure that seeing the leader of their planet, the leader of the coalition, *the queen herself,* so exposed would lead to some inevitable doom. His knees hit stone.

- Are the gods not just? -

- Oh no, child. What would become of us if they were? -

C.S. Lewis, *Till We Have Faces*

SHE IS THE END

BOOK ONE OF THE VADA CHRONICLES

SHE IS THE END

A.C. WESTON

She Is the End
Published by A.C. Weston
Copyright © 2018 A.C. Weston
Cover art by Kavya Tiwari

ISBN 978-0-9998716-0-7

Published by A.C. Weston
First edition, March 2018
This book is also available in print at most online retailers.
Visit www.sheistheend.com to contact the author or find her on Twitter @acwestonwrites.

For Tallulah, Rosie, and Nellie.
Space!

CONTENTS

EPISODE I:

WAKE

SHE WOKE BLIND to the scream of a siren.

Naked and encased in a standard travel pod, Relai spat out the dead breathing mask and heaved in a panicked breath. She pulled her face wide and horrified until her sealed eyelids tore open, blinked, and recognized drops of condensation forming on the gray plastic above her face. She was lying on her back.

Her pulse throbbed in her neck, in her temples, and she knew she wasn't getting enough air. *Slow down, slower, then—*

No light and no air meant the pod wasn't receiving power. She wrenched her hands out of the fluid-filled trough molded to her body, feeling the nutrient needles tear out of the skin on each wrist, and hit the cold forward shell of the travel pod.

These pods opened at the head. Relai buried her terror and tried to clear her mind. Her wrists hurt, sharp like a slap, and the pain helped her focus. No power. The pods sealed electronically; she only had to push open the cap above her head to get air.

Claustrophobia was not a problem for her, though fear of drowning certainly was. Drowning probably felt similar to this.

She kicked her feet out of the trough, wiggled and pushed up on the balls of her feet to loosen the material around her. The forward face of the pod curved only a few inches above her, too close to bend an arm at the elbow.

Fear began to win out, wracking her limbs with sharp jerks and loosening the pod's hold on her body. Her muscles were getting desperate, no matter how calm she tried to keep her mind. They were panicking all on their own.

Relai managed to pivot one arm across the front of her body, caving in her stomach and then her ribcage, reaching desperately up to where the cushion around her conformed to the pod wall. Stars lit up her vision, multi-colored, warning that she'd soon lose consciousness. Her chest heaved in and out but the meager air that filled the pod no longer held any oxygen. She could take a breath but it did nothing, gave her *nothing*—her wrists were bleeding and the wetness helped her arm slide further. She felt the space opening wider and her fingers met a seam—her muscles screamed—the cap gave way—

She gasped—

Letting out pitiful wails with each flush of new air, Relai grasped the lip of the pod and pulled. Little by little, the rubbery material relaxed further, allowing her other arm to snake up and aid her escape. She heaved, rocking her body up and sliding on her sweat and blood to the rhythm of the wailing siren, and with a cry she slid entirely out of the pod and crumpled three feet down. Yellow light marked her vision for a split second before the back of her head hit the floor and she blacked out.

∘∘●∘∘

Four floors up, Goren Dray nearly dropped his gun from fright. He scanned the darkness of the vineyard stretching out past the wall of what would appear to any passersby to be an ancient, eroding Tuscan town, searching for signs of the villains attacking their base. Nothing.

"Is that smoke? I think I see smoke."

Captain Fass ignored him.

"It's too dark to see smoke," Goren told himself. "It's nothing."

They'd lost communication with the fifty or so other guards currently posted at the eastern hemisphere base just before the security system went down, while Goren had been patrolling alone, so he'd run to the closest commanding officer looking for orders.

"It's been a half an hour; why isn't the system back up?" Goren said. "It's weird not hearing anyone else in my ear."

Fass sipped his tumbler of illicit honey-colored alcohol, his face beginning to flush from it. "Mellick is working on it. Don't expect much."

Goren expected a lot. The base had been only sparsely staffed in the decades following the Tennan War, but it still had its uses. Enough negotiations needed neutral territory (and enough High Court members needed vacations) that the coalition still maintained military bases on the protectorate planet of Earth, and Technical Sergeant Tannor Mellick, known genius, had arrived just a few weeks after Goren to bring them up to date. She didn't come soon enough.

Goren was barely out of training and he'd never even fired a live weapon at a real human being. He was not prepared for this.

"*Shit*," he muttered slightly hysterically, pacing from window to window. Why hadn't they replaced this colored Earthan glass with unbreakable stuff? This base was such crap.

Fass had the better weapon, so he could relax against the mantle and stare into the fire like a handsome philosopher or something. Goren's generator gun only shot pulses of plasma-bound electricity that could be tweaked to shock or penetrate the skin, or both. Fass's needle gun, on the other hand, held poisonous slivers of metalock. Metalock would kill you instantly if you even touched it. Why did Fass carry such a dangerous weapon? Goren wasn't going to ask. He valued his face.

"How are you so relaxed?" he blurted out. "Who could get past our systems? Do we really have valuable documents stored here? WHY?"

The captain finished his drink, stood, and swiftly gripped Goren's collar in his massive hands. "Cross in front of me one more time. "

Fass was four inches taller and thirty pounds heavier, and he probably sharpened glass on his jawline. Goren shook his head, mouth open.

"I think this fun tonight will be good for you." Captain Fass released Goren and smirked as he tugged awkwardly at his shirt, trying to get it straight under his close-fitting jacket. "Now get out there and search the street, building by building."

"But—but we're supposed to stick toge—"

Fass glared. Goren shut up.

"Get going. Maybe you'll do the coalition a favor and get yourself shot."

Fass shoved him into the hallway and slammed the ancient painted door.

Goren stood frozen like a tensed rabbit for a moment, then decided that speed was his best option. He had to run into other guards eventually, right? The walls loomed unnervingly dark, the ubiquitous bands of interactive tape blank against the restored Tuscan masonry. It was like being transported back in time to a terrifying other universe where he'd been born on Earth instead of Arden.

He couldn't hear his own footsteps with that useless siren wailing, not that it would matter if these enemies brought even the simplest sensors, and he did no more than peek inside each room, gun tucked to his chest. Every doorway, another chance to get shot in the face.

He'd already triple-checked his gen-gun's power, but he flipped out the charge tab and frantically pulled the cord, sending the cylinder spinning to build up the stored energy just in case. These weapons had been selected for off-world bases because they didn't require ammunition, but right now Goren was cursing the lack of good, solid bullets. Who needed ammunition, anyway? Not disposable seventeen-year-olds.

Their building was empty. He had to face the street next.

Goren eased his head out, looked left and right, then forced his body to follow. It was a narrow street of cobbled stone, not much to hide behind save a few recessed doorways. He immediately wished he'd chosen to travel over the rooftops instead. That's what the invading criminals were probably doing—they might be looking down on him and laughing *right now*. He whipped his head up.

Nothing.

The adrenaline alone was going to kill him at this rate.

Then he saw a foot poking out of a doorway down the street and he forgot about himself for a second. He dashed and found a pair of guards unconscious—or dead—just inside an unlit stairway.

He felt his face go all tingly and he nearly threw up as he crouched beside them. He was new here, but he *knew them*. These were people he played slateball with during their off hours. And sometimes during work hours. They were older than him—Fil Tars by five years, Sorret Palia by one, but she sparred like a junkie on smokepowder—and better guards in general. Goren didn't stand a chance against whatever troop of enemies had descended upon their quiet little base. He was going to die.

He whispered every curse word he'd ever learned as he shook Sorret, then Fil, glancing up and down the stairs nervously. She didn't move, but Fil groaned and stretched like he was waking from a nap.

"...Hit me upside the head. Didn't see who, how many. They were headed setward, did you see them?"

They both turned in the direction of this planet's sunset, realizing together: they weren't far from the security room. It made sense; anyone trying to restart the security system would be a target. Then again, that was also the direction of the armory.

Goren heaved Fil to his feet, so elated he wasn't alone anymore that he extended his life expectancy by at least an hour. Fil was taller, broad-chested, and heroic-looking, and he always seemed to know what he was doing.

"I haven't seen anyone," Goren whispered. "I hope they're going to the documents room, 'cause I left the captain in there alone. He shoved me off to check for intruders building-by-building and die. Do you know where everyone is?"

Fil winced and steadied himself. There was a little blood on his head, but not enough to worry. They both flinched when a small explosion from a few streets over rattled the windows. "Dealing with that, let's hope. We're going to get the main power back on, since no one else has bothered."

"Because they're dead, I bet," Goren pouted.

"I'm not dead, if that's any encouragement." Fil felt Sorret's neck to find her pulse and, seeming satisfied that his partner would live, reached for his holster. Empty.

Fil turned back to Goren and wrenched the gun out of his hands.

"Hey! Give me back my—"

"It's not yours anymore," Fil said, turning around. "Come on, we're going over to security. Pretend it's a game, like in training school."

"No one got covered in blood in training school!"

Moving quickly down the street, Fil flashed Goren a grin. "Then your cohort clearly never had any fun."

Goren glanced back at Sorret.

"Do you think it's okay to leave—"

But Fil was nearly out of sight, so Goren hurried after.

That gun was definitely still his.

∘∘●∘∘

"Ha! At least I got the siren to turn off!"

"Sure, Mellick. We wouldn't want to wake anyone during the attack."

"Shut up. Everyone's already awake." Tannor Mellick attempted to steady her hands so that her partner, Lorn Vesnick, might not notice her nervousness. He was busy peering into the dark street from his spot against the security room wall, grumpy and silent after the alarms wrenched him out of bed; Tannor hadn't been sleeping when they went off. Strands of her curly blond hair stuck in the sweat on her forehead and she slicked them away with the back of her hand.

"Heat—sectors three and five—locking mechanisms—air flow—generators—" she rattled through the list in her head, evaluating multiple systems at once. The wall in front of her flashed diagnostics bubbles, dead video feed, and error messages.

Lorn was not the tech sergeant here, so he wouldn't have caught the pattern, but Tannor was following a delicate order. Her hands flew across the rippling metamercurial surface of the desk in front of her, the key fields shifting as she progressed. She was a musician playing her instrument, and if her partner had bothered to notice he might have been awed by her skill. Lorn, however, was busy watching for the threat of death lurking just outside the security room door.

He was also busy glancing at her chest, or her ass—whichever faced him at a given moment. Men had been that way since she turned thirteen, grew three inches taller, and developed breasts in one year; they were all exhausting and boring and they could ogle themselves or full-life celebrity entertainment feeds for all she cared. She'd stick to computers.

Then Tannor's brain processed a piece of information caught on the slightest edge of her attention. She slowed her fingers and murmured, "Accessory power... where did this come from?" She asked the system and it responded with a screen of details. "It just showed up a couple months ago, buried under the extra power we needed for dock repairs... The captain signed off on it. Wow, it's a huge amount of power. Leading to what? Sub-basement auxiliary..." She pulled her way through the map of energy expenditure across the base, zeroing in on the mysterious red blip. "What is that? A storage room? There's no storage room in the catacombs."

She turned to Lorn. "Right?"

He scoffed. "Not high on my list of priorities right now, Mellick."

She turned back to her screen, glaring at the glow. She was one of the soldiers responsible for the base's security program—how was she supposed to do her job when they didn't tell her everything about the base?

Her superiors were under the impression that they could lock certain information behind passwords and other more creative security measures. They were mistaken.

Like a wild beast tamed, the system told her what she needed to know: "A transport pod?"

Tannor could think of a few scenarios in which a travel pod would be hidden at Arden's less-popular Earth base, and none of them boded well for the unlucky soul trapped inside. An ill courtier awaiting the development of a treatment for an embarrassing disease; a political prisoner kept silent by the Aydors until the right time for execution; the daughter of someone important waiting out an unacceptable pregnancy; like a stone skipping across a calm pond, Tannor's mind moved quickly to a conclusion:

"We've got to get that person out of there."

Lorn snorted. "Protect the security room, actually, is what we've got to do. You sure you're reading that data right, *Sergeant?*"

Tannor briefly considered slapping him in his callous face, but Lorn was a dick and she wouldn't mind getting away from his presence.

"Fine. I'll go myself." She drew her gen-gun and pushed past Lorn into the darkened hallway. The short girl from the poorer side of Kilani hadn't made it this far in life by hesitating.

Tannor didn't make it ten feet before she caught sight of two figures creeping stealthily toward her, silhouetted in the shaft of light from one of the window slits in the wall of stone. She trained her weapon on the first person's head and ordered them to identify themselves.

Then the emergency lights flashed again and she let out a small groan of relief. Corporal Fil Tars waved, an amused expression on his face and a glowing gun in his hand.

○○●○○

To Goren's shock, they reached the security center without a sign of trouble. Fil had no problem leading the way and Goren went through severe bowel pains taking up the rear, but it all worked out because Goren probably would've accidentally shot Tannor Mellick before he gave himself a chance to recognize her.

"Very fierce, Sergeant, I like it." Fil approached her quickly and Goren stuck close behind, willing himself not to cower.

"I am so glad you didn't kill us!" he exclaimed.

"Why aren't you armed, Private?" she asked.

He scowled at the wall.

Tannor pushed past them both, speaking quickly. "Come with me. There's a travel pod hidden in the catacombs next to the dock and with the power out someone might be dying right now. There'll be guns stocked in the dock."

Fil followed, drawing up beside her and matching her pace. "A hidden travel pod? I didn't know anything about that, did you?"

"No, just found out while I was trying to turn power back on. It's been there for months—"

"—Since that time the dock was closed for maintenance," he finished. Their superiors were hiding something down there. Someone.

Goren took up the rear, agitated for a whole new set of reasons. "Why would anyone hide a travel pod here? Shouldn't we deal with the enemies who have infiltrated our base before we go searching for an imaginary person who may or may not be dying?"

"Shut up," Tannor snapped. "We're not going to let you get killed if that's what you're worried about."

"What if *I'm* not going to let *you* get killed?" he countered. No one bothered to point out the ridiculousness of his question.

The dock sat underneath the property's immense vineyard, six concentric blocks away and six stories down. That was one of the advantages of choosing such a remote city—no roads passed close enough for spectators to see the vineyard drop, split, and reveal a pit filled with alien ships. Goren knew exactly what they'd find in the dock: a diplomatic groundship, the small jumper they just used for traveling between the Earth bases, two bomber drones that had never even been deployed, and a small fleet of single-person skimmers.

They heard another explosion, back in the direction of the security room, and Goren almost elbowed Tannor in the back.

(He wished he were only sneaking into the dock to borrow one of those skimmers, instead of slinking along in the spooky darkness to find a crypt demon or something. He'd slip silently over the outer wall, put down the front shield, and set the machine to hover just above the treetops as he glided lazily through the hills with the wind on his skin and only the threat of a halfhearted reprimand waiting for him when he returned. And as long as he was daydreaming, Tannor would show up on a skimmer next to him wearing a low-cut dress. With a midnight picnic in tow. And mention how much she liked younger men.)

They made it to the elevator leading down to the dock without coming across any dead soldiers, and thankfully this power grid was still functioning. Tannor pressed a series of icons on the elevator door and the unit dropped them at a stomach-churning speed. The door slid up to reveal reflections of the flashing emergency light retreating into endless dark, and Goren steadied himself by focusing on the curves of—

"Do you have our backs or are you staring at my ass, Goren?" Tannor whispered without turning her head, and the quiet of the cavernous room swallowed up her words.

"Uh, no?" he tried.

"The clever man does both," Fil muttered, then scampered forward before Tannor could retaliate.

Goren couldn't help but admire the massive diplomatic groundship as they snuck along the wall. It was black with silver accents, more masculine than the base's last model but streamlines in a way that disguised its bulk. It was the perfect vehicle for shuttling diplomatic personnel from the planet's surface to interstellar ships waiting at Oliver Station at the edge of this solar system. He'd probably never get to ride in it.

At least this place was a resort planet now. Back when the bases were first established, the Vada Coalition had been busy driving out the last vestiges of the Sevati, the nasty alien overlords who'd snatched humans from Earth in the first place to use as slave labor to colonize the other habitable planets in this galaxy. The galaxy was now properly Sevati-free and Goren was grateful, because serving back then would've been no fun.

They reached the section of wall concealing the storage room. A bulky mechanics rig sat in front of the entrance, but Tannor switched on its hover and pushed it aside easily. They saw the faint outline of what must be a door.

Tannor looked it over carefully, switched her pad into diagnostics mode, then mumbled about being locked out of wireless access and found a contact point along the tape instead. The door slid down and away.

A long, dark tunnel, shoulder-wide and carved by hand into the bedrock a millennium ago, stared back at them like a gaping throat. Cool, moist air rushed over them like breath.

The passage was lined with shelf-like pockets which held piles of artfully arranged human bones, the victims of some long-ago plague. Earthan religious practices must've prevented them from atomizing their remains, and Goren couldn't fathom how this planet wasn't entirely composed of dead bodies by now. What did they do with them all? No wonder these people feared the corpses rising up. Trying to ignore the toothy grins of the skulls he passed, Goren reminded himself to be thankful that he had been born on a developed planet.

Goren once again took up the rear as they crept through the catacomb. More danger lay behind than ahead, but he split his fear between criminal attackers and the long-dead skeletons and tried not to completely lose his mind. The walls were not watching him. *No.*

What if the attackers are shusa, he thought suddenly. The unholy offspring of human and Sevati, shusasevati were the strange and powerful creatures of horror that his mother used to tell him about when he'd beg for war stories from the past... Sometimes they were giants, all fifteen feet tall with an extra set of arms; in other stories, they could slip out of this dimension and into another one in the blink of an eye. Some of them could fly. They were infected with Sevati blood to serve evil ends, able to look human but just *wrong* enough to terrify any real human.

Goren brushed a wall and nearly yelped in fear.

They entered a larger room lit intermittently by the emergency light. Lines of piping and wiring on each side led to a focal point at the far end of the small room: a makeshift unit covered with bottled liquids, meters, wiring, and tubing, all converging at the center. The hidden travel pod.

It sat heavily on a low base, black and sinister, and at its feet Goren observed through yellow flashes the body of a young woman.

Tannor reached her first. She kneeled down, Goren panting over her shoulder, and rolled the woman gingerly onto her back. Fil took the other side, feeling for a pulse, watching for breathing. Dark blood covered the woman's torso in streaks, distracting at first from the realization that she was naked. Goren shifted uncomfortably, unsure how to help.

"She's breathing. She has a pulse," Fil said.

Tannor swept thick dark hair away from the woman's face.

And they recognized her.

Fil whispered, *"Gods in stars—"* just as Goren yelped.

Relai Mora Aydor. The queen of Arden.

Goren followed instinct and looked away, sure that seeing the leader of their planet, the leader of the coalition, *the queen herself*, so exposed would lead to some inevitable doom. His knees hit stone.

The focal point of the galaxy itself was *here*, unconscious in an ancient tomb? Four planets' worth of people seemed to be staring at them, judging their every decision, and Goren couldn't stand that pressure. His brain went mute.

Fil peeled out of his uniform jacket and Tannor tucked it around the queen, then zipped it up with her arms bundled inside. Fil watched from the corner of his eye and turned as soon as he could. He lifted her urgently, her head lolling back as he adjusted to make sure she stayed bundled in the jacket. Tannor said, "Hold her head, Goren," and he did. *Stars above, he held her head in his hands,* his fingers tangled in the sticky pod wax and sweat in her hair. She hadn't given them permission to touch her and they were doing it anyway.

They rushed back through the hall lined with skeletons, scraping stone as they huddled along, tense and silent.

"My room," Tannor whispered.

∘∘●∘∘

ii.

In the documents room, just below a temple belfry, a light began to blink on Captain Fass's tablet. It took him a moment to notice it from his position reclining in a leather chair, dwelling on the qualities of his whiskey. He'd left the tablet on an end table across the room, and he sighed as he pulled himself up to investigate, his needle gun leaned carelessly against a wine rack. He lifted the tablet and read the warning notice.

He'd set up this alarm himself, separate from the base's computer. It had been tripped.

"So they've opened up the storage room," he murmured, and gave a short laugh. He couldn't believe things could be so simple. "That's the end of that."

He strode back to his drink and his chair. Outside, rain began to splatter against the stained-glass window.

∘∘●∘∘

Goren barely breathed until Tannor pulled the door to her room shut and turned its meager single lock. She lit several candles, and the comforting light helped Goren get back on steadier ground. He'd never been in Tannor's room, obviously; it was larger than his, and she didn't have to share. She hadn't decorated much since arriving a month ago, if he didn't count dirty laundry, circuits, and alumeta power cells as decoration. The candles were her only native decor, and now they were melting away.

He positioned himself at the door while Tannor pulled undergarments, and then her robe, onto the queen's body. How glad was Goren that Tannor chose to wear bras, even though their regulation undershirts were supposedly designed so women wouldn't need them? *Very, very glad.*

(He would have been even more thankful if Tannor had any clean shirts for the queen to wear, instead of just underwear, but it was hardly the time to argue about chores.)

"How much time do we have?" Tannor whispered.

Fil moved purposefully from window to window, shutting the curtains. "If no one comes soon, we're going to have to move her." He lowered his voice and spoke only to Tannor, although Goren could hear every word. "Did you know she was here?"

She shook her head, curls bouncing. "I thought they just wanted data."

Fil glanced around grimly. "I don't want anyone to die tonight. Understand?"

"Yes."

Goren tried to chime in, agree, but Tannor went on whispering as though he didn't exist. He picked up her gen-gun and took up watch at the door.

"Someone must have known she was here—why didn't anyone check on her?" Tannor snatched up her tablet. They all knew she couldn't restart the security program from there, but it looked like she was going to try anyway.

"Maybe she hid herself. Maybe no one on base knows she's here," Fil muttered. "Or the ones who do ran, or the intruders killed them already. Did they mention anything, whoever told you to—"

"No!" Tannor's eyes darted to Goren, then back to Fil. "I'm not a part of this!"

Fil pulled the cord to charge his gen-gun. "We're part of it now."

Goren felt a chill creep over his back. They trained the best guards for three extra years before they got to join the Regent Service and protect any of the royal family—this was too much responsibility. He thought he might be sick.

Tannor nodded toward Goren. "And him?"

Fil huffed. "Three months out of training? He's with us. He'll listen to me."

An unexpected surge of annoyance helped Goren focus, and he frowned. "I can hear everything you're saying. What's going on? You're not—you're not Unity, right? I mean, ha, uh, I mean—" He inched the gen-gun up.

They both stared at him.

Then Fil batted the gun down and huffed. "No, we're not Unity. Someone has invaded our base and they're trying to kill our queen." He hesitated. Glanced at Tannor. "We might have accidentally helped."

Tannor glared back at him but didn't disagree. "I had no idea, Fil." She turned her back to Fil and addressed Goren, pleading. "I had no idea! I got an order from a—well—from an authority I trust very much. I disabled our computers using a randomized code eater so I wouldn't be able to put it back together right away." Goren gaped in horror and she rushed on, "They just needed data! We're not violent. We're not terrorists!"

"And what about you?" Goren demanded to Fil.

"I, ah, I uploaded a virus into our communication systems so our comms wouldn't work for a short time," he sighed. "They're not on yet. Should be soon, though!"

"And you didn't know she was here?"

"No."

"Of course not!" Tannor fidgeted next to their queen, busying herself by cleaning and bandaging the bleeding spots on the young woman's wrists.

Goren wrung his hands around his gun, sputtering. "Why would you ever—how can you just—we're all gonna—" Then light dawned on his face. He relaxed.

Tannor glanced from him to Fil and back. "What?"

"Oh, I always thought I'd die from my own stupidity, not someone else's." He let his gen-gun come to a rest against his leg. "It's kind of a relief."

•

Tannor rubbed her eyes and willed herself not to strangle him. He was only seven inches taller. She could do it.

Then she turned their focus back where it should have been anyway: their great and damaged queen.

Tannor used a corner of her silk bed sheet to dab away the vernix on the queen's face. "Nothing in my kit is going to fix whatever's wrong with her. We need a med scanner." Scanners were scarce on Earth, so some guards had started exploring native medical techniques. She knew just enough about them to be very skeptical.

"Nah," Fil grabbed the med kit from the floor next to Tannor and she stood back. "Something in here might wake her up."

Goren stepped a bit closer. "Do you need me to—"

"No," she and Fil replied in unison.

Fil reached a long plastic packet of single-dose drugs and started breaking out capsules. Tannor watched him twist off the end of one and reveal its tiny needle. "Epi, sure, amphet... morph, she's probably in pain, right? Let's wake her up, kneel and bow and so forth, and then ask what the hell she's doing here."

Goren gasped. "Don't let her hear you say 'hell!' She's the *queen*!"

Fil raised a fist, needle down. "She's not awake yet."

He plunged the needle into the queen's thigh and squeezed until the clear liquid disappeared, then twisted open another capsule.

"Do you—do you know anything about what you're putting into her?" Tannor asked.

Fil shrugged and jabbed again.

Tannor and Goren shared a nervous look.

Then Fil gave her the third drug, then a fourth he didn't identify.

"Are you trying to kill her?" Tannor exclaimed. Goren moved from one foot to another.

"Water!" he cried suddenly, and both of the other guards jumped. "When she wakes up she's going to want water." He ran to Tannor's private bathroom and she debated chasing after him, but then the queen moaned.

Goren scrambled back, splashing water everywhere. They watched, tense and quiet, and Tannor knelt close, put a hand on her shoulder, and shook gently. "Mora . . ." she murmured, using the name of most respect. The second name given only to the queen. "Mora, wake up. Can you hear me?"

The queen's breathing sped up. Her head lolled toward Tannor, she moaned again, and then she began gasping. Tannor pressed gentle hands to her shoulders as she dug her heels into the mattress and clawed at the sheets, and then the leader of the galaxy finally opened her eyes. She clutched at Tannor's jacket and pulled herself jerkily to a sitting position.

Tannor slid from the bed to the floor. On her knees, not in her arms. Proper.

"Where am I?" Mora Aydor looked hazily from person to person. The soft candlelight would be better for her eyes, anyway, so soon after waking up. "Is my mother here?" She panted a couple breaths. "My mouth tastes disgusting."

Goren leapt forward. "I got you water! Here!"

The queen couldn't hold the cup, not like this, and Goren almost elbowed Tannor in the face trying to help her drink it, so Tannor grabbed it and shooed him away. She put the glass between the queen's palms, then wrapped her hands over the queen's. They locked eyes.

Mora Aydor, her own bones and skin, here and vulnerable and Tannor was touching her—

She'd never felt so close to death. It was nothing like the sight citizens memorized in every news relay—rounded lips, pale instead of tinted, skin waxy and stiff up close. This wasn't a perfect, unflinching dictator. Tannor saw no threat in this woman's fear. Mora Aydor had condemned so many to suffering or execution in the last year, and yet—the pod had been hidden there for two months?

Then Fil cried, "Comms are working again!" He tapped the device under the skin behind his ear, using a simple finger slide to limit the proximity channel to only the three of them. Tannor was brought in automatically; anyone else, he'd have to add in by name.

"Get Lorn!" she said. "I left him in the security room alone."

Fil nodded, tapped. "Lorn Vesnick, can you hear me?" They all winced at the sudden blasting sound of unintelligible shouting and raucous gunfire. "We're in Tannor's room! Listen, stop them if you can. Whatever you have to do! Stakes are higher! *A lot higher!*"

Meanwhile, Tannor addressed her queen. "Your mother's not here, it's just us. We're guards—"

Goren interrupted: "The place is under siege! We don't know how many there are, or how many they've killed, but they're after *you*!"

"We're in Tannor's room," Fil repeated. Tannor couldn't hear a reply— it might not be working.

"Lorn, don't lead them here!" she said. "Can you hear me? Don't—"

The queen swallowed several gulps of water, then rested one eye against the heel of her hand. "After me. Of course. Where are we? What's the date?"

But Tannor's door burst open and Lorn stumbled in backwards, firing frantically, and Fil leapt and slammed it shut again.

"A little help, here?" He glared, mostly at Tannor. She noticed a wound on his arm. Difficult to tell what weapons they were using.

"How many?" Fil asked quickly.

Lorn jerked a shoulder. "Four, maybe. Hard to say."

Fil advanced, raising his gun. Goren moved himself between the door and his queen. The door loomed. They waited.

After a tense pause, Lorn muttered, "Maybe they won't bother following me in here. I'm just one guard. Maybe they'll move on."

"Lorn."

"What?" He didn't turn.

"*Lorn*," Tannor repeated, urgent enough to turn his head. He frowned at her.

"What?" Then he noticed the woman on the bed. Dirty, slick with sweat, bandaged wrists. "Who the hell is HOLY—"

He didn't have time to finish. The door exploded off of its frame, flying in several large pieces across the room and knocking Lorn heavily to the floor. Tannor hooked her arms under the queen's, dragged her roughly to the door adjoining her room with the next, and heaved her through.

•

With a quiet thud, Relai landed on a giant rug. The guard's desperate face disappeared behind a slammed door, and the stillness of this room weighed heavily on her as gunfire cracked next door. She had no idea where she was, no idea where she could call safe. Was she still on Earth? This was supposed to be Arden.

She felt destroyed and elated and dizzy and high. Her heart no longer seemed pinned down in her chest, bouncing around and churning up her stomach, and why didn't her muscles hurt? She always felt stiff after a trip in a travel pod. They must have given her something. Of course they would have.

She was leaving for Arden when she lay down in that pod—but this air tasted nothing like her home planet. Not Oeyla, either—too dry. She looked at the floors—not Titus. Gastred? She'd only been to Gastred once. She was having trouble thinking clearly.

Ardenian tech. So this was an Ardenian base, either on Earth or on Gastred. If she could just make it outside, she'd know. And perhaps she could find someone to help her.

She dragged herself shakily to her feet and looked around. It was a dark room, laid out the same as the previous one. Dresser, bed, nightstand. A guard's bedroom.

They're after you, he'd said.

•

Tannor flattened herself against the wall as Goren and Fil fired blindly into the hall through the newly opened gap. A string of return shots spattered the wall behind them, leaving the dark scorch marks of an electric shotgun, then stopped. Tannor spotted her gun where she'd stupidly left it ten feet away. The shooting had paused. She wanted her weapon, then she wanted to get into the other room with the queen without the intruders seeing her. The urgency ached in her muscles, hurt her down to the bone.

She moved.

A second round of shots from another angle made Goren dive to the floor, but Tannor's momentum brought her in line with one charge. It hit the side of her head and she fell. The pulse penetrated the skin down to her skull, but no further, and every muscle in her body momentarily clenched in an excruciating seizure. She didn't regain her sight in time to see what came flying into the room next, but whatever it was, it exploded in a wave of concussion that had to have taken down Fil, the only one still standing when Tannor fell.

The floor was wood, old and unkind. She was glad she'd chosen to put down rugs.

As soon as she could move, she eased a hand up and pressed hard through the pain to stem the bleeding. Head wounds bled. She knew that.

She also knew enough to tell that they'd been firing charges too weak to kill a person, even with a hit to a vital area. With her vision still grayed out, she rolled to face away from the door with her wounded side to the floor. Tannor had landed close enough to reach out to her gun and she knew without looking exactly where it lay, but she kept completely still.

It took a moment for the roaring in her head to subside.

Then she heard voices.

•

Goren was still recovering from the bone-jarring explosion when a hand gripped the back of his uniform and dragged him off his belly to his knees. The owner of the hand circled him and shook him by the collar.

"Where is she?" the intruder snarled, pointing an electric shotgun in Goren's face. He was young and dirty, one of those disgruntled revolutionary types that always seemed to be eran, not that Goren was racist. Wild black hair, dark eyes, monstrous beard, speaking low-class Erayd Ardenian but dressed in Gastredi clothes—the worst type of detestable trash.

"I'll die before I tell you!" Goren declared. The man hit him across the face with the barrel of his segmented electric shotgun (one with most of the barrel segments removed), opening a long gash in Goren's cheek. As he sprawled on the floor and clutched his face, he looked up to see a second intruder kneeling over Fil and securing his wrists. This one was older, and shorter, but still unfortunately taller than Goren. No way he was Ardenian, either—Goren couldn't place the man's dark features, but his clothes were also Gastredi. He tried to remember as many details as possible, in case he lived through this.

The second man observed himself in a large mirror, fixed his hair, and then swiped up Fil's gen-gun as he moved to Lorn. He tossed the weapon to his partner. "Generator gun—just shoot him in the leg. It'll go faster."

"Good idea," the younger one agreed, and he raised the second weapon.

"No! Don't! Wait!" Goren shrieked. The man paused expectantly, and after a few deep breaths, Goren explained, "I've never been shot before. Okay. I'm ready."

He shut his eyes tightly and clenched his jaw in what he considered a very brave manner.

His captor pressed the nose of the gun to his thigh and pulled the trigger.

·

The snap of a gunshot startled Relai, then she heard a scream.

"Where is she?" The demand was brutal. *Gods in stars*, they were torturing them.

She refused to have their blood following her.

·

Goren failed to keep bravely silent, instead screaming and writhing on the floor. An inch-deep pit had opened in his thigh, soaking his pant leg in blood, and the blast of electrical energy had sent shocks of seizure throughout his body.

"Where is she?" the man barked again.

"Milo," the older man snapped from across the room. "Look." Goren turned his head to follow the voice and saw the man hunched over Tannor's still body. Goren couldn't see any part of Tannor past her legs, but he watched the man roll her on her back.

The younger intruder's—Milo's—voice came low and tight. "Is she dead?"

Goren's eyes widened. *Tannor.*

The older intruder cursed flatly in a language Goren didn't understand. Then he sighed.

But a loud, demanding thud from the adjoining room wrenched away his attention. That was where Tannor hid the queen, and the younger thug bolted like a predator towards prey—

·

Relai overturned the dresser and shoved it sideways to block the door, but she wasn't fast enough. She stumbled back as the door slammed against the dresser, open only a few inches. Another blow to the door shoved it further. A man struggled through the gap.

He was tall, he was *huge*, and Relai frantically sent the bookshelf toppling into the door. It pinned him, but not for long.

Relai did not wait to get a look at his face.

She turned and she ran.

·

Tannor heard Goren's strained voice repeat the question: "Is she dead?"

She jabbed her gun at the intersection between the intruder's legs and narrowed her eyes.

"Not dead, Goren," she answered.

"That's the last time I shoot *you*," the intruder grumbled, not bothering to reach for the weapon slung around his shoulder. He seemed more annoyed than angry. "You've got that pointed at an area vital to my happiness. Could I negotiate its safety in exchange for my gun?"

Tannor sat up, trying not to appear as dizzy as she felt. The whole side of her head was thick with blood. "Throw it to him." She motioned toward Goren.

The man had the audacity to admonish, "Be nice to her," as he slid his gun over to the shaking guard. He was older than all of them but still younger than her father. Olive skin, dark eyes, black hair, accent difficult to place.

When Goren had the enemy's gun in hand, Tannor pushed herself up. She pointed at Fil and Lorn, still unconscious amid pieces of her door.

"Release them."

He obliged, talking lightly as he snapped off the bindings. "Not to overstep my captive bounds, but I'm concerned about my associate finding your queen—assuming that was her in the next room?"

This was not how assassins were supposed to act. Tannor pursed her lips.

"We aren't going to give you any information," she snapped. Then, after a pause, she added, "Why are you concerned?"

He finished untying the unconscious men and placed his hands gamely on his head. "It's just that he has a powerful hatred for your queen (I'm impartial, of course) and he's a little low on sleep, so he might react rather, hmm, *violently* when he finds her."

Goren asked the obvious question before Tannor could open her mouth: "Is he going to kill her?"

The man twitched to the left faintly, apparently trying to find the right words.

Tannor bent to shake Fil, then smacked his face a few times without taking her eyes off of the intruder. He came to, shaken but all parts still working, and swept his gaze over the room.

"The queen?"

Again, Goren answered first, wincing as he twisted off a tight bandage around his thigh. "She was in Lilya's room, and the other guy went after her, and I haven't heard anything in there so I think they're gone."

Fil found Lorn's weapon on the floor.

"I'm going after them," he declared grimly.

"Like seven hells you are," Tannor exclaimed. "You don't know where she is, or how many more of them are out there."

Fil kicked a chunk of door across the room. "He could be killing her!"

"And you running around chasing branches for your rank tattoo isn't going to help her, Corporal!" She pulled out one of the metaplastene binding strips integrated into her jacket and wrapped it around the intruder's wrists.

Lorn sat up, glanced around woozily, and demanded a hand up from Fil.

"Goren and I are going to the dock control room," Tannor said. "I can find the queen if she's still on base. You and Lorn go to the hangar and take out skimmers. I'll tell you where to go. Pick her up and secure the other man."

"Yeah, okay," Fil growled. "But if we run into the captain and he tells us otherwise—"

"He outranks me. I know."

She turned to their captive. "Are there others?"

The man smiled. "Would you believe me if I said no?" When Tannor glared but didn't answer, he added, "I wouldn't believe a thing I say, if I were you."

She almost wanted to laugh—a sure sign she needed to get back to a computer. Goren took one solid arm, she took the other, and she refused to look at the intruder's face.

Fil tapped behind his ear and called, "Keep in touch!" and then he and Lorn disappeared into the hall.

Tannor adjusted her grip nervously and prodded their captive over the debris and out the door. Goren followed behind, grumbling, "*Shoot him in the leg, it'll go faster.*"

iii.

Relai felt the threat of pursuit through every nerve in her body. She moved on the balls of her feet, eyes dashing from the floor to the wall, down the hallway, behind her. She reached a set of wooden stairs and leapt, skipping steps and tripping once, thudding and yelping. She heard someone pounding down the hallway toward her in savage pursuit. Someone wearing shoes.

Lucky.

She chose down by instinct, maybe, and she was right—she tumbled outside onto a narrow cobblestone street. Timeworn stone buildings with crumbling plaster facades loomed on either side. A steady drizzle pattered down. Earth.

The robe they'd dressed her in was black, a thin silk that stuck to her skin, clinging and pulling drop by drop, but better than nothing. Her arms and legs looked paler than normal, raw and exposed, but her skin didn't register the cold. She turned on instinct, noticing a slight slope in the street, and chose down once again. Maybe she was just tired and didn't want to run uphill. Maybe up meant a summit, meant trapped, and down meant out.

Relai emerged into a larger street, this one banked by subtle sidewalks, and she caught sight of a high wall. This was a walled city, very old but scrubbed clean. Buildings and streets like this did not exist in the developed galaxy—they kept everything new, swept the old away with no sentiment. She knew it was Earth, but she didn't know this place. Not all Earthan towns were the same.

Relai ducked into a recessed doorway, heaving in air from the exertion. She felt like she hadn't moved in months. Years, even.

Maybe she hadn't.

Her memory ended only a few minutes ago, when she had lain down to sleep, counting down from forty with deep, even breaths. She'd been *so ready*, set firm in her choice to finally return home. She missed her mother, her chef, and her city. Most importantly, she thought she'd gotten to the point where she could look her father in the eye, where she could face him. Where he couldn't hurt her anymore.

The trip from Earth to Arden took three weeks; she was supposed to wake up at the Kilani Naquia dock, greeted as Orist despite her rejection of the title. Instead she was here, mud splattering up her aching legs, holes torn in her wrists, probably a concussion. Maybe she'd been asleep for decades.

She saw movement far down the street, heard voices. *Move, go*—she inhaled and kicked up desperately for the wall. The other side held more safety than the side with those men, the ones doing the torturing—

She slipped on the wet, uneven pavers and scraped her knees and looked back and she saw him.

He was coming, *oh, gods*— She dug her fingernails into the grit of the street and pulled herself up. He was gaining ground.

Gate, let there be a gate—no, no gate—she ran along the wall, had to come to one eventually. The street veered away ahead of her, and the ground was built up against the wall and grown over with thin vegetation. She didn't need a gate. She scrambled up the incline.

The city walls were shingled with red half-cylinder tiles that cascaded down with each step Relai took. She heard a rival downrush of pottery, thrown loose by her pursuer, shatter against the ground as she slid to the edge and leapt out into the air.

The ground met the outer wall a merciful ten feet below—centuries of accumulated earth softened the original height of the ramparts. Her landing turned rapidly into a roll and then a tumble down a steeper, increasingly rocky hillside. Her head missed the corner of a boulder by a few inches and her hand caught it instead.

She'd feel these bruises later. Now, *run*.

Relai found her feet and stumbled onward. Her hunter slowed himself on the hill, taking it more carefully, but he came out steady and unharmed at the end of it. She tore through a field of brush, thistles snatching at her robe, at her skin, and she burst onto a well-defined lane. She saw ordered rows, heavy branches, and she knew this, she could remember what this was—a place for growing fruit for wine. A vineyard.

Haadam Base.

Through hazy darkness she made out a stone pathway, slick in the faint light cast behind her, stretching down a center lane. She could lose him in the vineyard. Maybe, maybe—

Then her pursuer reached the path. He took a shot, missed, and she could hear him drumming closer and closer, an immense thundering monster bearing down on her—another shot—

Relai fell, hit by a spray of sizzling plasma in the shoulder, and rolled through the mud. She had no time to recover before he was on top of her. She couldn't see his face, couldn't clear the rain and mud from her eyes, from her nose, and he flattened her on her back. She struggled but he pinned her arms against her sides between his shins and sat on her stomach and wrapped his hands around her neck. He pressed down. She felt his whole body quake.

She couldn't speak. He didn't, for a moment. She couldn't see, could only feel, could barely breathe. She kicked uselessly.

He growled, "You should know the pain you've caused."

Relai saw light, light in her eyes.

"You should suffer. For your crimes, for what you've done… you should die in the mud…"

Rain splashed down on her face, running in a stream from his head looming over her.

She was supposed to be better than this; she was supposed to be stronger.

Everything—bright—and it hurt—

Stars—

And then he let go. His weight lifted off of her and she heaved in air, rolling onto her side with one hand curling around to cup the wound in her shoulder. She lay there, breathing and regaining her mind, and the noise of the rain made her want to sleep.

Now she felt the cold.

She looked up and saw him in the light from the city, just barely. He sat hunched next to her, close enough to touch. His arms were resting on his knees, head resting in his hands. His body was still shaking, the rhythm like a song, one-two-three, rest, one-two-three, rest.

Relai felt a tightly stretched wire inside her loosen.

What day is it? Where am I?

And what the hell was he talking about?

Still high on whatever pain medication they'd given her, Relai sat up. The man immediately trained his gun on her again, inches away.

She heaved forward and vomited.

Relai had little time to ponder the color of her stomach contents because the ground jolted in what appeared to be a mechanized earthquake. Relai turned to get her bearings and saw that the hilltop behind them was rising.

The ground she sat on was vibrating and she watched the hill and the city walls lift higher, higher, and, *no*—to the left and right, dark edges rose in equal time. They were sinking.

The entire vineyard was sinking. They dropped ten, twenty, thirty feet, and then Relai tumbled sideways as a gap split blade-sharp down the stone pathway. Two tracks of lights dotted the edges of the new seam, and she'd seen these lights before, from the windows of groundships coming and going from an underground dock. This was the entrance to the base's dock. The doors were the vineyard itself, drawn underneath and safely untouched while vehicles came and went.

The jolt rocked the man sideways, too, but where his right foot and thigh had been resting he found only open air. Relai saw his arms flail and he tried to spin, fingers scratching stone, and then he fell. She felt the sudden plunge in her stomach like she herself had fallen. She gasped.

Relai rolled onto her chest to look over the edge. Luck had caught him— he hung by a forearm slung through the strap of his electric shotgun, which had snagged on a rod protruding from the vertical edge of the vineyard door.

The lights glowed on either side of him, bright on his soaked skin, on the painful dig of the strap into his hand and the crook of his elbow. He kicked violently, trying to gain a foothold and stop himself from slipping from the strap, but with every move the strap inched closer and closer to falling. How deep must the dock be? Deep enough to kill him. Relai leaned out further. It was so close, only three or four feet away—

She tested her grip on the edge of a pathway stone. The edge jutted out enough for her to hold securely, so she slid herself out and hung her weight on that stone. She could reach it, she could *just reach* the rod that held the strap.

He looked up and his body tightened when he saw her reach out. His face clenched through desperation and fury and then bitter resignation, and he refused to look away. Relai threw out her hand and managed to touch the strap. She clawed with her fingernails, pulled, and moved the strap back onto the rod.

She pressed her hand over it and held it fast.

"Climb up!" she managed to call out. "I can't hold it forever!"

He swung his free arm up and gripped the rod, then slapped another hand over the lip of the door. His arms were much longer than hers, his hands much bigger, and she shuddered at the sight of them. Just as he dragged himself up and scrambled gracelessly over the edge to safety, the vineyard creaked to a stop.

The roof of the recess cast empty blue light over them and covered them from the rain. They were underneath another part of the base now; the entire vineyard had retracted.

Relai pushed herself back at an angle, away from the chasm and away from her attacker. She kicked herself off the stone path and scraped along soggy earth, never taking her eyes off of him, until she collided with a wall of vines. The leaves were soft, the branches scratchy, and they spattered her with more raindrops as she settled.

The man remained hunched at the edge. He'd brought his gun up with him and he held it to his chest as they sat back and stared at each other. He was much younger than she'd expected, but it was hard to guess his age past the heavy beard.

He glared at her, still furious, but now with an edge of uncertainty.

Relai finally found her voice. "Who are you?"

She watched his chest rise with the breath it would take to answer and he opened his mouth in a snarl, but then two glowing skimmers rose like fireflies up out of the pit. They carried one guard each, helmets obscuring their faces. Relai couldn't tell if these were the guards she had met for only a few seconds back in that room, but it hardly mattered. Their job was to protect her.

She let out a shriek for help and waved her pale arms in the darkness.

oo●oo

EPISODE II:

ALLY

EDNAR FASS UNBUTTONED his white collarless shirt, pulled out the tail, and loosened the black cuff slides. He checked the wall for the time—still blank. He huffed. That tech sergeant bitch thought she was something. *Not much against a real challenge, huh?* He gulped the last of his whiskey and shrugged the shirt from his shoulders. He'd compose a message for the good Lady Redas, another for the High Council, and then he could melt into bed.

The rebels attacking the base should have left him the courtesy of a clear relay channel, but no. He didn't blame them for doing their jobs well, and he could use the pretense of ignorance a little longer. Kastroma would reach Gastred with the most valuable cargo in the galaxy in sixteen weeks, and that would be the end of all this.

Fass wondered if the people would love him more if he were to mourn the death of the queen, or if he were to cleave her head from her shoulders and bless Earth with her blood? He paused. He should make sure they left enough of her body for it, just in case.

He lifted the shirt from the arm of his chair and slid back into it.

"Captain! Captain Fass! Sir!"

Fass rolled his eyes high over the antique woodwork of his flat in disgust as Lorn Vesnick and Fil Tars thundered up his stairs. He thought they'd be dead by now.

Tars rattled out, "Mora Aydor is on base! We found her trapped in the catacombs and there are men chasing her—"

"Where is your partner, Tars?" Fass could see the annoyance in the soldier's pause.

"Palia? She's out. Unconscious. Listen, the queen—"

"Strength to Unity, sir?" Vesnick cut in.

"Strength to Unity, Corporal," Fass replied. He bent at the waist and raised up his needle gun.

"Fuck!" Tars cried as Fass pulled off a clean shot.

He died easily and Fass set down his gun to finish buttoning his shirt.

"Where is the queen now, soldier?" he asked as he rolled his shoulders into his rich grey uniform jacket.

Vesnick blinked at Tars' body. "Uh."

Fass retrieved his weapon. "The queen. *Soldier.*"

"He…" Vesnick mouthed like a fish. Pathetic.

Fass shoved him aside, fisted the back of Tars's jacket right over the stitching proclaiming his name, and hefted his body halfway off the ground. He dragged it beside him as he descended the stairs to the entrance, the hands and legs thudding along and Vesnick quacking behind him.

"The queen, um, she's on foot, I think. Mellick was going to get the dock up and she wanted us to go find her. She had one guy in custody, but he was Oeylan—is this us, sir?"

Fass grew tired of the body and just heaved it the rest of the way down. The night looked to grow longer and longer and he was losing the pleasant thrum of intoxication.

"So I was led to believe. Until we're sure she's dead we need to maintain our roles. Do you understand? We are loyal until we're sure she's dead."

"Don't we, uh," Vesnick stepped over the body at the foot of the stairs and into the rain on the street, "stay loyal until the rebellion really gets going? Somebody has to survive the first volley. I mean, they're just going to pick off the ones who—"

"The promise of battle," Fass said, needle gun resting on his shoulder as he walked, "often shows a man's true worth."

"Well, Captain, I exchanged fire with these guys, how's that?" Vesnick grumbled. "I went through a compression bomb, too."

Fass stopped. "And they let you live?"

"Uh. Well, it wasn't—they didn't *let* me—"

It wasn't Unity. He'd let them stroll in and take her, and they weren't Unity.

Fass looked to the sky. He stroked the smooth skin of his chin. Vesnick knew about the catacomb. What were the chances that he wouldn't think this through enough to wonder why their vicious queen needed rescuing? Rebellion only required boredom and youth, but Captain Ednar Fass thought further than rebellion. He needed more than just defiance if he wanted this to last. He needed to inspire absolute faith.

Absolute faith in Ednar Fass, and not the slimmest chance of hope in Relai Aydor.

Fass bumped the gun off his shoulder, caught it with sights lined toward Vesnick's panicked face, and pulled the trigger.

He let them come in and take her, and wouldn't Corven Ector find that interesting? Fass ground his teeth.

Then he tapped his ear. "Horten. Lilya. Get to the dock. Now."

oo●oo

Tannor shoved their captive against the wall just inside the dock control room, far from windows and weapons. His mouth curled into a grin as he grunted from the force. He might have been eight inches taller and thirty pounds heavier, but she was the one with the gun. Tannor reached out behind her to find Goren's slender shoulder and dragged him over to root him in place.

"Shoot if he moves an inch."

Goren's knobby fingers worked over the dials of his gen-gun. "Okay."

Tannor crossed the room and settled in front of the massive transparent screen covering the wall of windows overlooking the darkness of the dock. Give her a few minutes, she'd bring the whole system back to life.

But first, to find the queen.

She peered through the control room's glass across the empty expanse of the dock; only one jumper remained—a vehicle large enough to carry five guards, two captives, and a queen halfway around the planet to Daat, the other Ardenian base. She'd let them deal with this mess.

She swept through layers of code, keying up the dock for Lorn and Fil to take out single-person skimmers with one hand and building an algorithm to scan the base for the queen with the other. She tapped the proper window to wake up the vehicles, then flattened her palm to authorize the doors to open. High above, the ceiling split with yellow light as a gray sheet of rain bisected the hangar and spread like a gasp in a chest.

One skimmer, two skimmers, on. Goren held their captive against the wall, the nose of his gun pressed to the center of the man's chest, saying, "Ha, I didn't die! Ha!"

She tapped her ear. "Fil? You there?"

No response. Not even the whisper-hiss of an open channel.

"They should be out there by now," she muttered. As much as Tannor hated the constant chatter in her ear, she hated this silence more.

"Goren, can you—" she began, and then she saw movement.

Two tiny figures crept across the hangar, so far away she could only see the frosty white reflective stripes along their arms and legs.

"Okay, they made it out there." She glanced behind her. "My comm isn't working again, how's yours?"

Goren squinted at the ceiling and then poked the man again. "I can't hear anything. Is this your fault?"

Their captive blinked. "But I've been captured."

Tannor sucked in a nervous breath.

Deep in the darkness through the mist, the two glowing skimmers kicked forward and up, circling once as they rose out of the open mouth of the dock.

"How are they going to find her if you can't tell them where to go?" Goren asked. "What if there are more of these guys?"

"Skimmers have comm locaters, heat sensors, shields. They'll be fine. They'll find her and keep her safe."

"They'll kill that other guy, won't they? The one who shot me?"

Tannor paused, dread creeping up her back and grabbing her cheek to turn her head to look.

Their captive smirked at her.

"Don't ease off that gun, Goren," she said. She should map the locations of all the comms on base... her hands flew over the screen.

"Don't worry," Goren said, "I turned up to max and I'll shoot him if he breathes wrong!"

"Bloodthirsty," the man observed. "And after all we've done to make sure no one dies unintentionally."

"Shut up," Tannor ordered before Goren could get himself worked up. She glanced back again and the captive raised an eyebrow.

"I'm surprised to find," he drawled, "that I'm a little sorry about this."

Tannor drew her gun as she turned her whole body to face him. Goren let out air like a punctured tire and slumped over and Tannor pulled the trigger.

Nothing happened.

Tannor swore.

The man bent and somehow his hands snapped free and then he picked up the weapon Goren had been holding—his own original gun—and fired a warning shot to establish precisely who had control at this point.

No, not just at this point.

He'd seemed careless, even lazy, from what she could hear when she was pretending to be dead, but when the concussion blast flattened everyone in her room he'd sauntered around and disabled all of their weapons. He'd let her and Goren drag him here, let her unlock the skimmers and blink the dock to life. He'd seen everything he needed to see with those dark, sliver-sharp eyes. Since Goren had held the intruder's own gun, the kid had been his only threat.

Tannor could see Goren breathing.

"Away from the screen," her captor ordered, and she ran to Goren as the man took her spot. He never aimed his weapon away from her as he tapped through the screens she'd started and he didn't try to hide his intent: he was powering up a groundship.

Tannor shook Goren and searched him all over but she found no marks, no cuts, nothing but the purpling gash on his cheek from the other man's blow and the seeping wound in his thigh. She thought back, trying to remember—yes, the man had touched Goren.

He'd put something on him.

And he'd brushed Tannor's hair away to look at her head wound, too. Did he touch her skin?

She glared up at him as she swept an obvious hand up and down her neck; the man raised both eyebrows and bit down on a grin.

There, at the curve between her neck and shoulder toward her back: he'd tagged her with a smooth disk half the size of her pinky nail. Goren must have one somewhere, too. It felt like a mole, like part of her body, but Tannor knew her body. This didn't belong.

A drug tick.

"Shit," she sighed.

Groundship ready, the man walked back over, gathered her gen-gun, and slipped it into an invisible seam running down the side of his jacket. After it was gone she couldn't tell he'd hidden anything at all in the curve of the small of his back.

He crouched next to Goren. "You get the legs, I'll take the head."

Tannor stared at him. "What?"

His eyes flicked down to Goren's face, then back to hers. Another explosion sounded above ground, rattling the chairs, and his eyebrows inclined. "You two are coming along."

"No. Why?"

He smoothed his fingers over Goren's shoulder, eyes glittering. "I like his jacket."

Four more minutes until her code eater ate itself, but someone needed to be there to reboot the system.

"*No.*"

"I could drop you like I dropped him."

She barked a laugh. "Yes. Absolutely. Do that, carry both of us yourself."

He glared to the left, annoyed, and then pressed his hands to Goren's shoulders.

"I could kill him, instead. I don't need him alive."

Tannor tissed through her teeth at him, then shifted back and hooked her hands under Goren's knees. The man half-grinned as they stood, then spun them so Tannor would be the one to walk backwards.

She grunted as they shuffled down the dark hall leading from the security room to the dock, infuriated and confused about why he chose to bring them along. It wasn't long before Goren became so heavy she couldn't think anymore.

Rain speckled her shoulders and hair as they crossed the exhausting distance to the ship. She stumbled up the steep open ramp and the red panels of the ship glowed over them, ready and humming. The white interior lighting hurt her eyes, and she couldn't free a hand to brush away the strands of hair sticking in her eyelashes.

"I won't fly this thing for you," she said.

"Yeah, I hate flying, too," he replied.

They dumped Goren in the groundship's medical bay next to a massive central gurney. Goren started twitching as the man pulled cords from his sleeves and bound them, quick like snapping fingers, to the metal handles on one side of the gurney. He made sure to stretch the cords so they each had enough freedom to reach across the table—*why?*—and then he headed out of the room.

With one last burst of frustration, Tannor demanded, "Why are we here?"

He didn't look back as the door slid shut, but his response slipped through the gap: "Decoration."

She should have shot him in the balls when she had the chance.

○○●○○

The orange hover lights switched to cool blue, illuminating raindrops in a soft halo around the skimmer as Relai ran to meet the guard who floated to rest near the gaping edge of the dock bay doors. The other sped into the vineyard without a pause. Relief was in sight—soon she'd be warm, safe, clean, and she could look that raving man in the eyes again with more light to see his face.

"Thank you, thank you so much," she cried as she reached the guard. "Did you see where—"

"She'll get him, Our Glory," the guard assured. He stretched off the skimmer and, instead of saluting, held out a hand. She should have paused, questioned, but after four years on this planet she just met him with her own hand.

He jerked her off-balance as he lashed out with a heavy boot. A catastrophic pain tore through her knee and she fell where he threw her. He kicked her in the ribs, then his weight on her back pinned her chest against the cobblestone.

•

i.

Milo Hemm dove into the glowing rows of rain-slick greenery, tearing branches and skin and breathing through his mouth to stifle the rattle of snot in his nose. One guard would stay with the queen and one would go after him. He was glad he'd held onto that shotgun.

He was trying not to think about those last shaking moments when he cleared the fury enough to realize he was choking the life out of a defenseless girl, and then the ground had opened wide and tried to swallow him. He'd been close to the end, the end of this long, terrible journey, and then—

And then her hand stretched out, thin and glowing in the sharp light, and he thought he should have killed her after all. And then she'd saved his damned life.

Right now, his mission had reached its final paces. Either Ky would show up soon, or this would finish in the quick, sickening way he'd taught himself to expect. Ky had been so confident, Milo might have started to feel a flicker of his optimism—just enough to silence the part of his mind that wanted to live. The knowing part.

He'd placed his end point here, in this savage system, on this night. Who attempted to kidnap the queen of the civilized galaxy and got away with it?

Milo crept along, ducking under vines and dashing across another aisle. The skimmer slid along and he watched its light scan back and forth down each row, closer, now almost on him. He picked a post and grabbed on, planting his feet against the steady grain of the wood, and swung to the side opposite the skimmer as it turned down an aisle. He'd only made it a few hundred feet down, but Milo Hemm would not die running away.

The guard's voice carried clear down the aisle because her helmet didn't obscure her mouth. "...I don't know. I thought they were here to kill her." A pause. "Not with *your* gun. They're going to check." Another pause. "No, it definitely matters. We'll use his, there'll be no question."

Very close.

"I got him."

Milo dropped to the ground and fired up at her as a blast from the skimmer's cannon obliterated the post. His charge hit the shield of her skimmer and it bucked from the unstable electricity. Good enough—Milo leapt forward and covered the distance between them in three steps.

She tried to gain control and aim, but Milo surged too quick, too close. The shield would stop a blast, not the barrel itself—he pressed a shot to her chest and she seized up.

Milo thought he felt rain fleck from his face with his next exhale, but the drops spotted dark on the silver hull of the skimmer and didn't blend with the rain. He put a hand under his nose and it came away with blood.

"Earth," he muttered darkly.

He dragged the guard off the skimmer and pulled a locking belt from the row on his jacket sleeve. He slipped it around her neck and a wooden post, then connected the flat ends. The belt adjusted itself, tight and secure, holding her slumped body at an awkward angle.

She let out a gurgle and gained enough control of her muscles to claw at the strap.

He tapped his own neck. "The more you move, the tighter it gets."

It was a lie, but he'd found it felt true if you heard it before you tried to pull the thing off. She froze. Good.

Milo helped himself to her gun, shoved it in the last open holster on his chest, and gripped the handlebar of her skimmer. She'd set the hover too high; that was the first of her problems. He slung a leg over the seat and adjusted the steering to his knees so he'd have both hands free to shoot, and that fixed her second problem.

It took seconds to glide back to the edge of the vineyard and the light from the skimmer caused the other guard to turn and ask, "Lilya?" as Milo accelerated into him.

The guard flew back with a satisfying thud and skidded to a stop just short of the edge. Milo's skimmer swung over the edge of the abyss, and as he leaned into a spin he realized—he'd just flown over the queen.

The guard had been standing over the queen with his foot on her back, holding her down, and *that made no sense.*

Milo aimed the skimmer for the guard again, but the man had already found his gun. Milo barely reached ground before the guard rolled sideways and aimed a pulse at the skimmer's rear engine.

A hit—the skimmer bucked and Milo tried to pull around but the back end fell and scraped through the mud with the front end up like a rearing bull. It threw Milo off and slammed upside down into the mud. Milo took cover.

They traded shots, five, six, eight, and then the guard paused long enough for Milo to glance around the side and see him running for the queen, who was trying to get herself onto the second skimmer—something was wrong with her leg, it wouldn't hold her up.

The guard aimed a few careless shots in Milo's direction, then grabbed the queen by her hair and the back of her robe. She lost her footing, the guard wrenched her around, and Milo pitched desperately toward them.

He fired and hit the guard in the neck but the motion had already begun. The guard opened his hands just before his whole body seized and sent the queen reeling with no hope of balance. Milo reached out but it was too late— he saw the whites of her eyes, the gape of her horrified mouth, the useless grasping of her hands. She flew backward over the edge of the dock into the dark.

Milo sucked in a breath.

Then the wind picked up. The lighting changed from soft yellow to harsh red, the shadows turned, and Milo watched a groundship rise and lift the body of the queen up and out of the maw. He could see the angles of her body and the stillness of it. She hadn't fallen too far, but maybe it had been far enough. She might be dead and all of this might finally be finished.

For a second he felt the weakest bit of hope. Then the ship spun and the pilot became visible between the masses of the two main engines.

Ky.

He flashed Milo an impatient look and pointed at the queen's body as though Milo hadn't noticed. Milo growled and collected the incapacitated guard's gun, shocked him again to keep him down, and then shot out the engines of the remaining skimmer. The mud slipped around his feet as he pitched forward, kicked off the lip of the vineyard, and threw himself onto the hovering groundship. Ky must've turned on the friction to keep him from sliding off; it felt like stone instead of metal.

Ky lowered the top deck ramp as Milo dragged the limp queen over his shoulder. The rain made her body slippery, even with the robe, but he held on and stomped down.

The crisp image of Ky's face popped up on the wall just inside and followed him as he pounded down a shining white hall with the queen's arms flopping against his side.

Ky gave him a toothy grin. "Sorry that took so long, spark."

"Hell of a good timing, Ky. Is she dead?"

Ky's eyes flashed sideways, reading data from the ship that Milo couldn't see. "Not dead. Happy to be unconscious considering the state she's in, though." Milo heard the implication in his tone.

"Yeah, it wasn't all me."

He knew where he'd find the medical bay, not too far from the security hall. Part of him wanted to throw her in a locked room and let her body decide for itself if it wanted to live or die. After all she'd done, all that she was responsible for—and she was too busy relaxing at this resort to be bothered with the consequences—

Milo was gripping her hip too tightly. He forced himself to flatten his hand as he reached the medical bay.

The doors pulled open and the sight of two wide-eyed guards startled him. He took in the way Ky had chained them by the wrists to one of the patient gurneys and felt a rush of hot shame. Ky had known he would—Ky knew what Milo was.

The boy started yowling first.

"You better not have killed her, you dirty hill trash!"

The woman thought quicker; she started shaking her head almost the moment he walked through the door. "We're not medically trained, if she's really hurt you need someone with some skill to help her."

Milo unloaded his cargo on their gurney with a thunk. "You're all she's got."

"I—I feel like I haven't slept in two days," the woman pleaded, eyes her huge and desperate.

"Same," he replied.

Then he lashed out at the boy, landing a satisfying punch to his little reesh face.

"*Mountain* trash," he said.

He left for the bridge.

•

A damp hand flopped next to Tannor's and she jerked away, refusing to panic as the med bay door slid shut. That was the Monster of Eray—the one who'd decided to kill as many guards as he could when the relocation began. The one who'd escaped Arden and hit Gastred next, piling bodies under his feet everywhere he trod, leaving twenty dead before he disappeared. His face topped the kill-on-sight lists that no one wanted to take seriously because none of them ever expected to kill anyone during their guard service.

He'd found the queen.

"*Why?*" Goren moaned. Now his nose was bleeding in addition to his thigh, and she wouldn't look at him again until she got everything under control.

"Are you okay?" she demanded. Glanced at him.

"No!"

The table lit up, *thank the stars,* and Tannor tapped into the medical system—the older man must've opened it for her from somewhere else on the ship. Probably watching her every move, wherever he was.

"Hostages? Organ harvesting? Human shields for battle... neural data storage? Public sacrifice?!" Goren rattled on, fingers fumbling across the gurney keys as he swiped the blood from his upper lip with his gray jacket sleeve. He was probably trying to distract himself from the broken body before them, so she didn't tell him to shut up.

Tannor set the table to scan with her left hand and went to work taking control of the ship with her right—they were equally important, so she'd do both at once. The first thing any regulation scanner did was read the identifying pin embedded in every coalition citizen's chest at birth—it wouldn't heal anyone without a pin—and this one reported instantly that, yes, this woman was not just a clever imitation of the queen. Tannor ignored the confirmation she didn't need and rooted through the all programming she could access, searching for weakness or familiar algorithms or outright stupidity.

"Let me out," she muttered.

Mora Aydor looked dead, but Tannor knew better. When the second intruder, the Monster of Eray, had dumped the queen in front of them, Tannor had seen: he'd caught the back of Mora's head in one giant hand as he laid her down. Gentle.

None of this made sense, but the monster just saved the queen's life.

And now... *ah*. A change of command. She caught herself before she smirked, just in case they were watching.

"Are you sure you know how to run this thing?" Goren asked. He'd spread open the queen's robe, no blush, and flailed out to snag a med scanner hovering over the table. He passed it to Tannor without hesitation.

An array of readings flowed across the screen in pulsing bubbles—the larger and brighter the bubble, the more serious the problem. There were a lot of very bright bubbles on that gurney. Blood pressure, temperature, foreign substances, heart rate—and following each reading, the predicted success rate for treatment.

"You start with the table," she said, "I'll direct the scanner."

"How do you know how to do this?" Goren asked.

Tannor moved a mobile scanner to the brightest bubble. "I know our technology. I'll figure it out."

The table display pinged at them in condescending instruction as it finished its survey. DEATH IMMINENT, it warned, APPLY COLD LINES—then Goren found the straps that would cool her body to slow her decline tucked all along the rim of the gurney. He stretched them out and across, all up and down the queen.

The bands pressed like striped scars, white on her graying amber skin, as they brought down her temperature.

Tannor, now the new commanding doctor, rooted into the admin program as she keyed up the healing process. The queen was too far gone to even moan from the pain as Tannor pressed the waxy, ribbed interface of the med scanner against her forehead and started healing.

Hopefully they'd get her screaming soon.

"She can't die, she can't die, she's everything," Goren muttered.

Tannor swallowed. "You think there's no hope, if we lose her?"

Goren snorted. "Think? I don't need to think. I know! What are we going to do if she dies? King Ayadas is gone and there's no other heir. She's *it* for us. Who even knows what would happen without her? Bad stuff!"

"Bad stuff," Tannor echoed. "Worse, though?"

"I'm gonna pretend I didn't hear that."

Head, chest, and blood. The cold lines snapped away.

With her next breath, the queen let out a high, tight whine.

"It's working, she's getting better—"

"We should make her sleep, save her the pain."

Tannor felt a burst of energy driving the ship up and forward. They'd left the base.

○○●○○

iii.

Bevn Kyro, the name matched to a person, hadn't existed for twenty years Proper Time. No platform, no financials, no housing or service exchange or travel records. No military duty fulfilled. No pin. He didn't exist.

Hadn't existed.

When Milo crashed through his door (no, it was a day later, when Milo woke up and they finally exchanged names), Ky bit that bitter round and introduced himself right.

And Bevn Kyro came back.

Ky brushed crumbs from his chest and the console beside him, a weak attempt to tidy up before Milo stomped in. That loaf of local Earthan bread he'd slipped into his coat on their way through the base? Completely worth the effort.

He kept an eye on the medical summary he'd stashed in the corner of the bridge's primary screen: broken pelvis, right femur, and right arm. Torn tendons in the left knee. Scattered wounds across the shoulder and back. Concussion. Swelling in the brain.

Damn it, Milo.

And there were other findings, too, less obvious and more troubling: bizarre blood nutrients, subnormal bone density, and unusual hormone levels. Worst were the high levels of several badly interacting drugs. She would have been dead in a couple hours if Milo hadn't gotten to her first.

Didn't matter; right now he had other problems to address.

"Buddy!" he cried through a mouthful. "Welcome to our new ship!"

Milo looked like death. His legs and arms were caked with dark Earth mud and Ky saw blood mixed glossy black through the dense hairs of his beard. Milo leaned down alongside a chair, found the switch to release it from the floor, and slid it over to Ky.

"Her own guards tried to kill her and make it look like we did it."

Ky's eyes flicked to the video showing his two friends pawing over the queen's ragged body.

"Which guards?"

"Hell if I know, they all look the same to me. Why are her guards trying to kill her?"

"Unity?"

Milo considered it. "Think I should have asked? I wouldn't be surprised."

Ky laughed. "I think they would've killed you in the middle of your sentence." He threw the pilot screen over to Milo and stretched the med bay display larger in front of himself. Milo always took over flying; he probably needed it right now.

After a moment of quiet, Ky went on, "So they figured out the sit-back-and-watch code we sent didn't come from Unity, then."

"I heard one guard say they should kill her with my gun. They really do want everyone to blame Eray for Unity."

"You're tall. Easy targets."

"We're Erayd. Easy targets."

Ky smiled with half a mouth and checked on the queen's vital markers. The guards were doing their work well, especially the clever blond one. In fact—

"Uh-oh." He pressed two particular teeth together to trigger her tick. On-screen, Guard One flopped over unconscious just in time to stop her from subverting control of navigation to the medical bay. Guard Two howled and fumbled to adjust her body so she wouldn't hurt her shoulder joints. *Holy shit.* Ky was going to have to keep her away from this groundship's brain or he wouldn't be flying it much longer.

He made sure the med bay would stay nice and isolated when the queen woke up, then turned to Milo.

"Tell me." He tore off a piece of bread and tossed it over, but Milo just caught it and held it. "You ran off. What happened?"

Milo put the bread down and threw the pilot screen back to Ky. They needed to calculate a sneaky exit trajectory if they were going to make it out of orbit without getting disintegrated by the guards at Haadam, Daat, or Buzou. For now, though, they were safe under Ky's transmission blocker as they sailed silent and invisible through the dark, vacant hill country toward the coastal hideout Ky'd selected.

"She was in the adjacent room," Milo began. "She tipped a bookshelf on me." He cracked an empty smile. "I was expecting something more. I chased her down and caught her outside. I shot her and I pinned her down."

Ky watched his face. The last eight months—discovering Milo and pulling his wretched self back together; following bloody trails of worthless information to find those few precious names; then those long days and nights of travel without sleep, battling their way into a remote space port to find a single person who knew the careful secret, the truth about the location of the queen—it all came to a head here, now. The starving kid that had stumbled into Ky's dump of a Gastredian bar couldn't even form a sentence, and look at him now.

Milo had done it. He deserved his moment of confrontation. But this? Ky checked on the guards again; the boy, on his own, had resolved the brain swelling and moved on to healing the queen's broken bones.

He hadn't expected Milo to go this far.

Milo looked at his hands and said, "I wanted to kill her."

With a sweep of two fingers, Ky moved the video feed of the queen up to Milo's eye level. He kept his words light. "Nice try, but I'm afraid you just fell short."

Milo slammed his fist into his console, then stood and paced away from the image. He couldn't go far because the curve of the cockpit roof only allowed a few feet of walking space for someone so tall. Ky stared at the stretch of gray fabric across Milo's broad shoulders, at the charred edge angled along the bottom of his ribcage where the jacket had burned away in the fire when they crashed on Earth.

"That's the problem," Milo rasped. Watched the rain instead of the screen.

"What?"

"I had my chance. I keep trying to tell myself it's for the people, that I kept her alive to let the people of Arden condemn her. But all I can see is the look on my aba's face just before he died. I *failed him*."

Ky let out a laugh. "Right. Your father dreamed of his son one day beating a woman to death."

Milo turned back, his face crumpled in anguish. "No. I *had her*, and I *wanted to*... I had my hands around her neck and I—"

Ky waited.

Milo swallowed. "She deserves—"

He stopped, then glanced again, finally, at the screen where the queen's body rested. She looked like stone under the hands of sculptors.

"She destroyed us. She's *evil*. I shouldn't have been able to stop myself." His voice caught in his throat. "But I—do you realize... do you realize what I almost did?"

Made this a whole lot simpler, Ky thought. He hopped up and spoke with all the sincerity he could muster. It wasn't much.

"Hey. You—*you*, spark, out of everyone—you got her. You *got her.*" He tore at the bread so he could resist the urge to grip Milo's arm. "I'm not in this like you are. I don't know anyone who died. Hell, I just thought it'd be fun to make some trouble. Plus, you're pretty entertaining when you're mad, and I don't like dictators on Gastred *or* Arden. And I get itchy sticking in one spot too long. And business wasn't too great for—"

"Ky?" Milo interrupted, the creases on his face softening. "Shut up."

oo●oo

She was okay. Perfect again.

Goren rested on his elbows, forehead pressing into the clammy flesh of the queen's outer thigh until he realized what he was doing and jerked away in terror. This table should have a warming blanket, right? He flipped open the panel near her feet and, yes. He pulled it up and over her body, then tucked her in the way his little sister Fenla would've wanted.

She was fine. Sleeping a normal sleep. If he shook her she'd wake up, but he wasn't going to *shake* the queen.

Crap, his leg hurt.

He shook the uninjured leg where Tannor was slumped against him. She didn't move, but her head was tipped back so her neck pinched between her strung up arms. He wondered suddenly if the knockout drug thing worked for whatever amount of time the villains wanted it to... or if maybe Tannor was dead.

Oh, *hells*. He lifted up her head and—

He could see her breathing.

Goren tried not to give in and just cry. How was he supposed to handle all this? He was going to die, and then what would Tannor and Mora Aydor do?

Could he use a med scanner as a weapon? He mustered the energy to lift his head and locate it.

Wait! He could heal his leg!
Goren reached up and almos—
Everything went black.

○○●○○

iv.

Milo stood outside the dull white metal of the med bay doors. This was it. He was calm now, no weapon in hand. He needed to look her in the eyes and see the evil there and know that he'd stopped her.

Into his mind bled the faces of his father, his sister, his mother. Bry sipping his disgusting nettle tea and Shayla spooking him with her moss beard. Prayers that smelled of smoke and meat. Leaves crunching under his feet. Fire.

He wasn't going to hit anything and he wasn't going to try to strangle her. Not now.

Not again.

He stepped forward and the doors slid wide. Ky had knocked out both guards and laid them side by side on the floor at the end of the bed so Milo could do this uninterrupted. Face her.

She was laying still, light dusting the curves of her face, covered by a warming blanket up to her collar bones. One of the guards must have washed her hair—it seemed so much longer than in her last relay—or maybe bathing was a function of the automated medical service on this ship. They'd cleaned her skin, too, and redressed her in that tattered black robe. Her chin tilted up and he could see purple finger marks splattered down the length of her neck.

"Wake up," he ordered, and she opened her eyes.

She saw him. Sat up. Clutched the blanket to her chest and stared at him.

Then she recognized him enough to push herself off the table away from him, raising one hand to her neck, touching the rows of bruises there.

Milo felt dizzy for a moment, but it swelled back into the fury he was used to.

"Dear Mora," he said, throat full of gravel, "Our Great Glory. Forgive me if I don't bow."

Her brow furrowed. When she spoke, her voice came out rougher than his. "Why are you calling me that?"

Milo thought her head injury had been healed... but she'd come to her senses soon enough.

"Are you feeling disoriented?" She tried to answer, but he drove on. "Are you feeling powerless? Do you have a voice now?"

"What are you trying—"

"*Who is going to listen to you now?*" His fist pounded the med table and it clanged mightily around the echo of his words. "You have no advisers to whisper in your ears and affirm your every move. You have no fans fawning at your voice. You have *me*."

She looked terrified now. Milo was glad.

"Not just me." His voice rattled up from his stomach and out past his teeth and he tried not to let it shake. "We're going back. We're going back and the destruction is going to stop and you will face the people you've harmed. You will lower your eyes to every last one of them."

She didn't look *caught*, not like she should—she turned out her palm, fingers twitching like she could feel his words in the air. "No, no, no," she muttered. "No. You're not well."

Damn her earnest eyes; he had to turn and pace away. He knew his mind, knew the truth of the past in the snarl of missing tissue on his leg and the burn scars on his arms. She couldn't talk away his body.

She even stepped closer with her vile pleading. "Whatever you think has happened, it's not real. I'm not the queen, my mother is. Someone lied to you, or tricked you, or you're just—sick—"

One long-fingered hand, the same hand he'd watched reach out through the rain, lifted toward him. Like she was the rational one. Like she could help him, even, if he would only listen to her.

Tongue of a worm.

"Ruling from a distant resort instead of facing your people in person might help you play innocent," Milo said, "but the evidence is overwhelming. The courts will see the truth. You are damned. *Give up.*"

Her voice took on a higher pitch. "I haven't been ruling from Earth! I have no part in Ardenian politics any more. I left. I *already gave up.*"

He had to admit, he hadn't expected this tactic. She wasn't even ruling?

He shook his head and curled up his lip. "You'll have your day. I'll see you to it."

She let out a tiny impatient huff. "*Please.* Tell me what you think is going on. And please don't hurt me again." She spoke without flinching, though her knuckles were white, and damn her, she'd realized what she could use to temper him. *Don't hurt me again.*

He already felt like the thing they called him, Monster, and she could tell... but *she* was the monster, boring inside his head like this. Evil.

Heat was filling up in his mind again, memories screaming in his ears. The last smile his mother gave him. Little Shayla, six years old, in the middle of the street with a bloody head.

He'd been collecting video and images snuck into the commons before the censors deleted them, and he had hard evidence—real, solid, and irrefutable. He wanted to see her face when she couldn't deny it anymore.

Milo stomped around the table, his long legs bringing him to her side in less than a breath. He took her by the arm, firm but not vicious, and pushed her out of the medical bay.

They traveled through the ship without speaking a word and came to the conference room where Ky was eating.

"Show her," Milo said. He let go of Relai and she stumbled to a stop. No clear line to an exit, no objects to use as weapons.

Ky eyed him, impassive. "Now?"

"Yes, *now*." Milo took a deep breath to steady his nerves.

Ky snaked his hand back into the invisible seam in that depthless coat of his, rooted around, and then pulled out the bag.

Bry's bag.

Calfskin over metasteel mesh, treated with blueroot oil for softness. A few months ago Milo had added a magnelock and put the key under the skin in his finger. No one could open it but him.

"The first cohort of noncompliant families arrived in Kitya one month after you took the throne," Milo said, spitting out *noncompliant* like dirt on his lips. "Twenty days later, in the next cohort, you took my best friend. No communication, nothing, until he showed up wheezing at my door three months later with this." Milo shook the bag. They all heard a dull rattling.

She blinked between them, eyes shining. Still pretending.

He went on: "You have these people logged as living. Working. They're receiving food and energy rations. Where is that food going, Mora? What are you using that energy for? What did you use the energy from their atomization for? Because this is all that's left of those people—their carefully numbered pins."

He swiped his finger over the seal and filled his hand, feeling the weight like cries of accusation. He slapped them down on the table.

Sixty-seven pins. Dark silver, thick as a quill and as long as a fingertip, cylindrical with flat ends. Some of them still carried smudges of blood because Bry had smuggled them before washing and melting.

Ky instructed the table to read them and a list of identifiers scrolled across the wall, names included, sending a flicker through the room. Then Milo tore into his video files and pulled up a royal relay from a month ago. He scrolled through the viewline until he found the damning moments.

A perfect, glowing white queen smiled at them from all surfaces. She was saying, "…in Kitya, where the former disloyalists from Eray are learning to welcome the mantle of responsibility for paying back their debt to society by farming essential crops needed to feed those brave men who dare to leave their homes and families to mine—"

The feed cut from the queen to the gold-green fields of Kitya, where rows of dozens of people smiled through their teeth and waved. Milo's program paused the video, picked out a dozen faces, and matched them pin to bloody pin.

She couldn't deny this.

And then she did.

·

Relai stepped back. This was worse than waking from the travel pod— she felt sick in her stomach, in her blood, in that painful cringing layer right under her skin. The ship seemed to rock under her feet.

"This isn't happening. It has to be fake. Those are—" She sank down into a chair and her hands, still raw from the pod, jumped at the sensation of smooth, warm leather. "This can't be real."

The tall, scary one burst forward and dashed a chair to the side as he bellowed, "It *is* real and there's not a corner of the galaxy in which you can hide. *We have you.*"

Relai couldn't look at him, but she caught the expression on the older one's face and held tight. He didn't seem confident or condemning or hateful. He looked worried.

"*Crap,*" the man said. "Milo, she might not be it."

Milo reeled back. "What? She's lying. Ky!"

Ky pushed his chair out and, rather than taking the time to walk around the conference table, hopped up and slid over. She got an excellent view of the row of knives along his belt as he landed next to her. Relai jolted at the sight. *Knives.*

He prompted her up and led her around to the screen, pressing with the pads of his fingers between her shoulder blades. This one, Ky, stood only a couple inches taller than Relai. Fifteen or twenty years older. Solid.

He placed her next to the frozen relay and stepped back.

"Slide the video back. Get her face on-screen—good, there. Now, Aydor. Talk."

Relai opened her mouth. She couldn't believe how beautiful that thing on the screen looked. Her hair had never been that perfect a day in her life.

"Tell us who you are," Ky suggested.

She swallowed. Two dirty, terrifying men stared back at her.

"I... My name is Relai... Orist Aydor. I left four years ago and I was going back to Arden—when I, when I went to sleep—but I woke up here instead and I was dying. I don't know why I didn't go—I wanted to see my family. I wasn't supposed to wake up on Earth."

Please believe me, she thought. They would have no reason to hurt her if she could make them believe.

Ky shook his head, one brow angled high. "You see it?"

Milo glared. "I see a killer with a talent for lying."

Relai wanted to argue more, convince them, but words wouldn't come. Ky pointed one finger at her, then wiggled all four. "There's something off about it."

Relai felt her heart kick up at the barest chance they'd believe her, but Milo just cursed as he gathered up those precious, damning pins and sealed them back in their bag. "It's been touched up, that's all. See? She was made to look more... sanda, less barata. Paler, like a regent."

She wrung her hands and pulled at the wide cuffs of the robe. "No, it's fake. They would always lighten my skin before a public event so I'd look more like my dad, but I stopped all that when I left."

"And her accent's different," Ky added. Milo handed him the bag of pins and it disappeared into a seam along Ky's side.

Relai nodded. "Four years on Earth."

"She could be altering her voice right now."

"With such consistency, when she's terrified?" Ky's eyes bored into her as though staring hard enough would uncover the truth. Then he clicked his tongue. "Let's ask those guards, see if the travel tale matches up. The clever one might be able to link us back into the base's system so we can see the records for ourselves."

Milo frowned, but tilted his head in assent and took off with that same purposeful stride. He ducked through the door without breaking his pace. Relai watched it slide shut behind him without flickering. No security on the exits.

Ky stepped closer to her. She shifted, steadying her feet and loosening her joints to move.

"You know," he said, "if I hadn't tracked you down myself I'd think you weren't even her. Your manners are different. You aren't acting like royalty."

She clenched her teeth, flashed them, kept his eyes on her face and away from her hands. "I've been living on Earth for the past four years. No one treats me like a princess here. I'm not anymore."

Ky scratched his scruffy chin. "If you're lying... well. I will kill you."

Relai took stock of her body and tested the grip of her bare feet on the cold metal floor. Before she could allow herself to realize what any of this meant, she had to get herself safe.

"And if I'm not?"

After another moment of that piercing gaze, he smiled. "We'll see."

She took her chance.

Her hands were still quick and her muscles remembered, sure with the energy of a recent healing. She snatched the second smallest knife, one the length of her thumb with a sharp curve at the end. A knee to his hip put him off balance—he swung one arm out but she ducked, grabbed his gun, and flung it away—then she hooked her foot around his opposite knee, clasped his neck, and dropped him to the ground.

The tussle went quick and silent. Relai pinned him by the wrist and the neck, leaning most of her weight on the knee in his back. He swore with relish, ignoring the knife at his throat. "Where the hell did *that* come from?" He didn't sound bothered at all.

Her eyes darted from exit to exit. She wouldn't have to hold him for long.

She twisted his forearm and gasped, "I don't want to hurt you, but you keep telling these lies and I don't even know what day it is."

He tried to lift his head but she pressed in with the knife and he settled for waving a few fingers. "You could be damaging my spinal nerves, you know."

She frowned but still shifted her weight. With her luck, that would be all he needed to throw her off, so she angled the knife against the vulnerable crease running down the side of his neck and lodged her wrist against his shoulder. If he bucked, he'd open that artery wide.

The conference room door slid open and in marched those two guards from the base—first the boy, his face a swollen mess, then the woman—followed by Milo. Relai sucked in air, hoping they'd see and move, and *yes,* the boy dove right at Ky's gun, snatched it up, and turned it on Milo as *no,* Milo snarled and threw an arm around the woman's neck and put his gun to her head. Relai cried out, "No!" as his back smacked against the crisp white wallscreen and then everyone shouted at once.

"I knew it," Milo roared.

"Put the gun down, hands up, let her go! Gun down!" the boy barked, while the female guard shouted, "Nobody shoot anybody! Stop!"

"How about everybody *shut the hell up* for a second!"

For a man pinned to the ground at the mercy of his own knife, Ky had a sort of authority in his voice that cut through the noise.

Everyone shut up.

Then Relai answered Milo with her own growing anger. "If you were right about me, I would have killed him and gotten out of here. He's still alive."

"Ky?"

"Sorry, kid, she's quicker that I thought. Also stronger—nice job in the med bay, One and Two. I'm, ah, I'm surprised." Relai leaned just a little bit harder and he coughed out a laugh. "Fine, embarrassed. Second time in one day I've lost my gun."

The woman cut in, "He's got a trigger for a knockout drug tick and he might've put one on you."

Relai tensed. "Then I'd better lean so this knife will push through if I go limp."

"Do you want me to shoot him, Our Glory?" the boy guard asked as he ducked in an awkward bow.

"No!" Relai and the other woman both shouted. Relai couldn't see her name, but she caught the guard's eye and managed an appreciative nod as she flicked one hand to get the boy to rise. "And don't bow to me. That's weird."

Both guards froze.

No one had bowed to Relai in so long it felt bizarre, mocking. These guards had to know that she'd abandoned her inheritance—everyone had to know. Right?

"Weird?" the woman repeated.

Relai looked her full in the eyes. "Who do *you* think I am?"

The guard stopped straining against Milo's grip. Relai watched her wiggle her fingers and relax her hands against Milo's forearm, and then she recited: "You are our Glory, our Honor, and our Light. You are the best hope and the wisdom and providence of the four planets joined. We serve you without hesitation, without doubt, and without fail. You are our Queen. Our Relai Mora Aydor."

She didn't sound particularly sincere, but the young man beside Relai couldn't resist the pull of the oath. By the end of it he was down on one knee, his gun trained on Milo but his head bowed toward Relai.

Shit.

"Orist."

The woman's eyes widened, and then Relai managed to say, *"Orist.* Not Mora. My mother is queen." She looked from face to face and found no understanding. "What *happened?*"

It was the female guard who began to see through it all first. "That means…" Her eyes went vague and she spoke more to herself than the rest of them. "It hasn't been you, at least for a while now. I don't know how long… We can find out! We can still get access to the base records from this ship!"

"Ha!" Ky exclaimed from underneath Relai. He hadn't tried to throw her off, not once. "Good. Let her go, Milo."

Milo craned his neck to see the guard's face. "You can show us?"

She nodded against the press of his forearm and he let her go. Relai lifted away from Ky, knife pointed at the floor, and they all moved back to safer distances from one another.

The woman rolled her shoulders and rubbed her neck, glaring acid at Milo as she tugged heavy curls away from her sweat-sticky face. "So you're not Unity? And they didn't hire you?"

"No one hired us."

"Clever, clever," Ky said as he hopped to his feet. "We found a Unity code for sit-back-and-let-destruction-rain, so we sent it ahead of us in case it might clear the way a bit. Worked a charm."

The boy guard muttered, "Uh, Tannor, is that what—"

"Shut up, Goren," she snapped, and then she walked over to the table and brought up the ship's programming. "We're not Unity, either." Tannor noticed the confusion on Relai's face and clarified, "Anti-monarchy terrorists," as she tapped her way into codes and subcodes.

Anti-monarchy terrorists?

"Here!" Tannor waved through layers of floating information, but Relai couldn't make out what she meant. "See, this is the log of the work orders for energy and construction, and you can see how about three months ago there was a room dug out in one of the catacombs. Then here," she enlarged a separate window, "they transferred a travel pod. It doesn't say anything about an occupant; it says empty. They called it storage… but in these records, you see the room was receiving power and water the whole time. The right amount to run an occupied travel pod."

She turned, adamant. "That's where we found her. She's been asleep for at least three months, maybe more."

"What day is it?" Relai demanded.

"Proper Time 36-2-44. Earthan date is, ah, July something. Thirtieth?" Goren asked in the direction of his partner.

"Thirty-first. It's July 31st."

Relai felt dread eating up through her chest. "That means I've only been asleep for a little over two months. That doesn't make sense."

"I have an easy explanation: all of this is fake," Milo said.

"Or—" Ky spoke up, then stopped.

Milo shifted forward. "Or what?"

"Her bone density. I was checking the medical scan of her body, and it showed a warning about lowered bone density. Lack of movement screws your bone health, and ships compensate for it but it's not built into the pod, it's the *ship*. If they kept her here on Earth—"

Relai interrupted him urgently. "What year is it?"

The two guards looked at each other, apprehensive and silent. She stood up. "*What year is it?*"

"By Earth's count it's the year 2015," Tannor answered.

Ky bounced up and opened a window on the conference room wall showing the medical scan and they all saw the bone density readout. It didn't take a medical officer to understand.

Relai sat back down.

"Fourteen months. I've been asleep for over a year?" She stared at her hands, clenched them into fists and then opened them. "No wonder I've been feeling so strange."

"Can't fake bone density," Ky said.

"No, you can't," Milo answered in a hollow voice. He laid his gun down on the table and then he turned and looked at Relai.

•

Goren thought he might burst, and he'd been doing so well but he couldn't help it—his brain was banging around his skull and he couldn't take it anymore.

"*YOU MEAN YOU HAVEN'T BEEN RULING AT ALL?* WHO HAS BEEN IN CHARGE?! Did they kidnap you? We have to tell everyone! They won't believe you, either! What are we going to do?"

The queen—no, the princess, she was Orist, not Mora—sat there with the whites of her eyes showing, not looking at anyone. Goren couldn't believe that anyone would dare treat someone so revered, so important, so *glorious*, like a common victim. She was the next ruler of their whole side of the galaxy—the people loved her! Every artist used her as a subject at least once, and she'd been made into dolls for every year of her life growing up (his youngest sister had the first five). This woman was everything—glamorous, smart, so much more decisive than her father. She was the greatest leader the Vada Coalition had ever seen.

"Those bastards!" he raged. "Just wait until we get through with them! Wait, do you think it's the Tennans behind this? But the whole thing has been about preparing to defend against them! I bet it's those Gastredi jerkoffs. Or it could be the Oeylans, I always heard you can't trust an Oeylan—"

•

"Goren, please!" Tannor exclaimed, "I can't think with you rambling like that!" She flicked a finger toward Ky. "You: package all of that data into a relay and I'll encrypt it. We can't be the only ones with this proof. We'll send it to Oliver Station for transmission to Arden and then, no matter what happens to us, at least the High Council will know what they did to her."

"I'm capable of encryption, sprite," Ky said. Then he turned his back to her and did as she ordered.

Tannor moved over to the princess, sat next to her in a chair, and put a hand on the rain-damp hair spread across her back. People from Kilani normally wouldn't allow this kind of sudden contact, but Tannor was betting that Relai might see her as safe enough, considering everything that had happened. She could feel the knobs of the queen's spine under her fingers.

Tannor leaned her head in and whispered, "I can pause everyone and put you in control of the ship. Just nod."

Relai shook her head. Stared with blank eyes.

"I'm not in control."

Tannor held herself back from cursing and forced herself up.

What did they have, then? Idiot, rotten, and rage.

That left her.

Great.

•

Goren was relieved to see that Tannor watched Ky closely, then added her left handprint to rush the message past the normal civilian scans. Unity terrorists might have stopped spaceship travel to and from Earth when they bombed Oliver Block, but outgoing message transmissions still worked. The sooner the High Council knew about this whole disaster, the better.

Then Ky came over and offered Goren his forearm, fingers curved to cup his elbow like any normal, respectful Ardenian might. "Goren, is it?"

"I'm not going to shake your arm!" Goren exclaimed. "That guy shot me in the leg!"

Milo cocked his head to the side. "I also punched you in the face. I'm sorry I had to shoot you, but it was necessary."

"And the punch?" Goren demanded.

"Not sorry about that one."

"Nope!" Ky shoved between the two of them before Goren got close enough to threaten him properly. "That's all in the past! He's young, he'll forget about it eventually, and really," he turned to Goren, "the swelling improves your face. My name is Bevn Kyro, call me Ky. This is Milo Hemm."

Goren was NOT prepared to be friends. "Unity or not, you two still intended to—what? Kill her? Hold her for ransom? You're still lowlife dirty criminals and it's still my duty to arrest you."

Milo sneered down at him from his bizarre, gargantuan height. "What, are you going to tie us up and carry us back to your little base?"

"No, we're going to fly back and sort all of this out with the Captain!"

Tannor halted him with a hand on his arm. "Goren, we can't just go back. Someone at the base was keeping the queen there, and we don't know who."

"At least two of you tried to kill her," Milo said.

"Not *us*," Tannor snapped.

"Tower guards are all the same."

Goren went all tense and ready to fight, but Tannor didn't back away a bit. Her family wasn't anywhere near the greater class (Goren had checked up on her when she arrived on base... it wasn't stalking, it was being prepared), but she carried herself like more than an equal. The woman had *presence*.

"No," she bit back, "we are not. Some of our guards sat back and watched you two stroll in and attack, and if that's what you call trying to kill her then it rots you more than us!"

"He—" the queen's voice cut in. "He means they were really going to kill me. Not sit-back-and-watch, like your, uh, code said. Kill me. I think they almost did."

No one had looked her way for a few moments; they all moved to hear what else she might have to say, but she turned her head and covered her mouth with the palm of one hand.

(Goren was a little lost, to be honest. If Tannor wasn't Unity, what was she? *Rude* every time he tried to bring it up, that's what.)

Milo paced down the room. "Two of your guards tried to assassinate the queen of the Vada Coalition. That is not what we are here to do. We came to bring her back to Arden to face the people. I have all of the evidence we need to accuse her in a public trial. We came to see justice done."

"Ha!" Goren shouted, and Tannor laughed, too. He put himself between Orist and Milo so she wouldn't have to lay eyes on this mongrel. "You committed treason when you attacked her. The queen is never unjust. The queen *IS* justice!"

"Ignoring that nonsense," Ky interrupted, "let's talk about the plan. Get to Arden? To hell with proving anything to anyone—she's the rightful queen, after all. Power's power."

"Wait—" Orist stilled them with the crack in her voice. She'd squared herself at the head of the table like they were in a council meeting, except no one else was seated. "First. Tell me: *where are my parents?*"

For once, Goren bit his tongue. He hardly wanted to be the bearer of bad news—especially with how rotten her day was going anyway. He looked to Tannor.

Tannor was watching Ky watching Milo, and Milo was gripping the back of a chair, his face all in despair, his skin an ashen yellow.

No one wanted to say it.

Well, this was awkward.

·

Relai looked from face to face. Four people.

One, two, three, four.

She already knew.

Thick misery spread up from her heart and she recognized the feeling of dunking her head underwater, sinking down, water swelling around her throat and over her face.

Finally, Ky said it.

"Your father's dead." He spoke without emotion. "He was killed over a year ago, destroyed along with a fleet of Ardenians traveling to intercept the Tennans. He wanted to negotiate for peace, maybe trade, but they didn't even make it from Arden's atmosphere to Odys Block before someone set off bombs through the whole fleet. They call it the Overture Attack. Just after King Ayadas died, your mother disappeared. Everyone thinks she's dead, too, but no one can find her so no one really knows. You mourned a little, I think. S'hard to remember; you weren't high on my list of priorities at the time.

"Anyway, a Unity attack took out outgoing travel from Oliver Block, so you had to get on a spaceship and take the long way home. You're, what?

Maybe a year into the journey to Ketzal Block, now?" From the seat she'd taken at the word *dead,* Tannor nodded, rubbing the heel of her hand under her eye. Her knees wavered almost close enough to touch Relai's.

You'll be the death of us all, he used to say.

Relai forced herself blank.

"If I'm in deep sleep on a ship bound for Oeyla," she said, "then my cousin Voresh Regnaniban must be serving as Regent."

"No," Ky said. "You're awake, with a constant relay stream to the High Council. You've been ruling via transmissions like the one we just watched."

"Except—" Milo began, but Ky took back the burden of words.

"Except you—the false you—lied to everyone. The queen stayed on Earth. Even the High Council doesn't know."

"Somebody knows, or you wouldn't have found her," Tannor said.

Ky exchanged a long look with Milo. "Yeah."

Before Relai could face the implications behind that word, Ky continued. "You, Mora Aydor, claim to have evidence that it was Tennans hiding on Arden who killed your father. You froze travel between the provinces and then removed the governors as they protested. You put Regent Service guards in charge. Anyone might be hiding a Tennan, or sending information to the Tennans, or even shusasevati half-breeds working with them to overthrow humanity. No one says a free word."

Ky's eyes flashed to Milo. "Then Sol Hemm refused to export any more metalock, and you bombed Elik to rubble."

"What do you mean, *bombed?*" The creeping horror in Tannor's words dragged Relai's attention over. She had blanched. "There were only, uh, maybe a few dozen casualties during the relocation—"

She trailed off as Milo's fingers scratched marks in the headrest of the conference bay chair.

"Thousands, not dozens, died," Ky said. "They've moved the rest to camps in other provinces and brought in new conscripts to work the mines. The newbies aren't surviving well, of course, 'cause no one knows how to work with metalock like—"

"*Ky,*" Milo choked out, his face twisted away from the group.

"Anyway." Ky clenched his jaw, eyes hard and back to boring into Relai. "You're building new ships and uniforms and weapons galore. You sent a big crop of soldiers off to meet the Tennans and when they're slaughtered, which they will be, you'll finally get Titus off their asses and onto their tech. You might even convince Gastred to come out and play."

Like when she was a child cowering under a destructive tirade from her father, Relai found a single point and focused on it. Her eyes picked the buckle at the ankle of Milo's boot. She stared.

She didn't cry. She didn't want to cry. She was underwater.

Ky finished: "War. It's what you want."

War?

My father is gone.

"No," she answered with a voice outside herself. "As you said, I'm still the rightful queen."

The horror swelled too huge—and—

Relai couldn't. She couldn't.

The buckle might've been metasteel. Hard to tell.

She lifted her eyes. "There won't be a war once I take my crown."

"Good enough for me!" Ky turned to Milo. "What do you think?"

Milo dragged his arm over his eyes and shook his head. "Same goal," he said. "We're going back. I'll do whatever it takes to bring down whoever's been ruling."

It didn't sound like a vote of confidence in Relai's favor, but she wasn't looking for one.

My father is gone, she thought.

Finally.

○○●○○

EPISODE III:

TRUST

FASS REVIEWED THE state of his dock.

The jumper remained; the groundship and one skimmer were missing. Perhaps one of the absent guards had cowered off to delay the inevitable; it seemed like the sort of thing Private Dray would do.

"What now, Captain?" Sergeant Marejak asked from the back of the dock control room. Thirty-seven guards had trickled here after the communication system failed to reboot and Marejak was somehow senior behind Fass. She had no sense of humor and she never bent a rule.

Fass indulged her with a serious nod.

"Stay here and secure the base, Sergeant. We have six missing: Tars, Palia, Dray, Horten, Mellick, and Lilya. Find them."

"We need to get the system back up—" she nagged.

If she couldn't solve that problem without complaining, he had no reason to mourn the loss of her. "You have my orders."

He looked across the room for the appropriate faces; he counted nineteen Unity, but the jumper would only hold eight. He'd already sent Reddig for supplies.

Fass booted up the last jumper in the hangar and then turned to his people and called out the names of the six tallest and strongest men. As they pushed their way to the exit, he despaired of the tone of the crowd—fragile, nervous, and lost. Weak.

Off to one side Marejak seemed to be talking, trying to give orders, but most of the crowd was ignoring her. Fass tried not to laugh as he and his men tromped off.

Reddig caught up just as they reached the jumper. He was carrying a blue travel case the size of a dinner tray and thickness of an open-splayed hand.

"Got it, sir," Reddig said, barely short of breath. Reddig was fast and lethal and he knew how to operate an organ transport case. Fass liked him.

"Bulk it, Private," Fass replied. Some of these men might hesitate at killing the queen herself without trial, even with their loyalty to Unity. He'd have to be careful. Not many deserved his trust.

If only Tannor Mellick had spent a little more time with him; he could have drawn her in, used what skills she had. But she was gone now—neither her comm nor her pin were showing up on scans, which meant she was under some sort of masking.

She must be on the missing groundship with the queen—and groundships couldn't hide from Ednar Fass.

His soldiers sorted themselves out, Trima in the pilot seat, as Fass waved to the tiny brown splotch of Marejak's face in the control room and the jumper lifted off. The rain had faded and the night hanging over the jaws of the dock was just beginning to bow toward dawn.

Trima looked to Fass from the helm. "There's no trace of the groundship, sir."

Fass drew a tablet out of his jacket and delved into the connection he'd spent nearly a decade forging with his Earthan friends. Then as everyone watched, he laid the tablet on the console and allowed them all to see his genius: real-time satellite images.

"Even a masked groundship with no chem trail will appear under the eyes of Earthan satellites," he said. "Over land, the mask can disperse heat and light to disappear at close range, but from orbit the difference is clear. Over water, they'll find it impossible to hide." Everyone here already knew how all the regulation Vada vehicles avoided endlessly proliferating Earthan tech: Earth Monitoring and their planted agents in every government. Not just anyone could bypass Earth Monitoring to see the actual Earthan images, though.

"Strength, Captain," Trima replied.

"Strength to Unity!" the rest of them chimed.

Two bright marks appeared on the map and Trima pulled them open. "I got distress from Horten and Lilya, sir. Should we stop for them?"

Horten, they could lose, Fass mused in irritation. Lilya, though—she might prove useful later. He gave Trima a permissive wave.

Then he leaned close to Reddig. "Wait until we get the queen alone. You can remove the hand, but I claim the pleasure of the eye."

Reddig patted the blade on his thigh. "Thank you, sir."

Fass matched his smile.

oo●oo

When Relai went blank, it scared Tannor like nothing else that had happened so far. It was like the queen pulled her own stopper, drained herself from her body, and for a few nauseous seconds there was nothing there. Nothing.

Then Relai's eyelashes flicked and her eyes and mouth went tight. Tired, but present.

"Excellent!" Ky forged on. "How about you two? Are you in?"

Goren's whole face contorted in offended disbelief. "We're not following you anywhere! We're going back to the base and we're going to fully stock this ship and get more loyal guards so the queen—princess—so Our Glory is really safe!"

At the same moment Tannor snapped, "You should be asking if *you* can come along with *us*!"

"Words, words, sprite," Ky replied, snatching back his gun from Goren. "You're with us, we're with you, what does it matter? The important thing is who's in control of the ship."

Tannor smirked right back. "I think you know who'd be in control if we both stepped up to screens right now."

He hoisted his gun to his shoulder and gestured to the wall in cordial invitation. "Yeah, the one still standing."

"*Stop.*" Relai stood up. "Whether we like it or not, the fact is, you're all—" she swallowed, "you're all with me. So. Where are we right now?"

Ky looked over his shoulder, then up along the gently curving ceiling. "I, ah, parked us in a little cove at the edge of an ocean. We're protected on three sides by cliffs, fourth by water, fifth and sixth by open air. We're full up on fuel for a trip to Oliver, but there's nothing to eat and no travel pods.

Between me and this one, here," he inclined his head toward Tannor, "I'm confident your base can't follow us."

Tannor inclined her head in mocking return as she rested a hand on the chair behind Relai. "They can't follow us because I turned off the chem trail you didn't notice; you're welcome."

Ky tissed air through his teeth. "No you didn't. I've been watching your every move."

"Then I must know more than you about how to handle a ship." She cocked an eyebrow, waiting.

Milo hadn't responded to her prompt, and there were only two of them.

Ky went still, peering at Tannor with a crinkle in his brow, and then he yawned. "I must be tired. Feels like I haven't slept in three days."

Thank hell and holy valence, *yes.*

(A three? Tannor had never met a three before.)

She recited the proper response:

"Three? I can barely think after two. I go white as chalk with no sleep."

She saw, and she knew it was only because he chose to let her see, the surprise and intrigue and appreciation flit across his face.

"M'sure it looks nice with your yellow hair," he murmured. Three and yellow. Strategic planning, embedded. And no sleep meant active.

Feels like I haven't slept in three days. She'd trusted the orders, allowed for a breach in security, for a subversive, non-violent resistance. The resistance that altered travel documents, lowered mining quotas, redistributed food, and forgot to censor relays. For the Quiet.

Then these two had shown up and plucked the queen out of the hands of guards who were holding her captive. She'd been helping them.

She'd been helping rescue Orist Aydor.

Tannor felt a certainty sizzle through her, an energy and pride and a fierce drive—*she helped rescue the queen.*

So Ky was using Milo Hemm's vendetta… and Milo had no idea. Milo Hemm, the Monster of Eray, separatist, terrorist—and perfect cover.

I'm concerned about my associate finding your queen, he'd said. She met Ky's eyes and the glow from the wall screen flecked light in his dark irises.

Damn right, you were.

"Are you flirting with her?" Goren exclaimed. "This is a life and death situation and you're flirting?!"

Ky appraised the young man, flicked his gaze back to Tannor, and with a twitch of her head Tannor told him, *no. Goren's not Quiet.* But she shifted her body and thumbed a smudge of blood from the boy's cheek, and Ky smiled.

"Don't let him bother you, Goren," she said. "I don't think he can help it."

"Get off my face," Goren grumbled.

•

"*Okay.*" Relai shakily drew their attention with a wave of her hand as her eyes jumped from person to person.

They were dirty and greasy and damp, Tannor's blood caked thick in her hair and Goren's face swollen from abuse. The criminals, burn-marked and soot-smeared and crumbling dirt everywhere they went, didn't fit the warmth of the polished room. They were all staring at her. Expecting leadership.

Never let anyone in the room think they are more important than you.

She asked, "How were you two going to get me back to Arden?"

Milo grimaced and Ky scratched at the back of his neck. "We ran into some problems with our original plan," Ky admitted. "But don't get the wrong idea! Nothing has happened that we can't handle."

"We got shot down by this planet's military as I was about to land," Milo explained, leaning against the table with his arms crossed over his chest. "I underestimated this planet's defense capabilities. We snuck aboard a... a transport. It was bound to set metal tracks—I don't know—"

"Oh, a train," Relai guessed.

"A *train*." Milo repeated the word like wielding a club. "And then we walked the rest of the way."

They must be tired, she thought.

Tannor shifted, her hands twitching toward the nearest wall. "Why didn't I see you enter the atmosphere?"

Ky's smirk spread into a full-fledged grin.

Relai coughed and said, "So, you've got no plan now."

"We're making it up as we go along," Ky agreed.

"We've been through worse," Milo said.

Relai breathed deep, refusing to look back and acknowledge the misery behind his words. Forward held misery enough.

So she said, mostly to herself, "I get the feeling you're not going to be saying that at the end of this."

"Is that a threat?" Milo snapped. Time slowed, Relai stumbled back, and with one step Milo overwhelmed her personal space, all shadow and weight and wild brambles of brown hair.

"No! No." She put a hand up and left it hovering over his heart. "Just— feeling cynical."

He held her stare for another few heartbeats, glaring through the wave of residual hate.

"I'm sorry," she said.

He jerked back, jaw slack, and turned on his heels.

"We'll need food," he muttered, and left the room.

·

ii.

Tannor couldn't see them getting out of this alive.

If they went above four thousand feet their own base would shoot them down, and Daat Base in Hawaii would know by now, too. Both Ardenian bases sat north of Earth's equator and she didn't even want to think about dealing with Titus's Buzou Base in the South China Sea.

(Buzou carried maybe fifteen soldiers? Sixteen? It only took one to aim a missile. They didn't stand a chance if Titus decided to act.)

And yet… Ky and Milo got past everyone, and *how the hell?* They must have something, know something she didn't. It could be done. They'd do it again.

So, when Milo stormed off, Tannor hurried after. He showed only a moment of disorientation as he fled the conference bay and then the door clamped shut behind them. She knew where he was going: the cargo hold. It should be stocked with a few skimmers.

Tannor was terrible with social interaction, but even she could see that Milo needed rest and peace and time for mourning. He must have lost so many people.

And killed a lot in return. Tannor pushed back the thought with her own growing doubt. *Supposedly.* She couldn't trust anything she thought she knew about him from reports and telay, not anymore. She wasn't afraid, no—but she'd be prepared.

He noticed her but didn't stop barreling down the long, tight corridor.

He was eran, darker than anyone but some Titians, with a glow under the brown of his skin like he might be made of gold. She wondered if it was a regional thing that he was so tall, so broad-shouldered, so *giant*. She didn't know a single person in her region, Reyet, who'd grown so large.

"I speak a little Italian," she said to his back.

He paused, eyes flashing over his shoulder. Then he turned and—

"Will you stop doing that?" she blurted out.

He froze. "Doing what?"

She waved her hands like claws. "Looming. Using your size to intimidate us. I already know you could snap me in half, you don't need to remind me. I'm aware."

He looked down and let his shoulders settle back. "You healed the rest of her but left the bruises on her neck."

"Somebody needed to know," she replied.

Tannor saw a shadow of anguish in his eyes as he said, "I do."

He'd saved the queen from those guards, she realized. He must've done it when he thought she was his enemy, and now he felt guilty for scaring her.

She gave him a measured nod. "Good. So do I."

Then Tannor sidled past him and put on a professional voice. "Italian is the local language. They're used to tourists, so it won't be strange for us to stumble through conversation. I'll talk and you carry the heavy stuff."

She didn't hear him following, so she stopped and looked back to find a wary expression on his face.

"You're all right going out there with me alone?" he asked.

Tannor took off walking again to hide the conflict on her face. She'd always been taught to fear men who looked exactly like him—and he knew it. That knowledge didn't make him any less dangerous, but it did give her something to use against him: he didn't want to be the thing she'd been warned against.

"You need me," she said without looking back. "Besides, you're better for carrying food than Goren, and Ky thinks he knows what he's doing. I don't have time for that."

"He always thinks he knows what he's doing," Milo said as he fell into step beside her. "From each, according to their ability..."

"To each according to their need?" she finished in surprise. "I didn't know anything Earthan had reached Eray."

His cheek pinched in a half-smile and she watched the movement of his beard. She'd never known anyone with a beard. She wanted to touch it.

"People brought back all sorts of things after the Tennan War," he said. "The High Court can't filter out paper books."

They rounded a corner and reached a cut in the floor. Milo hopped right down, ignoring the hand bars, and he didn't try to help her as she climbed to the floor below. His hands didn't move in the direction of her body, not for a second.

"Where are you from?" Milo asked.

"Reyet."

"Ah. So you know."

Ah, indeed. Reyet was worse-off than almost any other region, though they didn't suffer the same antagonism that the Erayd did. It was hard to tell where a person hailed from until they spoke, but the Erayd made things easier with all that hair they liked to grow. Not that Tannor had anything against hair—she didn't even shave her arms and legs (to the constant horror of her family). Milo probably left hair on his chest.

Maybe he'd take off his shirt when they found new clothes.

Now Milo was peering at her with a faint bit of concern on his brow. "You don't need to be embarrassed; I don't care what class you're in. I recognize you."

Tannor frowned. She was careful about the use of her name across the commons after the trouble with Fordev, and he shouldn't know her face at all. Tannor kept her image out of the coalition's shared digital space because one look at her face might sour someone's respect for her accomplishments. *You couldn't have done all that yourself,* one teacher had told her. *No one who looks like you would need to. Now tell me who you copied.*

Tannor tamped down a flash of irritation at the memory and asked, "How do you know me?"

"I heard the way you recited your oath," he said. "She's your enemy, too."

"Whoever's been ruling," Tannor amended.

"The False Relai," he agreed. "So we're equals, you and I."

She smiled and Milo matched it. His eyes were a bit green.

"Equals."

∘∘●∘∘

"So…" Relai began, seated wearily at the conference table with Goren posted in the Regent Service guard position to her right. "What are we going to—"

"First, a question for you," Ky said. He was perched cross-legged on the table, poking around on his tablet without letting on what he was doing. Relai tensed. "Actually, a few questions." She tensed more.

"You say you weren't ruling. What *were* you doing on Earth?"

"Uh," her eyes met Goren's earnest gaze, then Ky's, then a nice, safe spot on the floor. "Traveling."

77

The silence told her that answer wasn't going to be enough.

"This is a big planet. I don't think it's really—I mean, right now we should be figuring out where—"

"What we really need to know," Ky interrupted, "is if you have any loyal contacts here, now, on Earth. Anyone who might help. Or who might—"

"No."

Relai had spent three of her four years traveling Earth with two personal guards. Their names were Gokoro and Aurseren and they'd glommed on to her when she left Arden at her mother's request.

"None?"

"No one."

Gokoro would spar with her using a different art than Relai's silata; she'd drill Relai with leg sweeps and in return Relai would dip blunt wooden dowels in red paint and demonstrate all the best places to slit ligaments. Aurseren would laugh at them both and snort smokepowder while she watched Buster Keaton movies instead of securing the perimeter of Relai's latest resort home.

Sometimes Relai would ditch them for a week or two so she wouldn't have to talk to a single human person for a while—she'd climb a mountain or pick a beach and just swim. Sleep. Not say a word.

Relief, if only for a time.

"No friends," Ky said. "Convenient."

Relai wrapped her fingers around her little knife blade and squeezed. Not enough to break the skin, just enough to hurt.

Then Ky eased back and his interrogating gaze vanished. "It's simpler this way, actually. We don't have to worry about any heroes trying to kill us to rescue you; anyone after you just wants to end you. Simple."

Aurseren lasted the first year, Gokoro, the second and third. After that, she'd been alone.

Goren said something belligerent, but she didn't hear the words. Ky was right; no one would come and rescue her. She would be alone, yet never alone again.

Relai didn't realize she'd drifted away until a head came level with hers.

"Hey." Ky crouched in front of her, one hand on her forearm, and moved to take back his knife.

"No, no." She drew it back. "I need this to keep me safe."

He smiled and she was surprised by the warmth. "But Milo and I will do that."

("Me, too!" Goren said. They ignored him.)

"Milo?" Relai's hand tightened against the sharp edge of the knife. "I'm sure he's nice when he's not strangling anyone."

Ky stretched his jaw. "He didn't kill you," he said. "He thought he should and he still couldn't. You saw him."

She remembered the way Milo's body shook as he sat next to her in the rain. *Pity won't rule our planet, child.*

Relai took a deep breath. She could bury this.

"I understand that. I just—" She wanted to go on but Ky stood and clapped his hands together.

"You hungry? I might have some bread left over."

"No, thank you." She attempted a smile. "I still feel sick."

She stood and swayed from dizziness as Ky turned his head and showed her the strong column of his throat. There was a spot of red there. A nick from her knife.

Relai didn't get the chance to apologize because Ky froze and his eyes went sharp and unfocused.

"Ooh, I can't believe we didn't see that one coming," he said after a pause.

"What?" Relai demanded.

His face only tightened. "Who cares? Same plan."

He was talking to Milo on his comm. Relai decided to keep quiet until something comprehensible happened, but then Ky let out a long, exasperated sigh and cursed.

"What?" she demanded.

He just shook his head and spun around, muttering, "Where's a good place to put a body?"

•

Two minutes earlier, Tannor had stepped up to a terminal and woken two skimmers.

"We need to get off of this planet as soon as possible," Milo said, rummaging through a supply cabinet. He found what he was looking for: a cargo extension. "It'll take the first relays twelve hours to reach Oliver

Station. Five, maybe ten minutes for security review, then six minutes from Oliver to Odys to Arden. They'll send every guard, bounty hunter, and disgruntled ex-terr on Earth after us. We have twenty-three hours left, and then all hell is our hell."

Tannor clipped up her jacket, glancing to make sure the cells held a full charge. One day left plenty of time to gather supplies, and they could decontaminate and system cleanse at Oliver Station... if the whole place wasn't waiting to kill them when they got there. She sighed, imagining the technical back bends she'd need to do to get them across the galaxy alive. "Mora Aydor isn't even supposed to be on Earth," she muttered. Since Unity bombed Oliver Block and destroyed outgoing travel, she'd had to take the slow way over to the next closest block, Ketzal, at Oeyla—

She wasn't supposed to be here.

Tannor and Milo turned to one another in unison.

"It's the perfect excuse," she began, but he rambled over her.

"They faked the bombing." Milo turned and stormed back in the direction of the main deck, tapping behind his ear. On comms with Ky, Tannor realized. "Oliver Block was never damaged, they just needed a reason she couldn't return to Arden. They're filtering her fake relays through Oliver. We'll find our enemies there at the station, maybe the ones really in charge—"

The relay. All the queen's medical data.

"Milo!" Tannor cried after him. "We just sent them our proof!"

Twelve hours. Less than twelve hours until their enemies received it.

Milo slowed, cursing. "They'll know exactly what we know. It'll never even reach Arden—"

"They'll twist it, erase it, lie," Tannor said. Her eyes lost focus. "No one will ever know what they really did to her."

The truth of it swelled in her mind and she concluded, quick and sure, that the proof would never be safe as a relay or a discrete package. They couldn't upload it to the commons, either. Too many soldiers had conspired to fake the block bombing, to hold the queen captive. Tech existed to wipe any storage device clean.

Milo charged back toward the others but Tannor stayed put.

Nothing could wipe a human brain.

She put her hand to the wall and opened up an interface with her comm.

"What are you doing?" Milo demanded from the end of the hall.

"It's not safe in any other format, and I'm not going to ask anyone else to do it."

Corpus cap, dissolve. She imagined she could feel the change in the neurons behind the knob at the base of her skull.

Milo started for her. "Stop. I don't know what you're doing, stop—"

Protection, off. Failsafe, off. Backup—backup—neural storage. Transfer. Hand—approved.

"Don't let me hit my head when I fall," she said, and tapped *begin*.

White hot liquid pain flushed through her body from her neck to her tail bone. She felt untethered, floating, lost the sense of her limbs in relation to her core. Her head hurt last and worst.

She barely felt Milo catch her as she toppled forward.

•

Thundering steps sent Relai's heart racing, and then Milo burst into the conference room with Tannor thrashing in his arms.

"She's downloading the data package into her brain."

"What? Tannor, no!" Goren clambered onto the table to cradle her head as Milo lowered her down. Her eyes skewed up and out and her fingers clawed at her neck. Goren grabbed her wrists and Milo held her calves to stop her from flipping onto the floor.

Relai looked at the door—should someone get a med scanner? No one else was going to get one—

"What will it do to her?" she asked.

Milo let out a grunt as Tannor nearly kicked him in the jaw. "Might be fine. Might lose her memory."

"That one guy ate off his hand!"

"Not helping, chaff."

Why would Tannor do this? What would evidence matter, if Relai couldn't muster the strength to lead? Relai sat close to Tannor's head, but didn't dare touch her.

Then Tannor went still and moaned, her eyes showing only slits of white. Milo released her and moved to the side.

"Tannor?" Goren begged.

She didn't respond, didn't respond, and Relai thought she should go and get a scanner from the med bay, but if she did Tannor would die while she was gone and she couldn't make herself go.

Seconds bled by. Goren petted Tannor's hair and grumbled trite, comforting things.

Then Tannor released a long, shuddering breath and opened her eyes.

Relai slid her knife against her ribs under the strap of the bra and bent over her. "Tannor? Tannor, are you okay? How do you feel?"

Tannor rubbed her temple and leaned against Goren. After a moment, she lifted her head. "It's okay. I'm okay. Once I stopped fighting it, it actually felt... fine. Not bad."

"Can you tell it's there?" Relai asked, afraid of the answer either way.

Tannor blinked slowly, the flutter of her eyelashes like movement in a dance, and nodded. "I know it. I mean, I know it's there, but now I know the data. I know every bit of it. I could tell you every line of code. I can see the images in my head."

Everyone but Relai seemed to know enough to be frightened by that. Goren gasped and Milo's mouth opened and closed.

"Yeah, that's weird," Ky said.

An alarm sounded.

Ky tore away and swept through window after flashing window as they opened on the wall of the room.

"*We're being boarded,*" he said.

•

Tannor scrambled to her feet, swaying as Goren fumbled for a gun that wasn't there and threw himself between Relai and the door—

•

Milo snagged the base of the chair he'd thrown across the room earlier with his foot, kicked it around, went to one knee behind it, and raised his shotgun to his shoulder—

•

Relai backed around the long end of the conference table and pressed her back against the wall, feeling small and bare and unprepared. *Anyone after you just wants to end you.*

Simple.

"Stop! What if they're not trying to kill her?" Tannor protested, resting against a chair on her way to the wall controls. "We weren't!"

Goren opened and clenched his fists, twitchy like violence eager to happen, as Tannor stumbled across the open few steps to knock shoulders with Ky. Her hands flew over his as they fought through layers of information.

Tannor brought up visuals of the jumper that had landed on the top deck of the groundship and the troops creeping toward them, guns raised. Relai had flown in those jumpers all over this planet; they only carried eight people, maximum.

The visual showed seven soldiers and a captain in the lead.

Tannor looked at Milo. "The guards who tried to kill her?"

He craned his neck to peer at each face from his spot on the floor. "It was dark, but—no. I don't think so."

Then he stood. "Ky. They'll want to kill her with one of our weapons."

Ky clicked his thumbnail across the hilt of a knife at his hip and inclined his head.

Relai touched the little knife at her ribs. She was terrified, but the fear felt outside of her body, like a cloud, and then it settled like a layer on her skin.

"Tannor's right," she said. "We should see who we're dealing with before you kill anyone. Give me a gun and put yours down. If they're loyal, they'll still want you two for taking me. And if they're not—"

Ky smiled. "Hand-to-hand works. I get bored with guns anyway."

Relai felt cold all over. The soldiers had entered now, the wall screen shifting rapidly between views as they passed checkpoints in the serpentine corridors. The squad moved as one group with a single goal.

"Can I have a gun? I need a gun!" Goren squawked, and Ky held out his weapon.

"So we're clear," he warned, pausing before he let Goren take control, "I have no faith in you. I'm taking her back if they even look at us wrong."

"Not if I shoot them first," Goren snapped back.

Milo cleared his throat and Relai realized he was offering her his electric shotgun, handle out and what was left of the barrel toward him. His eyes roamed over her face, intense and worried, and Relai hardly recognized him.

"Lay on your stomachs," Tannor ordered.

Milo growled, "Like hell I—"

Tannor shocked them both with mild blasts, just enough to send them writhing on the floor. Relai gaped, lost for a response, and then Tannor cued up a link and sent her own face up on the wall next to the conference room door as the guards arrived.

"Captain Fass," Tannor said, clipped and emotionless, "the ship is secure. We have the intruders subdued and you're safe to enter."

Their visual gave an overhead view and a direct conversation head, two different angles to a serious, handsome face and a pair of deep blue eyes. He seemed surprised.

"We'll see," he replied.

Relai saw Tannor's eyes narrow.

The door slid open.

Ky and Milo shivered down from their seizures as Tannor and Goren flanked them, and Relai stood back from the group, close to one of the room's rounded corners with the shotgun limp at her side. The conference bay filled with shouting as the soldiers piled into the room, gen-guns raised. Last came a tall man who hadn't bothered to draw his weapon.

He had an air of certainty about him and he looked Relai full in the eyes.

"Glory, Commander, Queen. Captain Ednar Fass." He put his right hand to the opposite shoulder and dropped to a knee. Utmost respect.

"Please tell your men to put away their weapons, Captain," Relai ordered as Ky and Milo dragged themselves to their hands and knees. "There's been a, uh, a misunderstanding."

Fass lifted his chin. "A misunderstanding."

"Yes. They put down their weapons willingly... and they're sorry for stealing the ship and kidnapping the three of us."

Milo looked up at her, incredulous.

"*Sorry?*" he growled, "Sorry I saved your—"

"*What I desire,*" Relai said, "is for all of us to go back to the base. We need to vet everyone for—"

"I need to run a full medical scan first, Our Glory." Fass pursed his lips as he paused. "You might be under some influence. Please understand, I am required to ignore your commands until I see that you are in full control of your decisions."

If that were true, how the hell did anyone take over in her name?

Fass signaled two guards. They closed in on her kidnappers and bound their hands behind their backs. One of the guards kneeled in respect and then took Milo's gun out of Relai's hands.

"We'll take these men back first. You," Fass pointed to Goren, who jumped up, "go along with them and help keep the criminals in line."

"Yes, sir!"

"They're under my protection, Captain," Relai warned.

He smiled. "Scan, first."

Relai watched them go with growing alarm. Ky's shoulders strained, compliant even as he tested his bindings, but Milo struggled and then wrenched sideways to look back to her. She wanted to call out but her words caught in her throat.

The door slid shut. She and Tannor stood there, unarmed, with three men.

"Sir!" Tannor piped up. "Did you speak with Sergeant Tars before—"

"We'll go over everything back at the base...." He stepped close and then reached out and unclipped the corner of her jacket. He pulled it to the side, little by little, his thumb pressing a shadowed dent into the stretchy white cloth of her shirt. The movement seemed to take ages before it finally revealed the black trunk and upturned branches tattooed at the join of her shoulder and collarbone. "...Sergeant," he concluded.

He hadn't checked Goren's rank. He hadn't *touched* Goren. Relai bristled as Tannor tilted her head down, deferential even as her eyes screamed rage.

Her instincts shrieked.

Her eyes flickered to Tannor.

•

Tannor hovered just barely closer to the queen, forcing herself to still. It wasn't the fact that the Captain was an utter bastard who always pushed the flirting and the touching too far, who *definitely already knew her rank*—

Relai had shaken her head and whispered:

"I'm not in control."

Tannor hoped that the queen would get past that phase of shock soon. They needed her to be in control; she was the one who mattered in the end. Tannor, Goren, the Captain, they were nothing at all compared to her.

And if Relai didn't do something, Tannor might have to punch Fass in his smug little square-jawed face, and then where would they be?

•

Relai tilted her head to one side. "This groundship needs to go back, too. Can we ride in here, Captain?" She blinked and ducked her chin the way her mother always had, looking up at him through her lashes. "Please?"

He grinned, dimples deep, and waved her toward a seat at the conference table. "Of course, Our Glory."

"Sergeant?" Relai drifted away and looked across the bridge. She tried to sound neutral.

"Yes, Our Glory?" Tannor replied.

"Does this ship have a scanner that can evaluate me?"

"I'm… not sure, Our Glory." Tannor moved to the wall and tapped a few buttons.

A few steps out of reach.

"Tannor."

Relai didn't need to say another word.

Captain Fass frowned, cast a sideways glance at Relai, then sprang toward Tannor—

Too late. He froze before Relai even finished her gasp because Tannor moved too fast, knew exactly how to slap down her palm and twist. Everywhere that pairs of feet touched the floor of the groundship, those feet stuck and their bodies stopped. The locking of her muscles didn't hurt; it just sent a buzzing thrum through her whole body. Relai could breathe and move her eyes and nothing else. Ardenians did not like cleaning blood out of their diplomatic vessels.

Only Tannor, who activated the feature, was spared.

She went to the glowing circle lit around Relai's feet and tapped the red square with her toe to release her. The Captain sent a low, angry growl in Relai's direction, but she shook her head.

"Fool me once, Captain. Can they override this?"

Tannor gave Fass another measured nod. "No, I'm the only one who can control the ship right now."

"Good. Let's get the guys," Relai said, and they hurried along the quickest path to the top deck.

"How did you know that you couldn't trust him?" Tannor asked.

She shrugged.

"What does 'fool me once' mean?"

But Relai didn't have time to answer, because they'd reached the ramp leading up to open sky. The guards had taken two prisoners and one Goren out to the early morning haze of the groundship deck. More guards must have been hiding in their jumper—

They'd frozen just in time.

Two of the biggest guards held Goren, disarmed and jacket askew and mouth open, as always, mid-shout. His face aimed toward a familiar guard— the man who'd kicked out her knee and then stomped on her back—who now stood over Milo and Ky as they kneeled on the deck. Milo's eyes were clenched closed as the guard's gun dug into the back of his head. Ky's head was tilted, one foot braced and his whole body beginning to turn, but he wouldn't have made a difference. Milo would have fallen, and Ky would have followed.

Tannor tapped Goren free and helped him pull himself away from the grip of the guards. He reclaimed the gun, ranting, "What the hell is wrong with everyone around here? Is *everyone* committing treason today? They wouldn't listen to me! They were just going to execute these men! Without a trial or anything!"

Relai crouched by Milo and Ky.

"Well," she said, looking them over in the early blue-toned light.

Milo embodied the epitome of an Erayd, from the shabbiness of his clothes to the snarled hair covering his head and face. Every inch of him cried *poor, uneducated, angry*; he was just the sort of terrorist assassin she'd feared as a young regent. She'd let them just drag him away.

And Ky... Ky seemed like the sort of man who should have been smart enough to keep away from this terrible plan. How had he expected any of this to work? He must have nothing to lose. Being here, what could he possibly have to gain?

A wind damp enough to chill passed over them, and Relai tucked her scraggly hair behind her ears. She tapped Ky's circle, then Milo's, and used her thumb knife to cut their hands free.

Ky hopped up and put his hands on Relai's shoulders. He held her out in front of him and looked her over in the rising light of dawn.

"Okay," he said.

"Okay, what?"

He gave her a big, toothy smile. "Okay, I believe you."

"It's about time," she replied. Then she turned to Milo. "Looks like it's two to one."

He scowled as he pushed to his feet. "Two to one?"

"I'm winning."

Tannor cleared her throat. "What are we going to do with these soldiers?"

Peering over the edge of the deck, Relai noted the waves—not too choppy—and tried to guess the distance to the shore through the haze. "Throw them in the sea."

She was giving orders! Like a queen or something. Throw them in the sea! Off with their heads! Relai felt laughter bubbling up but she swallowed it down. She could be hysterical later. Alone.

Tannor and Goren moved in unison to obey. Milo and Ky exchanged a complicated glance, then nodded.

•

iii.

Tannor wouldn't admit it to anyone, but she tensed the moment she saw Milo and Ky bringing out the Captain. Fass's body shook in their arms and she saw a shallow wound from a gen-gun in his chest.

And was she imagining it, or was Milo refusing to look her in the eye?

"You shot him," she said.

"Milo shot him," Ky clarified. "Your Captain's got quite a mouth on him."

Tannor closed her eyes hard against the onslaught of thoughts about what he might've said, then opened them again to watch as they shuffled out as far as their shoes could grip and then heaved Fass over. He thudded once against the curve of the groundship as he went.

"Try to wake up when you hit the water!" she cried after him.

Then she spun back to Ky and slipped her next words out without Milo hearing: "Why bring Goren?"

Ky nodded, scratched his chin, then caught Milo's eye and sent him off to deal with someone else. They moved back inside the groundship and made it all the way back to the conference bay before Ky replied:

"*Dray*. Recognize it?"

"Oh, uh," she stuttered as Ky stunned the last paused soldier and caught him over one shoulder, "one of the High Council ministers is a Dray. Environment, right?"

She didn't offer to help carry and Ky didn't ask.

"The Drays have more money than the worth of this entire planet," Ky said as they headed back to the deck. "They'll pay anything to get their kiddo back, and I'm betting they'll move stars to get the coalition to show restraint before killing us all to get to her. I like money and I like not dying. So. We keep him around."

Tannor sighed.

The world was noticeably brighter when they emerged than when they'd gone inside. Morning was creeping closer, and Tannor was utterly exhausted.

As she grabbed the soldier's feet and eased him down, feeling the burn of his weight through her shoulders and back, she finally asked, "And me?"

They swung once, twice, and heaved the guy in. Ky looked out across the water, ran an artful hand through his hair, then turned his eyes on Tannor.

"You're worth more than Goren."

Then he walked off to help throw the last guy in.

Tannor watched him swagger as he went, fluid like a song, and she swallowed. It was a good line. Very smooth.

Calculated just right.

∘∘●∘∘

"Wait!" Relai zeroed in on the last soldier left. The man was doing his best to struggle against Milo, but he was no match for a giant. "Take off your pants."

The tussle came to a halt. The guy was hardly the perfect size, but the sea breeze whipping over the deck of the ship was stinging her bare legs. Relai was tired of running around in only underwear.

"What?" the soldier squawked.

"*Pants.*"

"First time you've ever heard that from a woman?" Ky laughed. Milo wrapped his arms under the soldier's, locked his fingers up around the back of his neck, and lifted him six clear inches off the ground without any visible effort.

The soldier put in a pathetic attempt to kick but Ky crouched too close for him to get a good hit. "The queen wants your pants, you give her your pants." He unbuckled the soldier's belt, head level with his hips, and muttered, "Not exactly how I pictured my day ending."

Milo cracked a smile, and the sight felt like water in a dry mouth. He could have been anyone, anyone at all, when he smiled.

Relai slipped into the dark, stretchy slacks and tightened the belt as far as it would go, just enough to keep the pants hanging onto her hips.

Then the soldier (who had far too tiny feet for her to use his shoes) brought her back to the present.

"We won't submit to you!" he shouted. "Your time is over! You'll only make it worse for yourself if you kill me."

"We're not going to kill you. The shore's that way," Relai pointed. "I hope you speak Italian."

He bucked in Milo's arms and cried, "But I can't swim!"

Relai stilled. As the sun crept closer to rising, the crests of the waves swelled clear and relentless fifty feet below. These waves would carry him into the stark cliffs if he couldn't drag himself sideways to the shore, and if he didn't drown first. Even for a strong swimmer it wouldn't be an easy distance.

So, Relai, she asked herself. *How do you feel about throwing a man to his death? Water filling his lungs, crushing him as he sinks?*

She took in a deep breath. "Lock him up in the jumper; we can dump him on land."

Ky's eyes widened and he moved into the background as Milo snarled at her:

"We're throwing him in and leaving."

He still had the soldier in a headlock and Relai had to block him from doing it, her hands on the captured soldier's chest, her bare feet gripping the gritty surface of the groundship where it began to slope.

"Stop it! We're not executioners!"

Relai registered shouts from Tannor and Goren, but Ky interceded and their static faded away. The soldier thrashed, and as Relai tried to grab his legs and drag him back Milo stumbled and only narrowly avoided falling over the edge. They all toppled sideways, with Relai half-under the soldier under Milo.

Relai jerked her foot free and scrambled up, furious. "I am not going to just—just *murder* everyone who gets in my way!"

Milo flashed his teeth at her as he put most of his weight on the soldier. He had a foot of height and a hundred pounds of weight over the guy—it was up to him how much the man could even breathe. "He's obviously lying."

He wouldn't kill her, she thought, but he might do other things. He could hurt her again.

She perched on the balls of her feet, her stance wide and ready. "So you'd *prefer* I be the murderer you thought I was?"

Milo leaned toward her. "It'd make my next choice a much easier one."

"Life isn't easy," Relai spat. She looked to her guards. "Bind him in the jumper."

Milo clenched, dragging another cry from the soldier, then released. Tannor and Goren took the last rebel soldier away as Milo sent Relai one last murderous glare, then stormed off down the ramp into the groundship.

Relai caught her breath while Ky just stared at her, openly judging. She tugged at the sleeve of the dirty, sweaty robe. She needed to brush her hair.

And find some actual clothing.

•

Milo charged down the ramp, cursing without bothering to keep it under his breath.

Never mind herself, this girl was going to get them *all* killed.

In the last nine months, Milo had ended the lives of six men and two women. Each and every one of them deserved it, and seven of them had been attempting to kill him (or Ky, or both of them) at the moment of their deaths. Milo didn't consider himself the type to shoot first, but he did not hesitate when forced. The time for waxing poetic about the value of human life had shriveled up as he watched his aba bleed out in the town square.

Milo wanted to put his fist through something, but he settled for slapping an open hand against one of this ship's corridor walls instead. It blinked to life in protest, and Tannor must have locked the ship off from open access because the first thing he encountered was a smug little identification prompt.

He cursed that, too.

Relai Aydor might not have been ruling, but her head topped the monarchy still standing on the necks of his people. He would find justice for Eray in the broken body of the false ruler, and then he would turn to Relai herself, accuse the Aydor line, and demand their freedom. He hadn't failed. He wouldn't fail.

And in the meantime, Milo Hemm would make certain of one thing: she would not be in charge. Relai might be a queen, but she was no leader.

Then Milo observed an object which hadn't been there the last time he tromped through this passage. It was narrow and black and designed by the Ardenian military. They used these things in the mines, too.

Milo huffed, wondering what the hell else could go wrong in the immediate future.

Then he sprinted back the way he came.

Tannor jerked the soldier's arm closer as they set him on the floor behind the pilot's seat and bound his hands around a post leading from the jumper bench to the roof. She'd never been one for hand-to-hand combat and her skill with firearms was mediocre at best; she had no idea how she was supposed to be protecting the head regent of the Vada Coalition. If the queen herself had a choice, she probably wouldn't have picked Tannor, either.

"I still think we should go back to the base," Goren grumbled as he plopped down on the bench and clutched the muscle around the splotch of blood on his thigh.

Who at Haadam could help them? Marejak, maybe—she was a hardline genius who hated Fass more than most—but she could do little to change anything without Fass' approval. They probably should have killed him, if only to promote Marejak in his absence.

Tannor checked the soldier's bindings one more time, eyes flickering to Goren's wound. They hadn't had time to heal it in the medical bay.

"I don't think we can, Goren."

Their prisoner laughed. "Go ahead. Go back to the base. See what you find."

Tannor felt a chill. "What do you mean?"

He hesitated, but the chance to rub their noses in his revelation seemed too tempting to pass up.

"The Captain ordered it the second we left. The rebellion starts now—we'll leave no safe place for her to hide."

Goren put his gun against the man's neck. "*What* did he order?"

The soldier's face glowed with a glee that prickled the hairs on the back of Tannor's neck. "Plasma bombs. The base is gone by now."

Tannor reeled back. "*Why*—"

His eyes flashed. "Because the days of the crown are over! She's the *end*—will you be crushed with her, or will you join us?"

"She wasn't ruling!" Tannor exclaimed. "It wasn't her, since before Ayadas died."

The soldier's face scrunched in confusion, but he just shook his head. "Nice try, but I saw her there, relaxing in secret—the monarchy needs to end, and she's the last Aydor. Strength to Unity!"

She dove to a screen and pulled open a new message. "There are still guards there, we have to give them a chance—"

Goren bolted out to the deck of the groundship.

•

Relai found herself alone with Ky. The sea breeze felt solid, anchoring, and it left a complex taste of salt and life and the green of olive trees in the back of her throat. It was nice to take a moment to rest.

She wondered if she could say something about how beautiful she found it—if that would be inappropriate or awkward. If it would make her sound like a sentimental, silly little girl. Earth belonged to her just as much as any Earthan; she was purely human and she belonged here.

Sometimes life didn't give much, and often it only took away, but there was always beauty. Beauty helped. It was good all on its own, and seeing it and acknowledging it could soothe wounds.

Her father's death was a wound, but—

Her father was dead. The world wasn't supposed to seem brighter. More vibrant.

Oh, no—*no, no crying now*—

"Going to cut your hair, then?"

"What?" she croaked.

Ky scratched the stubble on his jaw. "I take it they let it grow the whole time you were under. You must be uncomfortable this way. You are royalty, after all."

Right. The hair nonsense. Four years on Earth and Relai had all but forgotten about it. She didn't peg Ky for one to be prejudiced against long hair; he clearly wasn't Ardenian. The other coalition planets weren't as obsessed with removing body hair as the greater class of Arden was; where men shaved their bodies and heads and women were only allowed a bit of length to compliment their features.

Relai wore her hair long. It was just one more reason for her father to refuse to let her be seen in public; at least they could both use the hair as pretense, so he didn't have to say it out loud again: no one wanted to look at her face.

No one loves a homely regent, Relai.

But she wasn't going to think about him anymore, right? He was gone.

"Actually, no. I've kept my hair long for years and I'm not going to stop now."

"Interesting." He looked her over, his face a suspicious sort of neutral, and she stared right back.

Then shouting from two directions split their attention.

"They're bombing Haadam Base!" Goren cried from the jumper.

"Those assholes set the groundship to blow," Milo shouted from the opposite side of the deck.

They bolted towards the jumper. Relai, Tannor, Goren, Ky, and Milo—six, they could fit, plus the rebel soldier—

From inside, Tannor screamed.

Relai saw Goren just manage to dive back in as the vehicle's left engine sprang to life. It kicked the jumper tail sideways into the air and the vehicle pitched, door still wide open, over the edge of the groundship deck and into the water.

Relai veered left and leaped.

○○●○○

iv.

Goren was, for a moment, floating.

The guard's foot jabbed into Tannor's neck, pinning her against the curving wall of the jumper as he twisted and pulled at wires in the busted casing below the pilot's seat.

Crap, *crap*—Goren shouldn't have left her in there with the guy, not even for a moment—he was so furious at himself as they sailed through the air, he almost wished the impact would kill him. Unfortunately, the spin caused by a single engine firing absorbed some of the force of the impact, throwing him up and across the ceiling as they splashed down. He didn't even break any bones.

The impact set Tannor loose, leaving the prisoner hanging for a few wobbly moments from the bindings around his wrists. The jumper crashed in the sea nose-down, open end still mouthing air, but they'd already been doused with stinging seawater and any second now the edge would tip and the thing would fill.

Oh, drowning, then? Goren did not wake up this morning thinking he'd end the day by drowning in a sea he hadn't even gotten a chance to visit yet. *Well, here it is*, he thought. *Scenic.*

Goren couldn't feel his weapon—Ky's weapon—and he was sure it wouldn't fire underwater anyway. The only thing that mattered right now was Tannor. She had to be able to take control of this thing.

He fumbled and slipped over to her, felt the rise and fall of a passing wave, and pulled her to her knees.

"Tannor," he gasped, "we have to save the jumper."

"The groundship?" she sputtered, clutching at his jacket.

"I heard Milo, it's gonna blow." If they abandoned this jumper now, assuming they managed to swim to shore, they'd be lost on a foreign planet, picked off by whatever lazy traitor bothered to track them down and execute them.

Tannor cursed. Goren agreed.

A wave crashed through the open entrance and they fell, smashed into one another, and pooled against the transparent front window. The water there rose up to Goren's waist.

Tannor gripped the lip of the dash with one hand and pawed at the pilot's controls with the other. Their prisoner kicked and jerked, trying to gain his footing and pull his hands free. Tannor ignored him, so Goren decided to only bother if the guy tried to kill them.

Another wave came, the jumper rocked, and the prisoner wrenched one hand out of his bindings.

"Tannor!" Goren shouted. He couldn't kill a fellow soldier with his bare hands—he'd have to drown him—

"Give me a second!"

"Shut the door!"

"I'm trying!"

Then he heard her exclaim, "Oh!" Her hand flew over a screen half out of the water. "That might—"

Then another wave bucked them sideways, the edge tipped, and the sea crashed in on them entirely.

·

Impact with the water stunned Relai limp. She felt as if one side of herself had just slammed into a wall, but then the groundship blew in a terrifying fury and she stayed under, opening her eyes to the blurry sting of the salt, and struggled away from the light.

She wasn't going to die drowning. She *wasn't*.

She surfaced. Behind her one half of the groundship groaned in flames, lilting to one side as the other half dipped into the Mediterranean. Clouds of flaming particles lit the sky, falling and fading like a celebration.

Congratulations, they screamed. *You lose!*

She saw the jumper.

Its back end gaped above the surface, interior filled with water but still clinging by an edge to the surface. She was close. She was going to make it.

A dark smudge of a head bobbed up and she couldn't see if it was Goren or the soldier who'd donated his pants. The haircut made them all look the same—

The 'Strength to Unity' soldier. She watched him and remembered the knife—*was it still there? yes*—pinned against her ribcage, but he wasn't looking for her. He started swimming the opposite direction.

He *did* know how to swim.

Focus.

She swam to the edge of the jumper, then took one more breath and clawed her way down. Through the white-blue glow she saw two figures at the bottom—her loyal guards.

Goren wasn't moving when she reached them, and when she latched onto his arm he turned shocked eyes on her and shoved her up toward the surface. She held tight to his arm as the final bit of water engulfed the jumper and then they were sinking.

A groan shuddered through the jumper and she looked up to see the door shutting. *Tannor, yes!*

Except they were still drowning, and now they were trapped.

Relai watched Tannor's hands work over the console as if moving in slow motion. Goren gripped Relai's arm in return, flexing his fingers tight and loose, faster and faster. She could do nothing to help here. *What was your plan, exactly?*

Everyone dies, Relai. They must die for you, and not the other way around.

Maybe this ship had auxiliary oxygen. It wasn't meant to travel outside the atmosphere, but it had to have something, didn't it?

She couldn't go very long without breathing. Most people couldn't.

Goren's grip relaxed and his hands drifted away.

Tannor, please...

Relai reached out to tug at Tannor's arm, to motion for her to open the back door so they could abandon ship, when a great white stream of bubbles burst out of vents inside the front of the ship. A smooth, mechanical tug righted the jumper and the air bubble grew and forced out the seawater.

Relai kicked up and treaded in the refuge of air until it grew large enough to set her feet back on a level floor. She and Tannor coughed and gagged, and then enough water drained away to uncover Goren. His body was caught at the waist, nearly bent in half on the strut supporting the passenger seating, and he wasn't breathing. Relai shoved at his shoulders until he flopped sideways and down.

Tannor clung to the pilot seat and worked at the screen, and when she saw Relai fumbling with Goren she said, "Roll him on his side! Slap his back!"

Relai had watched hundreds of Earthan movies and television shows to work on her English; she knew there was a way to breathe into him to wake him up, but she would get it wrong. She always got it wrong.

"Do it!" Tannor bellowed.

Relai rolled him and slapped *hard*.

His body jolted and he opened his mouth and vomited, then gasped. She kept striking more and more softly as he rolled to his knees and retched again and again.

"You're okay," Relai told him. He held onto the edge of the bench and rested his head on his forearms through more coughing as Relai rubbed his back and tugged her stringy hair out of her face. She caught Tannor's eye, exhausted and awed.

"We made it."

•

The jumper rattled beneath Tannor's feet and she put on her best brave face. They were in the air, wobbling more than hovering, wasting power with her every fumble. She'd done it.

Relai hauled herself to her feet next to Tannor and slicked her eyes clear. "What can I do? What do you need?"

The screen screamed at her.

"I don't know, I'm making this up as I go along!"

"Then you're amazing," Relai rasped out.

Goren managed, "I agr—" before the jumper tossed them all a foot in the air.

The wreckage of the groundship disappeared before their eyes, all the flash and crackle of the explosion succumbing to the sea. Tannor couldn't force the navigation imager to life no matter how she begged, but they could see out the broad front window and one of the mapping programs was working. As the interference of the wreckage sunk away, the map showed two spots of warmth sticking close and bobbing toward the jumper. Relai clutched the shoulder of Tannor's chair, her breath slowing.

"We don't..." Tannor glanced sideways and shivered. "We don't have to pick them up."

She was just offering the choice.

"Well," Relai said, "they came all this way."

•

Milo rested at the surface, shivering and shaken, legs limp and arms swirling through the ink under a hail of fire. He couldn't lose her like this.

He didn't get a chance to press his two metal-threaded fingers together and activate the draw, the simplest passive form of tracking tech in the galaxy, to locate Ky before the man reached him with a few swift strokes.

"You alive?" Ky called.

"Yeah." Milo splashed through a partial turn, searching for any signs of the jumper. "What plan are we on, now?"

"Oh, fifty-two," Ky said.

Milo's boots dragged at him like a call to death, but he'd rather die feet covered than have to figure out how to survive on this planet barefoot.

"Did you see where—agh," Milo choked on a mouthful of water, "...you could at least pretend to be tired."

"You know," Ky replied, "I used to dream I was drowning. It was really nice."

"What?"

Then the jumper churned free of the water a hundred yards away and fumbled airborne. *They'd made it out*—Milo steeled himself to watch it go, but Ky whooped and shouted:

"Here they come!"

"How do you know?"

Ky laughed as they rose in the crest of a wave. "On the run now, and they don't know how to be criminals. They need us."

The silhouette of the jumper drew closer against the grey-blue of the early morning sky, water spraying from the exhaust vents like sickened breaths, and Milo realized Ky was right.

He hadn't lost her yet.

○○●○○

v.

She called herself Runn.

The Ardenian diplomat at her feet choked on a mouthful of blood in a urine-soaked Tijuana alley without knowing that.

She had a longer name but it hadn't stuck. No one needed it here on Earth, and jobs paid the same no matter what. Lucrative, she called it, when she thought about it. Might've cost her an eye, years ago, but it was enough to keep her in sun and drink year round.

"Before you go," she breathed out as her target struggled, "I need help. I'm losing my game."

Runn liked to entertain herself by working out who hired her and why, and this one had her interested.

The diplomat was young, maybe thirty. Slim, easy to hold. Fear in his eyes, highlighted in the glint of sickly yellow electric lights they used to illuminate this planet. A normal kill. But Voresh Renganiban wasn't just an Ardenian diplomat; he worked for Fordev, and no one crossed Fordev. Didn't have any magic in his fingers that Runn could see, which meant he was either a Redas plant in the organization or one of the directors. With that surname? Director.

Best kill Runn had taken in a while.

"See, I tracked down who hired me to kill you, and I'm curious. Why," she lifted the man against the wall, fixed him high with the friction of the brick, "does your boss have it out for you?"

She liked it when they realized who took out the contract—sometimes they'd explode in the fury of the wronged and put up a better fight for a minute or two. Sometimes they'd cry. Sometimes they'd just crumble, their whole existence torn up before she did the same to their bodies. Renganiban was average in his reaction: confusion, disbelief, and betrayal. Nice little hint of anger.

He gurgled as Runn leaned a forearm on his neck. "I know you can't answer; I crushed your throat. I don't need your voice."

Renganiban tried to track the object in Runn's free hand but he couldn't focus or turn his head. Runn clicked the switch on her memory probe and one end splayed open, six little claws ready for skin. She jabbed it behind Renganiban's right ear.

It latched on and screwed in and the guy's eyes went manic and detached when the probe snicked into his brain. Runn glanced down at the knife in Renganiban's gut. Pulled it out. Two minutes to look around his memories, then he'd bleed out. It always went easier if Runn could get the mark to think about their secrets instead of digging through a mountain of memories with no help or direction.

A truck rumbled past the alley, kicking up dirt and broken glass and sending a cloud of exhaust over them. Smelled sweet, like home. Runn pulled back into the shadow of a recessed doorway and eased them both to the ground, then put her arm around Renganiban's shoulder. Local music pulsed through the door, muffled save for the *thum-bum thum-bum* of its endless two-note bass line.

"Why you came to Earth," she grunted in the guy's ear.

She closed her eyes for the ride, 'cause even with experience this shit made her queasy. Through a bright door textured like a coral-built Kilani building, under a black cloud of skin, weightless like unbound space—there, a voice:

—*Make a show of reviewing catches for Fordev and wait. It won't be long. We need you*—the source of the voice, distinguished, polished, perfectly still, Corven Ector at a desk without a speck of dust—*there to identify the body. Take on the mantle immediately*—

This asshole was the one putting out needs for Earthan children, Runn realized with disgust. Runn never took those jobs. Murder was fun; she wasn't into child trafficking. Kids were kids. She left 'em alone.

Inside Renganiban's head, Runn took a sideways roll through a swallow of hot water and:

—*Mora Aydor. Hand and eye*—the memory of an imagined scene, vague and curled with self-indulgence: Voresh Renganiban standing over her body and pledging to lead the Vada Coalition with ruthless equality—

"Do me a favor and I'll make you a king? Never a good hook to swallow," Runn mused. "So who's next in line for the throne now that you're dead?"

—Family celebration, new baby—teenage Voresh, bobbing with a baby girl in his arms, her mother, his father's sister—his cousin, Sana—irritation like wind—*Aunt Nay didn't choose a traditional name, that shallow, pretentious, disconnected*—

"So Ector wants her for queen, instead. She's pretty. Clean. Too young for him. Now," she twisted the blade to pull Renganiban back just enough to hear her next words, "since we both know she's not on a ship in the middle of fuck knows... where's Mora Aydor right now?"

—Tipsy, sharp and pungent—a perfect smooth-skinned body, wide-brimmed hat, bare skin darkening in the sun—*Haadam*—

"Haadam Base. What a lazy—"

She jerked forward under a gravel flood of deeper, swollen knowledge. *The queen. The queen, she sent her secret*—Runn felt Renganiban fading and she fought to dig out the last wisps of truth.

Everything went calm. Still. Gone.

Runn punched a button and retrieved her pen. Thirty seconds before the eyes would turn useless, so she didn't waste time: from her leather coat pocket she slid a small silver spoon engraved with a mariachi and the words *Bienvenidos a Tijuana*, which she'd bought from a souvenir stand when she arrived in the city.

She wedged it between Renganiban's lower lid and eye, and scooped the ball out.

She popped off her placeholder—a strapless eye patch—and inserted the wet, warm eyeball into her empty right socket. It only took a few seconds for the connections to form, her eyes clenched shut through the twisting, fiery pain, and then she could see. One dark brown iris, one amber-mottled green.

Runn patted the body's shoulder and stood up.

Then Renganiban's pocket trilled. Runn shuffled it back and retrieved a phone—no, an ex-terr tablet. Incoming relay. Runn crouched and picked up the body's right hand and slapped it over the screen. Still warm enough to count as living.

A little glowing green relay popped open. Runn read quickly:

Mora fled, recovering now. Atmosphere breach locked until recovered. Practice your king face, my friend. Don't trust anything from Erode.

Runn puppeted Renganiban's fingers to open metadata and just barely caught the name *Ed Fass* before a data chaser ate the message. Ed Fass.

Quick search of the underweb led to Haadam Base hierarchy of command, with Ednar Fass right at the very top. A jadissary. What the hell was a jadissary doing telling this barata suit to practice his king face?

Was there no loyalty left?

The insides of her cheeks tingled with a flush of saliva, and she swallowed into a smile.

She cleaned off the screw and claws of her memory probe and packed her bag, kicking the body over deeper into the shadows. Runn liked Tijuana. She wasn't eager to leave, but she wouldn't be gone long—no need to take a body cross-country, let alone cross-galaxy. Travel would go easier with a small parcel.

She nodded to herself. A Vadan royal meant all four planets would want her back. Meant a bounty coming. No mutters in the commons about Odene lurking in this solar system, and he'd've been the only competition. Runn would bag her before anyone else local could get their heads straight.

The proper royals would hire Applica, so she'd let them use their tech to track the queen down. Obvious, easy to follow.

Then she'd kill them and take their catch.

EPISODE IV:

EARTH

GOREN DRAY WOULD definitely be lowering his standards for what constituted a good day. Yesterday? Miserable. Got shot, taken prisoner, saw the queen naked and momentarily died of shame, base destroyed, almost drowned. Now they were on the run, he supposed. He couldn't tally all the people chasing them.

They collected the two vigilante elements of the group (who didn't even say thanks) and immediately began a massive argument about their destination. Jumpers couldn't make it out of the atmosphere—how were they going to get all the way to Oliver Station, where they could probably find (steal?!—no, by the queen it was lawful appropriation) a spaceship to bring them to Arden, if they didn't have a groundship to get off the planet's surface?

"We have to go back to the base—"

"No way—"

"Those guards need our help!"

"If we can get to Buzou, I think—"

"That'd just delay the inevitable."

"—we could ask for an escort?"

"This jumper won't make it that far, anyway—"

"They'll have a bounty out on you by now."

"There are other ways to get off this planet—"

"People are dying—"

"I don't care about a bounty."

"Well, *we* care!"

"How did they find us?"

"*I don't know—*"

Goren just listened. He had no illusions about his opinion mattering and he couldn't see how they were going to make it through another day, let alone all the way back to Arden. He saw his—no, Ky's—gun wedged under a seat, so he leaned on his uninjured leg to drag it free and then started pulling it apart as Tannor's frantic voice broke through the din.

"I need to pick a destination, people!" The jumper lurched and tossed them a few feet forward, but Goren was sitting tucked into the rear corner so he wasn't thrown. Tannor was flying on full manual control (and doing really well, all things considered). The vents had been able to drain the cabin, but one whole engine and a dozen automation systems were done for. Apparently these jumpers hadn't been designed to gargle saltwater.

He muttered to himself, but everyone heard anyway: "I just want to go home."

And now they all thought he was a toddler. Great.

Really, though… his mother would welcome everyone in and the house staff would set up rooms for each of them and bring them comfortable clothing (good clothes from Titus, where they actually appreciated fashion), and they could spend a week sampling different foods from the coalition planets. He'd buy them black rice from Oeyla—he heard the grains grew as big as your fingers—and pepperfruit from Titus, and gazpacho from Gastred. Then, after they were all fat-bellied and happy, they'd take a cruise over the city in a private party lift and Tannor would be charmed by him and she wouldn't think of him as a kid anymore.

"Tannor, can I borrow your tech pen?" Goren asked.

She peeled open her jacket and passed the heavy green cylinder to Ky, who handed it to him. At least she'd been somewhat prepared when this emergency began; Goren had had nothing in his pockets at all.

He found the wiring tip and turned it on as Milo took the opportunity to speak uninterrupted.

"We're going to have to find a way off this planet besides the military or diplomatic bases. We aren't safe on *any* ship that coalition forces could monitor leaving the atmosphere."

Goren brushed away a line of corroded wiring and redrew the tiny circuits one by one. The pen was full, thank Tannor, but who knew how long they'd need it to last?

"What do you expect us to do," Relai said, "wait around until Earthan space tech catches up with ours? There are no other ways off this planet." She peeled off the black robe and the soaked slacks to wring them out, sopping the water over the rear vent, and Goren reeled back to focus on the gun, *gun, gun. Hey, there's another gun. Let's clean that, too.*

Ky was shaking his head, resting an arm against the bulkhead nearest Milo and staring into the distance that ended about twelve feet away at the back of the jumper. He didn't need to undress because his stupid clothes were somehow completely dry. "I was a bartender back on Gastred. You hear things."

Gastred. Was that where he learned how to drug people?

"You hear all sorts of things," Ky went on. "Like how the Tennans and Hergryks need certain *products*. Things Earth can offer and the coalition planets can't. Salts, minerals, biomass… people. And if you use the right technology, the Coalition can't pick up your ships. Sure, they know it's happening, but they can't stop it unless they want to risk starting another all-out war. And Earthans aren't worth that."

Goren looked to Relai (still unclothed? Seriously? New clothing was now his first guardly priority) to gauge her reaction so he could be properly intrigued or offended. She'd lived here for a while, so maybe this sort of thing would bother her? Or maybe she would be mad that the Coalition wasn't getting its due portion of the profits—Earth was a Vada protectorate, after all. They could be taxing this stuff.

"That's happening?" she exclaimed. Anger, disbelief. Goren wasn't sure which meant what. "And my father knew?" Relai swallowed and shook her head. "One problem at a time. You mean if we could find one of these smuggler ships we could hitch a ride?"

Ky grimaced and whisked his fingers through his wet hair. "'We'd need to locate a black market dock—one hidden well enough that people like this genius can't find it." He indicated Tannor, but she was too focused on the unstable jumper to acknowledge him. "We could try hacking some of this planet's governments, see if they have any records of alien activity. It might take a while if we don't know the technology."

"No," Tannor said, and when she didn't elaborate Ky rolled his eyes. Jerk.

Goren pulled Ky's gun into pieces and rubbed at them carefully with pinched pieces of his shirt before setting them over the air vent to dry. Ky had retrofitted the thing with an extra ammunition chamber and switched out the barrel with some nonsensical piping that was weighted all wrong, and the original charge string had been replaced with a purple shoelace. A criminal menace in weapon form.

"We'll go to Xiong," Relai said abruptly.

"Xiong?" Ky asked.

"Uh. Gandred Xiong. He's my former guide. He taught me until I was fourteen, and then he left. He works at an Earthan research and development company now. He'll help us find a ship and get to Oliver."

The two criminals traded glances.

"Is he going to help *you*, or *us*?" Ky inquired.

"I, uh. I don't know if he'll want to talk to me... but he's a good man. A great man. He disagreed with my father a lot and I know he wouldn't support a tyrant. I'm sure he'll help me, and I'll ask him to help all of us. Okay?"

"Compelling defense," Ky said dryly.

Milo asked, "How do we get in touch with him?"

Relai swallowed. "I can send him a message from here. Tannor, you can encrypt it so no one can read it but him, right?"

"Of course."

"And *I* can add on encryption that will actually work," Ky concluded.

Tannor turned from the controls and flared her nostrils at Ky, who tapped his thumb knuckle against his brow in a mocking salute. "So where do we find him?" she asked.

"Fifth continent, Northus, in a central plains region called Minnesota."

"I don't know this planet," Milo said. "Show me where, I'll get us there."

He didn't sound very confident, so Goren added, "I think that's a brilliant plan."

"You would," Milo muttered. Goren threw up a gesture explaining exactly what the criminal could go do. (Screw himself, that's what.)

Tannor rubbed her eyes, offered a weak, "Okay, fine," and Relai entered something into the jumper's navigation.

Satisfied with his work, Goren rebuilt Ky's weird gen-gun and, just to see, turned it on. Ky glanced over to see his gun hum to life and his jaw sagged open.

"My baby! You fixed her?" Ky slid onto the bench opposite Tannor and tried to grab it but Goren elbowed him back.

"Yeah." Goren's fingers glanced over the sight, the battery, the safety. "You made some interesting *illegal* adjustments—will it really fire any ammunition?"

Ky peered over the gun, grinning. "'S'why I call it a spit gun: it'll even shoot spit. Doesn't really hurt past a foot or two, but she'll do it."

"Well, she's fine now." Goren handed her over and moved on to reconstitute the second gun he'd found.

Ky petted his weapon in wonder. "I thought I was going to have to build a new one."

Goren scoffed. He had always liked guns, but it wasn't anything any good soldier couldn't do.

Then Tannor slumped down across the bench behind Goren and closed her eyes, her head resting close to his as he sat on the floor. "I managed to route autopilot through the surviving circuits. We should be set for a while at this altitude."

As if in response, the engine shrieked and the ship dropped ten feet in the air.

"Or not," Tannor groaned. "Damn it."

"I'll fly," Milo said, sidling into the pilot's seat before Tannor could get up.

Goren shot a dubious glance to Tannor, but her eyes were shut again. Underneath them, purple smudges of exhaustion stood out on her pale skin. She'd be mad if he told her he was gonna take care of her, so he didn't say it out loud.

The jumper thrummed smooth and quiet now. Hells, his face hurt. His leg, too, though not as much as it should. Goren hunched forward and started work on another gun.

•

Milo settled into the steady, precisely-focused state required when flying a deathtrap carrying valuable cargo. The helm fought him every moment, strung tension through his limbs and his core, gave him something tangible to hold onto. To stay present. To keep from spiraling out of control.

Then the queen appeared beside him and asked if she could do anything to help.

"Unless you can fly this thing," he replied without looking at her, "no."

"Not at all," she admitted. "I don't know how to fly anything. It's not a skill anyone thought I needed."

The regret in her tone cut off the rush of bitterness he was expecting to feel. He paused a moment, then heard himself say, "If you don't distract me, you can watch."

"Really?" She sat down in the co-pilot's seat. "So what does that do?"

He allowed a stretch of silence, then answered slowly, "Making me talk… counts as a distraction."

But he wasn't willing her to go away, and she didn't.

They both shivered involuntarily. Milo had cut down on all non-essential power drains, leaving the jumper hazy-dark and freezing cold, especially in their still-wet clothes.

Milo needed to steel himself not to react with hatred at the sight of her. *I almost killed you,* he thought. His hands shook at the controls. It was probably the cold.

"You can help keep the right engine from overheating," he said after a moment. "Just ease open this valve when that gauge gets above here, and tighten her up if it dips below there."

It wasn't difficult work, and the queen didn't open her mouth again. Milo couldn't acknowledge it, but it helped.

He tried to ignore the fact that the target of his last eight months of desperate hate was sitting right next to him—except that it *wasn't her.*

But she was still an Aydor. Still an enemy of his people.

Focus. Milo tried to breathe evenly and clear his head, aware that one wrong move could end up crashing them in the center of this sea, hundreds of miles from any shore.

He needed sleep.

•

Hours passed before Relai had her answer. Xiong's reply—curt, formal, and frustratingly bereft of any hints at the Guide's thoughts or feelings—

arrived just as the jumper began its descent over the upper plains of Northus. They were to meet her old mentor at a test field owned by his company, MMN, six miles east of Minnesota, the City of Saint Paul. He'd clear the field and leave the security gate open and unattended.

They could fly right down and land there.

Relai's heart stomped hard and fast in her chest.

Did he know she'd spent years hovering in his orbit? Had he ever wondered about her?

He wouldn't even recognize her with her hair grown so long.

She would recognize him, though. What would she call him? Gandred? He'd always been Guide Xiong to her. He'd taught her for two years, and that was the longest amount of time any instructor had ever stayed with her. Eventually they'd all gotten tired of her and quit, every single one. *He refuses to teach a future leader who continues to show such ineptitude—such lack of skill—such stubbornness,* her father has told her. *As your guide, he would take some blame for your future failures, and you are not worth that.*

She'd tried so hard.

He'd quit, left without a goodbye, left the planet. In despair Relai had begged and threatened and dragged a story out of her favorite castle chef. Xiong had mentioned a city on Earth dedicated to a holy figure, Paul, where some ex-terrs had started a company after the Tennan War. It was a well-known destination for disgruntled coalition emigrants. Maybe he'd gone to find a job with them.

So when Relai herself finally gave in and quit, after—

After what happened—

Relai's thoughts fled abruptly as Milo crashed the jumper in a lake.

•

ii.

Milo lifted his head and heard lapping water.

"I think you fell asleep." Ky patted Milo on the back in either a reassuring or a condescending manner; Milo wasn't sure because he was so tired he could barely see straight.

The jumper swayed gently back and forth, and that was definitely water at his heels. More water. Great.

Milo blinked—it was dark, the cabin illuminated only by the glowing tip of Tannor's tech pen. He untangled himself from the crash webbing and stepped over the others to reach the back door.

"The engine burned out because *Orist* here couldn't keep it cool," he spat, loud enough that everyone heard even over the groaning of the jumper frame.

Relai kicked a splash of water right in his face. "At least we made it this far. I was doing my best!"

"We'll quote that on your commons memorial," Ky said.

Milo peered through the dimness at the oxygen filters, saw the chemical indicator strips all turned bright yellow. *Toxic leak.* And the alarms weren't blaring, so even the emergency circuits must be shot.

"Jumper's done for," he declared. "Grab what you can." He lifted the emergency release on the rear door.

"Wait, Milo, slow down," Ky said. "We don't know if there's—"

Milo kicked open the rear door and cold, murky lake water poured in and soaked their legs all over again.

"Are you mucking crazy?" the boy yelled. "I already drowned once today!"

"Air in here's poison," he answered.

Milo could only make out dim shapes in the hazy early morning light—their flight had managed to chase the same dawn they'd just left on the other side of the planet—but the shoreline looked close. Somehow, the jumper's exterior lights were still on, causing the lake water to glow. Milo blinked at it and frowned—vibrant green speckled the brown silt. Algae that color meant death in Eray, but this was Earth. For all he knew, this stuff would be lunch.

Milo pulled off his black Gastredi shirt, the one that had survived the crash and kept him from burning alive until Ky got to him, and wrapped it around two of the dry gen-guns. Then he eased out into the water, swearing softly as his body dropped shoulder-deep and his feet sank to the knee in muck. Everyone else would have to swim.

"Ahh! There's something alive in here!" Goren yelped as he splashed forward.

Milo spun as he suddenly felt it too—slimy, grasping tentacles—but he didn't struggle, and nothing tightened around him.

"What might be living in these lakes?" he asked in a low voice.

"Um, I'm not sure. Fish, I think?" Relai slid past him, horizontal in the water so that her legs didn't reach the tentacles. "I don't remember."

Ky rolled onto his back and laughed. "First one to the shore gets to live!"

Milo fought forward through the tangles and the sucking pull of the mud, ready for pain or a gasp and a pull at any second. As the muck turned to sand and the depth decreased, Milo's body lifted out of the water and he got a look at the tentacles: weeds.

Just weeds.

Goren stumbled into the shallows holding several pieces of the jumper's internal paneling over his head. He coughed and spit as he reached the grassy shore. "Thanks for the concussion, worst pilot ever!"

"Hold your head under the water for a few minutes, pain'll go away," Milo replied.

Goren spit into the water. "Die in a pit, pove."

Ky shouldered between them and slapped Milo's back before he could respond. "Won't it be fun, laughing about this one day when we're all good friends and we don't call each other disgusting slurs?"

"Just stop talking, Goren," Relai muttered, her arms wrapped around her miserable body and her hair strung in front of her face.

Tannor was tearing off her boots, shirt, and pants. "You know what? If you want to be friends," she bit through her teeth at Ky, "you can *remove the damned drug ticks from our bodies.*"

Ky cocked his head. "Hm, no."

"You're holding us hostage with these things, you *thug*. Let us go!" Tannor wrung out her pants, knuckles white and cheeks red, leaves and dirt sticking to her calves. Milo looked away as he stripped to his base layer to twist the dirty water out of his own pants. At least he wasn't cold.

"Yeah!" Goren added as he failed to hide his pale near-naked body behind a tree. The gen-gun wound seeped red in a stream down his leg. "You don't just get to knock us out whenever you want!"

Ky, clothes dry as ever, fussed with his hair. "Nope."

Relai clenched her fists at her sides like a spoiled brat and demanded, "Take them off!"

"Not my queen. Don't answer to you."

"Don't you hate it," Milo asked Relai, "when someone holds unearned control over you?"

Relai threw up a dismissive hand. "This has *nothing* to do with the Problem of Eray, Milo!"

"You think we refer to you as a problem instead of a human being?"

"*I am a problem!*" she shouted. "Bad example!" Then she heaved in a deep, furious breath and stomped away through the trees.

"You are helping nothing," Tannor said, finger right in Milo's face. "Force this now and you'll lose any chance of convincing her. And you," she turned to Ky, "don't think I've forgotten. I just know how to prioritize."

Then she bundled up her clothes and followed Relai without taking the time to dress.

"Maybe if I shave my head and bow just so, eh?" Milo called after her. "Maybe if I burn my skin to a lighter shade, she'll listen?"

She didn't turn.

It was different for Tannor's people, the Reyetim, people of plains and livestock and fields. They fed the planet, yeah, but they ate the food they harvested. Tannor didn't have to chop her best friend's fingers off because he'd accidentally touched the ground and med scanners were locked against use on 'choice illnesses.' Like Bry chose to trip and fall before he'd put on his gloves.

Goren dragged his shirt back down his skinny torso and asked, "How far are we from wherever it is?" He'd apparently already forgotten about the drug ticks. "Do any of those tablets work? How are we going to get anywhere? Can I drink that water? I'm thirsty. Why is the air trying to suffocate me? This place is disgusting." He limped after Tannor and Relai, making far too much noise and forgetting his jacket on the branch of a tree.

Foliage grew thick on this side of the lake, but across the water Milo could see intermittent buildings and boats. These must be lake and forest people. He wondered if this lake had fish. How would fish taste here—oily? Salty? Sour? The law used to say you couldn't eat of Earth or they'd never let you leave, but that was a long time ago.

To tide his hunger over, he closed his eyes and listened to the chirping morning music and the tall rustling trees. Almost like home.

"Jumper's a problem," he said.

"Go sink it, then," Ky replied, chomping on a reed.

"Earthans can't dive?"

Ky reached into his coat and tossed him their last remaining compression bomb. "Best I can do."

Milo sighed and tossed it right back. "You got to sleep on the trip, ass."

"No one's stopping you from sleeping right now," came the even more asinine response.

Milo sloshed back into the muck, swam back out over the underwater forest, and climbed back into the jumper. For just a brief moment he leaned on the helm, hung his head, and rested.

This would be the end of his control. He wouldn't be able to steal a vehicle to escape, and he couldn't talk his way out of trouble because he and Ky didn't speak any of the languages here. He would be at Relai's mercy, and that of this man, Xiong, who might help them home. How was he supposed to protect anyone when he knew nothing?

He set the last working ignition cell to fire, hit the final key, and leapt out the back, ducking under the water to avoid the heat from the engine. The jumper spun and skittered into a deeper part of the lake, sank below the surface, and then the cell finally blew with a muffled boom.

It was too early for most residents to be awake, he hoped, but Milo slicked the hair out of his eyes and watched the houses across the water as he dragged himself back out.

I'm too young to be this tired, he thought. He grabbed Goren's jacket on his way up the hill.

•

At the top, Tannor whispered:

"I need to fry the transmitters in our comms."

"You know I have that covered," Ky breathed. He made no sound as he moved, not that it mattered with the rest of them stomping through the foliage. The world grew brighter by the minute and these trees were too sparse to hide anyone; she needed to do this now.

"Yet they still found us," she said.

Ky sucked at his teeth and shrugged.

Relai led them to huddle in a copse of tall, spindly trees within sight of a wooden home with large, dark windows overlooking the lake. A property this large would've housed a three-family farm in Reyet, Tannor thought. She wondered how many families lived in this one—and whether or not they'd be armed.

Goren had fixed three gen-guns. She wasn't worried.

Ky mouthed *stay here* and then circled around the back of the house as Milo caught up with the rest of them. Tannor watched Relai pointedly ignore him as he thrust Goren's jacket in the kid's face.

Then a light flicked on inside the house, illuminating half of the open living area on that floor. An older woman, maybe Tannor's mother's age, shuffled into the kitchen portion with a blanket wrapped around her shoulders. She took down a mug and set it on a counter.

"Is anyone else itchy?" Goren whispered. "Why do they have a severed animal head hanging on their wall? That's disgusting!"

Then he slapped the back of his neck, and when his hand came away with a tiny streak of blood he gasped, "What in seven hells is this? It itches and—is that my blood? Are there blood-sucking creatures on this planet? Did it *poison me?*"

"You're fine," Relai said, but she sounded uncertain.

Then movement from the darker area inside the house caught Tannor's eye. The Earthan didn't notice, but a figure was moving closer and closer. Tannor squinted and realized it was Ky. He'd broken in.

Tannor couldn't breathe, watching Ky, a shadow, come within ten feet of this woman and her now-steaming mug. What if she—should Tannor do something? *Could she?*

But the woman didn't turn, busy rubbing her eyes and stirring the contents of her cup, and after a pause Ky slunk away. He even had the audacity to salute through the window just before he disappeared.

If the woman had seen him, would he have killed her?

Tannor spent the next thirty seconds before Ky reappeared imagining the different ways she could murder him. He flashed a smile when he saw her glaring.

"Vehicle in the back. Found these—" he tossed a set of thin metal slivers to Milo, "—and they have the same symbol on them as the vehicle."

"Does anyone know how to fly Earthan vehicles?" Milo asked.

"Not fly, drive," Relai whispered shakily. "Yes. I was learning before I left. And these are keys. They should turn the vehicle on."

"We're pinned to the ground here?" Milo muttered incredulously.

Tannor ignored him and raised her tech pen, the tip sparking with electricity. "Comms, first."

Ky raised a brow. "You gonna carve the pins out of our bones, too?"

Tannor grimaced. Along with a name and a class, every Vadan baby received a commons profile for their informatic life and a tiny pellet in their sternum to log their age. Without the profile, you couldn't do anything—get a job, attend school, watch telay, write a note to a friend—that required electronic data use. Without the pin, regulation med scanners wouldn't heal you, and it was really easy to lose track of how long your body had existed, even after only one space trip. And as long as they had their pins, they were easily trackable.

Tannor had no safe way to remove a pin. At least, not without a hell of a lot of pain and no unregulated med scanner to heal it.

"I had a ceramic deflector put in when I came to live on Earth," Relai said. She pulled open her robe and dragged down the stretchy material of Tannor's borrowed bra to show a rod the size of a fingernail and the color of her skin stuck flush, almost imperceptibly, in her flesh. "It stops distance scans of my pin." Tannor caught a flash of a smile on her face. "Xiong's company, MMN, sells them."

"But..." Goren began, and they all watched him choke on the words. *But those are illegal.* Relai brushed her fingers across the center of her chest.

"I wanted to be left alone."

"Good for you," Milo said dryly, "but what about the rest of us?"

"She's the only one who really matters," Goren, the idiot, replied.

Tannor pinched the bridge of her nose and raised her voice just slightly. "Stop talking. There's nothing I can do about the rest of our pins right now."

She turned to Ky first and brandished the pen. "Kneel down. You're too tall."

He smirked and dropped to his knees in the brush. She held him still with fingers in his wet hair, and she didn't have time for the look in his eyes so she shocked him and turned to Relai as he hissed.

"Will it destroy the whole comm?" Relai asked.

"No," Tannor said, easing the tech pen behind her ear. "Just the receiver and transmitter. Why?"

Relai looked at the ground. "Uh. Well. I store all my music on my comm."

Tannor jabbed, maybe a little less gently than she should have.

·

iii.

Thousands of deadly individual vehicles careening, without any automation, along ribbons of cement with random obstacles on either side? Driving had terrified Relai at first. In her current emotional state, though, the barely-changing scenery of the roadway provided a strange sort of comfort.

She glanced in the mirror at the cramped backseat. They'd taken the small sedan because it had been blocked by a larger vehicle from the perspective of the house, so maybe no one would notice it was missing for a bit longer. Goren was curled up drooling in one corner—he'd fallen asleep right away— with Ky in the other corner and Tannor wedged awkwardly in the middle. In his seat next to Relai, Milo looked even more cramped, his shins pressing against the glove compartment. He'd been staring silently out the window the whole drive so far.

As near as Relai could tell, they'd crashed about two hours north of the city of Saint Paul and its sibling city, Minneapolis. After aimlessly wandering a few back roads, she'd found a major highway; she knew how to get to the MMN testing field from there thanks to the nav map she'd studied in the jumper. They were going to be very late, but she had no way to notify Xiong.

They gradually left behind the sparse countryside for growing signs of suburbia. Billboards, lights, and restaurants lined the artery of concrete, cars buzzing around everywhere, each Earthan citizen in their own private glass and metal bubble. With any luck, they'd be able to get off this planet without having to encounter a single Earthan.

A pair of strobing red-and-blue lights in the rearview mirror dashed those hopes.

"*Oh, no,*" Relai said.

Milo instantly sat up. "Guards?"

"Y-yes. Local law enforcement. They want us to stop."

Relai saw his body clench, heard the dashboard creak where he'd braced his hand. "Can we outrun them?"

"No, I don't think that's the best thing to do—I'm going to pull over," Relai said. "I probably just violated some minor traffic law. It'll be okay."

"Exit here. Side road looks quiet," said Ky from the backseat. "Don't stop 'till you get past the first big batch of trees." They all heard the soft whine of his gen-gun powering up, then Relai caught Milo reaching under his seat. Another gen-gun. They rolled to a stop on a deserted stretch of road surrounded by thin forest on either side.

The police vehicle just sat there for several minutes.

"What are they waiting for?" Tannor wondered.

"Waiting for us to move so they can attack," said Milo.

"What? No," Relai said, smoothing her hair. "That's not how it works here. These vehicles have identification numbers. They're probably checking them against a database that will tell them if we're criminals or not."

Tannor grimaced. "Hopefully this car hasn't been reported stolen yet."

"Hopefully."

Relai noticed Milo's hands were clenched white.

"We should run," he said.

"I don't want dozens of these people chasing us every second of the way," she said. "No. Just...stay calm."

"Whassa?" Goren jerked up from his sleep.

"We've been stopped by Earthan law enforcement," Relai told him.

He settled back down in a shrug. "Earth's a protectorate. Coalition law trumps territorial law, and we have the queen with us," he said sleepily. Then his head lifted again. "But they don't know that, do they? But—we haven't done anything wrong, so... no, we stole this... We *have* done something wrong!" Goren's eyes widened. "What're we gonna do? Are we going to prison? Do they just kill you on sight?"

"No, ah—just stay calm," Relai insisted. She didn't have time to elaborate before someone stepped out of the vehicle. Beside her, Milo put his hands on the top of his head, ready for evaluation. He was shaking.

"Put your hands down, they don't do that here," she hissed as a thin, pink-faced man in a blue uniform paced towards them, gun holstered at his side.

"I've never been arrested," Goren said. "If I'm on Earth, will that show up on my Coalition record?"

"*Shut up, Goren.*"

Relai rolled down her window.

"Hi there," the officer said. "Do you think you maybe know why I'm pulling you over?"

"I'm sorry, sir, no," Relai answered in English.

"Looks like you got some expired tabs there," said the officer. (Tabs. What were tabs?) "They've been expired since May."

The officer peered inside at each of the other four passengers. His eyes were so pale they almost looked colorless.

"Who-all you got in there?" he asked. He seemed to be eyeing Milo in particular.

"Just my friends. We're just, we're just coming back from a week up at the lake."

"Uh-huh."

"Sorry, I didn't know about the tabs. We actually, we borrowed this car from my parents."

"I see. Well, I need to see your ID."

"Sure," Relai bluffed. "Hey, um, do you see my purse back there?" The others gave her confused or panicked looks. She feigned a search.

"Oh, no. I'm sorry, sir. I think—I think I left it back at our cabin. I'm really sorry." She gave her best innocent shrug.

The officer pursed his lips. "I'm gonna need you to step out of the car."

And with that, Ky leaned forward, pushed Relai out of the way, and let off a quick blast from his gen-gun. The officer convulsed and dropped to the ground.

"Ky, no!" Relai yelled. "What if there's another one?"

"Milo," Ky said instead of apologizing, and then they were both out of the car and carrying the man back to his vehicle before Relai could pull her head back together. She opened her door and leaned out, resting her weight against the seatbelt, to watch them load him back into his vehicle. There wasn't another one, thank the stars. There should have been, but there wasn't.

Another car might pass at any moment, though.

Milo tore into something inside while Ky circled the car and slashed each tire, one by one. They made it back in less than twenty seconds, and Ky ordered, "Drive."

Relai drove.

When they were back on the main road and her heart stopped racing, Relai gripped the wheel in her sweaty hands and said, "You could have killed him."

"He could've killed us," Milo retorted. The lines of his face were hard all over again, like the moment they met.

"How far are we from Xiong?" Tannor cut in.

Relai caught her eye in the rearview mirror. "I don't know, thirty minutes?"

"Drive faster."

"*I can't.*"

"It's fair to assume," Ky mused, "that once our friend wakes up, gets out of his own metal restraints, and finds a communications device that isn't ruined, the Earthan authorities will be looking for us."

Relai nodded grimly but said nothing. Hopefully they'd be off of this planet before that happened.

∘∘●∘∘

iv.

The day was bound to come when Goren Dray needed a shave, but today was not that day. He woke up the same as always: bleary and then shocked and then *five more minutes* and then off and running, and right now he was going to enjoy his five more minutes on this piece-of-trash planet. He rubbed his face wistfully, searching for those fine errant hairs that would eventually turn into a proper beard. Milo and Ky both needed to shave a year ago.

No one was getting the chance to shave any time soon, were they? First they needed to meet Xiong.

Goren yawned loudly and stretched into Tannor's space, earning himself a smack in the ear just as their sad little ugly car eased through some sort of security fence. They'd made it to the testing field without another incident, new sunlight just reaching the highest points of nearly-flat land as they pulled through a line of trees just inside the fenced enclosure. The security points sat eerily deserted, a barrier already lifted between two empty guard stations as they crept their way forward. It felt like they were the last people on the planet.

Goren scratched an itchy spot on his neck.

Relai stopped the car at the edge of a giant field. Grass covered one half, dirt covered the other, with the far section hilly and the nearer section completely flat. It reminded Goren a bit of the guard training grounds; he wondered if they tested weapons here, though tracks in the dirt hinted at vehicle testing. Maybe they'd gotten around to inventing their own hover vehicles? That would be cool to see.

The queen sat there staring and tapping the wheel for a moment while they all cleared the sleep out of their eyes.

"You're all welcome to—well, I don't know what's going to happen, but—if there's room you can all—I mean, unless you don't want—"

"Yeah, sure, get out of the car," Ky said. Tannor smacked Goren every time he tried to correct these scumsuckers so he just squirmed in his seat and said nothing. Relai was brave, as anyone should expect, but he couldn't understand why she wouldn't ditch these criminals. They were a disaster waiting to happen.

She opened her door.

Gross. The sticky air swamped his skin with heat and dust and unfiltered chemicals and how anyone lived here Goren could not understand. It might theoretically get this hot in Kilani on the worst summer days, but back home he didn't have to let the air outside touch his skin if he didn't want to. A proper climate was a human right, wasn't it? It was a health issue. Had to be.

As Goren climbed out, Ky pulled Milo aside and they whispered nefariously and then Milo just *walked off.* Somewhere in the stretching and shuffling as they woke one by one from their naps the three surviving guns had ended up with the three men, so when Milo left he was armed.

"You're not the only one who needs to pee, you know!" Goren shouted after him, clenching his thigh as he put weight on his leg and tried not to whimper. His torture wound had finally stopped bleeding, but everything felt so stiff and sore he could hardly stand, let alone walk. At least the pain took his mind off the itching from the bloodsucker bites.

"Don't cry, I won't go far," Milo threw over his shoulder as he disappeared into the trees.

"Where is he going?" Goren asked Tannor.

"Where are any of us going, really?" Ky mused, "In life? In love?"

"Oh, shut your stupid face."

Relai fussed with the jacket she'd borrowed from Tannor; it was a size too big and she looked just ridiculous. (Then again, it was better than nothing. Relai had been far too comfortable dashing around in a bra and pants, making everyone jealous of her abdominal muscles, but now they were about to face a professional man with High Court expectations. No showing undergarments here.)

Relai took a deep breath. "I think maybe we should just... wait? Tannor, do you want to follow Milo, or..."

"I'm staying with you," Tannor said.

Good, Goren thought.

Ky stepped forward first, like he thought he was in charge, and kept Relai just half a pace behind him. Tannor and Goren took up the rear, trying to form a weak excuse for a perimeter of protection. Only two of the three of them were armed; what was Tannor going to do? Dive in front of a gen-gun blast? Probably.

He hoped Milo and his weapon would be useful off in the trees somewhere.

Goren didn't feel too great about asking Gandred Xiong for help. Xiong worked for an Earthan company (which apparently made a habit of hiring extra-terrestrials and producing illegal things for Vadans to use) and he could just clap his hands and make their security disappear? What kind of power did he have?

And he was a renowned strategist. What if he knew about Relai's kidnapping and he wanted to take advantage of it? Maybe to take over or something? What if they were walking into a trap?

They were probably all going to die, that's what. Or Goren would, at the very least, because Ky would pull some crap and get himself out of there and they wouldn't kill Tannor because they'd know she was a genius the second she opened her mouth. Milo had run off, probably to snipe from the trees (no one bothered to ask if someone else was the best and only sniper in his training cohort, which Goren *was*, thanks). That left Goren himself. The dead one.

It occurred to Goren that maybe he should be thinking ahead. He should have a plan.

Maybe Tannor had a plan.

•

Tannor didn't know what to do with her hands if she wasn't holding a gun. She would have put them in her pockets, but the queen was wearing her jacket.

She felt totally confident, totally—except for the sick dread growing in her stomach.

Then Goren crowded right next to her as they crept further out in the open.

"Tannor," he whispered, "do you have a plan?"

"What?" she hissed.

"A plan, *a plan*! We need a plan in case this goes to hell!"

"This is the plan," she said. "We go see Gandred Xiong and he helps us."

"No, a *back-up plan*," he insisted.

"Goren," she said in a low voice. Relai was far enough ahead that she couldn't quite hear. "Fil and I turned off security and comms at Haadam for a non-violent resistance, remember?" He nodded like it was painful to admit.

127

"I don't just go around carrying out orders without knowing who I'm following. I did some digging and I found the head of the resistance. At least, here on Earth. It's him. Xiong."

"I… don't understand."

She resisted rolling her eyes. Sometimes Tannor wished she wasn't the only one who could listen and *comprehend*.

"If Fil and I were following orders from the Quiet and those orders let Ky and Milo get to Relai, that means the Quiet wanted to rescue Relai. Which means *Xiong* wanted to rescue Relai."

"Wait—does that mean Milo and Ky are secret resistance members, too?"

At least his brain made it that far.

"Ky. Not Milo. Don't tell Ky I told you; he wants to keep it secret."

"So why'd you tell me? Do you want me to join this thing?" He bounced a little as they walked. "Am I a spy now? A spy for the queen? A *royal spy*—"

"You're helping bring down whoever took over control, so you're resisting already. We all are. But… just stick with me, will you?"

He tried to shove his elbow into her ribs but she blocked him. "Tannor Mellick, are you worried about me?"

"Yes, Goren Dray," she whispered. "I am."

That managed to shut his mouth for once.

•

Milo wedged himself over a thick branch with his chest flush against the trunk. He leaned his cheekbone against this tree of Earth, took in the dry, dusty scent, and peeled away a piece of bark without taking his eyes off of the group. It came away more easily than the bark of the giant pines around his hometown. He put it in his mouth.

He pressed his teeth into the bark but didn't break it. His mouth watered.

Milo took a deep breath and his eyes fluttered shut for barely a moment. *No*—

Your head isn't pounding. You're not shaking. Not here, not now.

He spit out the hunk of bark and wiped his mouth on his shoulder.

He settled himself to perfect stillness, the same stillness he'd reached hunting sark birds with his brothers when they weren't stomping a ruckus just to make him mad. Milo didn't think they had sark birds here.

At least on Earth they didn't have to keep their skin covered and avoid touching bare ground at any cost.

Milo wished he'd been able to research this planet better before they landed here. The quick, violent moments of his journey punctuated long, bleak weeks of space travel with not a second of access to coalition libraries. He'd avoided going into the coalition commons entirely because he was sure they'd find him the second he logged on. Instead, he'd been crammed inside a cargo container or storage bunker with a cranky, sarcastic bartender. At this point he could probably recite every Gastredi folk myth, so that was something.

There was a time when the moon was food and the sand was water and the rocks were dragons…

He watched as the group drifted toward the center of the field; Milo could see the entire perimeter from his spot. He was a good shot by now, thanks to Ky, but gen-guns were not meant for long-distance accuracy.

(And he could pretend all he wanted, but he could no longer control the tremors in his hands.)

Milo blinked against a light breeze and watched a cluster of small leaves fall. They drifted through the field, most failing to make it even halfway. The leaves that drifted far enough, though, stopped abruptly in mid-air and fell straight down. They joined a small unnatural ridge in the grass.

He tapped on the cheap disposable comm he'd stuck behind his ear on the ride over after Tannor fried his real one.

"Ky?"

Peering out into the field, he saw Ky brush a bug away from his ear—tapping on his comm.

"Yeah?" came Ky's whispered reply. He heard Goren mutter something in the background.

"There's something masked five meters in front of you," Milo whispered, "center field. Looks big."

•

They'd reached a midpoint in the flat part of the field when Tannor saw Ky flick up a hand, and then he halted.

"There's something straight ahead of us," he whispered, squinting at the ground and then pointing into empty air. "There."

Tannor couldn't see a thing.

"Want me to shoot it?" Goren asked.

To Tannor's surprise, Ky said, "Yeah. Give it a little shock, see what it thinks."

Relai exclaimed, "You can't be serious—"

Goren let off a charge.

It connected with a solid surface and dispersed over several feet, revealing something flat leaning at an angle toward them.

Tannor jolted at a sudden sense of a small sleeping ship hiding behind a mask, resting and waiting.

The sense came so stark and certain she forgot where she was for a moment. She knew the ship was there and she knew it wasn't any ship she'd ever encountered before. It was exciting and foreboding and before she could regain the balance in her head the mask blinked off and—

There it rested, for all to see, silver and red and gleaming. This was not a ship converted from a Sevati vessel after liberation. She saw pieces she recognized from other ships—the loading dock at the front that Goren had shot, the chassis, the engines—but this ship was new. Unique. *Did he?*—he must have built it here.

Xiong built his own groundship.

(Where did he salvage the pieces from? Did it run off of metahydrocarbon? If not, what was the fuel and would there be enough to get to Oliver Station? Why silver and red? Did it have a metamercury interface? Could it pilot itself? Could they start sending encrypted relays to Arden immediately? Did the Coalition know he built it? Did it—)

The group shrank closer, Tannor's forearm brushing Relai's back, as the dock lowered and a man walked to its edge.

He wore a simple green collared Earthan shirt and brown slacks. She'd thought Gandred Xiong was in his sixties, but he looked so much older, with eyes like a snare waiting to snap. She wanted to assault him with questions. She held her tongue.

Tannor couldn't see Relai's face, but the queen's shoulders tensed and her back snapped stiff and tall. She'd twisted her hair in a tight bun, secured around itself by its own rough, salty state. Bare neck. Long hair hidden.

Xiong waited several aching moments before speaking.

"Relai."

The queen went through one breath before speaking. Her voice was steady.

"Guide Xiong."

She bowed. He didn't.

It was ridiculous. They just looked at each other, and looked, and looked, and Tannor realized they must be sending those endless tiny signals only the greater class could understand. She, a lesser, was lost.

And was it just her, or was there something really *off* about Xiong?

•

Seven years.

He looked so old.

Old, but definitely not tired. Hell, Relai probably looked more tired than he did. She probably looked disgusting. Embarrassing. He looked like a grandfather, maybe he *was* a grandfather by now—

The old anxiety hadn't changed and it was unfair, really, that she couldn't tamp out the clenching fear of receiving bad marks. Maybe he'd never really liked her. Maybe she was really as stupid as she feared.

Relai took in two small gasps, trying to calm her heart. Her fingernails were sharp against her palms.

Then he spoke and his voice was the same.

No, colder.

"This ship is only fueled and stocked to carry two people to Oliver Station. You, Mora, may come with me now, alone, and reach Arden quickly. Otherwise, I can send you all to Daat Base. It will be more dangerous, and I can't guarantee you will only meet allies there."

She swallowed and turned to Goren and Tannor. She already knew how Ky felt: he'd want her to stay with them so Milo could satisfy his vengeance fantasy and maybe even convince her to grant Eray independence. And of course, of course, her guards wanted her to go.

Or at least Goren did. Tannor looked sick. The corner of her left eye twitched but she didn't speak.

"I don't know what to do," Relai whispered. Xiong heard her and remained still. She had to decide now.

Relai could leave them behind and they'd be all right. They would be fine.

Or they'd be killed by those chasing her.

Or—

Relai realized it like tripping, like a sudden drop, and she stepped backward in surprise.

"I know this riddle."

It was a construct defense all over again and she remembered how this one went, she remembered her answer, and she remembered her guide's counter-construct.

Xiong's eyes gleamed in the morning sun.

But that was ridiculous.

"Are you—are you trying to tell me to *kill you*?"

.

v.

Milo cupped his hand around his ears, straining to hear the conversation with only Ky's comm to relay sound. He shifted uncomfortably in the tree, his muscles aching.

Relai stood at the center of a triangle made by Ky, Tannor and Goren as she spoke with the man who had emerged from the formerly masked groundship. Xiong. Milo could hear the timbre of their voices over Ky's comm, but not any words.

As he listened, another sound from the direction of the security gate drew his attention. A large white Earthan vehicle slowly crept up the entrance road and then paused, engine still running, and two figures in white uniforms stepped out. They held large firearms at the ready and split off in opposite directions through the trees around the field.

"Ky," Milo spoke into the comm. "We've got friends. Large white vehicle. Armed soldiers. Sent two out to flank; don't know how many still in the car."

"Hmm," Ky responded.

One of them was creeping swiftly toward him. Milo's heart pounded. He listened intently, hoping he'd catch a snippet on conversation that might resolve this before it went sour.

He checked the two dials on his gen-gun, cranking the charge to lethal levels and the penetration to maximum in case those uniforms were armored. His fingers shook as he did.

Don't fall out of this tree. Don't close your eyes. Hold still, gun up—

•

The riddles were supposed to be exercises in reasoning and strategy and they were never straightforward. Relai had learned quickly that Xiong expected more from her; he wanted creativity. He wanted ruthlessness.

The riddles were supposed to be a lot of things, but real was never one of them.

She *knew* this one.

A queen and her closest allies are traveling in dangerous lands. They come to a river that must be crossed in order to reach the queen's territory and they meet a sentry guarding a boat.

The sentry declares two options:
The queen may leave her allies and travel across the river with the sentry...
Or.
The queen and her allies may together travel far downriver to a larger port, facing further delays and the dangers of the foreign land.

The answer she gave Xiong did not satisfy him. He did concede that neither of the options given by the sentry were acceptable. If she had chosen to leave her allies the sentry would have killed the queen and taken her crown on the other side of the river. If she had traveled with her friends further downriver, the sentry would have passed in his boat and met them with murderous allies at the larger port.

Either choice was death.

So—so was Xiong trying to tell her this was a trap? His answer to the problem—

"Are you trying to tell me to *kill you*?"

This was the solution approved by her guide and the king:

A proper queen would kill the sentry and take his boat.

"Are we supposed to kill you and take your ship?" Xiong's face watched her like living stone as Relai stepped closer. "You know I never liked that answer."

Finally he raised one eyebrow, ruling on her failure. "It has been your answer these last thirteen months, Mora. Kill and take. I am ashamed to say I trained you well."

Mora. This again—she had been hoping Xiong and his strategic mind would have guessed her situation by now.

But he wasn't surprised to see her here on Earth? What did he think she'd been doing this whole time?

"Though you are more like your mother than I ever suspected," Xiong added.

What?

Relai closed her eyes for a moment. She had to figure this out. She had to figure this out because Xiong was expecting more of her and she had to make him proud.

If Xiong thought a dictator queen facing a rebellion had run to him for help, how would he react? With a safe ship and an offer of escape?

He wanted me to think for myself. He wanted me to be strong. I know, I know he wanted me to be kind, even if my father never let him say it.

This was a trap.

Relai bit back tears and looked at Xiong with all the honesty she could convey. "I haven't been ruling. I was sleeping. They kept me sleeping for the last year. My Guide, *Gandred*, please believe me. I don't know what to do. I *trust you.*"

If she were really smart, if she were the stuff queens were made of— she'd follow her own words and play out her solution to the riddle.

A stupid child's answer, a silly, nattering, naive—

If someone holds power over you and gives you impossible choices, you attack the power.

She'd declared, so bold at fourteen, that her answer was to travel upstream with her allies, dam the river, and walk the muddy riverbed until she reached the sentry. She would demand a treaty for the sake of his river, go home, and never get stuck in a foreign land again.

(They'd really hated that answer. She'd been torn to pieces for it. Nothing new.)

But Relai didn't know how to take away Xiong's power over her. She had nothing right now and she needed him—

Of course, the allies in the riddle never had a say in anything.

Here, in real life, Ky took three steps forward and pointed his gun at Xiong's head.

"I'm getting bored with your stalling, Xiong," he declared. "Let's tell everyone here what I already know and you can decide if you want to live or die."

Relai choked on her words as Xiong said, "Go on."

"You don't want this poison on your hands. You know everyone in the greater galaxy is going to be hunting her. You're stalling so your couriers can arrive."

Xiong gave him a sour smirk. "Out of the three of you, I think you, sir, are the one who impersonated me among the quiet in order to snatch her yourself."

"What?" Tannor exclaimed, and Relai whipped her head back to stare at her.

"Who's quiet?" she hissed.

No one bothered to answer her.

Did Milo know? She had no idea where Milo was. The tree line remained silent and still in the morning sun.

"It certainly wasn't the baby hugging his security blanket," Ky replied.

"Is that... am I the baby?" Goren whispered. He'd raised his gun halfway but hadn't decided where to point it yet.

Xiong ignored everyone but Ky. "You think you'll escape this planet with such expensive cargo?"

Ky snorted. "No, but if you're all that stands between me and that ship, I'll take an opportunity when I see it."

Xiong only laughed. "Titian jumpers are faster than you predict, hunter." (Titians. Was Xiong working for Titus now?) "I want her in the hands of the Coalition before some fool declares a rebellion or Odene takes an offer to kill her."

In the hands of the Coalition sounds pretty good, Relai thought. Titus didn't maintain an army; their soldiers were more ceremonial than functional and Arden outnumbered them twenty to one. It wasn't because they were pacifists, though; their automated weaponry was just that *good*. Their weapons were subtle and precise and devastating and they always saved lives because a conflict with Titus never lasted long. The cast-off weapons they'd used to stock their Earthan base had stopped nuclear war on this planet—twice. They'd be able to protect her.

But Ky said, "So they're taking her out of the generosity of their hearts? No."

"And you are so concerned for her well-being?"

"You think I'm going to hand her over to them for free, to sell at a profit? You don't know much about commerce, Xiong."

Relai exclaimed, "Nobody is selling me—what are you talking about?" Xiong wouldn't do that. He might think she was a horrific dictator, but he wouldn't send her to her death.

What was she thinking? *Of course he would.* If he thought it was best for the galaxy on whole.

"Relai, I think you should run," Tannor whispered.

She swayed, torn between the salvation of that open groundship door and unknown threats in every direction.

She caught Tannor's frantic eyes.

•

Tannor couldn't move.

Ky was a Quiet impostor. Milo was lurking out there somewhere. Goren had a gun and she didn't and there was something, *something* wrong with Xiong, with his body, his face, something wrong, something *wrong*—

If she wrenched the gun from Goren's hands could she really shoot their way out of this? Something was wrong with Xiong—Relai froze behind her and they locked eyes—and then they all turned to seek out the source of a growling engine.

•

Okay, so Goren was not exactly following all of this, but he could damn well shoot someone if he needed to, and since Relai was all nervous about perfectly pleasing her old guide (the tidy hair, the clothing thing, the bowing, all so obvious it was sweet) he didn't really want to shoot the guy just for threatening to hand her over to some Titians for the trip home. Did that even count as a threat? He hated the Titians as much as any Ardenian (mostly out of envy) but they were coalition—they had to protect her. Ky, on the other hand, could probably use a decent wound or two. He was scaring Tannor.

But then a large white car thing slid to a dramatic stop and out jumped six soldiers in Titian military dress with six Earthan guns at their hips and finally, finally everything was going to be okay.

Goren and Tannor moved in tight around Relai just to make her feel safe, and he angled himself in front of the queen so she could see everyone. For some reason Tannor refused to turn her back to Ky.

Five privates and an aggressively nervous sergeant (all with stupidly impractical, stupidly handsome white uniforms) surrounded them.

And they didn't even greet the queen first. Disrespectful!

At least Relai had a safe ride home now. Goren wondered if he and Tannor would just be reassigned to Daat Base after all this—and just when he was starting to learn Italian, too.

He wondered if they'd be considered heroes. He did get tortured a bit for information, after all.

Goren resisted scratching his leg with the gen-gun and tried to glare at these Titians with competence. Competent glaring. Yes.

•

Ky sighed. *Titians.* Always shortchanging their footsoldiers. Always big tech in place of tactical skill and cohesion—but his transmission jammer would drop any sleepies buzzing around before they got close enough to sting them to sleep, and he didn't hear the telltale hum of a stomperbot. They didn't bring their fancy stuff. Interesting.

And why did it have to be Earthan guns? Ky hated pulling solid bullets out of people.

"So you're the buyers," Ky started, and when the sergeant opened his mouth he solidified Ky's authority.

"We'll be escorting Her Majesty, Their Glory to Arden," the man replied. He sounded all sorts of guilty.

Ky fingered his gen-gun thoughtfully. "Maybe she already has an escort."

From his position left of the field midline Ky saw Relai's jaw open, but before she could speak the sergeant snapped:

"We're not cutting anyone in, *Gastredi.*" Good, they picked up on the accent. Six here, plus Milo's two…

"Oh, is a—hmm, eight-way split already too much?"

The sergeant squinted, tightening his grip on his gun.

Thankfully Milo chose that moment to crackle into his earpiece:

"Got one."

Ky smiled at the sergeant. "Well, it *was* eight. Now it's seven. See, we're already helping increase your cut."

"Soldiers!" the guy barked, and just like that everyone was pointing their guns at everyone. And they had no cover whatsoever. Ky sighed. The nearest Titian stood eight steps to his left and Ky could use him as a shield until he made it inside the groundship. Tannor and Goren had nothing.

The sergeant continued, "Hand her over and we won't kill you all."

"Hey!" Goren cried.

"You're not going to kill her," Ky said with absolute certainty. At least Titians avoided personal combat at all costs—an Ardenian unit would have opened fire in glee by now.

The man sneered. "No. They want her alive. But we can kill the kid, and then the woman, and by then we'll figure out where your dog in the woods is hiding, so call him off now and you can all go home."

Ky laughed. "The man believes he has leverage. Tannor? Goren?"

The two guards turned at their names.

•

Relai's ears registered the hiss of Ky's gen-gun as she watched Goren fall, and on the downbeat of her heart a second hiss and a second thud followed.

Goren's white shirt turned red right over his heart, body twitching. His eyes were open and his body was far too limp to be only stunned.

Tannor's mark bloomed right between her eyebrows and she was limp, too. Her eyes were open.

Relai stared at Ky in disbelief.

Then she reached over Goren and snatched up his gun and aimed at Ky and—

It *wouldn't fire.*

He'd given Goren a dead gun.

Relai swore and flung the weapon furiously at Ky as she dashed forward to the open ramps of the groundship.

She saw Ky lurch to the side as more than one of the Titians opened fire on him with their deafening weapons.

•

Milo had waited for the Titian to get close enough to take a shot but his hand had shaken. He'd missed.

The next few rough seconds of struggle after he leaped down should not have worn him out this much. He had four inches on the Titian, yet he could barely catch his breath after they'd struggled for control of the gen-gun and Milo had managed to fire a shot into the man's head.

"Got one," he told Ky.

Seven left.

These Titians were carrying small Earth-sourced guns that required solid ammunition; once they ran out of bullets, they were out. Generator guns were his favorite, but they offered so little long-distance precision. Besides, killing people with their own guns left less of a trail.

He had no idea how many bullets this gun held, no time to take it apart and figure it out.

Milo moved, hell, he pushed his body because that's what his body was for. He did it. He wanted to give up but he didn't, struggling through the brush to the edge of the trees just in time to see Ky shoot their two erstwhile guards.

Two fewer things to worry about.

Relai ran for the groundship and everyone started firing at Ky. There was no way he wouldn't be hit. Milo raised the Earthan gun and took aim.

After another missed shot, surprisingly loud, Milo managed to take out one soldier (six) then another (five) before any of them returned fire. The crack of the shots rattled in his head.

Ky dove and snared a private, clutched him flush against his body, and dragged him around the corner of the groundship. Four. Milo ducked behind a tree to avoid fire and downed another.

Three.

One disappeared after Ky (two) on the far side of the ship and the other bolted for the groundship. For Relai. Another shot, another miss.

He couldn't see Relai.

·

They were all *so close* when the soldiers started firing, Relai thought, that Ky couldn't possibly have avoided getting hit. She focused all her energy propelling herself forward until she landed inside the shelter of the groundship. She dove to the floor and rolled to the side and saw that Xiong stood at the cockpit now.

When had he moved? Why wasn't he armed?

"You can't fly this ship, Mora," he said. He remained very still considering the firefight that continued outside (firefight? Why were they still shooting? Was Ky somehow still alive? Milo. It must be Milo. Gods, *did Milo know he was going to kill them?*)

She pushed up to her feet. "You'll fly it," she said, hoped, begged.

"No. I won't be any help to you."

Damn it, *damn it*, and all she wanted was—

They died so easily—

Everything sounded brittle and distant and Xiong couldn't see her, anyway, he only saw the lie. The False Relai.

She pounded a fist against the bulkhead hard enough for the pain to help her focus. "I'll figure it out, then."

Then she whipped her head around to see one of the Titian soldiers stumble his way onto the entrance ramp.

•

Tannor blinked.

The sky above hung blue and cloudless and the heat so heavy she could almost see it. Then she registered the noise.

She lifted her head and saw Goren—he was waking, too, and the red over his heart shocked her until her own forehead twinged and she felt blood slide down the side of her nose and it all made sense. *That asshole did it again—*

A dead Titian lay a few feet away and Tannor caught movement and gunfire footward and left. She smeared the blood away from her eyes and rolled onto her belly to grab for the dead guard's gun.

Goren scrambled for a weapon further away as Tannor sat up. She saw Ky's leg sticking out from under a body but she couldn't see the rest of him because another soldier was in the way, bearing down on him. She squared her shoulders and fired, the gun kicking wildly in her hand, and hit the Titian in the arm and the back of the knee.

She was aiming for the center of his back. Damn projectile weapons, so heavy, and the recoil was terrible—

Goren gained his footing and moved into formation next to her (two-person combat, something she barely remembered from training). Tannor pushed herself up, not as weak as she expected to feel after a dose of whatever it was in the drug tick, and she focused in time to see the soldier she'd wounded jerk back and fall from another shot. Ky. He shoved the limp body of a Titian off of himself and just sat there for a second, breathing heavily. She couldn't tell if he was injured.

From their right Milo came thundering across the field, gun raised, shouting one word, and Tannor couldn't believe she hadn't seen and reacted yet:

There, inside the open groundship. *Relai.*

•

The soldier gained his footing on the ramp and aimed his gun with both hands.

Relai moved to grab Xiong's sleeve. "He'll kill you." They wouldn't kill her and she wouldn't let them kill Xiong. No.

"That's unlikely," Xiong replied.

Relai's hand touched nothing—empty air—and she blinked and watched it disappear into the image of his body.

He wasn't even there.

He didn't come. This was a projection.

Xiong smiled like he used to when he out-thought her, and she let out a strangled noise.

He thought so far ahead of her, how could she hope to—no. *No.* Next time she'd show him.

Which meant she needed a next time, so she clawed at her shirt to reach the knife stuck sweaty against her ribs, and it was already bloody from digging into her own skin and maybe that helped a little. She held it low and backed toward the pilot's seat, spinning the knife in her hand to dry the blood a little and find a decent grip.

The projection stepped to the center of the walkway and held out his hands toward the Titian. "You can't fly this ship, soldier. Step back and take care of your fallen."

She'd trapped herself. Just helping Xiong at every step, wasn't she? If the Titian backed off, Xiong would seal her in and he could surely pilot this thing remotely and bring her wherever he wanted her.

She kind of wanted to stab him a little.

But the soldier said, "I'm not splitting this bounty with anyone," and fired four times. Relai ducked as the bullets lodged in the bulkhead and pitted the forward window, but Xiong's projection didn't even have the courtesy to flinch at the shots.

This Titian *probably* wouldn't shoot her. She was just delaying the inevitable, delaying the press of her knife into his skin and muscle. Silata was just for stress relief, *she'd never wanted to hurt anyone*, but she was going to need his gun.

Relai advanced, knife out, only to hear another shot and see the look on the soldier's face as he jerked and fell, groaning a little and turning on his side, and beyond him both Tannor and Goren were rushing forward.

What?

...*What?*

Goren's arms were raised and his gun was still pointed where he'd fired. He'd shot the guy right in the ass.

They were alive. *Oh.* Relief washed cold across her shoulders. She didn't understand what she was seeing because they were both still bloody and those were real wounds, but they looked awake and alert and they weren't moving like injured people so she was going to have to trust what she saw.

Trusting what she saw had let her think they were dead.

Forget my eyes, she thought. *I need people I can trust.*

She tried to move past the wounded Titian and throw herself at her guards but the soldier caught her leg and she fell down next to him. His knee cut a vicious arc into her chin and she dropped the knife, reeling. He was struggling with something inside his jacket as he held her, and she kicked and twisted but he held her tight.

The something turned out to be a black and brown case shaped like a flattened egg, and the moment he brought it into view a lot of things happened at once.

Tannor and Goren reached her. She kicked one more time and knocked the egg out of his hand. From somewhere far off Milo screamed, "*No!*"

The case slapped open when the soldier lost it. Something fell out and rolled across the floor of the groundship, something small and dark, a pellet or a bead.

Relai felt arms around her waist, grabbing her and dragging her back, and she kicked one last time and broke free, sliding fast as her guards lost their footing.

She saw Xiong's projection frowning over the thing. His lips went tight with that same annoyed look he used to give both her and the king.

"Get away from it!" Milo shouted, but he didn't reach them before it went off.

Went *in.*

A bright light cracked over them. Relai ducked her head into her arm and Goren twisted into a shield for her, and when she looked up the space was empty. A breeze rushed past them, air filling the voided space.

A cubic area of matter was just *gone.* The space didn't quite reach the edges of the groundship, so they were treated to a perfectly-cleaved view of the internal workings of those sections left behind, before the unstable pieces tipped and piled into the hole with a muted crash. The top of the groundship was completely gone and the bottom of the void reached several feet into the ground. A perfect cube of emptiness.

Milo reached them, tipped onto his knees, and settled back to catch his breath.

"What. Was. That?" Relai breathed.

Milo rubbed his forearm over his sweaty brow once, twice, then lifted his chin at the missing space. "Condensing seed. We use them in the mines to shrink down loads of metalock so they take up less space for transport. They just... eliminate the extra space."

Goren pulled back, plucking his sweaty and bloody shirt away from his chest. "Sorry I grabbed you," he muttered, focused abashedly on the ground, so Relai smiled and whispered, "No. Thank you."

"Where did it all go?" Tannor asked.

Milo looked around with hazy eyes. "He didn't stabilize it, so it's probably just going to sink into the planet as deep as it can get." Everything was quiet for another moment and he put his weapon down. "Did it take your guide?"

His eyes showed sorrow and Relai felt pain twist in her chest. "No, he was just a projection. He didn't come in person."

Milo nodded like that was to be expected, and they were going to have to work on their group communication so Relai wasn't so damn shocked by everything.

Then Ky trudged up from the left. She didn't see any wounds on him, though his clothes were dark, and how in this world did he manage that? At least he looked terrible—dirty, pale, deeper shadows on his face.

"Looks like Xiong is going to have fun cleaning this up," he said. "Milo?"

"One. You?"

"One. Damn." Ky turned and started for the woods to their left.

"Stop!" Relai lunged at the gun in his hand and stumbled in surprise when he relinquished it. She didn't aim it at him. It wouldn't have stopped him.

He looked to the sky and smeared a hand over his eyes. "I can kill him without a gun, you know."

"They didn't do anything this whole time," she said. "There might not even be anyone there." Ky looked to Milo. He stared back, eyes dull, and twitched his hand vaguely.

The heat and everyone's exhaustion finally worked in her favor. Ky sighed, snatched his gun back, and then shouted toward the woods: "Good luck, friend! You're going to need it."

·

Tannor took Relai's hand to get up as Ky offered his to Goren. With the settling calm came awareness of how very dirty and stained and sweaty her whole body had become. And—she checked her forehead—bloody.

She was so *thirsty*. They needed to get out of here.

Tannor hoped her appearance made her incredulous glare more effective as she approached Ky. He was kneeling between two bodies and rifling methodically through their pockets.

"You knocked us out." She meant it as a demand for an explanation. "And shot us. *Again*."

Ky just arched a brow without even looking at her. Goren had followed his lead, collecting tech and neat folds of local money from the dead soldiers' pockets.

Milo mumbled, "No cover. You were good as dead. He killed you first so they wouldn't."

Which—okay. That was probably true.

She poked Goren in the ribs. "And how come you're not mad?"

"Oh, I saw him dial his gun down to skin-deep," Goren said. "I don't know why nobody else noticed."

Ky snorted and Tannor turned away in irritation. Goren's head was empty enough for him to catch small things like that? Good for him. Tannor was busy trying to keep the galaxy from falling apart.

She glanced over at the fallen Titian soldiers and felt... nothing. *We can kill the kid, and then the woman,* he'd said. They chose their end.

When they reached the Titians' white vehicle, Ky asked, "Anyone want to bother rooting out all the tracking devices?"

No one answered; it would have been pointless to try. Titian tech was better than Ardenian tech, and Tannor didn't know it well. Unless she had the Titian source in hand, she wouldn't be able to stop their tech from finding itself.

Ky carried out his tire-slashing routine yet again, and then Tannor sparked its engine with her tech pen until it caught fire. Relai had the presence of mind to remove the metal plates that displayed their own vehicle's identification number and replace them with the plates from the Titian's vehicle, though. Earthan vehicles didn't have intrinsic markers for law enforcement to scan, and eyes could be fooled. Simple.

Every second of blooming daylight blanketed them with thicker heat, and the last thing Tannor wanted to do was pack herself back into a metal can like a chewed wad of sour meat. It was better than throwing herself in with the dead bodies, she supposed.

As Relai tightened the tiny pieces linking the metal plates to their little car, Tannor eyed Ky until he sighed and looked at her over the rim of an open car door.

"Thanks," she said.

"We call it the Jaya Point," he replied.

Milo smiled, opening the car door and folding into the front passenger seat. "Glad it wasn't me this time."

Relai settled into the driver's seat and the final door shut. "Hospital?" she asked as she started up the engine. Tannor peeked behind Goren's head to see Ky's reaction.

"We need food," was all he said.

Tannor didn't miss how Milo eyed Ky for a moment, his green eyes glassy as he peered over the headrest behind him, but after a beat he just echoed, "Yeah. We need to get food."

"Okay. I'll find a place," Relai said, starting up the engine, "and that money should be enough to pay for somewhere to hide until we decide on our next move." Her words were steady, not frightened, not exhausted. It sounded like she'd shut off that part of herself again.

Tannor glanced back through the striped rear window as they sped off.

A field of dead bodies and a burning car. What a nice morning.

○○●○○

EPISODE V:

CONSEQUENCES

OSOSI TENA WAS not bleeding, not a bit. She was very much alive.

Wind unsettled the fallen leaves around her. She heard it and felt it, but she didn't see. She did not open her eyes.

The Quiet operated on Arden, not Titus. It was a group moderating Ardenian conflicts, operating within Ardenian circles. It should not have concerned Ososi, their discontent with the established monarchy, but for the fact that her mother was born Ardenian. Ma had been visiting her family on Arden when the Overture Attack came, and after that... nothing. The queen of Arden—and overseer of the farcical Coalition that theoretically included Titus—forbid non-military travel, and all of Ososi's frantic relays were met with silence. When Ososi received her transfer to Buzou Base six months later, she still had no idea where Mami was, or if she or the rest of their extended family were all right.

And somehow, *somehow*, Andrew Xiong had known all this when Ososi landed on Earth.

Andrew claimed he didn't know where Ososi's mother was, but he could find out. Perhaps if Ososi sent one more message for him. Perhaps after just one more package tucked into the hidden seam of a Titian groundship. One more.

For four months, Ososi had done as Xiong asked. His machinations all had something to do with Ardenian politics—which she was inclined to stay out of, as a Titian and a quiet sort of person—but for now she was stuck on this backwater planet and it couldn't hurt to be on the good side of someone who may be in a position to help.

So she told herself.

The staff of Buzou was not large, nor was there ever much to do, but Ososi kept to herself. When Andrew had called for a team to come to his aid, she'd still had to learn half their names, despite having seen their faces everyday. The hours of small talk on the jumper ride over here had been the most she'd conversed with her fellow Titians since arriving on Earth.

One of the team had introduced himself as John Paul Yora, which amounted to an aggressive religious declaration in Titian terms. Ososi didn't judge based on parental proclivity for syncretic religious adoption. Or translation, or—what would it be called? Conversion. So elemental. The essence of the self, changed.

John Paul had been shot in the head by the oldest of the group holding the queen of Arden captive. He was supposed to stand up in his older sister's wedding later this year.

Ososi gasped and pressed the heels of two shaking hands into her eye sockets until stars lit up and she couldn't think about John Paul and his complaints about wearing wedding robes under a hot sun, and how annoying it would be to smile until his whole face hurt.

Where was Andrew? Gandred, that was his Ardenian name. He'd changed it when the coalition excommunicated him. Where was he? Ososi had done exactly what Andrew Xiong had asked of her during their moment of secret contact after the team had voted to chase down the missing queen and deliver her to Unity for that tempting eight hundred thousand creds. Ososi had assured Xiong that the team had no choice but to stop at Oliver Station before leaving the solar system. "I want to see what she does," Andrew had said. "Either way, she'll come to me."

Ososi had started out nervous. "You go left, he goes right, and you take out everyone but Aydor if they move wrong," the sergeant told them. He didn't ask if they were at peace with that—if they would be willing to kill for a line of numbers of a screen.

When that man, that *vicious mercenary*, that *Oeylan*, had shot and killed the guards flanking the queen and then everyone followed along in violence, Ososi's nerves had clenched into panic. The Oeylan shot John Paul next, and after that Ososi had stumbled back and hid at the base of a fallen tree. *Andrew said not to interfere*—Ososi clung to that order and curled up behind a tree with a wretched Earthan revolver digging into the leaves and detritus under her hand but not raised because—killing? Murder? Self-defense, oh, A'lah, anything—anything would be too much.

Andrew said not to interfere.

Ososi had listened to all of those soldiers die.

They were not nice people, not even John Paul, and they'd been truly gleeful at the thought of selling the queen and retiring to the nicest ring of Titus, no matter how quickly her life and reign ended with their help.

Still.

Ososi had no concept of time but for the increasing, unbearable pressure of heat from earthsun above, and then she heard a voice.

Someone said, "Come on, kid, Xiong wants to see you. You're okay, you don't have to look. They're cleaning up. Let go of the gun."

Let go? She would never touch another gun again.

Now Ososi waited in an office like any other office in all these boring Earth buildings—mostly like the ones on television, only smaller, of course— except for the security gates and metal detectors and armed guards. Xiong thought himself very important on Earth.

How many minutes had passed? What would they tell John Paul's sister? What was her name? Probably Mary. They were that sort of family.

"Ososi," came Andrew's voice. He shut the door behind him and sat in a high-back chair on the opposite side of the desk.

"I'm here. Andrew—" Ososi's voice cracked, "what happened?"

"An astounding lack of strategy, child. I regret the loss of your fellow soldiers. Are you all right?" Xiong was a decade or two older than Ososi's parents, but not once did the man ever show fatherly concern. The question was not a genuine one.

"No, I'm not. I'm not all right. They're all dead! Why didn't you—"

"Why did one of your people have a condensing seed?" Andrew interrupted. Ososi blinked through tears.

"I—I don't know. I want to go home. Can I go home now?"

Xiong woke the screen in the surface of his desk and ignored the question. He tapped intently while Ososi hunched forward, forearms trapped between knees, and tried to breathe slowly and evenly to stop the panic.

"Soon. I hope. But events are unfolding that require us to act. I need you to do something first."

Ososi nearly wailed in exhaustion, but Xiong kept talking. No one ignored Andrew Xiong.

"You heard the news of the destruction of Haadam Base this morning, yes? A squad survived and they are currently in Earthan custody. I need you, Ososi, to go and gather them and bring them to Daat Base. I have arranged your authority. Some of these soldiers may be Quiet, and others may be open to joining. Evaluate each of them and contact me immediately with a report. I am leaving for Oliver Station now."

He stood and opened the office door before Ososi could even process the orders. "Now? You're leaving Earth? But I can't do this—I can't do this alone! Don't leave!"

"You will do it. Your mother is alive, Ososi. She needs you to be strong so you can make it back to her."

"She's alive?" Ososi chased desperately after him. "Where is she? What about my grandparents? Why can't she—"

He stopped in the anteroom where another employee, a woman with a pitying look on her face, stood holding a large parcel. "Clothing, documentation, weapons. You are sleepless, yellow, two. Shoua will take you to your jumper. Go now, Ososi Tena."

Then Andrew turned and left.

Ososi took the parcel, swallowed, and followed after the woman.

ii.

Thomas Wood (Tom to friends, Dr. Debunker to his listeners and readers, Thomas Benedict to his mother when he didn't call for more than two weeks) kicked a plastic trash bin across the studio. He was attempting to be intimidating.

It was only a little bin, though, and it just contained some crushed Summit beer cans, the torn remnants of a failed band's lyrics, and a few questionable tissues. The bin didn't even crack (because that's what IKEA was known for: durable products? *Come on.*). Tom really needed to learn how to be more threatening; no one was scared by tattoos anymore. Damn hipsters, ruining everything.

This was the last time he depended on studio time from a guy with a nickname that involved food.

"Damn it, Chippy, are you kidding me?!" he shouted, to no avail.

"Sorry, man, but I got bills; I can't keep letting you use my equipment for free. You're going to have to find somewhere else. Or, you know, buy a damn fifty-dollar microphone and plug it into your computer like every other podcaster."

"The audio quality on those things is shit, I told you. My listeners have standards," Tom said. "*I* have standards."

"Hey bro, no hard feelings," Chippy said. "How about I owe you a drink. Beer?"

"Some other time, man. I have *things to do.*"

The enormous bearded man threw open his arms. Tom reluctantly allowed Chippy to give him a proper hug, and then gathered up the crap Chippy had carelessly let him leave all over the studio—laptop, bike helmet, Gene Roddenberry biography, very bad owl carving—and grumpily shoved everything into his messenger bags. Everything barely fit in there, what with the towel he always carried.

He clipped on his bike helmet, picked up his fixed-gear, stomped down the three flights of concrete stairs with no disasters, and kicked off into the bike lane down University Avenue.

The breeze from riding his bike only helped with the heat so much; it felt like he was riding through a swimming pool. He sped through the northeast Minneapolis arts district, every pretentious converted warehouse reminding him of Chippy's betrayal, and then someone almost killed him as he pedaled over the Hennepin Avenue bridge. Wouldn't that have been a way to die? It was Tom's kind of luck. He called it Tom Luck.

He decided to veer east and take the Greenway bike path over to the river and ride along West River Parkway for a while; it wasn't like he had anything to eat at home anyway, and he knew all the spots to check for leftovers in dumpsters. Second-hand food reduced his carbon footprint, and that was all the dignity that Tom Wood required.

As he coasted across the Mississippi River from Minneapolis to St. Paul, his phone rang.

Very proud that he'd actually paid his bill this month, Tom dragged the phone out of his pocket and answered without stopping. He'd done enough drunk biking in his day, so this was nothing.

"Dr. Debunker speaking, please remember that the government is listening to this call," he said as professionally as possible, then he swerved to avoid an oblivious pedestrian and screamed, "GET OUT OF THE BIKE LANE!"

"Check your texts!" someone hissed, and then they hung up.

That warranted stopping, so Tom pulled over and rested one leg on the curb.

He had one call and six texts from frickfrackpaddywhack, one of his blog followers. She lived in St. Paul, so they got together sometimes to talk gluten conspiracies and debate GMOs.

Frick said:

u know that shape u drew for me? ppl here at Mickey's have it on jackets

five of em, look rough

2 in grey uniforms w symbol

not spkng englsh

smell weird

tom they don't kno how 2 use eating utensils gtf over here

He tried to open the attachment on the third text even though it was going to cost hella data points...

It wouldn't open.

Holy shit! If it really was the symbol they'd passed around on flyers, then it was *The Symbol.* The Symbol on those blueprints Hope sent him like five years ago. Alien technology! But, on the other hand—

"Why would there be aliens hanging out at a diner?" Tom shouted at the sky.

The sky declined to answer.

"Just in case," he concluded, and heaved forward on his bike. He could get there in twenty minutes if he ignored the laws of physics.

Tom flew off toward downtown St. Paul.

iii.

The diner was an oblong metal box, an old converted rail car, faded yellow with accents of red and covered in glowing lights. Most of the cramped single room consisted of one long row of stools arranged directly in front of the open food preparation area, with a handful of booths lined at one end. It couldn't possibly fit more than thirty or so customers; around ten were present when they arrived, and others were constantly coming and going.

Relai drew a deep breath into her lungs through her nose, reveling in the aroma as their waitress arrived with the last three plates.

Food. Gods in stars, *food.*

"Anything else I can getcha?" the waitress asked, settling her curious eyes on Relai, the only person at their table who could speak with her. Her name tag proclaimed, 'KJERSTEN,' which Relai wasn't even going to try to pronounce (and people thought Oeylan was difficult). Nevertheless, she'd spent her first year on Earth watching enough movies and television to wrap her tongue around American English with a near-perfect accent.

"This is good, thank you."

Goren shifted next to her, wincing as he bumped the tightly-wrapped wound in his thigh, and grumbled, "You had to pick an eatery with no cover in any direction? It's only been six hours and I'm already failing Regent Service."

Relai nudged a glass of water out of the path of his hand. "Keep your voice down. Eat."

"What's that?" Goren poked a small metallic box attached to the wall that held a stack of papers with lists of something behind a curved panel of glass. Then he picked up a stack of tiny white and pink packets held in a little black box. "What are these?"

"I don't know, and... I think it's sugar. Now, eat."

Milo stared dully at his plate. "What food is this?"

Relai looked over the overflowing table, tucking herself further into the corner of the booth to avoid bumping Goren again. Next to him, Milo had collapsed in the center of the bench reaching along the back wall from one side of the train car to the other. His legs stretched out past Ky and Tannor's side of the booth and the waitress had tripped over his massive boot twice in a row.

"That's chicken," Relai pointed, "a type of poultry on this planet. You'll like it. That one is called cow—I mean, beef, the meat part is beef—and it's worth seven days of grains, so enjoy it. Potatoes, you know what those are, and that's a pickled vegetable called cucumber."

Ky sniffed. "He eats my kimchi, he'll eat your pickle."

Relai raised her eyebrows and bit into her sandwich, too tired to eat properly around an equal. Milo would just have to see her hands touch food; it wasn't like he didn't already hate her.

At least she had a sandwich.

A sandwich and a knife, and three working gen-guns, six Earthan handguns, and a tech pen. And whatever else Ky held in that bag of his; they used bombs all across Haadam, probably had a few left. Money? Med scanner?

Her leg brushed Goren's and he winced again.

Inspire fear, or love, or both. Never allow them to ignore you.

Relai swallowed her bite.

"I want to figure out who's responsible for this," she said in a low voice. "Who has been ruling in my name?"

Goren blinked and glanced around. "Fass? He's the top official on Earth and he tried to kill you. It has to be him, right?"

"No," Ky said. "There's no way he arranged this all himself."

"Fass knows you weren't ruling and he's leading Unity on Earth anyway," Tannor cut in. "He's using the movement. I think he wants to take Earth. Not for Unity—for whoever he's really working with."

"Those finance guys on the High Council!" Goren threw out. "It's gotta be them."

Tannor hummed. "What about Winser Cabalto? After your father died he put himself in solitary mourning, holed up in his estate in Bilal, and refused all contact with Mora Aydor and the outside world. It seems suspicious now."

Winser Cabalto had been King Ayadas's primary adviser, and slightly more than that to Relai's mother (who was currently 'missing'). She laughed bitterly. "I'm sure he's enjoying himself."

Milo looked at her sharply. "Is he the False Relai?"

"Oh, no." Relai felt her stomach swirling at even the thought—but no. Winser loved Relai's mother, and Elavaani Aydor would never hurt her. Never.

Not willfully, anyway.

"I know it's not Cabalto. Absolutely not."

Milo raised his eyebrows.

"Eat!" Ky exclaimed. "We don't know when we'll get our next meal, after all. And I'm sure there are bounty hunters, a whole battalion of guards, Earth Monitoring, and maybe even some sinister suits from Applica tracking us down as we speak. You're lucky Odene probably isn't on this planet right now, but we can't be sure, so let's just get off this hellhole as soon as we can."

During this speech, Relai scoffed at the words *bounty hunters*, Goren asked if Odene was really real, and Tannor started listing off the reasons she knew they weren't being tracked.

"And yeah, Goren, Odene is very real," Ky added.

"Who is Odene?" Relai asked.

"Only the *scariest* master assassin in the galaxy—" Goren supplied eagerly.

"—Who will probably be offered a contract to kill you, and I'm still hungry." Ky nodded toward the waitress again.

Relai shifted to get Goren and Milo to let her out. "We're on Earth. You can't expect me to believe this nonsense about bounty hunters and assassins lounging around just in case someone notable comes along. It's *Earth*. Will you *move, please?*"

Milo wasn't sliding to let her pass. Ky went still and muttered, "Milo?" in a low and terrifying voice.

Relai eased one hand across her torso and under the hem of the jacket. Out of the corner of her eye she saw Goren slow his chewing and hold up both knives apprehensively while Tannor hunched further down in her seat as they scanned the diner and the street outside. She saw nothing... A young couple feeding each other fries, a rough-looking old man cradling a cup of coffee, Kjertsen at the cash register, a lanky fry cook with piercings all over her face, and a sweaty tattooed guy fumbling to answer a cell phone.

No one suspicious. Nothing.

Milo blinked, rolled one shoulder, then shook his head. "Second down. I thought—I don't know. Probably nothing."

Kjersten the waitress was watching them in open alarm.

"And now everyone in here thinks we're criminals," Relai whispered.

•

Tom tried to flip up the collar of his canvas jacket to hide his face as he answered the incoming call, but it kept falling down so he settled for slouching low enough on the red plastic-covered barstool to hide his face behind a cup of water. He put an elbow in a puddle of mustard on the plate of the guy sitting next to him, but it was worth it for the vantage point while he talked.

"Tom," the caller said, "it's Hope."

"Hi Hope! Sorry I haven't gotten back to you yet about the thing. I'm at Mickey's... *investigating*..."

"Why are you suddenly whispering?"

"Because I'm investigating!"

Hope was a government suit who used all her super-secret Homeland Security databases to contribute to the search for The Truth (when she wasn't doctoring reports and texting out warnings to help people avoid being deported). Once upon a time Tom had dated her sister, and they'd discovered a shared commitment to extraterrestrial investigation that endured long after Marisa moved to Oregon. Hope had drawn him a symbol—*the Symbol*—once, around five years ago, that she thought might be alien writing. Every time they scanned it or took a picture of it, the file went corrupt after a minute or so... and that discovery had cemented their bond forever.

Tom peered down the length of the diner to the booth at the back. Five people, all looking tired and bedraggled and dirty, were conversing quietly as they ate. Maybe two of them were in uniform like Frick had said, but maybe not—from Tom's position it just looked like a couple of dark gray jackets, and he couldn't see any instances of *the Symbol* anywhere on them. Balls. Frick hadn't taken her attention away from the hash browns and burgers she was grilling long enough to confirm anything yet, and Tom didn't want to interrupt her.

"Okay, I'll bite," Hope said, "what are you investigating?"

"Er, maybe nothing. Can't talk about it right now."

"Remember to gather evidence, whatever it is."

"Evidence! Yes. I will. Anyway, *what* is *up?* The planet is going insane! I know you know something, Hope Valdez. Did your Big Brother program turn up anything that points local?"

"Maybe. I'm on my way to look into something local now. Did you find anything on Italy? Or what happened this morning at MMN?"

"Wait—what are you looking into around here?!? Do you want to come have lunch with me? Also, yes to the first, maybe to the others…. Definitely a UFO they took down in Italy—or at least an ARV—"

"ARV?"

"Alien Replica Vehicle," he whispered, "keep up, jeez. Anyways, pics were posted of the crash site, but they were all scrambled as soon as they went up, and the OP said the originals deleted themselves. So that's legit. And someone posted video from a distance of the bombing, which is definitely related (and wouldn't there be something in the news if we were under attack from alien invaders? Huh? Maybe NOT. Maybe the aliens own The Media, okay?) This video's still up—just flashes from a distance. I got one written description of a symbol the military found on the UFO, did you see—"

"Yeah, it sounds right."

"Yeah! And there's something from a guy in Moscow about shape shifters, a herd of sheep supposedly got abducted in Kansas… a bunch of people shouting 'Strength to Unity' took over half of reddit, which wouldn't be weird except now the hashtag's trending on Twitter and someone decided to shout it while they tried to assassinate the chief secretary of Hong Kong and failed miserably, so it might be some sort of mass brainwashing? Or just run-of-the-mill fascists, hard to tell these days. Aaaaand… a couple aircraft malfunctions around Hawaii. I thought I might be on to something here," Tom dragged his eyes off of the corner booth to make sure Frick was busy on the grill and couldn't hear him, "but it's starting to look like my tip was just some good old-fashioned xenophobia. If I had a dollar for every time someone got scared of immigrants and cried alien, I'd be able to afford a dentist visit."

"Same thing for crying terrorist. Weird how people always seem to suck the same way, huh?"

"Oh, and I posted all this on my blog, and now Gecko's freaking out."

"Who is Gecko and why are they freaking out?"

"It's this buddy I have from the interwebs, his screen name is geckothegreco even though he lives in Argentina, so I call him Gecko. I posted the vid of the bombing and he's all, 'This is bad, must be Unity,' whatever that means. Either he's doing a really intense roleplay, or he thinks he's an alien and so am I.

"Then he yelled at me not to post anything more, like, 'You know they monitor the internet, not just the underweb, so take that down,' which, what the hell is an underweb? It sounds kinky and I'm scared to goog it."

"Stop trying to make 'goog' happen, Tom, nobody's—"

"It could catch on! Anyway, then Gecko asks, 'Are you trying to get a pass off-world?' as if I could. Then he says, 'I checked for passes and Daat's not even responding to inquiries.' What is *happening*, Hope? What's Daat?"

"*Goog* it. And just to clarify, you haven't heard anything about MMN?"

"Why, what's up at MMN? Isn't that where—*HOPE!* Isn't that where you got your first pic of the Symbol from?! The tech specs for that contraption I've been trying to recreate?"

"Yeah… I'm not sure if it's connected to any of this stuff or not. There were a couple reports of a column of smoke that the company hasn't, let's say, adequately explained. I'm headed there now to find out."

"Well, clearly you know *something*. What do you have?"

"…Nothing yet. We'll be in touch; I gotta go."

Tom put the phone away to finish his free toast and eggs, but then he remembered he promised to gather evidence. Frick might not have been imagining things, and 'twas better to have and not need than need and not have.

Just in case some partial shots of T*he Symbol* showed up when he *enhanced* the images. Just in case.

·

Relai turned back to catch Ky's glare. He curled forward and lowered his voice to a cutting whisper:

"We're not going to make it very far if you don't start taking this seriously. You don't know what the hell you're doing so you better listen to me, princess: you could've taken control of that shit with Xiong at any moment, but you didn't. *You are not in charge here, and you don't get to ruin this for us.*"

Relai took a deep breath through her nose. *Burn out any voice that—*

"Maybe that's true," she said. "I was too slow and I was scared. But you're not leading here, either—you're bashing your way forward and dragging us behind you. We're not going to make it very far if we don't start talking to each other and working together. I'll start thinking, and you're going to start listening. Deal?"

Relai didn't just mean Ky—she looked at each of them. Milo was the only one who wouldn't meet her eye; he was staring blankly at his plate.

She needed him to look at her.

The silence dragged on… and then piece of flatware clattered to the floor and startled them all.

Milo listed sideways and forward and he would have hit the ground if Goren didn't flail out and grab him by the sleeve.

He said, "I just…" and nothing more before his eyes closed.

Ky pushed forward and braced his hands on Milo's shoulders across the table. "No, Milo," he demanded, heaving the young man to his feet and ducking under one arm. "Come on, you big baby, you have to get to the car." Milo was too heavy, the largest of their group by far, and there was no way they'd be able to carry him without calling serious attention to the effort. "I told him to sleep on the train. *Milo!*"

Milo didn't open his eyes or speak, but he was still able to support some of his own weight on sloppy legs. Ky tossed a wallet over his shoulder and Relai caught it. She shook out all of the paper money and tossed the wallet under the table.

Goren shoved his shoulder under Milo's arm (or, three inches under his arm around his chest), griping under his breath, and helped Ky move him out the door. Relai hurried after them, avoiding eye contact with the dirty natives all around.

•

(And on the way out, Ky made sure to stumble when they passed the greasy man at the diner bar. He put an elbow in the guy's side, grunted a sort of apology, and came away with a cellular phone tucked in his sleeve.)

○○●○○

iv.

Agent Hope Valdez of the Department of Homelan
nearby table to slam her fist on, so she settled for poking the мь
security in the chest through the stack of files she'd just handed him as sн
repeated, "Every. Single. One of them."

"You have to understand," the pale, anxious assistant personnel manager
jumped in, "more than half of these employees have moved on to other work
in the last five years. Some may be attending conferences, or out sick. Give
us a few days, and we can set up a round of interviews—"

"Nice try, but the warrant says *now*," Hope said. "I'm not leaving."

(The warrant was a favor from a guy on Hope's broomball team who
happened to be a judge; her boss didn't even know she was there.)

Head of Security and Assistant Personnel Manager exchanged glances.

"I'll take you to a conference room," Head of Security finally said.
"You'll only have access to the bottom floor of this building. Your warrant
doesn't give you the power to search our facilities."

Hope grinned toothily. "I remember from last time."

"I will see if anyone on your list is on the campus right now," Assistant
Personnel Manager said, looking harassed and defeated. "I can't make any
promises."

Hope leaned right in the woman's face and narrowed her eyes. "If I find
out you sent any of these people home, you're in serious trouble."

The woman nodded. Then she ran off to start gathering people while
Head of Security led Hope away from the security desk and down a long,
open hallway of glass-walled conference rooms hosting various busy and
important meetings.

"We've remodeled twice in the past five years…" Head of Security
began; Hope zoned out and let her mind wander.

Five years ago, when Hope had been a junior agent with the FBI, she'd
been called to investigate a possible case of corporate espionage involving
MMN, a multi-national tech company based in St. Paul. A conscientious
employee had reported a piece of technology he'd been asked to reverse
engineer. This technology was nothing the employee had ever seen before.

As it turned out, it wasn't anything any of the specialists at the FBI had
seen before, either. Nobody could figure out what the thing did just from the

.otos the sources provided, and the authorities at MMN weren't admitting to anything. The only lead had been a logo engraved on one side: four crescent slivers, different sizes, bisecting a central circle. Below the design scrawled a line of loops and slashes—they were guessing the writing could be Mongolian, maybe Tamil.

No one could identify the company that the technology might have been stolen from, no company reported it stolen, and MMN R&D was more closely guarded than some state secrets. Then the FBI database started crashing every time an image search produced something, and Hope's computer got a virus which spread to the servers of the Minnesota branch of the FBI.

The day the virus attacked, while an outside team of computers techs swarmed their servers to troubleshoot the problem, Hope had taken a few bites of a delicious, flaky pastry she didn't know was filled with almonds and gone into anaphylaxis. She shot herself up with her epinephrine pen, took a jaunt to the emergency room, and when she came back to work the next day they'd closed the case. It was going nowhere, their source had suddenly taken a job in Bullshit, Nova Scotia, and none of the evidence survived the virus.

No evidence, except for a single trace line of code that had mysteriously appeared in the operating systems of every computer the files had been deleted from.

The destruction code.

A pair of voices caught her attention, and she tuned into a loud conversation between two MMN employees walking just behind them.

"...Or you could just start a pop band and then tell them you're singing nonsense instead of Gastredi poetry," a sardonic female voice was saying.

"Man, I hate those guys," a man replied. "Hopelandic? Idiots."

Hope scratched her ear and peeked over her shoulder. They were dressed like the kind of low-level engineers that played roller derby on the weekends, tattoos peeking out from under work-appropriate shirtsleeves.

"Calling it nonsense is better than telling them exactly where our bases are, though," the woman went on. "Now everyone wants to go to Europa."

"YES. If you're gonna make inside jokes, don't do it in a way that's gonna get us caught!"

"Then again," the woman said, "how was he supposed to know they'd go from theory to serious exploration in a few decades? We have maybe, *maybe* one year left. We're gonna have to either wake this place up or leave."

Hope managed to nod intelligently at something that Head of Security said without missing a single word.

"Their probe just passed *Pluto*."

"I know, I know, I was doing my two years at Oliver when it passed Europa and everyone flipped out. Only reason they didn't notice us was that one techie, what's her name?"

"Mellick?"

"Yeah, she did something weird with the wave shielding, I dunno, and they had to fry some sensors, I think. Close call."

Then they turned left and Head of Security led Hope right and it was over.

Hope thought wildly. She had no idea what Oliver might be, but Europa was a moon of Jupiter. This was either an absurdly elaborate and targeted piece of performance art, or the entire company was crawling with aliens.

Maybe they were just LARPers.

She needed *proof*.

oo●oo

Tom sat in the middle of his living room floor, a square of sun on his bare back and fan in his face, and popped open the cover of a new phone. The mysterious and beguiling Eris meowed at him and tried to distract him with her feline wiles, but he just raised his hands high in the air and kept working.

"Away, cat!" he said.

"Brrrow," she replied haughtily.

After the thrilling non-events of the diner, Tom had been in no mood to find his phone missing. He didn't exactly pay for the thing—no one knew what to do with their old phones when they bought new ones, so sometimes they gave them to Tom. He couldn't really tolerate the social class of people with phones nice enough to be worth anything second-hand, but thanks to the overlap on the Venn diagram between his commitment to the environment and his previous career as a soulless corporate engineer he now

165

knew how to fix hybrid car engines—and hybrid car drivers owned friggin' nice phones.

They were also unbearable, so Tom figured he came out even.

(If he couldn't get the phones to work, he'd just crush them up and extract the precious metals using the mushroom farm in his bathroom. He imagined himself a dystopian gold miner in a smoggy urban wasteland, painstakingly extracting precious metals from the grimy ruins shed by society's elite as they injected champagne into their eyeballs and laughed about stock portfolios on floating cloud patios.)

He snapped his back-up SIM card into the nice little retro flip phone from the pile—no camera or internet access this time; less likely to be stolen—and hooked it up to charge. He wanted to check with Hope Valdez to see if her government connections were searching for the people he found at Mickey's, but first he needed to check how things were going on the internet.

"Hurheh heh hah, hurr hurrhah, hah," said his computer, and Tom jumped up. (He'd set his text-to-email alert as Jeff Goldblum laughing in Jurassic Park, which helped him battle his existential angst and freaked out people in cafes, so... win-win.)

Speak of the devil—Hope's gorgeous latina face winked up at him from the screen.

Any more on Italy?

Tom tapped out his response:

aliens

Anything more specific?

extraterrestrial aliens

Useless as ever, thx

i know my role in the world

Did you gather any evidence?

NO, also, thanks for asking how I am

Ok how are you?

ROBBED

Oh shit, are you in the hospital?
Do you need me to come get you?

no, someone just snatched my phone. new
one charging, i'll call you soon w anything new

Ok. I'm at mmn interviewing ppl, maybe a lead

cool cool cool, keep me appraised

Will do

bye jeff

Stop calling me Jeff, why do you even do that

○○●○○

v.

Ky stared a moment at the abstract painting that hung in the clean but boring hotel room they'd rented, listening to Milo's breathing pattern change. He wondered if everyone in this part of Earth was suffering from existential despair, or if this place just bought cheap art.

Satisfied that Milo was finally getting some much needed sleep, Ky slipped through the door joining one room with another and tossed a shiny silver phone next to Tannor where she sat, legs crossed and back bowed, on a bed so ugly it didn't deserve her.

"Where did this come from?" she asked, casting aside the broken tablet in favor of this new, working tech. She examined it carefully, her fingers light and quick.

"Maybe a handsome stranger saw me in the lobby and gave it to me out of the goodness of his heart. Maybe I took it off of the guy Milo noticed watching us in the diner. Hard to be sure."

She snorted. Goren muttered something but Ky didn't bother to process the words. Relai was showering and—he peeked through the adjoining door—Milo hadn't woken yet, so as far as Ky was concerned Tannor was the only person there.

"Do you have an Earth cap, by any chance?" he asked over her shoulder. She hadn't showered yet, and under the lake muck and field dirt and the last vestiges of blood she smelled really good.

"I'm a tech sergeant, don't insult me," Tannor replied, already plugging one into the phone. The screen flickered and then reloaded, and the text switched to Ardi and the display rearranged itself into a more familiar interface.

Ky watched her smooth a curl behind her ear and said, "We should fix your comms so we can communicate without being tracked."

"You should take this damned drug tick off my neck," she retorted.

He saw, now, that her anger hadn't disappeared; she'd just left it simmering. He imagined her dead in that field like every other scrap of tinder on Milo's war pyre.

"I'll do what I need to do."

"You need," she said evenly, "to respect me."

Ky carefully kept any amusement out of his voice. "It's a strategy, not a threat. I won't use it to hurt you, Tannor."

She glared back at him. "You lied about being Quiet. Why should I trust anything else you say?"

The obvious answer was that she *shouldn't,* but she was smart enough to know that already.

Yet she was still asking.

"Xiong leads the Quiet on Earth, yeah, but he's not the head. I take orders from someone higher—someone who wants Relai to make it home safe. I'm still Quiet and so are you."

She considered him. "Forgive me if I don't take your word for it."

The tone of her voice implied she'd take something else instead. A bargain? Ky had never been so entertained. "Fix our comms and I'll think about taking off the tick."

"I don't see a med scanner around here, so I'm not going to do *minor surgery* to fix the tech embedded in our skulls. There are all sorts of ways for a small wound to kill you on this planet, and we know *nothing* about stopping that."

He smirked to himself because she'd gone back to the stolen phone, and that meant he was off the hook for now.

Tannor tapped into the device, frowning in concentration, and Ky stretched out next to her so he could study her face—the way her skin changed from peach to rose at the lips, the freckles on her nose, and the dark fan of her eyelashes. She was certainly distracting. He could return the favor and distract her for hours, if she wanted.

Not quite yet, though.

Ky let her feel the heat of his body but he didn't touch her as he asked, "Gonna find the secret black market dock on this planet's internet before we fall asleep tonight, sprite?"

"No," she said. "Milo was right—this guy was taking pictures of us."

Ky took the phone without sitting up and swept through the photos. Six in all, blurry and useless unless this guy knew how to use them.

"Well, our photographer friend didn't try to kill us or help us, so he's probably not an ex-terr. Maybe Earthan military, except the phone's crap and the guy smelled like bad decisions. Find out everything you can about him from that phone and give me a rundown after I shower."

Tannor eyed him, calculating. She lowered her voice so Goren couldn't hear. "You know where this dock is, don't you? I'm not going to spend hours searching for it when you already know."

Ky rolled onto his side, leaned on one arm, and hovered just shy of her ear. "I know when, but not where. My contact says we have forty-one hours until the next fleet of ships can leave from the dock. A bit more than two day cycles to figure out where and find a way there. In the meantime, I needed an excuse to get Milo to stop and rest."

"Who is your contact?" Tannor asked. "Why can't they just tell us where to go?"

Ky ignored her, hopping to his feet and heading to the other room. "I'm gonna go clean up. Kill anyone who knocks on the door."

He didn't look back.

•

"Tannor?"

It took a moment for Tannor to pull herself out of the depths of the stolen Earthan phone, but she managed to say, "Yes, Goren?"

"Can you... put this string through this tiny hole for me?"

Goren held up both hands in frustration. He'd stripped off his damp, bloody uniform as soon as they made it behind locked doors and thrown everything in the bathroom to wash later. He was now sitting on the bed in his underwear, surrounded by plates of plastic metalloy from the jumper and some of the clothing he and Relai had bought on a terrifying shopping adventure while Tannor and Ky checked into the hotel and tended to Milo.

On Arden, most material things started out available to everyone until claimed for justifiable use. Vehicles, tools, machines—they shared everything until a use was identified and an administrator assigned. (And if the greater class always seemed to make the final call, and end up with control, no one dared point it out.) Goren probably considered the bed and this room his property now. Tannor wondered if he expected someone else to wash their clothes.

"You mean you want me to thread that needle?" she said. "What's this for?"

She put down the Earthan phone and settled beside him on the other bed, shifting closer to the light to see.

"It's for Relai," he said, motioning over the clothing, seams torn out in strategic places, and she understood. She took the needle and held it against the light to spear the dark gray thread through the hole, then tied a knot at the end.

"Do you even know how to sew?"

He gave her a lofty look as he took it back. "I managed to find the materials at that market and I can figure it out. I'm not a complete lack-brain. I can see how threads go in and out and I can guide them with this needle thing. It's not like it takes skill."

Tannor sighed and picked up the broken tablet. She settled on her belly next to him, prying the device apart and laying the pieces out. "I thought maybe you had people to sew your clothes for you."

"Well, of course," he rolled his eyes, "but I'm not helpless."

He went back to sewing up Relai's jacket. After a few seconds of silence, he mumbled, "Do you think Fil made it out?"

Tannor paused, but Goren hunched over his work and refused to look at her. He was the sort of teenage skinny that promised a growth spurt at any moment, with lanky-broad shoulders and long-fingered hands. He'd be absolutely gorgeous in two or three years, and that thought made Tannor want to slap him a little. Like he needed looks on top of the wealth and power and obsessive intelligence; he was going to be unbearable.

He was already unbearable.

"I don't know," she said softly. "I sent the warning, but I don't know if anyone received it before that asshole kicked me."

Goren shuffled where he sat, then suddenly perked up, staring unseeing as he listened. Tannor stiffened. He tilted his head toward the bathroom where Relai was showering.

"Do you hear crying? I think I hear crying." He moved toward the door, but Tannor twisted forward and caught his arm. They'd already touched enough that he should be fine with it, and she was right—he didn't jolt at all.

"Leave her alone, Goren."

He sat back down grumpily. "She shouldn't be alone. It's not safe."

"We're right here."

"Us?" he exclaimed. "Two criminals who can't even commit their crimes properly, a soldier with no experience, and a tech genius with no working tech?"

"We're not dead yet," she scoffed as she eased a pillow behind her back. All the running, getting shot in the head, and nearly drowning had taken their toll. She felt like crap. "Don't bother her, okay? Actually, don't bother me, either."

She set to work reconstructing the broken tablet.

•

Now was the best chance Ky was going to get, so he locked himself in the bathroom and turned on the shower. He stripped off his shirt, ripping at the spots where it stuck to his body from the blood, and took a good look at himself in the mirror.

One of the bullets had passed through the muscle of his left shoulder. In and out. Another had just grazed his right arm; nothing to worry about. The last one, the one that had really been bothering him, was still stuck between two ribs on his left side. Ky felt around the wound, wincing in his mouth but not his eyes.

He pulled his favorite knife from the belt still around his waist—

No, better do this in the shower. Blood had a way of getting everywhere.

Ky peeled off the rest of his filthy clothes and dumped them in the bathtub. He'd scrub them and hang them up and they'd dry instantly, and then he could clean his boots. He didn't want to be stuck wearing Earthan crap if they caught a ride off-planet.

He stepped into the spray, hot as he could stand it, knife in hand.

One breath in through the nose, held for a beat, then released. He dug in and the blade caught metal and he clawed at it with a fingernail on his other hand. By the end of the slow breath the bullet squelched out, pinged off the shower tile, and came to a stop against the drain. The water ran red for a while.

He flushed the thing down the toilet and then took his time washing his clothes.

•

If Ky and Relai were both showering, and Milo was sleeping, that left Goren and Tannor on watch, Goren reasoned. No one had told him to keep watch, but he decided to do it anyway. If he started thinking down the path of taking a nap, he would not be able to stop himself and then Relai would probably be murdered by an assassin. So he didn't.

Once he finished Relai's jacket he stationed himself in the room where Milo was sleeping, to avoid the possibility of seeing the queen naked. (Again.)

He couldn't avoid the sight of Milo sleeping, though, and it irritated him immensely. It was like somebody went and carved the guy out of umber cherry wood or something—he should be lying in the Kilani Patropolitan Institute, all lit up with glows and shadows, with only the artists laureate privileged to sketch him. And if he were a carving he wouldn't have all this gross hair, either.

Goren wondered how Milo got himself like this. Special food? Probably from mining. These Erayan jerks didn't know how easy they had it, working jobs that made them all muscly without even trying.

Then Goren's eyes reached the leg portion of this idle observation, and he recoiled—something was horribly wrong with Milo's calf. The skin was a mess of dark scarring puckered along a deep, ugly dent, like part of the muscle had been shredded out by a jagged blade... or claws. Or teeth.

It was really, really gross, and Goren didn't want to look at it anymore, so turned and eased open the curtains to look out the window.

At the change in light, Milo flopped his head toward him, eyes opening to tiny slits. "You got shorter," he said in a rough voice.

Goren frowned. "I don't think so."

Milo just closed his eyes. "Must not've made it out, then, huh? Bad dreams."

"Er, what?"

"Thought I could make it out. Tell someone." He took a breath and his neck arched back and he twitched a few times. Goren didn't know what that meant, but it scared him. He stepped closer.

Milo flailed a hand out and touched Goren's arm. "M'sorry, Ozem. About Dad."

"Tannor?" Goren called out in alarm. He sat on the edge of the bed, feeling helpless, and didn't pull away from the contact. Milo's skin looked wrong, now that Goren was looking closer. Goren placed a tentative hand on Milo's shoulder, and under his palm Milo's body emanated a scary amount of heat.

Tannor cracked open the door joining the two rooms and peered in. "Yes, Goren?"

"Milo's saying weird stuff and his body feels too hot."

Tannor rushed to his side.

•

It was a nightmare come true.

"He's *sick*," Tannor said, palming Milo's forehead and neck. "How did we miss this? He's *on fire.*"

Someone should have noticed this sooner. Relai, Goren, and Ky had all touched him. They should have felt it, damn it.

"I don't understand," Goren said. "What's *on fire?*"

Tannor could only gape at him.

"What happened?" Relai asked, rushing into the room as she pulled her wet hair into a knot and cinched it tight, wearing only a loose white t-shirt and underwear without a hint of self-consciousness.

Milo's head flopped back and forth on the pillow at the sound of her voice. "Shayla, bird," he whispered, "m'sorry. Couldn't get to you. I'm sorry."

"Is he dreaming?" Relai whispered.

"Ky!" Tannor barked in the direction of the bathroom. In another moment he emerged, fully dressed and toweling his damp hair.

"Milo is sick," she said accusingly.

"No. It was really hot out there—" Ky began.

"And he's been in this cool room for hours. *Feel him.*"

Ky shoved Goren aside and put a hand on Milo's forehead, frowning in concentration. His face hardened. "He's not sick."

"This is illness," Relai insisted. "This is what it's like!"

"Have you ever been sick?" Ky demanded. When Relai only stammered, he concluded, "That's what I thought. You don't know."

Tannor thought back, tracing through their conversations, and her mind skipped to the likely conclusion. "You crashed in Italy. You didn't go through any of the health checks, did you? Did you get any of your vaccinations? Did you take *any* disease precautions, you *catastrophically stupid man*—"

"What did you expect us to do," he shouted, "stop by one of the med centers on Oliver before we sped over here to steal a queen? No, we didn't do any of that." Ky paced to the far end of the room, smearing a hand over his face.

Relai backed away from Milo. "You're going to make this whole planet sick. What have you brought with you? You *touched stuff* in that diner—these are innocent people, Ky. What have you done?"

Ky threw up his hands. "We scrubbed down on our way and I know we didn't carry anything xeno onto this planet. *I made sure.* Besides, he's not sick. So calm down."

Goren, who had been checking over Milo with a sort of academic interest, piped up: "He has a rash on his hands. On his palms. Look."

Relai waved her hands in panic and Tannor just shook her head. "We have to take him to a hospital. We don't have a med scanner. We don't have any way to deal with this."

"He burned his hands in the crash, that's all. He needs sleep," Ky snapped, "and he won't get it with you all hovering around him. Leave."

Relai launched into a furious rebuttal, but Tannor went still at the cascade of thoughts: this wasn't adding up. Ky wasn't stupid. He must know what was going on with Milo.

Tannor knew that med scanners couldn't heal everything. Milo had gone through a terrible trauma.

She wondered if grief could cause fevers.

Relai wasn't yielding and Ky was looking hunted, now. He wanted them to leave.

"Okay," Tannor cut in, and Relai shut up with a look of surprise. "We can give it until morning."

"But—" Relai began.

"He doesn't need you," Ky spat. "Out."

"Um," Goren said, but that was all he contributed before Relai saw the look on Tannor's face and relented.

"And stay in that room," Ky added with an edge of command.

They went.

•

A door swung in her face, and Relai spun to face Tannor.

"What the hell?"

"Milo isn't ours to watch over," Tannor said.

"That doesn't mean I don't care what happens to him!"

Tannor gave her a dry look. "You really think Ky would let him die?"

Relai could only throw up her hands.

"Yeah, he might be too stupid to handle this," Tannor conceded. "I'm betting he's not, though."

"Fine. He gets one hour. If Milo's not improving by then, we're taking him to a hospital."

Goren very loudly said nothing.

Relai was baffled by everyone's response to the situation, but she wasn't really their queen, was she? She didn't want to know how they'd respond if she tried just ordering them around. And for now... the criminals were occupied. She looked down at herself, thinking. "Stay in the room, he said."

"Yes," Tannor said.

"What do you bet the radius of his transmission jammer doesn't go much further than that?"

Tannor looked over to the closed door. "We need to be fast."

Relai shook out her hair and ran her fingers through it, crown to tips, over and over again. "Does any of the tech from the jumper work?"

Tannor shook her head, then hopped up and grabbed a cell phone Relai had never seen before. "Ky took this off of a man in that restaurant. He was taking pictures of us, but he's not ex-terr as far as I can tell. The phone works and I already plugged in a cap. I haven't started—"

A man was taking pictures? An Earthan? Why?

No. Relai couldn't process that string of words before she handled the pounding footsteps inside her head.

"It has a camera on it," Relai said, dragging on a new, cheap pair of gray denim pants. Then she looked down at the plain white Earthan t-shirt covering her torso: white, like perfection. Too thin, too—the line of her bra stood out underneath so clearly she might as well wear nothing at all. And as for the yellow thing Goren had bought, his face so desperate to please as he offered it to her, the neckline curved too low. Made her look weak, or cheap, or manipulative. No.

A guard jacket? Tannor and Goren might need a few precious hours more of anonymity.

She spun left, right, searching, and then she saw Milo's seamless black shirt in a crumpled pile where Goren had thrown it on the floor. Plain, black, high collar.

Relai stripped off the white t-shirt and pulled on Milo's shirt. The sleeves swamped her hands and she bunched them up her forearms as Goren uncovered his eyes and said, "Ew."

"Why do you need a camera?" Tannor asked.

Relai wiped her face with both hands, digging crusts from the corners of her eyes and mouth, then licked two fingers and smoothed her eyebrows and the rumpled hair framing her face. Good enough for a queen on the run.

"I'm tired of letting everyone else speak for me," she said. "Goren, stay here. We'll be back in five minutes."

•

"I wonder if," Relai began, dark and simmering, "they had trouble generating sincerity with a computer program." She leaned forward slightly, her shoulders squared. "You should be able to tell. Even if you've never met me, you should be able to tell. Look closely."

She stared silently for a breath or two.

"I'm on my way home. To those who are suffering: find strength in each other, and in the assurance that things will change soon. Wait. To those who took my name and hurt my people," she lowered her chin and turned her head slowly a quarter-turn to the right, "we will be speaking soon."

Tannor almost clicked off, but she saw Relai's lips peel open again, and she waited. Relai thought, eyes down and left, and then she said, "And if you need proof... seven arils."

She winced through a smile and Tannor saw a shine in her eyes. Relai didn't turn her head to catch the light for the sake of the video.

Relai finished: "I'm on my way home."

Tannor turned off the video feed. Relai wiped her face.

"What was that about arils?"

Relai stood up, shaking the intensity out of her limbs. "Oh. I only need one person at the palace to believe this is me. Now she does."

Tannor once again thanked the Ardenian educational system for training everyone to type one-handed. She pulled together the video file and encrypted it without missing her chance to reach out and squeeze Relai's wrist. It was a brief little movement and she didn't look up from the screen, but it was enough. Relai paused at the touch.

"Send it right away. They'll probably stop it at Oliver, but if you send it directly to Xiong he should be able to spread it." She headed for the door.

"What do you think Unity is going to do in response?" Tannor asked.

"Threats, lies, who cares? This wasn't for them."

The perfect silence of the windowless stairwell hung around them like comfort and promise. No light from the earthsun reached them here, no indication of their hemisphere, longitude, latitude. Blank wall ahead, blank wall behind. Tannor tapped *SEND*.

Then she asked, "Who was it for?"

Relai scratched at a stray edge of skin along one of her fingernails. "Anyone that might feel hope seeing it. Maybe not many. Maybe just one."

"Oh," Tannor remembered, pulling up a line of code she'd prepared, "and you need to promote me."

Relai smiled. "Promote you?"

"It might let me override Fass the next time we run into him. And it'll really piss him off."

Relai looked over the order, held up her eye to the camera, and said, "Well, congratulations, Colonel."

Tannor clapped a hand over her shoulder and felt the filaments under her skin rearrange as the order went into local effect. It would take another twelve hours for the update to reach Arden, but she'd set it to confidential and Earth operated on its own network (thanks to her own carefully planned security decentralization, of course). No one on Arden could override the promotion.

She pulled aside the collar of her shirt and saw the sharp, dignified downward point of a colonel's arrow. "Thank you, Our Glory."

Relai let out a disgruntled hum, and Tannor laughed.

○○●○○

vi.

The light trimming the interior of the Earthan jumper glowed red.

Andrew Xiong must like red, Ososi thought distantly.

She stared at the line of lighting opposite her position on the bench until the streaks melted into her eyes, her hand gripping the steady bar as the rest of the soldiers clambered in, half-bloody, from the nightmare of that Earthan base. Smoke smudged the Italian sunset behind them.

She'd gone in with a firm and quiet determination, ready to perform the lies she'd memorized on the way over or, at worst, stun a sentry or two. Reaching the soldiers had been simple… but they hadn't paused to even consider a stealthy exit. This squadron of Ardenian soldiers had taken her favor and clawed their way free with savage violence. She'd lost control.

She couldn't count how many people she'd watched die.

An astounding lack of strategy, child. Andrew's words echoed in her mind.

Someone dragged her and shoved her along until Xiong's jumper swallowed her again. The ship had never left its cloaked state, so the moment the doors closed they were safe from any pursuit. The small space flushed with sweaty man-smell and equally noxious conversation as the soldiers commended each other on their kills. These men (and they were all men, all but one) were dangerous. They chanted the slogans of revolutionaries even though those Earthan soldiers weren't oppressing Arden.

Andrew Xiong had sent Ososi into an unrepentant trap. She wasn't here to find out if any of these soldiers were Quiet, no—she was there to find out if they were Unity. And they were.

They *were*. She'd rescued a vile, frothing gang of murderers who shouted *Strength to Unity* as they shed Earth blood. By helping them, did she ruin herself? Was Ososi Tena now a murderer?

Your mother is alive, Ososi.

Ososi listened to the words lacing over and around her without really hearing.

"Clear?"

"Open, clear. Trajectory?"

"Five by seven, and solar at two-nine… five."

"What about her?"

"Toss her out the back," someone said, and Ososi felt terror gust through her. Before their leader responded, though, the one who'd taken the pilot's seat cursed.

"This thing is locked, Captain! It won't let me put in any new commands."

The one who must be the Captain grabbed Ososi's arm and pulled her to her feet.

"You—what's your name, soldier?"

Ososi gathered herself enough to focus her eyes on a face, the same bland face of every Ardenian soldier. They all looked the same. "Do I still have a name? I'm nothing to you."

"Unlock this jumper," the Captain ordered. He was hurting her arm.

She realized it that moment: "I'm the only one who can fly it." She let the statement hang in the air. Not a threat, simply fact.

The Captain shifted at once into a caricature of urgent sincerity, and the vice on her forearm turned into a stroke. "You came for us from Buzou Base, right?" he intoned. "Just fly us back there. We'll all be safe."

He had blue eyes, Ososi noticed. *Light eyes, devil's work*, her mother always said. Devils drain the good out of you and takes the color with it.

(Buzou Base. The most powerful weapons on the planet.)

"This ship is Earthan," Ososi answered.

He laughed because he was ignorant, so she explained:

"Ex-terrs built it here and if we take it back to Buzou they'll arrest us, or worse. We were going to collect Relai Mora Aydor for the bounty—" Ososi could lie this way, because it was true, "—and the ones with the queen killed my team. I have nowhere to go now."

"Ah," the Captain said, and she could see the slithering interest in his eyes. "So you're no worshiper of the Aydors, then? Did you come to us to bring strength to Unity?"

"I don't have anywhere else to go… and," her lower lip trembled without a need for encouragement, "and if Unity overtakes Earth, I want to be on the winning side."

He smiled a pale, rotten fruit smile. "It will save a lot of lives if you can put us in control of Buzou Base's weapons."

Stick as close to the truth as possible, Xiong always said. This required no lie at all.

"You must know I can't do that. It requires the highest ranking Titian and Ardenian soldiers on Earth to give final approval."

The rotten fruit split wider. "I'm the highest ranking Ardenian soldier on Earth and I'll give it final approval."

"Oh…" Ososi found herself dragged around to a wall screen. She didn't try to follow Captain Fass's movement through the commons; she knew that the remaining few soldiers at Buzou wouldn't agree to his plan. Titus's queen had declared neutrality in the fight between Mora Aydor and Unity after Unity kidnapped Lady Redas's daughter; they would neither help nor harm either side, and they would treat with the victor.

This left Earth ripe for takeover by Unity, of course.

But then something strange happened to Captain Fass's face. The rot shifted sour, bitter, and then furious as he stared at the screen. Ososi looked to where his eyes were fixed and saw the face of a pale blond woman. The woman seemed familiar, but Ososi couldn't think why.

Senior Ardenian officer: Colonel Tannor Mellick, the screen read. The woman's eyes were brown.

Fass smashed a palm against the screen, sending it blank before Ososi could understand.

"Then we'll go to Daat," Fass spat. "We can take it over before they even realize the revolution has truly begun. We've started early, anyway, because of… circumstances."

Ososi moved with the shove of his hand and sat in the pilot seat, praying to clear the death from her mind.

She didn't have to like Xiong, and she didn't have to trust him, either—but she could trust that he must have a plan. He needed her here, watching and listening to these men. Xiong knew where her mother was. He needed her to open her eyes and use the tech he'd put there at the start of their agreement.

Her Seer. A plate at the back of her retina linked to her comm that recorded visual and audio of everything she saw. Ososi closed her eyes and spread out one palm on the helm. She could link to the Seer itself, turn it on, and instruct it without a hint of activity on the jumper's screens.

She couldn't transmit anything for fear of these men and their tech detecting it, but she could record. And, just in case, she could set it to transmit the recording at the moment of her death.

Ososi was there to see.

•

Fass eyed the growing stubble on his soldiers' faces disapprovingly (had these men never heard of using med scanners for follicle elimination?) as he stroked his own perfectly smooth chin in thought. This Titian couldn't hand them Buzou, but she might lead them to something even better: the maker of this jumper.

But first...

"Reddig," Fass barked.

"Sir?"

"Your search program... the one that has failed to find anyone useful so far."

The man went pale but didn't flinch. "Yes, sir?"

"Can it find one of our own if he isn't under any blockers?"

Reddig didn't hesitate. "Yes."

"I need you to find Voresh Renganiban. He should be somewhere on this rock."

Again, Reddig snapped into action without questioning Fass. Good. Excellent. They'd find Voresh and Fass would have his figurehead for the kingdom of Earth, his friend crowned red and mighty.

Then he could return to his Lady and kneel and offer her an entire planet as a show of his devotion.

oo●oo

"They say, 'Strength to Unity.' We say: *No.*"

The words cut through the silence hanging around Tannor's head, but she'd managed to route the sound output of the Earthan cellular phone's sound directly into her comm so Relai and Goren wouldn't hear and wake.

She angled the phone so the glow wouldn't light her face and listened to Gandred Xiong's voice.

"We, the Quiet, must hesitate before we join with any plan led by Unity. Violence has been their banner and their violence will continue. We must consider what kind of leaders we wish to fill the void that once honored the Aydor monarchy. I ask you to consider this: will Unity stop once Mora Aydor is dead? Will they destroy anyone who rises in her place? What are their goals? Who is their leader? Let the leader come forward and state their aim before we throw in our lot with them.

"Hear me, Gandred Xiong of Earth, as I come forward as a representative of the Quiet. I am not the leader, only the mouth to speak for the head.

"We desire justice, and for that we demand that Mora Aydor stand trial. We will not murder her. We will maintain our civility in our resistance, and we will preserve her life to force an answer to her actions. Do not reveal yourselves. Wait, quiet ones. Watch, and wait, and report to your contacts."

Tannor put down the phone.

Across the room, Relai was sleeping.

Tannor got up and went to check on Milo.

Ky was sitting on the bed next to Milo eating packaged bars of Earth junk, and the light of the moon sparkled against inky black of his eyes as he looked up at her.

"He's fine," he said.

"Hmm," she replied. Milo's breathing wasn't labored and he wasn't groaning or shivering. She gently touched the center of his bare back and it felt cool.

Ky chewed smugly.

"Did you see the message from Xiong?" Tannor asked.

"Yep. Stand trial."

"He doesn't believe her."

"Nope."

Tannor sighed.

"It's our turn to sleep," she said.

○○●○○

vii.

Relai thought she'd bought enough food to last for days. She thought they wouldn't even have to leave the hotel room until they came up with another (better) plan. By the next morning, the food was completely gone.

How did they eat so much in the middle of the night?

So, unfortunately, they had to eat the hotel's food. Relai gathered small, disparate packages of food from a counter in a common area filled with metal chairs and pressed-wood tables, and sat down for the sake of a few minutes alone. It took thirty seconds for her to notice that Ky was already relaxing in a chair in the corner, pretending to read a newspaper.

"Oh!" she exclaimed. "Good morning."

He only turned a leaf of paper in not-too-subtle mockery. They didn't even use paper on Oeyla, what did he know? He couldn't even read English.

Tannor came next, nest-haired and sour-faced. She wasn't wearing any of the clothes Relai and Goren had bought her on their adventure to a local shop; it looked like she'd washed out her uniform pants and taken one of the new men's shirts instead. She grunted at Relai as a form of greeting.

"Good morning," Relai replied with a smile. "Pastry? Cereal? Muffin? Bagel? Coffee?"

Tannor just rubbed her temple. "I am not awake enough for a vocabulary lesson. Just give me food and I will eat it."

"Coffee first, then."

She held out a foam cup. "This is made from chiba beans."

"Why is it a drink? No. I don't care. Give it to me."

Tannor slumped back in the painted metal chair and took the cup, glaring at the brown liquid as she sipped.

"Why aren't you wearing the clothes we bought you?" Relai asked.

"Because you and Goren think I'm a smaller size than I am, which isn't a compliment. It's just inconvenient."

Oops.

Then came Milo.

Fresh and handsome and ten feet tall, broad shouldered, his hair clean and wild, Milo stepped curiously into the eating area and then focused on Relai and didn't stray.

He sat across from her and greeted Tannor without looking away from Relai.

"You look better," Tannor replied resentfully.

Relai took in a deep breath and poked the plastic salt shaker, accidentally tipping it on its side and spilling salt in a scatter shaped just like the friction glow around a groundship as it entered the atmosphere. The shaker was pale yellow to the pepper shaker's black, or maybe it was just the tint of the morning sunlight pouring through the windows.

Relai didn't know anything about Erayd negotiation etiquette. Her father had never told her the Erayd mattered.

So she said:

"I used to bite my lip. I'd tear right through the skin with my teeth, make myself bleed. Everyone could see and they'd heal it up right away." She brushed the edge of the salt spill. "I started chewing on the inside of my cheek or the side of my tongue, instead. It forced me to speak more slowly. Sometimes I slurred my words. Sometimes I couldn't eat."

Tannor reached the end of her cup of coffee, groaned to her feet, and went to refill it.

"Why are you telling me this?" Milo asked.

Relai braced herself, looked up, and found nothing but sharp, overwhelming focus in Milo's gaze.

She didn't flinch. "Because I need you to tell us, you and Ky, if you're sick, or—anything. If anything is wrong." Milo considered her carefully, dropped his eyes to her hands, and then reached out and nudged an errant grain into the pile of salt.

"Don't concern yourself with me. I won't be the reason we fail."

She sighed. "That's not why—"

"Set my people free," he murmured. He left his hand on the table, relaxed, palm down.

"You know I can't do that," she whispered back.

"But you will," Milo said softly. "It's the right thing to do."

She looked at him unblinking, trying to let him know how sorry she was. She couldn't break apart her planet—her Aydor blood ruled over all of their technology. If she granted them sovereignty, she could take it back at any moment and no one could stop her. It wasn't something she could reject, either; even the ruling Aydor couldn't assign equal power to someone else. The monarchy would only end in the death of the last living Aydor.

This was a High Council secret since the first Aydor king, of course. She was mandated to rule, and if the public ever found out the root of exactly why... *no.*

But it wasn't only that she couldn't. She wouldn't.

If Arden split—if Arden lost the unity of voices behind their coalition ambassador—Gastred would win their motion to take charge of the coalition and their next step would be to invade Earth. Titus would stand back in disinterest and Oeyla didn't have the stability or numbers to challenge such a move.

"No," she said out loud.

If anyone was going to secure Earth, it would be Arden, not Gastred.

Milo held eye contact in a manner so bare and open, earnest and pained, that Relai couldn't stand it. She had to look away.

Tannor returned to the table clutching one of the giant coffee carafes set out to serve the breakfast crowd and said, "I'm stealing this." Then she looked between them. "Are you two seriously... no."

She slammed down the carafe and clawed her hair out of her face. "Now is not the time. Neither of you are in any shape to discuss this." She grabbed the pepper shaker and shook it, dousing the salt with little black and grey flecks, and then swished her fingers through the pile.

"Now put all the salt back in the salt shaker and all the pepper in the pepper shaker and don't make one single mistake. Then you can talk about Eray."

Relai glared at the mess on the table and didn't reply.

Tannor left with her coffee and Milo stood and followed with his bare feet. Relai sat in silence for a few moments, running her fingers through the tiny flecks and grains.

∘∘●∘∘

The message finished and Ky set the stolen phone down.

Milo stared at the final image of Relai's relay and rose to his feet. If Ky didn't know better, he would've been afraid.

"Why—" Milo gasped, "why would she do this?"

Ky wanted to go find her and wring her neck himself for putting that look on Milo's face, but he still wasn't sure.

"I can see it two ways," he said. Neutral words, neutral face.

"How can this be interpreted in any other way than—" Milo's mouth moved, but no more words came out.

Milo wanted so badly to let himself soften, Ky knew. This was no time for soft.

"She wants to let everyone know that she's tamed the Monster of Eray. That she controls you. That you… belong to her."

Milo swore. "She saved my life, Ky. Our lives."

"What better way to defuse Eray than convince one of their own to defend her?"

"But what about the evidence?"

"Some people can fake anything. I bet Tannor could fake it."

Milo grimaced like taking a punch to the stomach. "Tannor, too?"

"I don't know. I've met some pretty impressive liars," Ky said. "Or Relai's telling the truth."

"But then why—"

"Maybe she just needed a shirt."

Milo stood for a moment, then he picked up his boots.

He slid them on and pulled the buckles tight.

"Let's ask her."

•

Relai opened the door to the room and walked into a crackling thunderstorm. Milo stood at the window, arms folded across his chest and feet planted, lit from behind by morning sunlight so she could barely see his face. His profile—the strong brow, straight nose, full lips, beard—belonged on glass in a temple. Ky leaned against a dresser holding a phone.

"Hi," Ky said. The emptiness in that word scared her.

She shut the door behind her but didn't come any further inside. "What?"

Milo scratched his beard, settling his hand to hide his mouth. After a moment of silence, he said:

"Do you remember how you looked on the day you gave the Onarden speech?"

Relai stopped short at the absurdity of the question. Her Onarden speech… the one where she was supposed to speak for an hour, but her father pulled her from her the podium after ten minutes because she went off script. She'd tried to name the Cabalto family—second to the Aydors since the revolt, since independence, since Arden became one. Winser Cabalto was her father's key adviser and closest friend. He was worth mentioning, and yet—

No one freed Arden but the Aydors. No other name.

"How I—looked?" she stammered, "I don't…"

Milo turned and faced her, finally, square and giant, like a statue come to life.

"Your ear was painted with a little notch of gold, remember? Your left ear?" His eyes marked the spot like a wound.

"Uh, yes—I remember, that was a style then—"

"A *style*," Milo spat.

Relai wondered if she should run.

Instead she stilled her body and said, "A… fashion trend?"

"Let me tell you about your *trend*," Milo said. The edges of him seemed to be shaking. "Ten years before I came of age, your Regional Guards took a liking to shaving the heads of anyone who looked at them wrong. Stand too long in one spot? Late on a tax? Mouth off? They'd shave your head."

"What does—"

"Shut up," he barked. "*Listen.* They used solid shears for cutting, not tech blades, and someone thought it would be funny to *accidentally* snip a notch out of the ears of these Erayd thugs. Resisting consequence, they called it. No access to a med scanner, no healing. They probably kept score."

People could be so cruel, Relai thought, no matter where they stood in society. Everyone was capable of it.

"They did it to men and women, boys and girls," Milo went on before she could form words. "Always the left ear."

Relai heard her own voice come out high and strained. "That wasn't—it wasn't policy. We didn't tell them to—"

"It only stopped when we started doing it on purpose," Milo went on. "Cutting our ears ourselves. I was little, and I watched the toughest of the big kids fill their notches with colored clay or gold resin, or they'd pierce across the gap and tie it up with string or metal clips." Milo let out a long, bitter breath. "Done by a guard, it was a consequence. Do it to yourself? Mutilation. They'd moved on to a new way of torture by the time I got old enough to land on my knees in the street, and then your artists laureate found inspiration for a new *style*."

Relai stared unseeing, and then she looked up. "What did they do to you?"

Milo just clenched his jaw.

"Okay." Ky flipped the phone toward her. She picked it up, recognized herself against a bland white background, and Ky asked:

"What the fuck were you thinking?"

Relai winced at the harsh curse and looked at the ceiling to avoid staring at the image of her own ugly face. "You can't stop it and I'm not sorry."

Milo shifted and Relai's back hit the door, but Ky threw his arm across Milo's chest and held him firm. "Let's just—let me try, okay, buddy? Okay. Relai: we're going to need an explanation."

Milo... he'd gone back, Relai thought, to that place in his mind the night before last, when killing her seemed like the right thing to do. He went back so easily, he hated her *so much*.

"I'm not like you," she said. "I'm not going to creep around silently. They kept me sleeping for a year, and the False Me is probably going to release a statement—I don't want to always be reacting, I want to—I need to initiate. And I told my people to wait because maybe it'll stop some violence. Maybe some people will decide not to—"

"That's great," Ky interjected, "very noble—"

"—join Unity if they see that I'm coming home, and we did everything we could to make sure no one would be able to track us."

"—But we're not worried about getting caught."

Relai faltered. "What?"

Ky jabbed a finger at the image. "Why did you wear Milo's shirt?"

Relai realized that Milo hadn't changed into Earthan clothes; he wore the very same black seamless travel shirt, the one that still smelled faintly of lake water and blood and charred meat, that she'd draped over herself.

Oh, no.

She'd screwed up—it must be special to him in some way. Warrior clothes that carried him through battle? In Kilani everyone maintained strict boundaries for when and how people touched one another; maybe the Erayd had something like that for touching a person's clothing, too?

Or was it as simple as taking what didn't belong to her? She'd worn the gold on her ear without knowing the significance, and now she'd taken his shirt. She'd screwed up.

"I'm sorry," she tried, "I didn't know—"

Ky blocked her view of Milo and said, slow and clear like she was stupid, "Explain this."

Relai felt her blood swelling inside her skull. *Stupid.*

"The—I'm sorry—the white shirts we bought are too thin and—and the yellow one shows too much of my skin, I felt uncomfortable, and—and besides," she latched onto a new thought, "what if they could look at the stitching of the Earthan clothes and somehow know where we bought them?"

Milo stared, incredulous, from across the room.

Relai closed her eyes, squeezed tight, but didn't lower her gaze when she opened them again. "I'm sorry. I won't take anything of yours again."

Stupid.

Ky's cold eyes swept over her, judging her white shirt, gray jeans, and the itchy purple jacket Goren had given her. It was too warm, but she wore it because Goren asked her to.

Then the fight faded from Milo, leaving an exhausted sort of confusion. He stared at his hands as they stretched and relaxed, and then he looked up and found her eyes.

"I shouldn't have touched you," he said. Acknowledging how they met. "I thought I was ending the reign of a tyrant. I... Hear me now so we can speak without confusion: I will never hurt you again. *I will not hurt you.* I won't touch you at all."

Relai realized she'd moved her feet in anticipation of an attack. *Asshole,* she thought. She forced herself to square her stance and rest her palms flat on her thighs. She wanted to say, *until I make you angry enough.* She said nothing.

He took a shaking breath.

"I don't know how you think about clothing," he said, "but it's clear you don't understand what you've done."

She felt her pulse high in her chest like the beat of it was trying to crawl up her neck and into her head.

She asked, "What have I done?"

Milo came forward and she saw him put a hand on Ky's back. Then he looked her over (stupid, ugly) from head to toe and said, "I'm going to keep watch outside the building. I'll send Goren in. You should sleep."

And then he left.

Ky followed him, but stopped at the door with a pitiless sneer. "Let me know when you start thinking."

Relai stood there numb, watching herself from a distance as she said, "I'm going to get a newspaper."

She pocketed the phone as she went.

She didn't even pause when she walked to the lobby. The hint of freedom outside those doors set off a claustrophobic panic inside her and she had to—she had to go. She felt the tension in the backs of her calves and the center of her chest, the panicked need to *go go go*. There were hundreds of thousands of people in this city, and her pin was blocked; how would anyone find her?

Not that she didn't intend to return.

She just needed to be alone.

○○●○○

viii.

After six hours of interviews, the last useless engineer on the list scampered out the MMN conference room door and Hope debated throwing a potted plant at the wall. Just allowing herself to think about it made her feel better, but it didn't add anything to her progress.

The mood among the MMN employees ranged from anxiety to amusement to scowling suspicion, all of them yielding the same empty non-answers. They knew something, but damned if they were going to tell her what.

More than that, though, Hope got the sense that something had *happened*. *Was happening*. Hope checked her phone for messages, alerts, and news reports. There had been a terrorist attack on an embassy in India, seventeen dead, and another college campus shooting in Texas, only three this time (and how bitter a number to feel relieved about?)... and her cross-referencing query lit on both events.

In Hindi and English, the murderers had shouted the word for *unity* as they attacked.

She checked the report on the assassination attempt in Hong Kong that Tom had tipped her off on this morning...

Strength to Unity.

A new terrorist organization? Cult? She'd have to dig into this one further when she got back to the office.

Then, while on her way out of the complex, Hope took back her confiscated belongings at the security checkpoint and found something that wasn't there when she went in. It was an MMN employee key card. The photo ID on the card showed Shoua Fau, the assistant head of personnel— the woman she'd mercilessly harassed for the last half a day.

"This isn't mine—" she started, but halted when she discovered a note posted to the back.

It read: 'Meet me in 3A-LL-217B.'

What the hell?

Moving before her train of thought fully caught up to her, Hope simply began walking, first out to her car to ditch her purse, firearm, and Homeland Security badge, then looping back around to another entrance at the side of the complex. This was building 3A, that much she knew.

The side entrance was smaller than the front, but had just as thorough a security checkpoint. Hope strode confidently forward, watching as the woman just ahead of her tossed her bag onto the x-ray a conveyor and casually swiped her key card. The metal detector beeped in alarm, but the guard, glancing at a photo of the woman's that had appeared on a screen in front of him, simply waved her through. "You're good."

"Thanks, Dave," the woman called.

Hope took a deep breath. She did not resemble a black-haired Hmong woman named Shoua Fau. Odds were, this was going to be a real short trip.

Hope strode confidently up and swiped Shoua's badge.

She walked on through, without so much as a beep from the detector, surprised to see her face (the photo from her Homeland Security ID, no less) appear on the screen. Apparently, she wasn't the only one who sometimes hacked her own employer's system. As she passed, Dave the security guard never even broke from the vacant gaze of the professionally bored.

It took her a while to find her way through MMN's labyrinthine corridors, which, thank God, were mostly empty. Her ankle boots padded quietly through the 1970s ceramic-tiled halls, and she recalled the giddy thrill of roving unsupervised through her middle school with a forged hall pass.

LL-217B turned out to be an office one level down from the ground floor. Hope paused, debating whether to knock, then barged in. Shoua Fau sat on a swivel chair in the middle of the room with a look of immense struggle on her face. The computers behind her were all disassembled and draped in dust-protecting covers.

Hope raised her eyebrows and said evenly, "Yes?"

Shoua got up and shut the door behind her and asked a question, her voice full of fear, in a language Hope had never heard before. Hope prided herself on her ear for linguistics, but couldn't recall anything quite like this. Not Hmong, Vietnamese, Tagalog, Karen, Somali, Oromo, or any of the other dozens of languages spoken in the Twin Cities.

Maybe an *alien* language?

Oh shit, oh shit.

What were the chances that was a yes or no question? *(Are you one of us? Do you know what's going on? Can I trust you?)*

What did Hope have to lose?

She sat back in another swivel chair with an air of confidence and answered, "Maybe."

Shoua seemed to take that as some sort of confirmation, thank God, and she rushed forward. "Listen, I don't know if I'm doing the right thing or not, but the planet is falling apart and I think Xiong is handling it wrong. And I thought, if Earth Monitoring sent you…" She trailed off.

Hope had never been so relieved to hear a person resume speaking English.

"You shouldn't have to carry this responsibility alone," Hope said soothingly, handing Shoua's key card back to her. "Let me help you."

The woman's face tightened in undeniable fear, then she nodded. "Come with me."

They traveled through a series of buried hallways and passed between buildings, air conditioned to the damnable heat of the day, Shoua opening doors with her key card the whole way. They came to a building that seemed more like a storage facility than laboratory and Hope watched Shoua hover her hand over the access panel instead of her card.

She waited a moment, then the door mechanism audibly unlocked. Shoua swallowed as she grabbed the handle. "I'm showing you this because… it's not right. It's not right for their families to lose the chance to know what happened to their loved ones." The door opened with a rush of air—negative pressure inside this building—and just inside the building they came to an inner set of swinging doors. "Xiong told us to atomize them, but I can't do it. Please, can I hand them over to Earth Monitoring instead?"

The doors swung inward at the pressure of Shoua's hands.

Hope took in the high ceilings and chilly air, no windows, and long stretches of pale yellow shelving lining each wall… but the whole of her attention zeroed in on a row of oblong metallic palettes, each bearing the still body of a person.

Seven bodies.

Hope felt goosebumps creep across her neck.

∘∘●∘∘

Just outside the old munitions plant that ex-terr suits used for fueling up and passing time, Runn heard tires on gravel. She sat up and eased an empty beer bottle to the soft heather without making a sound, then put her phone to a brick wall and used it to look right through.

An SUV had arrived, engine still running. One by one, Applica agents filed out of the jumper and met the ones that had gone off to pick up a more convenient vehicle to use in the city.

Weird, she thought. They'd brought the crappiest old pile of junk jumper she'd ever seen. She shoved the last few sour gummy worms in her mouth and peered closer. Apathy, she guessed. Didn't care much for the cargo they were chasing.

The phone counted seven agents. It looked like six would be leaving for the city, just one left behind to bring their jumper whenever they found the queen. Runn sneered. So easy it wouldn't even be fun.

Then Runn's phone beeped: a new contract.

She popped the cap off another beer with her lower incisor and read the message. Then she laughed out loud.

First client, Ed Fass, hires her to kill a queen and deliver her hand and eye to Curragh Dock. Once delivered, payment would go through. Contract over.

Then she could fulfill this contract just come in: kill Ed Fass.

What would she do with the hand and eye, then?

Runn wasn't sure, but it'd probably involve a hell of a lot of money.

She graciously accepted the contract, setting into play the code to trace back and reveal who hired her this time around. If she didn't know, this job wouldn't be nearly as entertaining.

EPISODE VI:

TOWER

A *PIECE OF STOLEN tech from six years ago, a fire in the testing fields, missing data, computer viruses, destruction codes… and a row of dead bodies in a storage facility.* Hope had bluffed her way into this and she was going to bluff her way out of it, and nobody was going to stop her.

"Who are these people?" she demanded.

Shoua laughed humorlessly. "Those uniforms aren't a disguise."

So I should know who they are just by looking at them, Hope thought. *Okay.*

"Who killed them?"

Shoua wrung her hands in front of her chest. "I—I don't know if I can tell you. I don't know if I believe what Xiong told us. He's gone to Oliver to stop Gastred from getting through the block, but I don't know if he can, and no one has been able to contact anyone at Daat—"

Hope felt like she was back in grad school, trying to force her brain to act as tape recorder, wishing the lecturer would slow down as her hand cramped from note taking. Xiong. Oliver. Gastred. Daat. So many names, so little context. So many questions.

"Tell me what Xiong told you," Hope said.

"He said it was Unity, but…"

Hope burned each corpse's face into her mind, thinking furiously. At least she knew how to pronounce Daat now. And Unity was a fucking terrorist group.

She asked: "What were they doing here?"

"I don't know! Buzou has gone neutral because of the declaration from Titus, and they haven't even declared these soldiers missing. It's madness! One of them survived, though, and Xiong sent her off right away, poor girl."

Survivor. Okay.

She eyed the garage-style door at one end of the room, the oil stains on the floor, the forklift pallets piled up in one corner. A loading dock. She did her best to imagine the layout of the complex, specifically where that door opened to…

Hope turned to Shoua with her best sincere gaze. "I need to take these bodies."

"I—can't you analyze them here? We have med scanners and I can set up a commons interface…"

This place was swarming with people Hope couldn't trust and Shoua might figure out she was bluffing at any second. Hope pulled up the number for Darcia Rowan, her contact at the Hennepin County morgue, as she shook her head. "No. You took a risk showing me this, and now you're in danger. Can you be sure there's no… Unity here?"

Shoua's face went from pale to faint green. "Oh, no," she breathed.

"I'm calling in help to take these bodies away. That door—opens up outside the complex, right? For deliveries?"

Shoua nodded.

"Do you have a safe place you can go until things settle down?"

"I can put on a pin deflector… but Xiong will find out I helped you if you bring more agents here. No one else has realized where you're from."

Ha ha, Hope thought. *Perfect.* "My people will be very discreet. A white van, unmarked. Could be any delivery. They can pull right up here, and I'll give explicit instructions to deal with you *and only you*. When you meet them, they'll have IDs from the county coroner's office—just in case the van gets stopped later, that'll cover the presence of seven bodies—but they're with me." *Who am I with, again?* "Earth Monitoring has this."

"Oh… all right." Shoua spoke like someone utterly overwhelmed. "I can change the delivery logs so that the people watching the loading dock feed are expecting a delivery van."

"Great. Now give me your cell number and *answer if I call*, okay?"

Shoua nodded and tapped Hope's number into her phone, then her head snapped up. "Wait—do you want to examine their jumper? We brought it to building 3C after the incident."

Hope swallowed. *Jumper. A teleportation device? I hope it's a teleportation device...*

"Yes."

○○●○○

ii.

Relai left.

No one had any way of knowing where she was. Her pin was shielded and her comm was dead. If she got into trouble she could do the native thing and use the Earthan phone she'd taken to call the hotel room using the seven digits she'd memorized when they settled in. She felt invisible and safe—safe for the first time since she'd woken up. The others could wait for her to get back, or split up and move on and leave her to fend for herself like they should probably do anyway.

The sun wouldn't reach down between the skyscrapers until late morning, but the day was blooming bright and hot already. She kept walking, surrounded by suits and bicycles and shouts and honks, and with every step the fear and suffocation faded.

Alone again, if only for a moment.

Relief.

She walked. She walked until she saw a storefront full of paper books—room after giant room stacked with paper, beautiful paper, filled with words and voices to drown out the noise in her head. The land of a thousand fantasies.

These coffee bookstore places always served an exotic mix of whirring sounds and rich, dark smells and harsh overhead lighting and bumps of crowded seating, so quintessentially Earthan; Relai knew she could disappear completely here. She just had to act the part.

Relief.

Life was lighter with her father dead.

Relai tried not to feel it, tried to deny it, but it was unavoidable. She had loved him. She even *missed* him. She'd cried her tears out over his death and the lost chance to reconcile, and now she could let herself feel these other, shameful things: relief. Freedom. Release.

For once, it felt like all her bones fit into place. Like her own skeleton could hold her up properly now. Like she was real.

Gandred Xiong had always treated her like someone real, with faults and strengths and value, but now he thought she'd gone rotten.

He was wrong. She was going to prove him wrong. She'd *show him*.

Maybe she was ugly and maybe her father thought she wasn't good for anything but—

But—

Relai realized she was staring blankly at the floor in front of a magazine rack and a bookseller was starting to look worried.

She tamped down the dirt in her mind and turned away from the little plot of soil that held sad, buried, forgotten things. Rotting things. Things that might spread inside her, if she stopped pretending they didn't exist.

She flipped open the first book she found and started reading.

oo●oo

Tannor let the door click shut behind her and leaned against it. "I think we should tell Relai about the Quiet."

Ky, warm and gorgeous like an invitation, wrapped his mouth around another piece of sweet bread as he reclined against the edge of the window, staring at the skyline of glass and metal towers in the near distance. He was wearing the clothes she'd met him in, freshly washed and clean.

He chewed slowly and then brushed off his hands before turning, catching the morning light across the shift of his shoulders, to regard her.

"You're looking refreshed." He grinned, and she tried not to be annoyed by the deflection. "Nice shirt."

Tannor ignored him. "The Quiet haven't done anything to hurt her. We've helped her."

"She should already know about us." He moved to start packing. "She can claim a title, but if she doesn't do the job, does it matter?"

"That's not fair. She just woke up."

"And Milo didn't get to sleep through the last fourteen months, so who got the better side of luck?" Ky clipped his knives around his waist and then faced her head-on. "Look, I'm not here to help her learn how to be a good little queen. I'm here for Milo."

Tannor heard a lot in that last word—real emotion, whether he liked it or not. He really didn't care about what Relai knew, she realized. It was Milo.

He didn't want Milo to know he was lying to him.

Idiot.

She'd deal with her own secrets, then. In the meantime— "Where is Milo, anyway?"

He tipped his head to the window and Tannor looked out.

From their second-floor room she saw Milo crouched within shouting distance in the vehicle lot, reverently inspecting a skimmer-type thing. Two wheels, no hover capability, single engine. The Earth skimmer's owner, a man not much older than Milo with shockingly light blond hair, stood a pace back and watched in awkward amusement. Milo couldn't seem to keep his hands off the thing, his movements reverent and his face relaxed. He'd pushed his sleeves up to his elbows, and no one had ever complained about bare forearms on a strong young man. A slight breeze ruffled his dark curls.

She hummed in appreciation, then blushed and glanced at Ky.

He smirked, then slid open the window. "Maybe he'll show you how to ride!"

Milo flashed him an exasperated look and shouted back, "I'm keeping watch. Stop calling attention."

"I'm not at fault for that one," Ky said quietly. "He can fly anything, and I bet he could ride that motorcycle after only looking at it. They trained him well growing up."

"Trained him for a revolution?"

Tannor glanced sideways at Ky; his gaze didn't leave Milo.

"He's not going to stop asking her to let them secede," Ky said.

"He will if one of them dies."

"Did you know," he said, his hip resting on the windowsill, "that in Eray they have their own currency? Or that they've built their own schools and they ignore the teachers Kilani sends? Did you know they've been raising their own military?"

"That's—*hells*—" Tannor gaped. She could understand why, of course, but it all meant more violence, bloody and inevitable. Even Relai wouldn't be able to stop it. "How—why would the Aydors allow that?"

He just glanced at her, silent, and they both went back to staring at Milo.

"Maybe they didn't know," she thought out loud. "Or it's the metalock. The Erayd were willing to mine it, they know the techniques, and everyone else was too scared. It's our only source of it in the galaxy. They had the leverage they needed to keep Kilani inspectors out."

Outside, the cycle owner swung on, revved the engine, and pulled away. Milo stepped forward in the sunlight to watch it glide away, lifting an arm to shield his eyes.

"I had no idea," she whispered. "I should know things like that. They're going to start a civil war."

Ky shrugged. "Who suffers when an Erayd miner dies of metalock poisoning? Who still gets paid? They tried things the peaceful way, stood their ground, and Elik burned."

Ky turned his whole body now, looming larger though he didn't take a single step closer.

"Eray didn't have a strong leader until Milo's father came along. Everyone rallied around Sol Hemm. He would have been their king, lord, whatever they wanted to call him, if they'd succeeded." Ky's eyes burned into her. "You guards made him and his whole family an example."

Tannor shook her head, thinking of every program, every piece of code she'd written that might have been used to help slaughter those people. She should have questioned sooner. She could have written broken code or sent trigger eaters ahead of the bombers or—

"They murdered our own people…" She gripped the windowsill. "We—the Ardenian guard—we murdered them."

"The Erayd are dangerous," Ky said, stepping even closer, "to anyone who stands in their way."

For a moment, her apprehension almost tipped into fear. Almost.

"Why is he helping Relai now?" she asked.

"He's not." Ky's words came out deep and soft. "She's helping us. We're going to stop the False Relai and right the wrongs against the people of Eray."

"And start a civil war."

One eyebrow flicked up. "Better than a slow massacre."

She held his gaze for a moment, looking for any sign of doubt. Nothing.

"Maybe Relai will change things," she said. "once she's really queen. She seems gentle."

Ky tilted his chin, watching Milo again. "Gentle feet on their necks still won't let 'em breathe." He gave his thickening beard a scratch and then curled a loose hand around the back of her elbow. He didn't trap her against the window and she could've pulled away if she wanted to. "We both joined the Quiet. You went up against the monarchy just like I did."

Tannor ducked her head. "I never wanted to hurt her."

He gripped just a bit more tightly, the pads of his fingers pressing into the soft skin of her inner arm. "*I don't want to hurt her, either.* It's her choice to rule or not, and she left. She doesn't want to be queen. I don't blame her—I can barely last half a year in any one place, and if four planets full of a couple billion people were looking at me to smile and wave and tell them how to think I'd shoot myself and be done with it."

"*Ky.*"

"We're going to finish this, Tannor, and we need you with us."

She let one corner of her mouth quirk up. "At least you're aware of it."

He pulled back, smirking in return, and then marched to the door adjoining their rooms, clearly intending to burst in and ruin Goren's rest.

Tannor yawned. "Relai and I get to sleep next."

Ky's eyes narrowed. "She isn't sleeping now?" He shoved open the door, revealing a quiet room containing one lump of a snoring teenager. "Where is Relai?"

"The lobby? I don't know—"

Ky growled in his chest, slung on his pack, and barked, "Get up!" as he dragged Goren to his feet by his shirt. Goren stumbled and sprawled on the second bed, panicked and flailing.

"What? Where—" Goren sputtered. "Relai?"

Then the hotel phone on the end table trilled and all three of them jumped.

∘∘●∘∘

A voice broke Relai's reading concentration.

"Lan!" someone exclaimed, "My phone just got scanned! Something is wrong."

She was speaking in Ardi.

It was a young woman at the other end of the bookstore's cafe, one hand tugging at a toddler and the other arm clutching a baby to her chest while she wrestled to look more intently at the screen of her phone. She was calling down one of the aisles in panic.

"Lan! *Lanoer! Where are you?*" she went on, stupidly and conspicuously speaking an alien language.

Relai reached her the same moment that a man—Lanoer—emerged from an aisle of books. He was young, like the woman, and by all appearances they were an average Earthan couple. The hair, the clothes, nothing gave them away. The woman had even been speaking Ardi with an *American* accent. What the hell? Lanoer scooped up the toddler and the two shrank close together and gaped as Relai huddled in the aisle and rushed her words. "What do you mean, your phone got scanned?"

The woman's eyes flashed wide and frightened. "Are you...? You can't be—" She sent a panicked looked around the store. "You're not supposed to be here!"

Then she handed her phone to the man, who only blinked at Relai, stuttering, "You're—the—"

"Yes, I am," Relai snapped. "Tell me about the scan of your phone."

The toddler waved a chubby arm, trying to grab the bright thing from her daddy. Lanoer craned away from the child in his arms to read, and his eyes widened.

"Someone just sent a cripple signal through the building. All the non-Earthan tech's shut down. It's Applica; I recognize the program that pinged the alert."

Relai sucked in a breath and took a few steps further back into the cover of the shelves.

Fleeting views, glances—that's all she remembered. They'd be meeting with her father behind closed doors, or standing in the back row of a High Council meeting, faces impassive, or she'd catch just the edge of a shoulder, a suit, lurking in a screen shot of a new technology launch. One or two standing outside a coalition summit meeting. Shaking hands with a diplomat from Gastred.

Applica. Those shady bastards.

She still wasn't actually sure what they *did*—her father had said they were economic development facilitators, which meant nothing; she remembered Xiong referring to them as information mercenaries. Niko had just called them spies. But if they were criminals they'd be linked to crimes, wouldn't they? And Applica had never been charged with a thing.

She knew one thing: they worked by contract.

Relai must be a contract.

I'm flattered, she thought darkly. Maybe they wouldn't kill her right away.

She asked in English, "Who are you? How do you know they're here?"

"I work at MMN," Lanoer said. "Applica buys a lot of hardware from us and we keep up with their developments, too."

He probably knew Gandred. Maybe he helped him build that groundship. She probably couldn't trust him.

But she grabbed his shoulder and demanded, "If it comes down to war between Arden and Gastred, how will MMN side?"

"*War?*" he exclaimed. "My kids are here, you can't bring war to Earth. Please!"

"How will MMN side? Are you for Arden or not?"

"I'm for Earth! We're with Andrew Xiong. Do you understand?"

Relai released him.

She hadn't realized. Arden had thrown her guide into space—uncivilized, sleeping space—and out here he'd built himself a home.

She could work with that.

Then a teenager with a chunk of blue hair stomped up and whined in English, "Ellen, my laptop like, stopped working or something. What the crap were you yelling about?"

"Eva, be quiet and go sit down!"

But Eva noticed Relai and— "Holy crap, is that the QUEEN?" —pulled out a phone and held it up. "Intsagrammed."

Relai snatched her phone away. "They will kill you—"

"Ugh, give me back my phone! You'd need an Earth cap to see it, and royal suits aren't on Instagram, anyways—they use the underweb... or, like, Facebook. No one's gonna care but my ex-terr friends. Jeez!"

Lanoer seemed frozen in horror, but Ellen just smacked the girl on the shoulder and told her this was serious.

"Whatever," Eva mumbled. "I'm totally tweeting it to Dr. Debunker and you can't stop me. Besides all the crazy he's right like half the time about ex-terr stuff and it's hilarious."

So *this* was what it felt like to want to throttle someone. "No... *tweeting!* What is wrong with you? You need to get out of here!"

"No way, if you're gonna get bumped I want to be here to see it."

"*Eva!*" Lanoer exclaimed.

Then all the electronics in the store went dark.

Relai stepped up on the bookshelf and poked her head over it to look at the entrances. She could see both the Nicollet Avenue and 8th Street entrances and the walls between were full glass windows. People drifted past the building in a gentle stream… the agents surely knew how to blend in. They could be anyone.

"Ugh, whatever," Eva said. "If this is gonna get, like, scary I'm gonna go pack up my stuff." She waved at Relai and then tripped her way back to her table. People were starting to get up and grumble about the darkness. It would be a disastrous place for a shootout.

"What's going on?" Lanoer whispered.

Relai shook her head. "Too much. And thanks for not bowing."

The woman poked her head around from behind her husband. "We don't bow to dictators."

Relai coughed out a laugh. "Neither do I, good for you."

Just then the toddler managed to squirm down and bolt off, but before Ellen could give chase Lan nudged her into the aisle with Relai and went himself. Ellen continued to glare, holding her baby out of Relai's reach, but there was a definite curiosity in her eyes.

"What are you doing on Earth? Why is Applica chasing you?" she whispered.

"I haven't been ruling and now everyone is trying to kill me and I don't have time to explain this to you. Are you Earthan?"

The baby grabbed a loc of her mother's dark brown hair and yanked. Ellen winced and gently peeled the baby fingers away as she answered, "We moved here when I was three and my sister Eva was born here. I say we're Earthan."

Relai hadn't even known people like this existed.

"Don't wake Earth," the woman blurted out suddenly.

Relai blinked in surprise. "Why?"

"You know why," she hissed. "If they find out we're not from here, they'll round us up. They will round us up and I don't know what they'll do with us, but it will destroy our lives. I love this planet. Don't wake it."

Relai couldn't help but stare at the little baby with her wide, round brown eyes and perfect brown cheeks and innocent, toothless grin. She swallowed. "You should leave. I don't know how far they'll go to take me."

Lanoer reappeared, towing a fussy girl on the edge of screaming. He heard Relai's last few words.

"I'm sorry, I can't risk this—"

"Go, go," she urged. The young couple faded away, American as any of the other customers, bland and unremarkable.

She backed herself against the wall and stood on her tiptoes to see over the shelves.

There—a young man in a business suit outside tapped behind his ear and whispered. She might have been seeing things. He might have been scratching an itch.

How did they find her here? Maybe she had some sort of tracking device embedded where Tannor hadn't been able to detect it. Maybe her pin deflector was broken? If so, she stood no chance.

But she was not panicking, no, no, no.

She crouched back down and pulled out the stolen phone she'd taken from Ky just in case it somehow survived the cripple signal, and to her shock it turned on.

She dialed the number she'd noticed on the room phone as soon as they checked in. It rang three times before anyone answered.

Silence.

She whispered in Ardi, "Hello?"

"Relai," Ky said. "*What the hell.*"

"I'm sorry, okay? Applica are here—"

"*Shit.*"

"Did Tannor get that tablet working again? It should have a translate function and then you can follow—"

The connection cut out.

Relai felt for the thumb knife; it was safely wedged flush against her ribs, but she had second thoughts and crouched and moved it to her boot.

Just as she was straightening the edge of her pant, two proper, shiny shoes stopped abruptly in front of her.

She raised her head. Over and over again she repeated to herself, *it's okay. It's okay.* As she straightened up she scanned the room, left and right around a pair of broad shoulders. The family had disappeared.

If she went quietly they'd have no reason to hurt anyone here. She'd go quietly.

Finally, she looked the Applica agent in the eye.

He was tall, but not enough to stand out. His dark blue suit and thin black tie looked slick and expensive. He was a shade paler than her, maybe kecha Ardenian, with brown-black hair cut in a professional Earthan style. His eyes were wide and worried.

The agent stared intently for a moment, then jerked his head sharply when she opened her mouth to speak. He lifted a hand slowly as though she might startle and run, which she really should be doing but she wasn't sure what his thoughts were on shooting cowards in the back. He stepped forward and to the side, and Relai knew this type of movement from years of Regent Service. This was *protective*. He stretched his hand out and curved it behind her and placed it between her shoulder blades. Then, without a single word, the agent ushered her out of the bookstore.

∘∘●∘∘

I am from Earth Monitoring, Hope told herself as they marched from the bodies to building 3C. *Buzou is a person or a place. Daat is a person or a place. Unity kills people. Xiong went to Oliver to... block something. You can do this.*

Block what?

The walk took nearly half a mile, ending in a hangar that held various large pieces of equipment, work tables with electronics and tools spread everywhere, and at least ten people. Hope glared at them all like they should be afraid of her, and they responded perfectly.

Shoua scattered them all with a few of her alien words, and then a ship appeared out of nowhere in the center of the hangar.

Hope did her best to hide her awe.

The alien spaceship was about the size of a Black Hawk helicopter without the tail, with two cylinders running down the length of the base on either side. Hope couldn't see any sort of windshield, at least not one that allowed her to view inside, but it didn't matter because Shoua led her around and opened up the back—she opened it by melting it open, somehow.

A hole just *spread open like the vehicle was a liquid metal motherfuckin' Terminator.*

Hope closed her gaping mouth and walked inside.

211

Ky might be too late to fix this. He might have to—

He blinked, trying not to show his increasing anxiety. It was all going to fall apart, just when he started figuring out how he might be able to spin it right.

He stared at the hotel phone. It wasn't going to give him any more answers than the dispassionate dismissal he'd just received. He cursed.

But he still had one trick left, one suspicion that might be instinct or intuition or a hint at the bigger picture: Tannor.

He turned and shoved the broken tablet into her hands.

"Find Relai."

She gaped at him. "I have no way to find her."

He growled low in his throat and raised his voice. Goren tried to pull him away but Ky wouldn't be moved.

"You didn't blow out her comm's receiver, right? Just the transmitter. Do it, Tannor! Find her!"

"I—can't—I couldn't get it to work—"

Ky wrapped his hand over hers, pressing her skin tightly to the tablet's smooth white surface. He gripped her shoulder with the other hand, shaking her a little, then slid his hand up firmly behind her neck.

"You know how your eyes focus on something without you having to think about it?"

She gave a jerky nod.

"Okay. Do that, except focus on finding Relai."

"I can't—"

"Reach in and ask the tablet to send her a message and then *follow it*."

She looked terrified, but he let her feel the steadiness that could be found in his grip. He was right there with her.

After a moment, she swallowed and he watched her choose to be brave.

"Okay." She put her other hand on the tablet, their fingers twisting together around the device. "Okay."

She closed her eyes.

Without the slide of a finger across the screen, without a tap, the tablet awoke. The screen shone blank, warm, and white. Tannor's brow furrowed and her eyes twitched back and forth under their lids. Her lips tightened.

"Relax," he whispered. "Follow."

Then her eyes flew open.

"I found her." Tannor's eyes were wide and unfocused, and she dug her fingers into the meat of his arm. "I know where she is. *How did I do that?*"

Ky pulled her into a frantic hug and her curls muffled his voice. "Good. Good job. Thought maybe you could."

Goren growled, "Can we go save our queen, then?"

They raced down the hall. Ky made sure to grab a wire hanger from a rack as they passed through the lobby.

"What just happened?" Tannor demanded. They burst from the cool of the hotel into the dragging midday heat, moving just slowly enough to avoid calling attention. "What did I do? It was like I—I pulled the information from the tablet. I wasn't just in my head anymore. I felt it."

Ky surveyed the parking lot. Now was as good a time as any to start bleeding secrets.

"It's something you've always been doing. You just didn't notice until now. *Milo*," he barked across the lot. "Can you ride that thing yet?"

Milo snapped around and reached them in three heartbeats.

"Not yet. Trouble?"

"Princess wandered off and Applica grabbed her."

"*What?*"

"Exactly." Ky tossed him his bag, because whatever Ky was willing to give Milo, manservant privileges weren't one of them. Then he led the way around the building to a quiet corner of the lot, far from a main road.

Broad daylight. Not ideal.

He spotted an older car that he hoped would have the right sort of windows and lock. He craned his neck—nobody watching (that he could see).

"Where is she? How did this happen?" Milo demanded. Ky ignored him and focused on shoving the bent hanger down through the rubber window seal.

"She ran off just after breakfast," Tannor answered. "I tracked her comm… with the tablet." Milo eyed her and the tablet, then looked to Ky for an explanation.

Ky smirked.

"TANNOR, you have MAGICAL POWERS," Goren said.

After a moment of fumbling, Ky yanked the hanger up and the door unlocked. He flung it open and laid back under the steering wheel, wrenching open the plastic cover to reveal the wiring inside.

"Magical powers?" Milo repeated.

The car growled to life.

"Not magic," Ky corrected, huffing as he twisted up and slid cleanly into the seat, "but we can talk about it later. Let's go."

They all scrambled awkwardly into the stolen car.

"Is no one going to ask how the hell Ky knows how to start and drive one of these things?" Tannor demanded.

Ky paused, making a show of adjusting the rearview mirror and buckling his seatbelt. "Magical powers?"

ᴏᴏ●ᴏᴏ

iii.

Apparently Applica rented space in the IDS Tower, the tallest skyscraper in Minneapolis.

Relai and six agents rode an elevator to the fiftieth floor and then filed through an eerily normal business office. The lead agent walked slightly ahead of her, alert and watchful, as they passed a long row of blue-grey cubicles with dutiful drones in button-up shirts typing and chatting over telephone headsets. She couldn't understand this abrupt, stoic treatment, and it made her want to scream at them.

"You're safe," the head agent muttered, so sincere, as they moved through a narrow hallway lined with filing cabinets. They squeezed into another, smaller elevator at the end, which brought them up another level onto a nearly empty floor with a panoramic view of the cityscape.

Sure, she was.

Another agent pulled out a handheld med scanner and aimed it at her head. She recognized both Ardi and Earthan tech strewn about the green carpet, with some equipment still being hooked up and oriented. Four with her, two setting up tech. Two looked like business professionals, two like college students, and one like an older housewife; good disguises. She wondered how many of them were planning to kill her.

Once the head agent was satisfied with her med scan he lifted the silence ban.

"You're safe," he repeated. "I'm Agent Olin Batar and we work for Applica. Our Glory, I need—"

"Don't call me that," she interrupted. "I'm not."

He frowned at her. "What am I to call you, then?"

"You can call me Orist. I'm not particular about friends or enemies using that name."

His face revealed the barest hint of surprise, and he looked her over yet again. "Fair enough. Orist. Now that you're safe and we know that you're not under any malicious influence, I need you to tell me what happened." She considered his precise suit (Westwood? Armani?) and the way his short hair made his ears look enormous. He was perhaps ten years older than her. What was he doing on Earth? She had assumed that most ex-terrs were there by force, not choice, but apparently she knew nothing about anything.

"How many of you are there?" she asked instead of answering.

He sat at one of two chairs bracketing a lone, bland folding table and stared at her until she sat as well. "Nine Applica agents are attending you directly—six of us are here in this room, and another are two bringing a jumper for transport right now."

Relai frowned. "That's eight."

Batar paused and looked at her quizzically. "You were already attended by an Applica agent before we got to you."

"No, I—wait—who?"

"Agent Raphe. They're a special agent, not part of any team, and we have no way of contacting them."

"Man or woman?"

Batar shook his head. "I don't know. I have heard stories, but not enough to identify them."

Shit. Who was it?

Definitely not Milo; he was Erayd and he'd hurt her. Maybe he was Erayd and Applica? Was that even possible?

Ky? But Applica wouldn't have let him tag along with Milo for nearly a year, not if he was such a valuable agent. Goren, well, his guileless persona might just be an act, and maybe he was older than he looked. Tannor was so, so smart, and Relai had thought she was hiding something. It could be any one of the three. Then a thought occurred—

"Just one agent? Not two?"

"One agent," Batar confirmed.

So it wasn't Milo and Ky together, or Tannor and Goren together, weaving a convincing lie. Just one of them.

Tannor, then.

"We flew in from California as soon we located your field," Batar went on. "We're coordinating with the Regent Service guards who were already stationed here for your protection."

"Then you must know something's terribly wrong."

He had to know. She was supposed to be on a ship halfway across the galaxy, not running manic across Earth. How were they trying to explain this? Whatever they'd told these agents, it probably made her seem even more horrible. If the official story put her on a spaceship, there must be an unofficial lie that explained why she was still on Earth. What excuse would seem believable enough to keep a queen from her people? Or was she just supposed to be that disconnected, distant, or selfish?

Relai drummed her fingers on her thighs. She suspected the man sitting across from her knew she was doing it.

He only stared. His eyes were large and dark and it struck her that he either wasn't a very good Applica agent, or he was deliberately wearing his thoughts on his face. Agent Batar seemed harried, exhausted, and confused. He was short on patience and wary of this woman across from him, queen or not. He refused to break eye contact.

She decided to match him, letting her own fear, anger, and very justified paranoia show.

He put both hands on the table, fingers curled in a circle in front of her, leaning forward.

"Yes. I know something is wrong."

He leaned on the *I* just enough for Relai to glance at the other agents who were adjusting their computers or talking in low voices over comms. Batar just clenched his jaw.

He went on, "None of the Regent Service guards know where you are. Their story didn't match up with the other information we've gathered and I wanted to talk to you before we handed you over to their care."

"How did you find me?"

"Your heart," he answered, glancing at her chest without pretense. "We narrowed you down to this city after you sent your..." the corner of his mouth quirked up slightly, "message yesterday, and then we were able to track your heart's electromagnetic wave signal to the bookstore."

"How romantic," she muttered. "Does that mean anyone can find me at any time if they're close enough?"

His smile grew. "*We* can. The High Council can't demand access to technology they don't know exists, so your lackeys don't even know how we found you."

"Fantastic, but I'm still not sure you're not trying to kill me, too. Can we run a truth drill on your agents using that med scanner?"

He pursed his lips. "Would you trust that?" Truth drills were notoriously unreliable.

"Just a little bit more than I trust my intuition." She stood, chair scraping raggedly on the carpet, and he mirrored her. "I want to contact my—my friends, but if I can trust you, I won't say no to more allies. I need allies right now. I need help."

"Very well." Batar tapped the med scanner and readied the program. "It must be hard to be queen."

"I'm not anyone's queen."

The furrow between his brows deepened. Relai took the scanner and pointed it at him. "Can you hear my voice?" she asked. Green patterns flickered across the man's face as the tool's diagnostic array—a mix of lasers, infrared, x-rays, and magnetic resonance—mapped out his every muscle movement, capillary action, heat variation, and cluster of neural activity. "Yes," he answered calmly. The small display on the back of the scanner flashed an incomprehensible graph of the data gathered, glowing neutral yellow.

Relai raised her right hand in the air. "Which hand did I raise?"

"Your right hand."

A new graph loaded, still yellow. *Baseline established.* If he was neurotypical and telling the truth, the screen should remain yellow (assuming he hadn't been trained in the art of deceiving truth drills). The display would turn orange or red to indicate any of the neural or physiological activity that typically accompanied a lie. A green or blue screen would indicate an inconclusive reading.

"What is your name, rank, and affiliation?"

"Chief Agent Olin Batar, Applica, Earth Unit." *Yellow.* True.

"To whom or what do you owe your highest allegiance?" she asked.

"To you," he answered. *Orange.* His face tightened. "To what I believe is right."

Yellow. Relai felt some of the other agents in the room shuffle uncomfortably.

"And who do you think I am?" Relai asked, nervous about how he might answer. He inhaled, thinking a moment. The screen briefly wavered blue-green as who-knows-what thoughts ricocheted through his head.

"Relai… Orist Aydor." *Yellow.*

He believed her.

"Are you planning to kill me or sell me?"

"No," he answered without a pause. *Yellow.* The other agents were turning, standing, orienting themselves toward Relai.

True.

"Who hired you to find me?"

"We're never told." True.

"What were you told about me?" Relai asked.

"The official public story is that terrorists stole something from Haadam and destroyed the base, and one of the terrorists is posing as you," he answered. "We were told that story is a cover; you're the queen herself and you were kidnapped by the terrorists. We're to escort you safely to Arden via Buzou Base. Daat would have been easier, but they're locked down with the rebellion," Relai's pulse quickened at the word, "and I don't know if they're going to come out of it under coalition control."

She wanted to ask more questions, but that could wait. She nodded. "Next."

"Agent Kish," Batar called, and a shorter, stocky woman with grim frown lines stepped forward.

She repeated the process, and Kish passed as well. "Okay, next." Batar nodded toward another agent.

"Agent—"

She didn't get the chance to learn the third agent's name because the man stepped forward and lifted the gun off his hip and pulled the trigger before Batar had a chance to finish speaking.

Relai was hit square in the chest; she fell backward and lost focus at the rush of pain and loss of air. A shout followed, more surprised than anything.

The ceiling was gray.

○○●○○

As she stepped inside the jumper, Hope got the impression of walking into a giant aquamarine lava lamp, or maybe an aquarium. The interior of the spacecraft had a seamless silver-white surface which softly glowed with sea-green light cast by lines of light running along the ceiling and floor. Different shapes protruded softly from the main surface; controls and seating, Hope guessed.

"A lot of our engineers are Titian, but I don't know this tech very well," Shoua said. She ran her hand over one of the extrusions from the wall, and cryptic computer displays instantly glowed onto the semi-transparent surface.

Physical buttons rose up out of the liquid metal to meet Shoua's typing fingers.

"As you can see, the travel logs and all stored data are locked, but maybe your people have a way around that?"

Hope nodded noncommittally.

"I wanted to ask…" Shoua said hesitantly, "could we just link our comms so if something goes wrong I know I can get through to you right away?"

Hope clenched her teeth and took her time sucking in a breath, desperately trying to think of a lie about a piece of technology she knew nothing about.

Shoua seemed to take her hesitance as refusal, because she went on. "I took a real risk showing you this. I could lose my job, or something even worse could happen…"

For the first time, Hope stopped to really look at this woman. Who was she? What did she want, really? Hope could fake her way through this, but she couldn't be there if Shoua Fau ran into trouble.

She'd lied herself into potentially screwing over someone who'd helped her. So… what could she do?

"I can't give you the assurance you're looking for," Hope told her honestly. "I can't tell you whether you should trust Xiong or not. But I can tell you this: I will make sure those people you showed me get the justice they deserve. And you have to do whatever you can to keep yourself safe. Is there somewhere you can go… just in case things get complicated?"

Shoua wrung her hands. "I have family. I could disable my comm and take a few days of vacation?"

Hope's phone buzzed—an agency-wide text. Developing incident. Downtown Minneapolis.

She glanced around one last time, drinking in the sight of this insane vessel. She'd give herself away if she stayed any longer.

"Do it. But first—be at the front gate to meet my contact, Darcia Rowan, in twenty minutes. I have places to be."

○○●○○

"Right! No, no, here!"

"—Like when you worked the med bay on that groundship with no prior knowledge. Or when you taught the Haadam system to trust you over everyone else. And then the download into your brain—no one accepts a neural download like that."

Ky rambled over Tannor's frantic driving directions while Goren readied the weapons and Milo learned how to drive by watching.

"Left! Then forward, forward!"

Engines whined, brakes squealed, and vehicles honked alert horns at their car as Ky barreled it through the oppressively linear streets into the heart of the city's central district. He vaguely remembered how lawful traffic was supposed to conduct itself here, but now wasn't the time. He'd drive on the sidewalk if he needed to.

"You think you're bad with people," he continued, "but you're not. You're fine with people. You're *damn great* with computers. Absolutely astounding. You understand them, you know how they work, and you can push their bits of information around with your mind."

She wasn't disagreeing. Her hands on that tablet were firm, not shaking one bit, even with Ky's admittedly terrible driving.

Good start, all things considered.

"So can Tannor kill people with her mind?" Goren wanted to know.

All three of them looked apprehensively at Ky.

He shrugged and narrowly avoided a young man on a bicycle. "You never know until you try."

Tannor gave a low whimper, then her eyes went vague for a moment and she stammered, "I can feel it coming closer. The signal's going higher, really high—she must be up in one of these buildings."

They were right in the midst of the tallest buildings in the city, weaving through the grid-like canyons of glass and steel. It had been a while since Ky had needed to read English, but the basics were coming back to him quickly enough for this short trip. He made a mental note every time they passed a layered structure of stored vehicles—parking ramps, the perfect place to ditch this stolen car and find another one.

"It has to be this one!" Tannor pointed up. "This one we just circled— at least, I'm pretty sure…"

"This one it is." He whipped the car into a U-turn, swerving past several motorists and plowing straight into the entrance ramp they'd just passed. His passengers screamed and lurched forward as he slammed hard on the brakes.

"See why I said to buckle those belts?" he grinned, rolling down his window and taking the ramp entrance ticket. They probably could've smashed through the flimsy barrier, but there was no sense in risking it. The gate rose and Ky slammed the accelerator down once more, zooming up the rectangular helix of parked vehicles.

"What if I'm wrong?" Tannor said, doubt creeping into her voice. The others remained focused on gripping their seats tightly. "I don't even know how I'm—"

"You have an ability," he explained as they circled higher and higher. He wouldn't say the word in front of Milo or Goren, because the word was an abomination to them. The dirty mix of alien oppressors and human slaves. The scourge of the galaxy. The last traces of the Sevati, still left to be purged.

Ky couldn't stop himself from grinning as they pulled out into the sunlight on the highest level. Ky wasn't alone in this group.

He wasn't alone.

"You have an ability," she realized, eyes sharp on him. "What can you do?"

Ky laughed and skidded the car to an abrupt stop at the edge of the rooftop. "You don't know yet? Let's go."

iv.

Four, five more blasts came in quick succession, and then Relai felt hands on her body.

"Orist, Orist," Batar repeated, low and calm, as he unzipped her jacket. She coughed, writhing, and lifted her head to look down at her chest. Then he let out a laugh. "You're wearing armor?"

A still-hot lump of metal sat embedded in the flap of her jacket just over her heart.

She felt the panels of the jacket in wonder, noticing the clumsy stitching and recognizing the stiffness for what it must be. It had to be Goren—he must have cut up those pieces of paneling from the inside of the jumper and sewn them into her jacket. She loved him *so much* at that moment.

"Apparently so," she coughed, rolling over onto her knees. She might have some bruised ribs, but she wouldn't be complaining. Batar helped her up.

Three of the six Applica agents were now dead or dying. The one who'd shot her was dead, taken down by Batar, though not before he'd shot two others. One was already dead, and the second, Agent Kish, was gasping through her last moments. Both lay in spreading pools of crimson, the edges browning on the green carpet.

"Since when do you people use Earthan guns?" Relai said.

"We don't," Batar replied grimly. "Surai, will Kish make it?"

The young barata guy who looked like a hipster and moved like military pulled off his jacket and pressed it to the gunshot wound in Kish's neck. There were flecks of blood on Kish's cheek and all the way down her plain blue tie, and her eyes were bulging red and desperate. The agent looked up and twitched his head—no.

Batar's gaze remained fixed on the bleeding victim as he gave orders to the remaining agent, a tall, fair woman with red hair. "Linnet, go outside, secure the perimeter. Stay on comms." The woman nodded and left.

Relai grabbed the med scanner and thrust it into Surai's hands. "Save her."

Surai (who looked more like her than anyone she'd met in the past few days, and for some reason that made her chest ache) took it but didn't move.

223

He just looked to Batar and swallowed. "This wound would take all of the med scanner's power. We might need it for Orist later."

Batar went stiff. "*Are* we going to need it for her later?"

Surai's brows drew up, he blinked a few times, and said softly, "Oh, no. Olin, you—"

Relai looked between them, completely lost, and the she gave up and jerked the scanner away. She'd seen one used enough times; she could figure it out herself. "If I am the queen then you answer to me, and so says the queen, we are healing her!"

After she went through a moment or two of frenetic poking and tapping, Batar hit his knees next to her. "I thought you were no one's queen," he said, but he powered up the med scanner and pressed the contact points to the injured agent's forehead. Then he glanced at Surai and muttered, "Me. Huh."

Relai helped stabilize the woman's head and neck while Batar ran the scanner and Surai held her legs. It was a painful thing, artificial healing, and her body bucked and shook as the scanner did its job.

Relai rambled through her worry. "You should've come better prepared. What is wrong with Applica? Your reputation led me to expect more professionalism and—and maybe more murder attempts—no extra fuel cells? Don't you prepare for the worst? I was kidnapped! What were you expecting?"

Batar's hand slipped in the blood and he snapped, "We're the *Earth* field team. We're expendable, every one of us."

She realized she was holding the injured woman's head too firmly between her hands and she nearly swore. "No one is expendable. What kind of person is running your organization? No! Don't answer that."

Kish groaned raggedly.

"She's back," Surai said, heaving his fellow agent into a wobbly sitting position. "Sir?"

Olin Batar nodded to himself, running his clean hand through his hair and sending pieces curling madly in every direction. He touched the bloody agent's shoulder. "Kish? Are you with us?"

"Can you see me?" Kish gasped in reply, pressing a hand into the blood on her neck. "Did Rugo just shoot me?!?"

"Yes—I'm sorry, I didn't see it coming," Surai said.

Before Relai could make sense of it all, the elevator opened and the other woman, Linnet, slipped back in. "No one down there heard the shots," she said as she drew up to the group. She looked Relai up and down with clear contempt.

"Thank you, Linnet," Batar said, grabbing a tablet from the table and crouching next to the body of their would-be assassin to scoop up his gun. "Surai, water. We have to clean the blood off so Kish can walk out of here. Earth Monitoring will have to come for their bodies."

He switched the tablet into a scanning mode and passed it over the killer's head. "He was transmitting an optical feed from his comm when he took the shot," he said. "He wanted his actions seen."

"Was he Unity?" Linnet asked.

"Probably," Batar sighed. "Though I'm beginning to think most of the Vada Coalition is out to kill you, Orist." He spun around to face Relai. "If Unity or any other factions have infiltrated Applica…"

"What?" Relai asked.

His brow furrowed. "The agent who attended you before…If the stories are true, you're dealing with someone ruthless. Some agents are known for the harder jobs, the ones where people die, and Raphe's one of those. Applica agents don't serve the Vada Coalition or the line of Aydor. Whoever it is, they're not loyal to you." He paused. "None of us are loyal to you, but we've been contracted to bring you back to Arden alive and safe, and you can trust me. You *can*. I can't guarantee that the other Applica agent, Raphe, has an assignment with the same protection."

He fixed her with his eyes, imploring. Relai had never met anyone with such expressive eyes.

In her periphery, Relai registered Linnet pacing, muttering into her comm.

You can trust me. He had the weight of a rich, resourceful, independent corporation behind him. He could escort her to Arden, help her avoid checkpoints and dock searches. And despite his claim that he wasn't loyal to her, he'd shot his fellow agent without hesitation.

Plus, she had a good feeling about him.

"Batar, listen," Linnet interrupted. "Regent Service guards are on their way here."

"*What?*" Batar turned and put himself between Relai and the elevator.

"They went straight to the Executive. There was nothing we could do."

"We have to assume those guards will kill her on sight. Orist—"

Relai pushed the fear onto her skin, like normal, and focused. She had to get out of there. "No one new is coming near me. Agent Batar, please. I need to get back to my friends."

"Call the Executive," he told Linnet as he held out placating hands. "Tell her we're leaving for Arden. She can send more agents if she wants the kidnappers found."

"No, they'll be killed! Don't do anything—say I escaped." Relai skirted around him and rushed toward the nearest door. Would stairs be faster? Safer? They were high, fifty floors up. The elevator would be fastest, but she'd be trapped in a tiny box...

Batar followed close behind her. "They kidnapped you. Why do you care what happens to them?"

"They didn't kidnap me, they *saved me*. I was being held captive at Haadam Base. I've been a prisoner since before my father died. I haven't been ruling. Someone took over in my name." She pushed forward but he managed to stop her just before she burst through the door into the stairwell. He was muttering *no, Orist, stop,* and ducking to catch her eye. Finally he caught her shoulders between his hands.

She glared up at him. "The people you think kidnapped me are the only ones I trust right now."

He shook his head, fierce and certain. "You can trust me."

Relai tried to pull back from his hold but he followed, gentle and persistent. It didn't hurt, and she probably could have shaken him off, but her heart just wasn't in the struggle.

"They won't get to you," he insisted.

She sensed something there in his grip, an implication of safety, of rest. She craved it and despised it and she didn't want to think about it. It would be gone soon.

"Are you willing to take me to my friends?" Relai asked.

Batar surveyed her carefully. "Yes. Who are they?"

"An Erayd seperatist, a Gastredi bartender, and two Haadam guards."

Batar barked a laugh, then slid one hand down her arm to pull her along by the wrist. "Throw in an Applica agent and you've got a great joke. We're going to the roof."

Then he nodded to his fellow agents. Only Linnet joined them; Kish sat there pale and shaking as Surai sopped a wet towel against her neck. Relai, Batar, and Linnet moved into the stairwell—heading *up*, not down.

To the roof, she told herself. Sounded like *trapped*.

oo●oo

Milo heard the craft first.

He clambered out of the car, shushing their guards as they ducked in a line behind a larger vehicle on the open roof of the parking garage. Milo looked toward the distant sound.

It was moving quickly, an insect buzzing insistently toward the city center, and he saw it for its true nature as soon as he could make out the shape.

"Why does that jumper have a disc attached to its roof? And a tail?"

"Shouldn't we be running to the street level right now?" Goren interrupted, trying and failing to hide his gen-gun under his obnoxious Earthan checked shirt. "You said she's up there, right?" The boy pointed up at the giant glass monolith across the street. The parking structure was thirty odd stories, but the tower still soared another one or two hundred meters above them. "Unless you can jump from building to building and you just, oh, haven't bothered to mention it yet."

"There's a reason we're crouched, idiot," Ky answered. He motioned across the roof of the parking ramp to two lurking figures wearing the unmistakable red jackets of Regent Service guards.

Milo shoved his jacket at Goren to cover the gen-gun. Goren grumbled but put it on, and it swamped the boy's slender frame.

"I look ridiculous, thanks."

"There are two masked skimmers right next to those guards," Tannor said. "I can... not *see* them, but..."

Milo snuck a glance. "Damn. Look."

One of the Regent Service guards had turned and activated the skimmers, dropping the masks. They were getting ready to move.

"So, do I have any magical powers?" Goren asked.

Milo snorted. "No."

227

"They're not magical powers, Goren," Ky said. "No spells, no curses, no potions. No magic."

The jumper drew closer in the sky.

Ky said, "Is that helicopter heading for—"

"*Helicopter?* That's a jumper," Milo corrected. Ky frowned and they all squinted at it. The sun was behind them so the craft was well-lit and steady as they watched it approach. "It's a jumper with something on its roof, can't you tell?"

"You're right," Ky said. "It must be Applica coming to pick up our princess. Let's borrow it, shall we?"

"What about those guards?" Goren asked.

"You know my opinion on guards," Milo replied, "All the same."

"We're not—"

"Of course, you two aren't guards anymore," he said, "you're fugitives from the law."

"Relai *IS* the law!"

"Goren," Tannor groaned, tucking away her tablet. "These guards might be... helpful or unhelpful. Let's just try to avoid killing anyone, okay?"

Ky yanked the string to charge his spit gun a little harder than necessary. Tannor eyed him sternly.

"Looks like they're waiting on orders," Milo said. They almost looked bored. If these guards were working purely for the good of the queen, they'd be straining with every breath in their bodies to find her and keep her safe. He checked his gen-gun's charge.

Goren, though, was peering at the sky.

"Hey," he said, "that jumper is opening weapons…"

•

Relai stepped into the sunlight just behind Batar, with Linnet following. The wind blasted her face as she looked around, seemingly on top of the world. The horizon wrapped around them, geometric rooftops laid out below like stepping stones. The only things higher than them were a couple of gray sheds and several spindly antennae—and, circling above, a jumper.

The craft turned to face them head on. Batar waved and said something into his comm. The jumper came in low, still facing forward as it drew closer to the gravel surface.

Batar abruptly spun and thrust the killer agent's Earthan gun into Relai's hands.

"Something's wrong. I need you to—"

They were both thrown the ground and pelted with gravel as a blast from the jumper's plasma cannon struck mere feet from them.

Relai landed partly on Linnet; the woman jumped up and shouted, "Back inside!" as she dashed sideways toward the nearest shed.

·

Milo stood and barreled toward the guards, cranking the dial on his gen-gun to a non-lethal setting.

Ky, slower to move, shouted behind him.

The Regent Service guards were watching the jumper in alarm; they'd seen it firing in broad daylight at the roof of that building, too. One hopped on his skimmer. Milo stopped, raised both arms, and took aim.

Head shot for one—*direct hit*, number two turned and tried to react—*face shot*. Ouch.

Milo had to get up there, and he kept his eyes up even as he reached the skimmers and threw a leg over the one already running.

They were close enough, everyone watching, the others running behind him, blood thumping…

Close enough to see a body go flying off the roof of the tower.

Milo could do it—he had time, his body knew what to do—

He squeezed and twisted and leaned and the skimmer shot up and forward, racing up the flashing glass of the skyscraper—

Catch her in an arc, a direct interception will break her—

He swooped up and dove at the falling body, fast enough that she appeared to be drifting, limp and unconscious, and he leaned with his knees clenching the skimmer and reached with both hands, grabbing at the material of her jacket and pulling her to his chest, righting the skimmer with a jerk of his hips.

It wasn't Relai.

He saw before he caught her that this woman was older than Relai, with shorter red hair, far too fair skin, and different clothes. She was bleeding from small cuts on her face and hands but she didn't appear to be hit; she must have been thrown off the roof. Her nose was bleeding.

The buildings stood too close in this city, unsafe for flying vehicles, too little clearance. He struggled to steer and keep his grip on the limp body as he avoided the tops of trees and circled a building, ignoring faint shouts and honking horns.

Milo dipped low with the skimmer and slowed just enough to deposit the woman on a strange mound of grass amid a flat expanse of gritty stone. Then he twisted up and around, climbing the air to join the fray on the roof.

.

Goren did as the others had asked before they left him behind—secured those Regent Service guards, took their weapons—and then he ran like hell.

People were stopped in crowds, gasping and holding tablets up to the sky, when he burst out a set of glass doors on the ground level of the parking ramp. Goren couldn't see the jumper in the air anymore. Everyone up there was probably dead by now—but still.

He raced across the street, narrowly missing being flattened by more than one hulking ground vehicle, and charged into the revolving entrance at the base of the tower. (Stupid Earth, with their gross buildings made of all different materials, all different heights and designs, no uniformity at all—)

He had no plan but to get up on that roof, however possible, as quickly as he could.

Two people in uniforms, guns on their hips, stood behind a desk in front of him. Both of them were occupied, one speaking into a handset at the end of a spiraled cord and the other into a black rectangle with a stick pointing out of one end. They were just realizing something was going on, Goren guessed. He tucked behind a tall indoor plant, raised his gen-gun, and stunned first the guards and then the other six people in the building's ground floor lobby. The charges he used wouldn't leave a mark on the skin; they'd just look like everyone started having seizures at the same time. Plenty of trouble to distract the locals for a while.

Just past the guard station was a set of six elevators, three on each side facing one another. Goren dove into an open lift box, pressed the topmost button, and the doors closed on the shouts of people discovering all those seizing bodies. He felt himself begin to rise.

Terrible, *terrible* music played overhead.

He could hardly breathe deeply enough, his chest tight and pounding. For all his boredom on Haadam Base, there was plenty of time for exercise and Goren was in excellent shape (if skinny counted as a shape). He watched his progress as the red glowing numbers above the door rose higher and higher. How many floors did this building have?

Finally, the elevator doors opened and Goren darted out into a hall with doors and confused people and windows and a view that revealed that he was most definitely *not* on the top floor.

Crap. This was the highest floor the elevator reached.

He needed to find another way up.

•

The jumper was parked on the rooftop by the time Milo reached the scene. Various metal air ducts and scaffolding littered the roof, some of them torn to shrapnel by the plasma cannon blasts that had left blackened pits on the otherwise flat, gravel surface. Parts of the roof had been torn through, revealing the charred struts of the structure below, but the jumper still looked steady.

Ky, with Tannor clinging behind him, arrived on the other skimmer moments later.

"What the hell took you two so long?" he shouted as they both landed.

"Goren got stunned by one of the guards, had to hit all of them again to make sure he loosened up first and could get away," Ky explained as they took in the layout of the battle-strewn roof.

"And Goren's more important than Relai?" Milo demanded.

"We thought YOU had Relai!"

They both stopped yelling at the sight of blood.

A tall, dark-haired man lay mangled and unmoving near a rooftop door. No movement. From the positioning of the body Milo could tell the man had been defending the doorway from the pilot of the jumper, and he'd given his life. He'd died protecting the queen.

Maybe he'd bought her enough time to get away from the attacker.

Milo ran for the blast-torn door, threw it open, and narrowly avoided being shot in the face.

•

Relai had a gun, one that shot metal bullets instead of electrical charges, but it wouldn't fire. At least she knew how to operate a gen-gun. This one was dead weight in her hands.

Or, it had been.

Relai was three flights down when she was hit with a binding grenade. It bounced down the steps and collided with her calf; from there the spindly fibers swarmed out and enveloped her whole body without a breath of opportunity.

She pitched forward and fell four steps to a landing, caught herself with her shoulder to cushion the crack of her head, and skidded to a stop against the stairwell wall.

Oh, it hurt, it *hurt*—

"Hi."

From her tilted perspective, she saw her attacker amble down the stairs. She was tall and overly-muscled, with gruesome scarring and discolored skin around one eye. She could pass for Earthan by her clothes and hair but Relai wasn't fooled. She'd handled that jumper like old military and her accent was Ardenian.

The woman looked greasy and mean and Relai wanted her old kidnappers back.

Relai's head was caught and held bent unnaturally to one side, exposing her throat. The woman crouched and scratched behind her ear, observing through two differently-colored eyes.

"Broken shoulder," she decided, poking 'til Relai screamed. "So I don't have to cut you to keep you hurting. Less messy."

"Happy to oblige," Relai managed through gritted teeth. "Who are you?"

"I'm going to release this and you're not going to run," she replied.

"Or you'll shoot me?"

The attacker's face jerked close to Relai's and she struggled to stop her from touching her face, to escape the smell of her breath.

"The only reason you're alive right now, *Queen*," she hissed, "is that I don't have the supplies on me to pack your eyes and your hand for transport. Otherwise you'd be a lot less talkative."

Oh. Oh, no.

Relai couldn't seem to slow down her breathing after that.

The woman released the bindings and Relai tried to curl in on herself, to protect her shoulder, but she was yanked to her feet instead.

When she caught her breath she gasped, "I have money—"

The woman cut her off by wrapping the crook of her arm under her chin and dragging her up the stairs. Relai flailed, clawing for a position to lessen the pain in her shoulder as her heels skidded on the stair edges.

"I'd never get another job if I turned on my clients for a bigger offer from the target. No, my little queen, you'll come with me and Unity'll show us what they think they can do as rulers of a fucking planet."

Job. A bounty hunter.

She reached the top of the flight of stairs and tossed Relai on the landing.

"Unity?" Relai groaned.

The bounty hunter smirked. "Guys who hired me. You should know the people who hate you. So tell me, how long did you think you'd last before someone overthrew you?"

Relai managed to push herself into a sitting position and ease back against a painted concrete wall. "They kidnapped me a year ago. Never ruled in the first place."

"Oh," the hunter said with little interest. "Well, now they just want your parts. I wonder if they'll use your hot cousin as a puppet queen. What do you think? She won't be able to rule worth a damn, but people will listen to anything that comes out of a pretty face."

She panted as she stared up at the hunter.

"My cousin? But—the Renganiban brothers are next in line—"

The hunter's smile broadened and she assaulted Relai with her breath again. "Yeah, except they're dead. I got one of them myself."

Relai would have stumbled if she weren't already huddled on the floor. Her nose was running from tears she hadn't noticed. "Why?"

The hunter ignored her.

They would be after her cousin Sana next, but she didn't have Aydor blood so the dirty little secret of the Aydor line would come out—and—and they'd kill her, too. Or, like this hunter said, they'd use her as a puppet. As long as they had Relai's hand and eye, they could control everything.

The door to the roof was just one flight up. Out there she'd see two bodies... because Batar and Linnet must be dead or she wouldn't be facing this bounty hunter. They'd only been trying to help her.

Then the door to the roof jerked open from the outside and Relai cowered as the hunter pulled her weapon and released four chasing shots before the door slammed shut.

Batar—it must be—

"Thought I killed him," the hunter muttered. She crouched down and Relai glared up at her as she considered the door.

Then from her coat she pulled out two small black rectangular objects. From one side of the first one she pulled a tab and peeled out a strip of shimmering silver tape. She wrapped it deftly around Relai's neck and attached the tab to a slot in its case. It clicked into place, locked like a necklace. The tape sat on her skin, heavy for its size, the plastic growing warm with the contact. Then she grabbed Relai's left hand and placed the second strip around her wrist. With the tap of a few buttons the devices lit up orange, coordinating with a thick black band on her own wrist.

"Pay attention," the hunter growled. "These are linked incision rings. If I take my hand off of your neck, these will set off charges aimed inward and they'll sever your head and hand. Your head would be enough of a threat, but I might as well get ready for the trip. Less to carry."

Relai wasn't sure blood was actually reaching her brain anymore. She was seeing spots.

The bounty hunter wasn't going to keep her alive for convenience. Once she got Relai onto that jumper she was going to take her hand off of her neck and take her parts back to Arden and they were going to use them to authorize more horrible things in her name.

Less than a minute. She had less than a minute.

But the hunter's hand was on her neck now. The thing was set.

Think of something, anything—

The hunter wrapped her other massive hand fully around Relai's upper arm and shoved her out into the daylight of the roof.

•

Tannor suspected Relai was already dead, but she didn't want to say it out loud. How would they transport her body back to Arden? They'd all be tried for treason. She might even be blamed for the queen's murder.

No, that would fall on Ky and Milo's shoulders. She watched the men bickering and wondered how they'd ever thought their plan would work.

Only one fate awaited these criminals, both if Relai had been queen and if she was dead now: execution.

But they'd have to get the body back first. She'd just opened her mouth to propose they bring out the grenades when the door opened and they saw Relai.

She stepped out with a look of excruciating terror on her face, her body curled in on itself with her arms folded tightly against her chest. After her came a burly woman with one hand gripping Relai's neck.

Tannor followed Milo's lead and fanned out so the three surrounded the two. The bounty hunter shouted her terms with her second step into the open.

"My hand leaves her neck, her head'll blow off. Give us a clear path to the jumper."

Tannor saw the device and sucked in a breath. If only she could touch it, maybe she could stop it from working—if she tackled them maybe she could get her hands in the right place quickly enough...

Her awareness of this ability was so new, she was sure she wouldn't be fast enough. She needed practice, training, knowledge. Tannor couldn't risk it.

It didn't end up mattering.

Relai caught the Tannor's eyes, frantic, and then settled on Milo. "End it now," she said. "It's my choice. Shoot her."

Milo choked out a desperate noise. Both of his hands were on his gun. Tannor saw him crank the settings all the way up to lethal.

Ky shouted, "Tannor, do something."

"I don't know—"

"TANNOR!"

Relai barked, *"Milo!"*

Then Tannor looked and panicked and reached out and *gripped*.

Milo fired.

The world faded around her and Tannor held them, each and every tiny spinning bit of energy in that device, in the palm of the hand of her mind. She stopped them from flowing and doing their duties as programmed. She stopped the explosion.

Or, the one at the neck, at least.

She hadn't noticed a band around Relai's wrist.

The bounty hunter fled into the stairwell, wounded but not dead and with Milo right behind her, as Ky watched Relai stare at the stump of her arm until she keeled sideways to her knees.

Her hand was gone.

No, it was lying several feet away.

Ky grabbed Relai's hand (it seemed so small, unattached) and threw himself onto the ground beside her. She wasn't crying yet, not even really breathing. He cradled her arm in his and positioned the hand at the stump. The incision ring had worked efficiently, searing the skin so there was less blood than he'd expected.

He squeezed the pieces together and threaded his fingers and pushed.

"Of course," Relai mumbled.

"What?" Ky asked, breathing through the drag of pain. He needed to concentrate.

"No, I," she slurred. She swayed backward and he followed the movement so they both slapped down on their backs in the gravel.

Ky groaned. He tightened his grip around Relai's severed wrist and closed his eyes. Tannor put her hand on Relai's neck and the band popped free. Ky saw her stuff it in her pocket. Smart.

"You're insane," Tannor said. "What made you think I could do that?"

"Almost done." Ky's hands had paled, his skin flush against the bones of his hands as though he were wasting away. He saw Tannor's horrified stare and winced into a smile. "It's too early for her to die. She's got more to do."

"*According to who?*"

"I can't bring a person back to life, so I figured it must be you who'd save her…"

"This is what you do," Tannor whispered. "You heal."

"Healer, yeah. That's me." He grinned and tried to stop himself from groaning.

One last push and it was done.

Sirens squalled far below as Milo lumbered over, flushed and grim. Ky rolled his head sideways over the grinding pebbles to gauge his health and came out satisfied. "Where's your friend?" he asked.

"Locals'll find the body," Milo replied. "We should go."

"Tannor will start up the jumper, won't you?" Ky asked with a twitch of his brow. She held eye contact, frowned in concentration, and the jumper hummed to life.

"Good," Ky whispered. Then he dropped his hands away and lay still, closing his eyes to the brightness of the sun.

.

Relai helped Ky stumble drunkenly into the jumper. She had no idea what was taking the local police so long to respond to all this commotion, but it must have been less than ten minutes since the bounty hunter attacked.

They needed to find Goren and get out of there, likely not in that order.

"Where's Goren?" she asked.

"Probably trying to get up here on foot, if he has any sense," Tannor answered as she laid her hands on the deck of the jumper. Her eyes went vague and Relai looked on in wonder. "I can find him."

"So you saved me with your mind?"

Tannor quirked a smile. "I suppose so. Looks like the tail and the blades are just imaging for the locals; I can mask them and hide us."

"Do it," Milo answered. He was leaning over Ky, inspecting his hands unhappily. "I'll pilot."

No concern for Relai's own recently-removed hand, then? She flexed her fingers and the movement was perfect, no seam, no trace of pain. A *healer*. *Stars*. Relai stared out the open jumper door at the scene they were leaving— a surprisingly subdued sight, but for Olin Batar's body. She didn't see Linnet anywhere.

The police would find them and Applica would catch wind and pick up their bodies for their families… she hoped.

Then Olin Batar's body moved.

"He's moving! Stop, STOP!" Relai shouted, bounding out toward Batar. No one followed her.

She moved one hand over him, the other folded to her chest to keep her collar bone still. His body was a disaster, cheekbone crushed and holes all down his chest; he shouldn't be alive, and yet he was. He was breathing.

"Olin, Olin, I'm going to help you," she whispered, then she screamed to the jumper, "Why aren't you helping me? Help me!"

•

Milo rose to his feet, but Relai was fooling herself if she thought he was leaving the jumper. He still had Ky's arm by the wrist.

"We're getting out of here," he declared, and everyone else seemed to agree. Ky should've echoed but he didn't, and Milo didn't understand. They did not stop for injured strangers.

"Ky. We don't have time."

Tannor grimaced and took half a step. "We don't. But maybe we could load him in the jumper?"

"Look at him," Milo snapped. "He'll die before we move him ten feet. We get him into the jumper and then we have a body to deal with."

From outside Relai shrieked, "*Please!*"

Milo bellowed, "Get back in here!"

But Ky, unbelievably, was already stumbling his way back out into the sun.

"I'll just heal him a little, okay?" he called over his shoulder. "It'll take less time than arguing."

Milo drummed his fingers on his gen-gun and growled deep in his chest.

•

Olin Batar heard words with his ears but he couldn't make sense of them, so he reached out with his mind.

What happened?

He heard, just above him:

Damn. She was right, you're alive.

Who are you? Olin asked.

Gonna save you, but only just.

Who are you?

He felt his body coming back to him, and with it, he became more aware of the pain. Oh, right. He'd been shot. The man above him thought:

You're Applica, but you tried to die defending Relai Aydor?

Yeah. Well. She seemed nice.

Very funny. The Executive is a conniving wretch and she's not worth your time. Does she know about your ability?

Yeah. Only reason I even made it out in the field. Nothing serious ever happens on Earth, they said. Everyone on my team is shusa.

His ears finally made sense of a sound—the man above him laughing softly.

Shit, what is she planning to do with you? Listen, this is... it's the end of what I can do right now. Earthans will have to patch up the rest.

Olin only mostly felt like he was dying now. His heart still screamed in his chest, but still he thought, *Thank you. Who are you?*

The man answered:

Tell the Executive that Raphe says hi, and I found someone better, and she needs to retire or I'll retire her. She's not using us anymore.

Raphe. No, Raphe, don't leave me here—

You're near-dead weight, and I have things to do.

Hands lifted. Olin was alone.

•

Relai crouched next to Batar in relief as he groaned and shifted without quite gaining consciousness. Milo had both arms wrapped around Ky's chest,

239

fully supporting his drowsy, gaunt body; his gen-gun rested on the ground beside them. Tannor had drifted a few steps out of the now-invisible jumper, the interior still visible so it appeared she was standing next to a doorway to another dimension.

Relai saw the stun grenade fly out of the stairwell and she could do nothing, say nothing, before it exploded.

The bloody, wretched bounty hunter dragged herself slowly out of the doorway. The open air had reduced the power of the blast so everyone was thrown back from its epicenter but still conscious. Not hurt, only stunned.

There were no weapons within reach.

The hunter took five steps to reach Milo, who was trying to raise himself up enough to dive for his weapon, and kicked him in the face. Relai watched in despair, raised up on one elbow, vulnerable and ignored as seconds crept onward.

In their short time together, it appeared Milo and the bounty hunter had grown to dislike one another.

"Nice. Fucking. Try," the hunter spat, and kicked Milo again. Then she picked up Milo's gun and shot him in the chest. Then again. And again.

Then the hunter turned to Relai. "Now I'm frustrated."

She advanced.

•

Ky was empty, empty, Milo was dead, dead, *dead*—

•

Goren stumbled out of the stairwell.

His feet hurt and his thighs burned and he was out of breath and there were probably Earthan police chasing him but *he'd made it.* He took a sweeping look at the scene and lifted his gun, twisting shock and penetration to their highest settings as he moved, and shot the bad one.

Tannor could say what she wanted about helpful and unhelpful; this was not a hard call to make.

The woman bucked backwards, Goren fired again—and *again,* and *again,* pushing her further and further—until she pitched over the edge of the roof. Tannor clutched her head and let out a strangled laugh.

Goren waved in weak celebration. "I got to help!"

Then he saw Milo.

•

"Can't you heal him?" Relai begged.

Ky clawed his fingers into the gravel of the roof and dragged himself over to Milo. He put his hands on the still body's chest. "There is no... new energy," he breathed. "No creating something from nothing. It takes substance and energy... to heal a wound in regular time. It takes more to push the healing faster. And I. Am. *Spent*."

"I didn't know—"

Ky pounded a weak fist into the gravel. "The first time I listen to you— and he's going to die. You don't know what you've done." He ground his forehead down and let out a formless wail. Relai was shocked to see him so unraveled.

"I'm sorry—can't you—"

"It's too much, too fast. I wasted the rest of myself on you and that fucking Applica agent. I hope he was worth it."

Ky bathed his hands in Milo's blood and slumped, so exhausted that he couldn't even hold his head up, and started pushing anyway. Relai threw herself down on Milo's other side.

"You can use me. My energy, my—my substance."

Ky glared at her but his breathing slowed. He stopped breathing entirely. Then he sucked in a chest full of air and said, "I've never done that before."

But before she could argue he was already grabbing her hand and laying it between his palms and Milo's wounds.

He gave no warning before she felt it. It began as a push and a pull, terrible, painful like a bruise traveling up her arm. Soon the pain outdid her broken shoulder and she was almost grateful for that, and she cried out but she didn't pull away. She was glad. She'd wanted to help Milo heal.

Then Relai felt movement, the brush of skin, and pressure unlike the pain. Other hands pushed under and over hers, a large and fine-fingered one and a smaller solid one.

Goren. Tannor.

They wedged their way in and added their energy and so it became the five of them, together, sweating and crying.

oo●oo

EPISODE VII:

PROPHECY

THE 'TERRORIST ATTACK' turned out to be something like a shady corporate deal gone wrong, if Hope was going to believe the story that the other Homeland Security agents had worked out before she arrived.

She did not believe the story.

Somehow a helicopter was involved—but there was no video, even though Hope was pretty sure that if it looked like a helicopter was shooting at the roof of a building, the first thing anyone down on the street would have done is pulled out their phones and started recording. They'd found one man on the roof in critical condition, gunshot wounds to the chest, a woman dead in a tree in the IDS Center courtyard after falling off the roof, and another woman with serious internal injuries who... didn't fall off the roof, because that would be impossible, but it sounded more possible than the reports some witnesses were giving: that a man on a flying motorcycle had *caught her as she fell and left her on the ground before he flew away again.*

Not to mention the eight people in the IDS Center ground floor lobby who all experienced simultaneous seizures.

Why mention those? Nothing was connected, of course. Hope's fellow Homeland Security agents were complete idiots. Hope was just a crazy conspiracy theorist who probably had an 'I WANT TO BELIEVE' poster up in her office (she did *not*), right?

Hope was now shouting in the face of the agent in charge, aka Asshole Ben.

"I want to talk to everyone, on every floor!"

"You want to personally interview... fifteen hundred people?"

Condescending motherfucker— "Not me, *personally*. I want *us as an agency* to talk to everyone."

Ben actually crossed his arms in response. "I don't even know why you're here, Agent Valdez. You're not in charge, no one needs a Spanish translator, and—"

"That's not my job and you know it—"

"—the incident doesn't have any connection to Islam, ISIS, Al-Shabaab, or your Somalis anywhere."

Hope nearly murdered him on the spot. "They're not *mine* and you have no idea what I'm working on, *Benjamin*, because you never come out for Thursday night happy hour!"

He put his hands on his hips. "Let's call Maggie and let her decide what you're working on, huh?"

Maggie was their supervisor's boss, the division director. She would not be happy to hear anything coming out of this guy's mouth... Hope would be screwed if she lost her job. She'd lose her queries, her data sources, her authority... *what if Ben was in on it?*

Before she could form a reply, her phone rang. She glared at him as she backed away, snapping, "I need to take this call."

Dr. Darcia Rowan from the Hennepin County Medical Examiner's Office was on the other end.

"Hope. Hi. I need you to come down to the morgue. This case just went from weird to... really weird."

Besides the fact that they're aliens, Hope didn't say. She watched uniformed officers stretch out another spool of caution tape and tried to keep Suspicious Ben in the corner of her eye. "Why?"

"It's these people's teeth. We did the x-rays and then I made molds just to be sure, and now I'm freaking out and I have a really bad headache. It's probably anxiety."

"What's wrong with the teeth?"

"Nothing! They're perfect and—and identical."

"So, good dental hygiene?"

"No," Darcia said. "They're *identical*. These people *all have the same teeth*. Different races, different ages, and they all have identical sets of false teeth."

Hope had to take a moment to let the phone hang limp and rub her eyes. This was good. It was evidence. Maybe these aliens could just bio-print human bodies to inhabit, and they were clever enough to vary the overall appearance but too lazy to differentiate the teeth? In the meantime...

The local police might talk to her before they realized she wasn't supposed to be there. She could still learn more without pissing anyone else off, and she could do it before Ben heard a word about it.

"I'll be over in a couple hours, Darcia. Breathe deeply until I get there."

ii.

The rustling wind and dimming sky let Tom know that he had about half an hour before the rain destroyed everything within a two-foot radius of his open windows, so he made sure they were all open wide. It was still disgustingly hot and he was going to keep them open as long as possible, renter responsibility be damned.

The mysterious and beguiling Eris was nowhere to be seen. She was going to be pissed if she got caught out in this rain, poor thing. And Tom hated wet cat smell.

He leapt up the stairs to the door three at a time and stuck his head out. "EEEERIS! GET YOUR MANGY BUTT HOME! THEM BOYS AIN'T WORTH IT! DADDY WANTS YOU BACK"

"Shut up, you psycho!" a girl yelled from a window of the second-floor unit. It was one of the blond ones, which meant nothing because three of them looked exactly the same (though the Nice One, she was a brunette) and they attracted the same lounging, scrawny-bearded hipsters with non-functional thick-framed glasses and parents that paid for their wasted lives. They spent more than Tom made in a year just to look like they dug their clothes out of their grandparents' garbage bin.

"Cats can sense evil!" he screeched back.

Neighbors properly incensed, he left the door open a crack for his kitty and wandered back inside. His computer desk was a disaster, two laptops humming amid a monstrous snarl of cords, external hard drives, old computer towers looted for parts, and the occasional cracker. (Somebody had to feed the mice.)

He'd have to clean at least a little bit before the marathon of research he had planned for tonight. With the planet freaking out like this, he was going to have a lot of late-night chat sessions with friends and bitter enemies in other time zones. Gecko was the only guy he consistently didn't hate; maybe it was the hilarious alien roleplay thing the guy had started when they met. He'd message things like '*Last post such a sick burn, they felt it 870LY away*' after Tom wrote a blog post about aliens coming to Earth just to steal velcro. Plus, he was great at World of Warcraft.

No time for WoW tonight, though. Gecko didn't want to play, anyway; he kept freaking out about the crash in Italy. *Unity, Unity, Daat's not responding,*

Unity… Everyone on this planet was terrible, so unifying terrible people would be… terrible.

Someone knocked on his open door. Tom frowned, leaning back and craning his neck to see up the stairs. Beyond the edge of the stairwell ceiling Tom spied two pairs of feet. The legs attached to them wore dirty jeans and very new shoes, and those legs looked *nervous*.

"Better not be Jehovah's Witnesses," he grumbled, considering the last ones he let in stayed for two hours. Ending awkward conversations with strangers was not something Minnesota taught its children.

He dragged on pants to be polite and stomped up.

It was a gorgeous Southeast-Asian-looking girl, maybe early twenties (friends with the American Apparel models upstairs?), and a scowling teenage white boy. They both looked exhausted. The boy could have pulled off the model thing, too, all skinny and cheekboney, except he was dressed like a confused lumberjack ("fashion," perhaps?). Neither of them had a chainsaw, which was a good sign.

"Yeah?" Tom asked in what he considered a neutral manner.

He noticed now that the girl also appeared to be covered in blood. She stared deeply into his eyes and said:

"Are you Tom Wood?"

She had a bit of an accent which he couldn't place. The boy just alternated between glaring at him and glancing over his shoulder toward the alley.

Tom crossed his arms. "Who's asking?" Fidgety Boy was now trying to peer inside his place. Tom shot out a hand to block his view.

"Well," the girl said, "I need your help. You were taking pictures of us with this," she held out Tom's stolen phone and he gasped—it was two of the people from Mickey's! Shit!— "…and we looked through your blog. We found this world map you posted, and it looks like you guessed the location of all of our bases. There are more spots marked, and we're looking for another secret base. We need to know how you came up with these guesses. We need your help."

Map? Map? He recognized the image she showed him, but it was a map of heightened alien activity… "What? Who are you?"

She shook the phone for emphasis and said: "We're not from Earth."

Tom found himself laughing, high pitched and deranged, for lack of a better response. It ridiculous that this hadn't happened yet, really. He was asking for pranks, and Frickfrack was probably in on it, of course she was—they were messing with him.

The girl sighed and called out, "Tannor?"

A few yards aways, a door opened in mid-air.

Just, just *right there*—in the middle of nothing in his backyard, a door opened. A tiny blond woman leaned out from a space that cut back into the air and the grass of his yard as though there was a second reality on top of this one. He could see white lights and pale curved paneling and a thick ribbed walkway stretching back toward the alley.

"We are not from this planet. That's our jumper—it's like a, uh, a shuttle. It can hop continents but it can't really go into space and that's why we need to get to a groundship. My name is Relai Orist Aydor and this is Goren Dray. That's Tannor Mellick inside, and we need help moving Milo Hemm and—I forgot his last name—Kyro inside."

Tom couldn't reply because he was not actually physically existing at that moment. He was literally a giant conglomeration of screaming nerve cells which had all spontaneously combusted into glitter and the opening lines of *Bohemian Rhapsody*.

Okay, maybe not *literally* literally. But definitely *figuratively* literally.

Aliens aliens aliens on his doorstep and they looked human (BODYSUITS?) and they had a spaceship—

"Is it bigger on the inside?" he blurted out.

"It's—you can't see how big it is, it's invisible—my friends need help!"

"Are they dying of the common cold?"

"No!" She let out a frustrated noise and called out something in their alien language. The boy had somehow transported into the ship (or maybe Tom just wasn't paying attention for a second there) and he was helping the blond lady struggle out with a giant unconscious man slung between their shoulders. "We're going to come inside while you panic, if that's okay."

"Yeah, yeah, of course! Anything I can do to assist you in your journey home. Do you like Reese's pieces?"

"I think we're all hungry, thanks."

Fidgety Boy and Blondie wrestled their fallen comrade (who was very bloody, he realized) down the stairs and Tom air-traffic-controlled them to his own bed. His bed got alien blood all over it. ALL OVER IT. It wasn't green, though, just a normal sort of brown-red. Bummer.

Boss Girl stuck with Bloody Guy and sent Tom back to the ship to drag one last dude in. The spacecraft was beautiful and glorious and, okay, kind of scratched up when he tiptoed inside. But still! Every inch of the interior appeared to be covered in faint patterns of geometric swirls and interlocking lines, like an etched version of Islamic tile art.

The final guy lay slumped across a row of seats. This one was around Tom's age, had very respectable facial hair, and appeared to be… maybe Korean or something. (Did that mean these aliens were originally from Earth? PLANET ZERO? That didn't mean his own theory about super-intelligent pre-humans leaving to explore space a million years ago was wrong.)

Tom was able to just hook him by the armpits and drag him awkwardly across the yard and down the stairs. It was embarrassingly difficult; Tom was never going to be a clean-up guy for the mob that maybe existed in Minneapolis.

Right in the middle of the near-disaster of the stairs, the guy said something. Tom slipped, overbalanced, and clunked down the last couple steps, cushioning the guy's fall as he landed flat on his back with a head bruising his ribs.

"Ow," Tom groaned. "What did you say?"

"Food."

At first Tom didn't realize it was English. Then Sleepy went on, eyes half-closed, "Feed me. I need food."

"Feed me, Seymour," Tom croaked, and pushed the guy off of him.

"Name's not Seymour," Seymour said.

"Yeah, and Frankenstein wasn't the monster." Tom went and rooted through his fridge. Maybe Seymour was diabetic. (Could aliens be diabetic? Why not?) He still had a tube of frozen pineapple juice left over from that night of too much vodka and poetry so he just grabbed a spoon and fed it to the guy like Italian ice. After six spoonfuls Seymour opened his eyes.

It was weird. He was getting more color in his skin, just from that little bit of juice. He spoke more clearly: "Good. Protein, too?"

"I have some eggs, but it'll take a minute—"

"Raw."

251

"Ew. Okay." Tom was pretty sure raw eggs were not a treatment for diabetic shock, but he got the last three eggs in his fridge and cracked them down Seymour's throat.

After a minute, Seymour sat up. He winced and took a few very deep breaths; Tom couldn't see any major injuries, but who knew how these alien bodies worked? Seymour grabbed the slushy tube of juice concentrate and chomped away, there at the foot of Tom's stairs, sprawled across Tom's shoes, until it was gone. It struck Tom that Seymour might not be an alien, what with knowing English with no accent and everything.

"Are you one of—them?" Tom was already slightly jealous that they might have brought in another Earthling to help.

The man let out a tired laugh and wiped a sticky line from his lip. "Yeah, man, I'm not from around here." Then he heaved himself to his feet and demanded to see the kitchen.

Fidgety Boy was doing something weird to all of the windows, feeling them or something, while Blondie was tapping away at a computer tablet of some kind.

"Where are you from?" he ventured as he led the guy to his tiny kitchen, which was not in any way stocked for visitors. Tom kept salami and cheese, phở (the embarrassing packaged kind), gummy bears, and not much else. There might be a loaf of bread somewhere growing mold. Hope's abuelita had insisted on giving him massive bags of brown rice and dried beans the last time he'd visited her house so Tom wouldn't pull an *Into the Wild* in the middle of Uptown Minneapolis, but that was it. The cupboard was bare.

Seymour didn't answer.

"Sorry—" Tom began, then stopped himself when the guy started dumping the uncooked rice right in his mouth.

"Good enough," Seymour groaned through a full mouth, crunching and mashing the grains with not a hint of concern for etiquette. "Now you need to go get us more food. We need more eggs, oil—good oil, and vinegar… does this area have chanh muối? No? Fine, kefir or tempeh."

Tom snapped out of his horror and into irritation. "I don't have any money! How am I supposed to feed you all?"

From somewhere on his person Seymour produced a suspiciously large wad of cash.

"So I'm supposed to just leave you here at my place all alone?"

"What are we going to do, burn the house down? Go! Now!"

Tom glared at the man as he grinned through a revolting mouthful of rice flecks. "Am I going to come back to a house full of dead bodies?"

Seymour shrugged.

Tom thought for a moment, then his last-second brilliance saved him yet again. "Okay, I'll let you stay here and use my stuff and I'll feed you, but I want something in return."

Seymour went scary-still and then cocked his head. Tom allowed sufficient tension to build as he psyched himself up for rejection.

"I want you to take me to your home planet."

Seymour snorted unattractively. "Sure, buddy. Just get us some food first, then we'll take off."

Tom fish-mouthed at the blatant sarcasm. Okay, then. He aimed a stern finger at the guy and said, "I'm willing to negotiate. In the meantime, the rain better hold off, *Seymour*. And I'm going to have to borrow the next-door neighbor's wheelbarrow to carry all the food because I don't have a car. I'll be back in about two hours—this place better be here when I get back!"

"Thanks, buddy!"

Tom received a slap on the back and then he stumbled into his sandals and out the door.

•

Tannor settled in a faded, well-worn chair made of synthetic fabric so bland it could hardly be called any color at all. She took out the pack of seca mints she'd found in Ky's jacket as the door to a side room eased shut with Milo, Ky, and Relai inside. She'd taken them on the jumper ride here, while Ky was unconscious and couldn't object. She'd sensed her way to them.

She was so, so tired, but she had a job to do.

She shook the tiny, shine-glazed beads into her hand one by one and, with a tentative courage similar to her first time at a shooting range in guard training, wielded the newfound power in her mind.

She searched for energy. Metal, power, still or flowing… she searched and she found it. The world around her faded like light mired in fog as one tiny bead lit up brightly in her head. The transmission blocker, disguised under a layer of hard sugar.

Tannor folded it in her palm and allowed her eyes to close. She sensed the little thing's design, recognized the art of the circuits as Gastredi, and felt exactly how much energy it contained. Then she tilted it, nudged it with whatever this new talent inside of her must be, and amplified its range.

Swelling, bigger. Outward. More.

She rested her head on the back of the chair, a flap of torn fabric tickling her cheek.

She looked—like looking with eyes, but eyes had to focus in one direction, and her mind didn't have to choose. She looked out and she saw energy all around her, shining bright: the limping electronics in this poor little hovel, the media and the appliances above them, music traveling in packaged bundles from wire to vibrating of panels and out into air...

Had she truly never tried this before? It was like realizing she could speak a language she'd never heard before, like she'd been wearing a mask her whole life, with only edges of light peeking through from time to time before suddenly, finally, she tore it off and realized she could see this whole time.

See. Feel. Hear. Taste. Balance, up and down and everything her body could control. It touched every sense she'd known before.

(This must be her mind trying to interpret a new source of information, she thought distantly. Why it felt natural to move her hands when she thought out her power, why her mouth watered whenever she reached out.)

She needed to sleep.

She needed to figure out how this ability of hers could save them all.

Who was Tannor Mellick to decide what saving them meant?

She could absorb more information than before, she thought, based on how the neural download went. Or maybe she could always take in more information than other people. Tannor had always suspected she was more than just naturally smarter than... everyone, but what was the use of it? She didn't want to rule anyone, or destroy anyone, and she knew enough to doubt the absolute evil or absolute good of anyone.

She considered the bomb she'd stopped from blowing off Relai's head. It had been so simple, but so terrifying—just the thought of stopping. *Stop.*

No.

Tannor could do more than make things stop or go. That moment there'd been a word in her mind (no), but words were just one representation of meaning. She could do more than flip the state of a piece of data between binary states. The data she'd downloaded had been stored in heptadecimal format, and now if she wanted to she could bring up the records in her mind and see the information. She could know everything—

Tannor's eyes tore open.

She sat there, frozen.

It couldn't be true.

·

Relai was finally calm.

This tenement was filthy and cluttered with Earthan tech, books, piles of clothes, clumps of animal fur, and gods-knew-what-else—but at least it held the comfort of undeniably being someone's home. The egress window let in a little light, and under the rhythmic din of an oscillating fan she just wanted to crawl onto the rumpled bed and sleep. If Milo hadn't been laying on it, bloody and unconscious, she might've asked permission to do it.

Ky shut the door to the bedroom and turned, slow and weary and steadfast, to tend to Milo.

Relai blurted out, "You've really never used someone else's energy to heal before?"

Ky unsheathed one of his knives instead of responding.

Starting at the waist, Ky sliced up the front of Milo's plain black skin-hugging shirt, shoulders barely shifting as he moved, skimming the skin of Milo's throat as he finished. He didn't leave a scratch.

"I think he liked that shirt," Relai murmured as she rummaged through piles and found plain bits of clothing to use as cleaning rags. Ky peeled open the shirt and, arm by arm, tugged Milo carefully free.

She could see, the blood thick but not dry, where each and every bullet had entered Milo's body before Ky sealed his leaks.

Relai took a glass of water from a nightstand and soaked one of Tom Wood's shirts; the water was cold but Milo didn't react when Ky began to clean away the blood on his chest. Relai knelt and leaned forward against the bed, ready to sleep where she sat as soon as Milo woke up whole. She couldn't let this happen to him again.

"You're right," Ky said, finally. "I should have tried it before. I'm usually the one causing the injuries, and I'm not inclined to heal those. When I'm not—well. No one ever offered before."

The white cloth had turned rusty with blood and Relai lost herself in staring at it, then Milo's half-clean chest.

Ky asked her something. Relai blinked herself back to awareness and listened to the words he just put in her head.

"Don't feel like helping?"

"Oh." She frowned. She thought Ky understood. "I can't touch him. He hasn't given me permission."

Ky gave that neutral hum he liked to annoy her with, and she couldn't help but check his face for judgment or disdain. Pity? They were both so tired, she couldn't muster the energy to feel offended. The rules were straightforward and it wasn't personal. It wasn't anything.

Milo was cleaner now, free of his own blood, laid bare. She'd never let herself look, just really look at him, but it was finally calm and she was so tired...

Milo didn't remove his hair. She's never seen such a thickness of it on a man's face before, nor on a head. Relai had her own long hair, but she couldn't grow a beard; they were *different*. Fascinating. It wasn't just the beard, either; the skin with hair continued down his neck, only thinned a bit in a band around his shoulders and the hollow below his larynx, and then returned across his whole chest and stomach. It wasn't as thick there as the hair on his face, but it grew denser again in a trail below his belly button that disappeared past the thick canvas of his pants, so different from her own stomach.

Relai needed to focus on something else.

Feet. Once again, Milo's feet hung off the end of the bed; Ky pulled his boots off and set them aside.

Milo's height was the sort of thing that people wrote songs about—the giant, the warrior, the kshatriya poised above his vanguard. She could see that his muscles had formed through physical work, not sport or luxury training. He must have worked in the mines.

He was young, but she could imagine people pledging themselves to him.

She could imagine him leading an army against her.

Then she saw marks on Milo's side which hadn't disappeared with the cleaning. Most of his wounds had healed under their hands, but one point remained open and raw and red. Ky had passed out before Milo was perfect again.

Relai put out a finger, aware that Ky was watching.

"You didn't finish."

He came around to her side of the bed to see. She breathed in copper and sweat as Ky nodded, then he leaned against her to fit his index finger along the edge of the wound. Relai watched it all with her nose nearly touching Ky's hand—she saw no strange colors, no bursts of light, nothing. The skin stretched and pushed up old torn layers and finished with new, healthy, unmarked ones. Curls of dead skin built up and flaked away as Ky's fingers went pale, Milo gasped in a breath as he slept, and that was that.

Ky withdrew his hand and looked down at her.

"You're incredible," she whispered.

His head dipped, eyes shadowed. "I'm hungry again," he said.

Relai swallowed.

She stood and Ky shifted back to give her room, but only just. She wanted to steady herself with a hand on the bed but it sat too low.

"You can always touch me, you know," he said quietly.

Ky stood four inches taller and he was slouching here, almost touching her from arm to hip to knee, his head tilting so his whole body turned into a well, waiting, and Relai whispered, "Oh," and let herself drop forward. Her forehead rested in the space he made for her along his collar bone. She closed her eyes.

•

Ky's instinct hadn't failed. She was desperate.

He realized he could hook her if he wanted to, here, at this stopping point. Ky used every resource at his disposal without hesitation, and his body was a resource in more ways than one. No one ever said no, given enough time and the right kind of smile; he hadn't considered it for Relai… but this could be the way to free Milo's people.

He could get her alone sometime soon, distract the others, smile. Give her the scraps of attention she craved. People were more pliant when he was fulfilling a need, Ky knew. People turned weak. Emotional. Stupid.

His chest clenched and a rushing sound swarmed inside his head. He kept still and realized that this—this sick feeling was coming up from his stomach.

He didn't *want* to do it.

It wouldn't be—what? Nothing was right, so it wasn't an issue of right and wrong. Milo would stop him, maybe fight him if he followed through with this chance. Further, or maybe separate from Milo, Ky realized he didn't want to do it.

As he stood there doing nothing, Relai's body settled more and more slack against his. She was falling asleep.

He wasn't going to do it. He wasn't going to bide his time and leave himself open until she softened enough to ask him to slip his hands under her clothes. He was letting her do this, fall asleep, by doing nothing... but he would need to raise his arms and hold her soon or she'd fall.

Ky thought to himself, *shit.*

Thank every deity that every planet had ever bothered to worship, Milo chose that moment to wake up and grumble,

"Should I leave you two alone?"

•

iii.

Milo shifted up onto his elbows, groggy and stiff through his torso like things hadn't ended well on that rooftop. Relai pushed away from Ky and said, "No," in a voice too loud for the confines of this tiny room.

Healing always left Milo warm inside, sensitized without a trace of pain. He sometimes wondered if Ky fiddled with his emotions while erasing his wounds, because afterward he always felt calm. Relaxed.

Peaceful.

Maybe that's why all he did was glare at Ky after Relai gave him a startled, bleary glance and then fled the room. Ky glared right back.

From the angle of Ky's shoulders Milo knew that there was no need to search for a weapon, no pressure to check the exits or parse out enemies. The room was square and dark and personal in ways the hotel hadn't been: pictures of people and animals on the walls, crumpled metal cans under a desk. Someone's home.

Milo swung himself to his feet, letting out a groan at the deep gratification of new stretching sinew. The floor under his feet consisted of dull, lifeless stubs of cloth, and as he dug his toes into it he felt crunching. "All alive? Those bullets fucking hurt."

"All but the bounty hunter. Goren killed her. Saved us."

Goren? That must have been his first kill. Milo's surprise turned weary as he thought about how Goren might react. Milo didn't want to deal with a kid cracking apart.

He stood, pressed his palms into the ceiling, groaning more, and then started searching through drawers. He found a small thing—metallic mechanism with one prominent gear, tubing, and a tiny tank of liquid—and threw it to Ky.

Ky held the thing up and demonstrated how to make a flame. Milo huffed. "This planet is so strange. Where are we?"

"You have no idea," Ky said, throwing the fire-light back to Milo. He put it in his pocket. "Remember the guy you caught taking photos of us in that diner?"

"No."

"Well, he's an ex-terr groupie and we're crashing with him. Princess made the call while we were both unconscious. I know, I know—don't worry, the guy seems fine. Next exit window from the black market dock is fifteen hours from now. Tannor's layering security perimeters, my transmission blocker is working fine, and everyone's safe."

"Did we recover the—"

"Jumper's shielded and parked three doors down in the back lot of an empty house."

"Fuel?"

"Enough."

Milo nodded. Ky picked up a shredded black rag and tossed it in his face; it was Milo's black Gastredi shirt, he realized.

He counted the bullet holes as he straightened the material and rubbed the torn edges between his fingers until they melded together again; four this time, and then he started on the long, clean slit up the front. Milo glanced up to catch sight of Ky's bare back as he changed his shirt and noticed how much muscle and fat the man had lost just over the past few days. They were sucking him dry.

"So Tannor's like you, then?" Milo remembered. Ky barely hid a smile as Milo pulled on his mended shirt. "I know I killed that hunter in the stairwell. And how am *I* alive? You were spent."

"It worked out," Ky replied in his lying voice.

"What did you do?"

"You were going to die."

Milo was always going to die, and he told Ky exactly that with the look on his face.

"I'm not just gonna let it happen," Ky replied. "We didn't have time for anything else and she offered. Turns out, I can use other people to heal."

Milo blinked, shook his head at the nonsense inherent in that sentence. But then he realized—

"It hurts you when you heal someone. Did you take something—*did you hurt her to heal me?*"

Ky shrugged. "She might have felt a twinge of something, but the point is you got better. And One and Two jumped in and helped with her broken shoulder, so everyone is fine. Just tired."

The impossibility of it all did nothing to stop Milo's belief, or the rush of anger. "I promised not to hurt her again."

"Too bad!" Ky exclaimed. "You're in this together now, you can't get out of it. You want to give up and bow to her?"

Milo glanced at the door, wondering how thick it was. It looked thin as cloth. He lowered his voice. "I don't want to take anything from her and I don't want to be in her debt."

"You covered each other's *lives*. Doesn't mean you're in her debt. This is something else." Ky pushed forward, aggressive, forcing Milo to look at him. "She didn't just touch you, buddy, she's in you. You took her *health*, her *energy*, and now she's living inside you, *beating your heart*—"

Milo balled his hands into fists, turned his back on Ky, and went to find Relai.

○○●○○

"…A sacrifice."

Ososi had been drifting back to sleep despite her resolve to listen to every conversation that occurred among these rebels, but the tone in Fass's voice jerked her mind into stark alertness. He'd been speaking with his favorite, Reddig, when his tone turned quiet and unusually serious.

"We had to begin the revolution too early," Fass was whispering. "We need to be able to show the people an appropriate truth, even if the situation requires a different set of circumstances for her removal. Do you understand?"

"A hanging," Reddig suggested. "It will remind people of the victory of human liberation, and we can obscure her face with her hair. The dynamic rendering won't work if you want to do it live, but no one is going to believe it anyway until you can show Mora's pin."

"We'll get her pin."

"I know, I know," Reddig assured. "I have no doubt. But in the interim, we may want to—"

"We won't do it live, you lack-wit. We'll use Earthan tech to obscure the exact time and place and adjust later to match the circumstances of Mora's death."

"At Daat, then?"

"Yes. Find a bare area that could be anywhere and we'll do it after we gain control of the place."

Ososi opened her eyes.

Dynamic rendering would allow a person in a video relay to appear to be someone else.

Like, for example, a young woman with the same long black hair and pale brown skin and slender form as Mora Aydor... the only woman Fass had brought with him. Lilya. Asleep with the others in the rear compartment.

Fass was keeping her around only to kill her for his victory narrative.

Ososi froze mid-rise. Did Lilya know? Was she willing? If Ososi told her Fass's plan, would she laugh, or shrug, or retaliate against Ososi's betrayal?

Would Lilya smile as she died?

The Earthan jumper hummed in peaceful silence as they descended on Daat Base.

oo●oo

"I have a job to do," Tom told a package of bagels at the Wedge Co-Op. "Aliens have descended and chosen me as their Earth Friend. They have requested food. My role..." he wandered on to the next aisle, "my role is caretaker. I am the innkeeper of heavenly travelers."

(What were they thinking? Tom wasn't capable of caring for people! They were probably going to kill him before they left. Or what if they were dead already? What if someone was waiting to kill him, too, when he got back? What if the government was already *in. His. House?*)

Against his sense of self-preservation, Tom pulled out his latest phone to call Hope.

She answered after five rings.

"What."

"What you too, Hope! And a happy new year! I mean. What are... the haps. What's up? Wuzzuuuuu—"

"No, absolutely not. Are you on drugs, Tom?"

"How dare you! I get high on *life*. And pot, but not right now. How about you?"

"I'm in downtown Minneapolis right now, so if you've seen the news you probably know what I'm working on."

"Good, good. Agent Valdez, on the case. Excellent. I knew you had it in you."

Hope paused. "Wait. What do you mean? Do you know something about this?"

"NO! I am Jon Snow-ing over here, I know nothing." Tom chewed off a hangnail and made himself bleed. "Just wondering if you had any updates on... anything. How was MMN?"

This time the line was silent long enough for Tom to think maybe this was a bad idea. If Hope was already on the case, she might realize he was involved. She was too smart. He never should have called her.

Finally Hope said, "Tom, how likely are you to die in the next twenty-four hours?"

"Oh, maybe a seven," he said without thinking.

Hope made a frustrated noise. "Look... I'll call you later, okay?"

Tom frowned. "Okay. Make good choices."

"...You, too."

They both hung up.

The wheel on his cart squeaked, and Tom jumped.

Hope would've told him if she knew that government forces were convening on his house that very second, right? She was a good, nice government friend. She was not The Man.

(What if Hope had turned into The Man?)

"Stop freaking out, Me," Tom snapped. "You have a job to do, and you're gonna do it! Now, shop."

He snatched a box of wheat cereal off a shelf and peered at the ingredients with an air of incisive critique.

Maybe he should avoid allergens? Peanuts, tree nuts... his cousin was allergic to strawberries; no strawberries?

Nah, these people were *aliens*. They could be allergic to anything! For all Tom knew, they might be allergic to all sorts of normal stuff: cinnamon... lettuce...

"Water," he said aloud, and then he laughed long and hard enough that someone came and asked him to leave.

Luckily, Tom knew one of the cashiers, Bekki, because she used to serve at Bryant Lake Bowl where Tom sometimes performed unsanctioned spoken-word poetry about the evils of late capitalism, and she let him check out.

The key to a good lie was in the details.

"*These* groceries are for my friend who is visiting from Wisconsin, but she fell down my stairs and sprained her ankle so she's stuck at my place. *These*," he made a chopping motion at the end of the groceries to divide out a jar of peanut butter and a bag of tortilla chips, "are mine."

Bekki stared as he unloaded the wads of probably-stolen cash to pluck out enough to cover the alien groceries, then he took out his wallet to pay for his own food with his own legitimate money.

He passed her a crumpled handful of bills and coins. She eyed him in judgment. "No salsa?"

"Community garden, whaaaat," Tom retorted. She nodded approvingly.

"Hey," she said as he bundled the last of the groceries into shameful paper sacks, "did you hear someone jumped off the IDS Tower? Crashed right through the glass ceiling of the Crystal Shopping Court and landed in a tree."

"Holy crap," Tom said. "Splat. Guess I've been too busy to check Twitter."

Bekki rolled her eyes.

ºº●ºº

iv.

To be honest, Goren's hands were shaking. Tannor had fallen asleep curled up in the giant comfy chair with a tablet in her hand, and he didn't want to admit it, but he couldn't quite find the energy to stand up and wash the blood off of his hands.

It wasn't even the bounty hunter's blood; it was Milo's. The kill had been clean. He could fall asleep right here, he was sure, as soon as his body decided to stop vibrating.

He kept replaying the moment over and over again in his head, scrutinizing his memories to more and more granular levels to try and recall every detail that, in the moment, had passed in a blur. The blood smears on that last stretch of stairwell. How he'd feared the worst. How, when he'd pushed through the rooftop door and taken in the scene, his training held and he did the right thing.

He wasn't sorry.

Still, the shaking hands.

Relai hurried out of the bedroom, bleary and wide-eyed with a blush on her cheeks. She looked so lovely, it was almost like she was shining.

"Are you hungry? I'm hungry. I'll get us something," she said.

Goren should have jumped up, he knew, but before he processed that thought she was already back and sitting next to him, perched on the rim of the couch. She handed him a few slices of bread.

"I brought you water, too—oh—"

He hesitated when he realized his hands were still all dirty. He didn't want to touch his food like this. He didn't want to touch it at all in front of her.

"Here." Relai twisted onto her knees in front of him as she reached for a cloth strewn on the end table. She tipped some of the water into the cloth and grabbed his hand.

"Thank you for today," she said. He stared in dumbfounded shock. Her fingers were touching his, the cloth brushing rough and sure over his skin. "We were lost, and you came."

She wouldn't meet his eyes. He tried to pull his hand away but she held tight.

"No," she said. "Let me do this. Please?"

"Everything is for you," he croaked.

She kept her gaze down, working out the grime from around his fingernails. "I know. I don't—I don't want it to be, but I don't think I can stop you."

She smiled and he could see her bitterness. It made him angry.

"Why are you like this?" he blurted out.

Now she looked him in the eye, startled. "Like what?"

"You're not... regal, or refined. You shouldn't be kneeling at my feet. I'm nothing. You should be wise but you doubt everything you do and you change your mind all the time and—and—you *ran away*."

His voice was too loud, he was waking Tannor up, letting his emotions take over, but he couldn't seem to help it. Relai sat back on her heels, eyes wide.

"I just needed to be alone, I was coming back—"

"No, you *ran away*."

He wasn't talking about that morning.

"You were our *Glory*, our *Hope*, and you left us. I just want to serve you and you won't let me and now I killed someone and I—I—" his voice cracked. He was going to regret this later.

"Goren..." Tannor began, pain in her voice.

He clenched his fists. "I don't regret it. I don't. But why did you leave? Why did you leave us?"

Relai struggled to her feet, the wet cloth still tight in her hand. "Because this is all I have to give and *it wasn't enough*. It wasn't the right thing—it wasn't what Arden needed. I was never enough. I failed, Goren. *I am a failure*. And I would have stayed, I really would have, even knowing I'd probably drive the planet to ruin, but I couldn't, not after—I had to—"

Goren leaned forward, elbows on his thighs and clean hands dropped loose between his knees, but Relai wasn't seeing them anymore. She backed into a bookcase and jolted at the impact.

From behind him, Goren heard Milo ask, "What happened?"

Dirty brown water dripped from the cloth in her hand onto the floor.

·

Relai leaned forward to clench against the pain in her gut.

She didn't want to think about it, but they wanted to know.

And didn't she want to tell them?

She was ashamed.

She wanted to scream it and she wanted to run *(you ran away)* and she wanted to sleep. Outside the house, a sudden heavy rain began to drum a patternless beat.

She didn't know how to do this right—how to tell something so stupid, so shameful. How to do it without sounding pathetic.

Oh. Oh, just—

In her head Relai lifted a shovel and struck into the ground. She'd buried this one a long time ago, suffocated it and silenced it and walked as far away as she could. Left it to rot.

Now, she told herself, *it's not me digging it up. I'm Relai and I'll tell them about Orist.*

I'll tell them what she's truly worth.

•

Goren watched the dirty water drip until Relai opened her mouth and spoke.

"You want to know." She was talking to all of them, but it sounded like she was reassuring herself. Milo came and stood at the couch next to Goren but they didn't look at each other. "You asked. Okay." Goren noticed she'd gone very pale.

"I left when I was seventeen. You all know that. I don't know what story they came up with to explain why I left."

Goren opened his mouth but she waved him quiet.

"I don't care. I didn't want to leave but I couldn't stay after what happened."

She swallowed.

"You know I refused Nikotus Yansa of Titus. You know I had that right. My father didn't own me so he couldn't sell me or trade me. Arden doesn't do that."

Children weren't considered property or assets on Arden, but the king would have had huge influence on her marriage prospects... Maybe her father had tried to marry her off to a prince of Titus to convince her to leave Arden? But why wouldn't King Ayadas want her around?

She went on:

"Then, when I was seventeen, the Gastredi Minister of Trade was visiting. On Gastred they don't have staff, they have bond-servants. Masters expect—" The words caught in her throat and she swallowed. "The minister was going to leverage their mining production against the—it—no, it doesn't matter. The king told me he'd bargained me to the Minister. I was to entertain the man during his stay. Arden needed it for the negotiations. If the Minister was satisfied, if I submitted *just right*, everything would be fixed. He said I might need to cover my face for it."

Goren didn't want to believe it. She said it like she was quoting him, like these were real words a father said to a daughter.

Then she went on:

"He told me all this after he sent the Minister of Trade into my room. *After.*"

Her voice cracked on the last word and Goren's vision fogged white. He was so furious he felt dizzy.

"I fought," Relai said. "Don't think I didn't. And I left because... because I couldn't do it. I had nothing of value to offer my father and I won't offer myself like that, I can't. I left, and all I have is what I can do to help and that's *nothing* and—"

She looked at Goren once, then turned away abruptly, muttering, "I'm sorry—sorry—"

Goren and Tannor followed her into the kitchen, the others close behind.

They found Relai tearing through the place, dragging out drawers and whole stacks of dishes and shattering them against the edges of the counters and the wall.

"Do you know what he said when I told him I was leaving?" She gripped a cupboard door with her fingernails and looked right at Milo. "He said, '*Finally.*'"

She threw a glass and shattered it and tried for another, but then Milo reached out and she shrieked, "Don't touch me!"

Goren would've shoved between them, but Milo backed away immediately, shifting his bare feet around shards of glass, and then crouched with his back against a cupboard door. Goren looked to Tannor—her distraught expression, tears welling in her eyes—then to Ky—

indecipherable—and finally back to the Their Glory, the High Queen, the most powerful figure the galaxy, falling to pieces in front of them.

Goren didn't know what to do.

•

Ky remembered now what it felt like to really *want* to kill someone. Not just for practical reasons, but for hate.

"Here's a theory," he said. "Your dad was a lack-wit coward who couldn't let his daughter be smarter than him. He never wanted you to succeed."

"But *why?*" she demanded.

Milo hummed. "He could've just killed her."

"Ayadas never made the decisive move, remember?" Tannor said.

"You—"

"Shut up, Goren. He's dead, and he was shipshit when he was alive. You know it's true."

"You can't question Our Glory!" Goren insisted.

"You were just shouting at her!" Tannor exclaimed.

Relai wiped snot off of her face. Her hair was rumpled, her face swollen from crying, and she looked terrible. "*Why?* Why did he hate me so much?" and everyone shut up for a moment.

Ky stared at her.

He cleared his throat.

"It wasn't about you," Ky said. "He needed to drive you from the throne."

Milo leaned forward. "What do you know?"

Ky was beginning to see the pieces fall into place. He thought he could pick out the Lover, maybe even the Prophet. The Guide was probably Xiong; they'd just have to win him over. He could guess at the Warrior, and of course he knew the King. One would be the Sacrifice.

"Because," Ky said, "he thought you were part of a prophecy. And he was right."

•

Milo glared at Ky and rose out of his crouch. His feet tested and settled delicately into spaces clear of broken glass.

"Prophecy?" he repeated. He'd gotten over the whole healing ability thing once they established that Ky was willing to save Milo's life on a near-daily basis. Ky had gone out of his way to assure Milo that this wasn't some mystical spiritual thing, which Milo hadn't had the clarity of mind to even consider at the time; his religion held spiritual healers in highest regard, but they were a long way from Elik and Ky was no holy man. Ky had said his ability came from a drug they gave his mother while she was pregnant with him, and that was it.

Milo didn't want to think about it more deeply than that.

"You never mentioned anything about prophecies," he said.

"Well, it's also a children's song. Does that make you feel better?"

"Worse, thanks."

"You'll have to forgive our predecessors for their storytelling flair," Ky said, "but they knew what they were doing. Think of it this way: they experienced rational visions of probable future events, compared what they saw, and then shrouded their conclusions in poetry and mysticism. Call it space-time probability interpretation and no one cares. Call it a prophecy? They'll never forget."

"That is... ridiculous," Tannor said as she stepped up and wrapped an arm around Relai. The touch prohibition didn't extend to her, Milo realized, because Relai sank against her without a complaint. "Wait—look." Tannor pointed and they saw blood smearing everywhere Relai stepped. She lifted her foot and they all saw a deep seeping wound in the arch.

"I'll get a—" Goren scrambled off.

Relai glared at Ky and said, "Don't you dare come near me."

"Relax, Princess," he replied. "I don't heal scratches."

Tannor helped Relai hobble across the floor and then she hefted herself up on the counter to rest her foot in the sink. "Sorry," she mumbled. She seemed tired, still, but calmer now.

Goren reappeared, thrusting a clean shirt over the field of broken glass. "Will this work?"

Milo grabbed it and tugged the material between his fingers. "Yeah." He began tearing it into strips as he glanced at Tannor. "Clean it first."

Relai let Tannor run water over her foot and inspect it for glass, then she took the cloth strips and wrapped up her foot.

"Not too tight," Milo said. "And cinch the knot right over the wound." She met his eyes and nodded. When she swung her foot down he used his words again, because he couldn't touch her. "Don't put your weight on it. Let Tannor help you."

"Listen to Milo," Goren added. "…I can't believe I said that."

"Into the central room," Milo decided. "She needs to elevate it above her heart to slow the bleeding."

If they were going to start talking ridiculous old prophecies and visions, they were going to be sitting down face to face.

"All right. Tell us your story," Milo said to Ky when they'd all settled.

"Just don't fall asleep," Ky replied. "Who knows the one that starts with the Lover and the Prophet?"

"Do you mean, 'The Prophet and Guide, the Prophet and Guide, will there be love, or will they hide?'" Tannor chanted.

"No, that's another one. That one is a problem we're not going to worry about."

Tannor glanced nervously at Relai.

Goren said, "You mean: 'Poor Lover yearns, Prophet is wise—'"

Milo was surprised to find himself singing the proper response: "Poor and wise, poor and wise…"

Goren sang on, nodding at Milo in excitement.

"Mad rebel rules, Sacrifice dies!"

"Mad and dies, mad and dies."

"Guide teaches, Warrior cries!"

"Teaches and cries, teaches and cries."

"The King will divide and unify!"

"Unify, unify."

"That's the one," Ky grinned.

"I have little sisters," Goren explained.

Milo nodded. "I had one, too." He felt an ugly satisfaction in the way Goren lowered his eyes.

"Good job," Ky went on. "They were just trying to get the people to remember the basic verse when they started that."

"*They?*" Relai asked.

"The Keepers of the Words. They were the—historians? Futurists? Keepers. It probably took a lot of them to spread that rhyme around." Everyone stared at Ky blankly. Milo only vaguely remembered something about keepers from one of Ky's stories. "They've maintained the history, prophecies, and predictions of the Vada Coalition for thousands of years."

"But the Coalition only started four hundred years ago, and we only added Oeyla forty years ago," Relai argued.

Ky smiled. "Prophecies involve seeing the future. It's not magic, it's just—shusasevati on the four planets saw this unification before it happened."

"Shusa?!" Goren exclaimed. "We can't listen to monsters! What is wrong with you?"

"You should shut up about things you know nothing about," Ky replied evenly. "Some shusa could see probable futures, and some of those were decent poets. They've been keeping their currents of history, and as each planet is added, the records are combined. They check for partnered prophecies and line everything up. They saw this coming. They saw you, Relai."

She stared at him, her fear showing bare on her face.

"Just tell us the damn prophecy," Milo exclaimed. "Stop dragging it out!"

"Okay, okay," Ky laughed. "It's not 'rebel' in the original prophecy. The words are more formal:

> The Lover will risk, Prophet to hope
> The Prophet will seal, Defiant to claim
> The Defiant will crawl, Sacrifice to shield
> The Sacrifice will fall, the Warrior to mourn
> The Warrior will learn, Guide to teach
> The Guide will call, the King to hear
> The King will divide and unify."

"Oooh," Goren gasped, scrambling for paper and something to write with.

"Why do you think that's about me?" Relai asked.

"Because that verse was spoken the night you were born," Ky said.

"*Oooh!*"

"It was spoken by a keeper on Oeyla. It matched up with two other prophecies, one from Gastred and one from Arden. As far as I know, they haven't found anything from Titus."

"*And?*" Relai demanded.

Ky scratched his chin. "And what?"

"The other verses?" Milo reminded him.

"Right! Hmm," Ky tapped his fingers along his stubbled jaw.

> "She is the End
> She, the Defiant
> The last of the Aydor crown
> She is the End.

That's from Arden, from about a year before you were born. Actually, nine months. See? It makes sense! And this is from Gastred, at least two hundred years ago:

> From disgrace she will rise
> Against her own rotten blood
> With a Lover, a Warrior, a Guide,
> With a Sacrifice, a Prophet, and a King
> Against her own rotten blood.
> She is the End."

Relai transitioned through shocked and sharp faces while Goren scribbled. "I'm the Defiant?"

Ky nodded. "Last of the Aydor crown."

"So I *do* fail." She sighed. "No wonder my father hated me from birth. He didn't want me to be our family's downfall."

Goren cut in before Milo could argue. "Actually, if you think about it, you're not ruling now, so you already *were* the end of the Aydor crown. I mean, the legitimate one. So it's okay, it wasn't your fault! Now we can go fix it."

Tannor looked doubtful. "It's so vague. How can we trust that they understood what they were seeing correctly? What if they just made up lies to manipulate the future?"

"The role was sacred, Tannor," Ky said softly. He sounded disturbingly sincere.

Milo wanted to ignore every word… but the greatest nonsense could still become self-fulfilling, and these rhymes had wormed their way into heads across the galaxy. They were important whether or not they were true.

They also meant…

Well.

They implied that the Aydor monarchy would end.

He glanced sideways at Ky. "She has already gone against her own rotten blood. Sounds like it's already coming true."

"So who's the King, then?" Relai said.

"Your guess is as good as mine," Ky said.

"Does this mean I need to go find these people," Relai wondered, "or will they just do their prophesying and sacrificing all on their own?"

"Hell if I know," Ky replied. "I say we just keep going."

Milo almost missed it: an evasive twitch, an avoidance of eye contact, then a perfect mask came over Ky's face.

Liar, liar.

Ky clearly already knew who some of these people were. Milo doubted that the two of them were involved in the mystery and revelation of it, but if there was a chance of changing things, making a real difference, he'd be whatever stupid archetype the poem needed him to be.

"We keep going," Relai repeated. "But if we're really safe right now, first we need to sleep."

oo●oo

v.

An hour later, soaking wet from rain, Tom burst back into his apartment (refusing to carry any of the mountain of food down the stairs) to find three aliens asleep on his couch together. Boss Girl had her head in Blondie's lap and her feet across Fidgety Boy, who sat slumped in the opposite corner. It took Tom another minute to notice the Alien Formerly Known as Bloody, now wearing a blood-free black shirt, asleep on the floor in front of the couch.

Except he wasn't sleeping at all by the looks of those peeking eyes—Tom yelped, "I live here!" and the eyes closed.

Tom inched away and turned around. His kitchen was completely destroyed.

What.

The.

Hell?

"This stuff cost like twenty-five bucks at Goodwill, you deadbeat planet-surfers!" he exclaimed. None of them moved a bit. "That's a lot of Earth money!"

Why did Tom think that alien kids would be less annoying than Earthling kids? Or less expensive? At least they hadn't abducted him or tried to suck out his brain, but *still*. They could at least clean up after themselves.

This was going to require a conversation.

Tom went and got the separate bag of food for himself and popped open the jar of peanut butter. He was shoving a spoonful in his mouth, wondering if these aliens needed any space nutrients that Earth couldn't provide, as he walked into his bedroom and found alien number five: Seymour.

Shirtless and sharpening a bunch of big-ass knives.

"I would've put him in the tub, personally," Seymour said without looking up. Tom had to take his eyes off the one two three *four FIVE* **SIX** scary blades in ascending length laid out across his floor in order to look around and realize his bed sheets were stripped and lying in a clump in the corner. On top of those sat a pile of wet red-brown cloths. Smears of blood covered his bare mattress, too.

"Gross," Tom groaned. "Is this how it's going to be?"

"Don't worry," Seymour said, "I'm gonna pay you."

Tom couldn't help but perk up, even though that sounded like something you'd hear right before you got stabbed in the kidney. "Seriously?"

Seymour nodded. "I don't see any reason not to tell you every single thing you want to know."

"Everything?"

Seymour looked up with a tiny smile. "Everything." Tom clutched at his heart. Yep... took a second or two, but the thing was still ticking. "You just have to promise on your honor as a man of Earth that you won't tell anyone anything about us until we leave. That's all we ask."

"Pfft, a 'man of Earth,' okay," Tom snickered. "But will you help me flip the mattress first? This is frickin' unsanitary."

oo●oo

Hope slammed her palm flat on the desk. "BULLSHIT! There were seven bodies here two hours ago when I talked to Dr. Darcia Rowan."

"Dr. Rowan is home sick today," the receptionist replied frostily through a speaker in the two-inch glass separating them. "She hasn't been in at all."

Hope's entire being filled with incandescent rage, and she had to do a set of breathing exercises before responding.

"Phone records," she hissed, slamming her finger through a pathway of icons on her phone. "Look—you can see the call she made from here in my phone's..." Hope stuttered to a halt.

Her call log showed no trace of the conversation with Darcia. There was no trace of when she'd called to arrange the pick-up of the bodies, either.

They were erasing every trace of evidence, damn it.

Hope snarled. There was no chance the security tapes showed anything, either, then.

She'd lost them.

Darcia.

Hope tapped the woman's personal cell number in a frenzy and waited, pacing across the aseptic waiting room, through six painful rings.

Finally, she heard Darcia's voice.

"Hi, this is Darcia! Sorry I missed you! Send me a text because I don't check my voicemail, thanks!"

Hope had a bad feeling about this.

Car accident, kidnapping, hospital, bobbing down the Mississippi River wrapped in black plastic trashbags… Hope needed to get to her house and see if this was just a terrible misunderstanding, or if Darcia was really missing.

The man and woman in the hospital after the terrorist attack were California residents, not aliens, and she'd have to wait to interrogate them whenever they woke up. The body of the woman who fell off the roof of the IDS should be arriving here at the Hennepin County morgue whenever they finally got it out of the Crystal Courtyard tree. That body couldn't possibly just disappear—it was being covered on every news station. What could the aliens do?

She'd be there for the autopsy this time… or would she? Were they going to disappear Hope like they might've just done to Darcia? Hope fought down the urge to call her husband, John, just to hear his voice. She couldn't disappear on him. His guacamole was so bland without her input.

She could call him in the car on the way to… what?

Proof. She needed proof.

Everything kept getting deleted, but now she knew about the jumper's body in advance… Hope spun back to the receptionist. "You're going to assist Homeland Security by recording a live back-up of your security feeds on my laptop. My *special* laptop."

The receptionist lifted her telephone handset in resignation. "I'll call the chief medical examiner."

"You do that. Now."

Hope hurried back to her car to grab the laptop. It had been a gift from Tom, covered ("shielded," he insisted) in copper, with an operating system that hadn't been updated in twelve years. It was slow as shit, but somehow the destruction codes couldn't get into it.

Someone had been here. Her colleagues were inadvertently covering up everything downtown thanks to their own ignorance. What about the seizure victims? Three had gone to HCMC, two had opted for Abbott Northwestern, one went to their primary care for outpatient evaluation, and the last one refused to cooperate entirely. All eight of them had experienced a thirty-second seizure right in the middle of the incident. Any one of them might have seen something essential.

They were her next best leads.

First, surveillance on her laptop. Then, she'd track down every seizure victim.

No—laptop, then *visit Darcia to make sure she was alive*, then find the seizure victims, then hopefully she could observe the autopsy of the person who landed in the Crystal Courtyard tree.

And whatever happened, she wasn't letting Tom Wood go anywhere near any of this. Online he'd be fine, but in real life that idiot was a corpse waiting to happen.

oo●oo

Captain Ednar Fass screamed in rage and whirled up from the body of his friend, Voresh Renganiban. The soldier closest to him took a fist to the face and flew backward into the dust of the empty Tijuana sidewalk as Fass breathed through his mouth to avoid the smells of oil and metal and death.

Muffled music and faint clanking continued uninterrupted from the car repair shop across the street, while a group of young women laughed as they crossed from one distant corner to another. Fass glared in every direction; if the locals weren't too busy drinking and drugging themselves to death they were welcome to come confront his outburst, but no one approached.

While Fass might have found a quaint sort of amusement in this city's color and music and impoverished children, all he saw now was a dirty shithole that had killed his friend.

This did not fit into Fass's plan. This stupid, slobbering nothing of a planet, with its twitching, mewling sacks of flesh excused for conscious beings who would slash a man on the street for a few of their worthless coins—a good, decent, civilized man with nothing but help for this pathetic place! And now he was dead.

Voresh would have been a great king. He would have cleaned up this planet. He would have cleaned it, taught it, and led it into the galactic commons. He would have given it a proper name.

"We're going to melt this city into nothing," Fass seethed to no one and everyone, "the ash from its burning will fill this planet's sky as a warning to every other barbaric nation—"

"Sir?" Reddig interrupted from where he knelt behind a dumpster in the cloud of flies over Voresh's body.

"What?"

"There's a puncture behind his ear with a circle of claw marks... it's from a memory probe. The newest ones only have five claws, but this one has six, which means it's an old model. Probably black market, sir. He wasn't killed by Earthans."

Fass stopped, feeling his own sweat trickle down his spine. He clenched his fists tightly at his sides.

It was a contract. Someone paid to have Voresh Renganiban killed, and on Earth only one contractor offered the service of memory extraction.

Runn.

Fass's thoughts flew forward. He wouldn't have to pay the bounty hunter for finding the queen... if he killed the bounty hunter when she delivered the goods.

Of course, that had always been true.

The soldier he'd punched started to rouse. "Somebody heal him," Fass spat, turning to storm back to the jumper.

○○●○○

Naked. Cold.

Pain, tendon from bone, under her skin like fire if fire healed instead of charred. A scream as ground for thought.

Must've been a bad one.

Runn waited as long as she could. Healing took enough, had to focus on slowing her breathing. Ears whole. She listened.

Alone in the room. Cold, good. Would help with the burn of flesh reforming.

She didn't remember at first. Face destroyed, holes in chest, broken back and legs and neck. The shot to her thigh would have been enough to kill her from blood loss. Guy knew what he was doing.

Guy's gonna die.

She concentrated on breathing and moving carpals and tarsals to stand and move. Someone entered the room humming. She went still. Waited.

Runn's eye pulled back together enough. Cruor sealed her eyelids so she peeled them open, saw through slits. Didn't see much—a plastic sheet covered her body. Dark.

The fall didn't crack the med scanner embedded in her back or the nodes laced along her spinal cord. The doc did his job when he put it in. Scanner must be nearly out of alumeta now, healing all this at once. She'd have to find the doc first, before she went after the queen and her dogs again.

All gonna die.

Runn knew how to be silent through pain, but this was a morgue and she couldn't wait. They hadn't started processing her yet.

Yet.

The scanner implant had focused on her vital organs first, then got around to healing limbs later. Felt like there might still be a bone sticking out of her right calf; she'd have to reset it to get it to heal right.

Runn sat up on the table.

Someone screamed. Ran. Door swinging with little creaks and clips of receding footfalls.

She bent forward, shrieks plucking on the tendons down the back of her legs, and pulled the fracture straight. She had to push the bone back in.

They'd taken her toys, her clothes, I.D., tequila. Her spoon. Couldn't take the metal fibers embedded in her skin, though, and those were passively linked to the Applica jumper. Couldn't be blocked. If the queen and her dogs were as stupid as they seemed they wouldn't have ditched it yet.

She watched the skin start to seal.

Gonna die. Gonna die.

Another forty seconds and the leg knit enough to stand on as a crowd of four poured into the room. Gaped. Someone said, "God."

They'd placed a tray of knives right next to her.

More screaming.

oo●oo

EPISODE VIII:

DOUBT

K Y GENERALLY SLEPT around ten minutes for every twenty hours awake. He could go for fifty-six days without any sleep at all, but he'd learned that the hard way and it wasn't something he wanted to repeat. Sometimes he'd sleep for weeks at a time. The dreams only came with longer sleep.

The old dream, the drowning one, hadn't come since he met Milo. Now his constant dream was a sort of opposite: instead of drowning, he was flying... or maybe it was leaping, except the leap took him across a vast ocean and the whole dream was a single moment of the journey. This one wasn't nice like the drowning dream, either. In this new dream, Ky *thrummed* with wrath. He felt he might burn the universe down, or eat it, or kill each person in it by tearing them apart with his bare hands.

Waking up after these ones was not a fun experience, so Ky decided not to sleep at all. Too little time, too much food to eat, anyway.

To Ky's delight, Tannor was first to stumble drowsily into the kitchen after a few hours of sleep.

·

"You're shusa," he told her in the quiet afternoon sunlight, and Tannor released a breath she didn't realize she'd been holding.

"Shusa," she repeated. "I'm shusasevati."

She knew the stories exaggerated. She understood how villains were necessary for victories to mean something. She was not afraid.

Ky cracked an egg into a bowl. Tannor had passed their host, who was talking feverishly to himself in fits and stops, on the way to the bathroom, but she wasn't awake enough to bother with him. She'd never gotten to know an Earthan before, and so far, she wasn't impressed.

She followed Ky's lead and began cracking eggs into the bowl alongside him. He'd taken out two cartons of twelve and she was sure they'd eat them all. Tannor never got to eat eggs; they were too high-quality a food for lessers to afford. The eggs from Tannor's family farm came in mottled blue-green, yellow, and fiery orange-red patterns, and nothing smaller than the size of her open hand. Tom had chosen cartons with a range of white, tan, and dark brown eggs, each of them clean and smooth and tiny. They were beautiful. Perfect.

She wondered if Tom Wood could afford eggs when he wasn't using stolen money.

"Yeah. Shusasevati," Ky smiled, shoving an egg shell into his mouth. He crunched through his next words and Tannor cringed at the awful sound. "They always told me, one drop of human blood, one drop of Sevati, and you're shusa. They call us creatures. Monsters."

Us, he said. Such joy in his eyes.

On Oeyla they'd had Sevati rulers to the bitter end, to the last days of the Tennan War, and she remembered learning in school that their victory had involved purges. A lot of people had been exiled or executed and, even now, inhuman ancestry meant a person might meet with violence or worse. Not just on Oeyla, but on every planet, humans didn't recall their oppressors fondly.

"The Sevati rejected shusa as inferior," Tannor said, "and so do humans. *And in their rage at rejection, they lashed out against all the galaxy.*" The line was from the Epic of Ristlan. Tannor loved that story.

Crack. Pour. Rows of ragged-edged cups and a bowl of yellow suns.

Ky began to whisk and didn't reply. Tannor turned away to spread butter on bread, slice after slice after slice.

She wasn't particularly worried about being less than human; at this point she definitely felt *more than.* She felt like her life was finally making sense, and everything was more dangerous now but more *right.* Ky, too. Dangerous, and right.

She watched the methodical flick of his wrist as he stirred, how he didn't stop stirring as he shook in granules of salt and pepper and then something else. He poured the eggs into a sizzling pan and then he turned and just looked back at her, studying her in return, and she should have been uncomfortable but she wasn't.

Thanks to relativity drag, if he'd done a lot of interstellar travel he might be quite a bit older (Proper Time) than his body's age. Tannor was a little less than a year younger than her twin sister, who'd never left Arden. Their war ended forty years ago, PT, but with space travel it wasn't difficult to imagine that Ky might have fought on Oeyla in the war. He might have fought for independence. Or—maybe she was wrong about everything.

Gods, *what if he fought for the Sevati?*

Her eyes widened.

He noticed her face, put down his whisk, and wrapped a gentle hand around the back of her head, fingers carding up under her curls. "The Sevati are gone," he said. "The stories are wrong. We're human. Okay?"

He seemed to think she was going through an identity crisis, but he was wrong.

Tannor gripped his wrist and nodded. Ky withdrew and turned to stir the cooking eggs, and the mark of sweat left by his palm lingered on her neck in the heat of the day.

She took a deep breath, then she told him.

"I think she might be lying to us. I think she might have been ruling after all."

Ky pushed the flat edge of the spatula through the hardening egg without looking up. "Go on."

"You don't seem surprised."

He just glanced at her dryly.

"Fine. I found something in the data in my head." Tannor had to brace herself against the enormity as remembering brought it all back. She couldn't let herself dwell there. *Process*—she was explaining the process, not the content. Implications.

"My brain moves so fast, too fast for me to stop it from going through that information and finding things and realizing things. I found something. Goren would follow her even if she's been lying to us, and Milo might not... handle it well. If I say something before I'm sure."

Ky was staring at her now with bright eyes. "Are you telling me you're... starting to fall in line with Milo?"

"No! No. It doesn't have to be a choice between Milo or Relai, anyway."

Tannor paused. Ky waited.

"...Well. We don't know what's going to happen—no, stop looking at me like that! Don't start thinking I'm going to—to do anything—"

Ky grinned in glee. "You will, though. If we're working with rot, you'll do something about it. It'll be measured and it won't be violent, but you'll do it."

"Stop! I don't know what I'm going to do, so how could you?"

He speared a fluff of egg and held it up to her mouth. "At least tell me why you're suspicious."

She glared hard at the food, then at Ky. The light in his eyes was really incredible. Damn it.

She took the bite.

"Stars, that's good... I can't. Not until I'm sure. I want—I don't know what I want. *Help.*" Tannor reached out and found a fork without breaking the intensity of her words. "The transport storage data could have been faked. I don't know if I'm good enough to call it real."

Ky watched her eat for a moment, resting close to her against the flaking plastic kitchen counter. He glanced to where the others were sleeping and then he tilted his head down.

"Her nails," he said.

"What?"

"Her fingernails and her toenails. They're perfect. Have been since the moment we met her. Why would they maintain her nails so perfectly while she was sleeping? If no one was going to see her?"

Tannor swallowed and gazed at nothing. "They might've been about to wake her up and kill her."

"She stepped on that broken glass on purpose."

"*What?*"

"I was watching her. She scanned the floor, focused on one shard, and aimed for it when she walked."

That thought—if she believed Ky, damn it—sent dismay boiling up in her stomach. Finally, Tannor said, "You really still don't trust her?"

"I'm careful."

"What if you just don't know how to trust anyone? What if I don't?"

Ky shrugged. "You could walk away. Disappear. Let the coalition sort itself out."

"No. I turned off the security system at Haadam and now dozens of people are dead. And I don't run away from my problems."

Unlike Relai. It was petty and unfair but the thought was there.

"So confront her with it."

Tannor pushed her hair out of her face and stared out of Tom's high-set window at a sliver of sky. "No. What I found is—no. If she doesn't know… I don't know what it will do to her. It's *bad*, Ky. I don't know what to do with it."

"Damn, you're starting to make me nervous."

"How do you think I feel?"

"Terrified. Alone. Overwhelmed—"

"Okay, okay. If you're so perceptive why don't you tell me what I'm going to do next?"

Ky smiled. "Figure it out."

"Figure it out?"

"Or you might ruin everything. Hard to say."

"Oh, shut up."

○○●○○

Relai woke to blaring sunlight, oppressive heat, and a terrible headache. A glass of water sat on a low table near to her head.

"Good morning, Mora Relai Aydor of the planet Arden, leader of the Vada Coalition," Tom Wood said primly as he perched on a low table in the center of the room. Relai squinted up at him as she tried to process his words; none of his joints seemed to want to bend right, and he clearly cut his own hair. "Breakfast is ready."

"Title goes after the given name," she groaned as she eased to her feet. Her pants flaked dried blood in Tom's lap as he shifted so their knees didn't knock. "What day is it?"

"We let you nap for four hours. On Arden that's exactly…" he opened a notebook with a brightly-colored cat sliding down a rainbow on the cover, "…one eighth of a day."

"Wait, how did you—"

"Ky talked for two hours straight. Also Blondie, I mean, uh… Tallie? Tanna? Tannor—Tannor hooked me up with one of these babel fish thingies," he pointed to his ear, which held a disposable comm that must've come from Ky or Milo, "so now I can understand all of you, regardless of which of the four official Vada Coalition languages you're speaking! It's pretty rad, it even does your voices and everything!"

"Yes, they're very helpful," Relai said, distracted by a waft of coffee aroma. "Do we… did you show Tannor your maps?"

"Oh, yeah! She said, um, she said Ky already knows where it is, but, and I paraphrase: 'that *(untrustworthy person)* will not stop you from reaching it with his *(profane language)*!' I'm guessing the interpreter isn't perfect. Anyway, she looked at my map data and typed a lot on her *sweet fluid metal tablet* and figured it out herself. It's in Siberia! *Cool*, huh? Heh."

Relai stared at him blankly.

"Is that not a pun in your language? Anyway, you guys are staying here until dark and then leaving. Would you like some clothing that doesn't have blood on it?"

"Uh, yes. Please."

"Here's a clean shirt and a pair of sweatpants! They'll probably fit you just fine because I am malnourished."

"Oh. Okay. …Thank you."

By the time Relai emerged from Tom's bedroom, Goren had already cleaned up yesterday's mess and was standing next to an empty chair at the table next to the kitchen with a hopeful smile on his face. She had summoned the strength to face another meal with everyone settled together like at the diner, but Ky and Tannor were already eating at the counter and Milo had only nodded at her before inexplicably disappearing outside with a small plate of food. Perhaps she'd get to eat in blessed silence.

But then Tom sat down with a big smile right next to her and started shoving food into his face.

"So!" he began, with a full mouth, "let's get right to the point: are you guys invading Earth?"

Before she could even try to form a coherent, respectful answer, Ky drifted in carrying an armful of fruit.

"Maybe," he said, *in English*. "Why?"

"How do you know English?" Relai exclaimed. Goren was right behind him with a plate piled high with something yellow and eggish, five slices of buttered toast, and a pile of thinly sliced green vegetables that smelled strongly of vinegar. He set the plate in front of her along with a pair of knives and then backed into the kitchen, grinning.

Ky smiled lazily and kicked his feet up on the table. He ignored Relai and addressed Tom instead.

"Aren't you tired of sleeping on this sad little planet?"

"Did you notice the stuff he's working on over here?" Tannor interjected on her way past the table. She'd apparently finished eating on her feet. "That black thing there is a metacurrent potentiometer with Earthan adjustments. It doesn't work, of course, but it could work. I could get it to work. Innovation isn't *illegal* here. This is Xiong's jumper all over again—do you have any idea what we could accomplish if you'd let us create new tech? *We're the ones sleeping!*"

"Wait... what? Meta-what? I got that thing 3D-printed based on—on—" Tom sputtered.

"We're not invading, don't be ridiculous," Relai said as Tom grabbed the thing and paced away, muttering to himself. "And we're not innovating, either." Their entire society revolved around Sevati technology, and that fact wouldn't change in a day. Every time anyone tried to extrapolate new tech, people died. *A lot of people* died. That's why there were laws about it.

"Okay," Ky replied, looking supremely unimpressed. "By the way, the next batch of groundships leave from Curragh in thirteen hours."

"Curragh?" Relai said.

"Curragh's the Earth dock for those of us who need to avoid the official ones," Ky said. "Other side of the planet, near the polar sea. Four hour jumper ride."

"You *knew*—"

"I figured it out. We didn't need you," Tannor called over her shoulder.

"Yeah, yeah," Tom interrupted, "So what kind of engine would this thing work with?"

Ky shot back: "Who's Gecko?"

Tom gasped deep in his throat. "STOP MONITORING ME!"

"Stop messaging people about us."

"I—didn't—"

"Yeah, you did. But don't worry; you didn't send anything important. I don't have to kill you."

Tom dove from his chair to his laptop on the kitchen bar. Ky lunged right after him and slammed it shut.

"Gentle hands, you bag of dicks!" Tom yelped. "I don't even get to check how you've been screwing me?"

"If I'd been screwing you, you'd know, *lack thereof*."

Tom folded his arms across his chest. "You're mocking me for not having a bag of dicks? I have one and that's a perfectly fine number. Quality over quantity!"

Ky smirked. "S'pose we'll see."

"About my help, or my dick?"

"Enough!" Relai yelled. "Ky, let him have his computer. Earth can't sleep much longer, so there's no point in tiptoeing around. Tom: what did you tell this person?"

Tom smugly flipped the laptop back open as Milo tromped back down the stairs and began fixing a new plate of food. "Gecko's my friend in Argentina who is probably one of you, I just didn't realize it until now. I messaged him when I was at the store to ask if aliens need menstrual products."

Relai blinked. "What?"

"Ha! Gecko said you don't, and I knew it! You're just *kind of* human, aren't you?"

Relai didn't understand, but then Tannor put down the tech and said, "Oh. No, we don't do that. We're human but we don't do that."

"Do what?" Relai asked, just as Milo settled at the table and said dryly, "You do if you don't take the implant."

Tannor answered, "Women don't have babies until it's approved, so we don't menstruate. We don't need anything for it, thank you."

Tom pursed his lips into a sour little grimace. "Who gives approval?"

Relai understood now—it was the bleeding thing, so she answered before Milo could say anything sarcastic. "The Family Ministry."

"Say *what?*" Tom gasped.

"It's not a bad thing," Relai assured him. "Nobody goes hungry and everyone has a place to live. Nobody is unwanted. It's nothing like the chaos and—and suffering here on Earth."

"Yeah, I'm sure it's a utopia," Tom muttered.

"Hey, shouldn't we all change our appearances?" Goren interrupted as he sat down to finally eat. "I can't grow a beard and we don't have anything to change our skin or reshape our bone structure... Tannor, you know how they do searches for criminals on Earth, right?"

Tannor scoffed. "I destroyed the automated recognition coding already, so now it has to be re-written. It'll be the senior security officer at Daat who's writing it, and she's an idiot. We only need to worry about Buzou."

Ky shrugged. "Haven't shown up again yet."

"Wait," Tom said suddenly. "You pause between the a's: *Da-at*. Is that a base?"

He jumped to his feet.

"It is, isn't it?!" he exclaimed. He sat right back down again and typed on his computer. "Gecko told me he tried to get a pass off-world—" he slapped the words on the screen emphatically, "but Daat's not responding."

Relai rubbed her eyes. "Of course. Olin Batar said they're dealing with a rebellion. He said it so quickly I hardly registered it."

Tannor spun toward them and reached for her tablet. Her brow furrowed as she looked into the device. "If they win, Unity'll have a whole base of weapons and ships at their disposal."

Relai blanched.

"Unity? That's what you said, *Unity*—aliens! I knew it!" Tom muttered in glee.

"I was wondering if you were going to figure any of this out," Ky said. "Somebody's busy taking over Earth, Princess. Do you care?"

"Earth needs taking over," Goren mumbled, "but not by Unity. We just have to keep this planet stable until ships from Arden can get here."

"Not when I'm not in charge yet!" Relai exclaimed. Then her eyes flew to Tannor. "But I can freeze the entire base."

Tannor sat straight up. "Yes, you can. Let's do it." She dove into her tablet.

"I don't understand," Goren said. "Why wouldn't they freeze themselves if it would help?"

"Unity must have control," Tannor concluded.

"Mora Aydor's the only one who can override everyone," Milo said. The bitterness in his voice carried clear. "She could explode every bomb, fire every weapon, turn off their water and their heat—"

"Or I could just freeze all the weapons until we gain control," Relai said in exasperation.

"You're a genius," Goren said, glaring pointedly in Milo's direction as the man went into the kitchen and began to re-fill his plate.

"Got it! I'm in," Tannor said. "Ships, weapons, doors, anything else?"

"I don't know. What else might they use to rebel?"

"Let's turn off communication, too," Tannor said. "Stalling the bad is worth inconveniencing the good. Now just put your hand here—"

"Put a time limit on it or they'll starve to death," Ky advised.

Relai signed the order to freeze Daat Base and watched the command clear. Then she steeled herself and asked:

"What about freezing Buzou, too?"

Everyone except Tom looked at her in shock.

"That would violate the coalition accords," Goren said.

"If they kill her it'll violate the accords, too," Ky said.

"The Titian team from yesterday didn't bring any fancy tech with them," Tannor reasoned. "I think their commander's maintaining their neutrality."

Relai rubbed her chest where the bullet from the Applica agent had struck. "It only takes one person…"

"Two," Tannor said. "Any planet-level weapons require dual authorization now, thanks to my security revisions. The top Ardenian officer and the top Titian."

"And you just got promoted," Relai said. She sagged in relief. "Buzou can keep their tech, then. What would I do without you, Tannor?"

Tannor didn't answer or look up.

"Hey," Tom interrupted, "how about you guys share some of your cool alien technology with Earth, huh?"

"We barely have enough for ourselves," Relai replied, "and your planet has twice the population of our entire coalition—"

"Information doesn't cost you anything!" Tom slammed his hand down on the table. "Send us tech specs!"

"What do you think this is?" Tannor said, holding up the potentiometer.

"Wait, no, no, that was leaked—by—" Tom sputtered and then visibly, painfully stopped himself.

"Us," Tannor said.

"No," Tom insisted, "I... let's say I hypothetically know the person who leaked it to the world, okay? And that person is definitely not one of you. No. Ha ha. No."

Tannor said, "That person got it from someone," just as Ky leaned forward and asked, "Is this hypothetical person the reason you were taking photos of us at that diner?"

Tom looked between them. "Lo siento, no hablo ingles."

Relai let out an impatient huff. "Tannor, we don't release technology to Earth... do we?"

Tannor took a long breath and then shook her head. "The coalition doesn't. When I said 'us' I meant the Quiet. We're a non-violent resistance and we do whatever we can to lessen the harm that the monarchy is causing. If we could create a working metacurrent potentiometer, we could create flying vehicles that don't depend on Sevati tech."

Relai's eyebrows jumped in surprise. *The Quiet.*

"Did you know about Xiong?" Relai asked.

"Yes. He's the head of the Quiet on Earth."

Then the blood drained from Relai's face as she thought back further. "Did you know I was trapped at Haadam?"

"*No.*" Tannor's cheeks flushed. "The second I realized someone was down there, we went and got you."

"It was so scary," Goren said through a mouthful of food. He waved his hand at Milo and Ky. "You guys are really scary, you know?"

Ky nodded happily while Milo lowered his eyes.

"Xiong said, *impersonated the Quiet...*" Relai raised a finger at Ky, "to you. Is that true?"

"Yep, that's me. Liar. Can't recommend trusting me, if I'm honest. And I'm really not."

Relai tried to think this all through. Of course there was a resistance; it must have formed long before she even left Arden. An awful lot of people had hated her father's reign. "Do you know who the head of the Quiet is on Arden, Tannor?"

Tannor paused. "I could know. If I needed to know."

"Okay," Relai concluded. "That's who we'll aim for when we get back to Arden: the head of this nonviolent resistance. Maybe they'll even let me join."

Relai tried to smile at Tannor, but she was focusing hard on the tech in her hands again.

"What if they're resisting the crown itself, not just the False Relai?" Milo asked.

She met his eyes. "Then there's a prophecy they'll be happy to hear."

No one wanted to elaborate on that, despite Tom's exasperated demands.

oo●oo

The receptionist called Hope first.

She stayed on the phone with the woman through four illegal turns and a 90 mph sprint down I-94 to her office, listening to her wheeze and cry as she hid under her desk. Hope heard her use the office line to call the police and try to describe what had happened.

Then Hope stood in her office, panting and watching the security camera footage on her copper-shielded laptop in astonished horror. It had been sixteen minutes. Police were on their way.

Or were they? Shit.

She paused the video after everything in the image went still. A foot and leg protruded from behind a bloody gurney.

This—

This was—

She didn't even know what it was, but she knew what it would become: nothing, the second whoever took those other dead bodies got wind of the corpse's resuscitation and murder spree. This would be erased, too. That doctor, that security guard, whoever the other person was that this psycho lady murdered on her way out...

Hope clenched her eyes shut. *What would Tom do, if Tom weren't a total idiot?*

Her eyes sprang open.

"Let's see them bury this after I tweet it to every news network in the state," she said, and got to work.

oo●oo

ii.

One of the first things Ky had done with Milo all those months ago on Gastred was teach him how to shoot. The kid had held a gun before, of course, and he'd done some hunting, but Milo had been depending on his brute strength and size to make it from Arden to Gastred. He hadn't been far from death when Ky found him.

At first, Ky had had no intention of revealing his healing ability to Milo, so he'd dressed the kid's wounds and used that time of recuperation to improve Milo's aim.

Now, he set Relai and Tannor up with gen-guns in the living room and targets at the far end of the kitchen. It was about as far away as they were ever going to need to shoot, anyway. Then he poked Goren awake.

"What? Stop—no, what?" The kid flailed up and out of bed, reaching for the gen-gun on the nightstand and missing completely. Ky laughed and steadied him by the shoulder.

"How are your combat skills? Aim?"

"What? Ugh, I was having such a good dream." Goren rubbed his eyes. "My aim is great, and you're not even running away."

"We're playing with guns, want to join us?"

From beneath the haze of sleep a hint of interest piqued in Goren's eyes. "I could show you all how to snipe with a gen-gun," he offered.

Ky just laughed. "You can't snipe with a gen-gun."

"*You* can't snipe with a gen-gun. *I* can."

"When I say 'you,' I mean *everyone*, kiddo. No one snipes with a gen-gun. Come on, hit Milo in the face instead."

Goren looked like he wanted to keep arguing, but the offer was too good. As they drifted out of the room, they heard Relai exclaim,

"Why do you have a *sword?*"

•

Instead of answering her question, Tom shouted, "Ow!" and dropped a cat onto the ground.

Relai dodged. The cat ran up the stairs and out the door.

The floor was littered with strange objects, all dirty, half-broken, and old. Relai kicked aside a baseball glove and it knocked over a giant golden plastic kitty. The kitty's arm waved smoothly in protest.

"My ex used to live here and when she left she didn't bother with a ton of stuff because she went to work on this farm co-op in Portland or something, anyway, she left this—" he grunted, wedged halfway into the upper space of the closet, and used his meager weight to jerk back and heave out a long, weathered case.

It was black and over half his height, with leather straps and tarnished buckles.

"You're practicing with weapons, right?" Tom asked, then he lifted open the case to reveal a *gorgeous* sword, displayed in green velvet alongside a wooden scabbard. "Behold, the only weapon I own."

"What a terrible idea," Ky commented.

"Where is this from? How old is it?" Relai gripped it by the handle in one hand and rested the double-edged blade on the palm of the other. Silata didn't deal in swords—she'd trained with short blades and sometimes just wooden sticks—but she could appreciate good craftsmanship when she saw it.

"I don't know, it was in their family. I think it's nineteenth century Mexican, maybe?"

"I know swords!" Goren clamored over to Tom with greedy hands and took the sword.

Relai watched in surprise as his stance changed; his body went both straighter and more fluid, more confident than his usual manner. He turned the blade over, holding it carefully but not gently, touching the whole length with reverence. After eyeing his surroundings, he swung the blade back a couple times, hefting it to get his grip comfortable. Then he sliced a sharp arc and, switching the direction of his grip, brought it behind him, vertical, flush along the back of his arm. He stood ready, grinning and a bit smug. "Anyone up for a little sparring?"

Relai wanted to give it a try, but only if they fought outside, and certainly not with a real sword. She didn't have a death wish.

"You don't know how to sword fight," Milo stated, matter-of-fact, as though he couldn't recognize skill when he saw it.

Goren lifted his chin. "The training of an accomplished youth of the greater class," he intoned in what must have been an impression of his mother, "includes no less than: the primary languages of the coalition; three-tiered hospitality; formal dancing; song; mastery of two instruments; an understanding of the arts; athletic form; natural philosophy; and... fencing."

"So that's what greater kids grow up doing," Tannor said dryly. "I always wondered."

"It's what the greater class is suited for," he replied. "Somebody has to keep fine culture alive."

Relai didn't miss the way Milo stiffened and Tannor's whole face went sour, but Goren did.

"I used to wish I could just do mindless work all day, you know, lesser class stuff, 'cause I never got a break." He tried the sword with one hand, then two. "Wow, this thing is heavier than I'm used to."

"Mindless," Tannor repeated. Relai frowned; Goren definitely didn't mean anything by that—

"Like farming or building or something."

Milo stood up. "Somebody give me something to hit him with."

Relai sighed and looked around for a spare gun. "Please be joking."

"Sorry, we in the lesser class are too mindless to understand jokes," Milo replied. "We never learned to fence or dance, either, so we're probably not much use to you, except for the food we harvest and the metalock we mine and *somebody give me something to hit him with.*"

"You can use my broomball stick, it's metal," Tom offered. "It's okay if you get blood on the carpet; I'm never getting back my security deposit anyway."

Tannor took aim at a target as she said, "Goren, just put the sword down and say you're sorry."

"I'm not apologizing! I said the work is mindless, not the people, but if people are stuck doing those jobs it's because they didn't test into any better positions, right? So—so let's go." Goren assumed a formal dueling stance.

"You're going to slice someone open!" Relai tried to take the sword, but he twisted away.

"Come *on*, he's so mean to me, let me show him—"

"Is your lack of skill going to maim anyone? Think hard, kid," Ky advised. He was nudging Tannor's shoulders to adjust her stance. "I'm not healing anyone."

"I'll only bruise him a little," Milo promised, taking the offered broom handle.

"Sword up," Goren ordered. He and Milo crossed blades (more or less) in the center of the room, then stepped back.

"Enough!" Relai placed herself right in front of him. "So says the queen, put down the sword."

Goren let out a dramatic sigh, then handed the weapon back to Tom with practiced care. "So says the queen."

Tannor repeated it, too, in the deadened voice of a well-trained guard.

Then Milo tossed away his stick. "Fine. You want to know what I grew up doing?" He shifted his center of gravity lower and let his hands hover out just a bit.

Goren looked nervously toward the exit. "What?"

Milo rocked back and forth.

"*Wrestling.*"

Then he pounced.

.

"Get his—grab his chin!" Relai shouted. A few minutes of watching the guys practice physical combat techniques—that is, struggle on Tom's carpet and knock things over—had already offered more entertainment than the hundreds of tournaments she'd been dragged to in her youth. She and Tannor had given up on target practice for fear of accidentally shooting them. She went on more quietly, "The bounty hunter said Unity were the ones who hired her to kill me, but I don't think they kidnapped me. They think I was ruling. And—oh, Tannor. She said my cousins are dead. The Renganiban brothers. I barely knew them."

"So someone is killing off the Arden regents. After them, who's left?"

"Just my cousin Sana. She would never work with them... They're going to kill her, aren't they? I am the End, that's what the prophecy says."

Tannor shook her head. "I need to know more about how this *prophecy* thing works."

"And what about the rotten blood?" Relai asked a bit desperately. "Maybe the keepers saw all the things the False Relai has been doing and didn't differentiate between me and her? Maybe it's a mistake. Maybe I'm not part of this at all."

Or maybe I'm the Sacrifice.

·

Tannor thought:

Maybe you're the rotten blood. Maybe this is all your lie and you are not the End. She didn't say it out loud.

·

Meanwhile, Tom sidled into the kitchen where Ky was gulping down a bottle of rubbing alcohol.

"That might kill you, you know," Tom said.

Ky lowered the bottle with a slurp. "I'm hard to kill."

"Like a cockroach."

Ky ignored him, apparently more interested in watching Milo and Goren wrestle than conversing with Tom.

Well, he was a guest. Guests were required to converse, damn it! Welcome to Minnesota!

Tom grabbed the empty bottle and chucked it in the trash. "How old are you, anyway?"

That got a reaction—Ky arched an eyebrow. "By what count?"

"Uh, if you can convert it to Earth years that'll help."

"No. Do you mean, how many years have passed on this planet since I was born, or how old is my body?"

Tom narrowed his eyes. "Both."

If Ky thought Tom missed how his eyes darted around to make sure no one else was listening, he was a big dumb stupid idiot. Milo was busy cutting off Goren's oxygen supply, saying, "You're never gonna knock me down if you don't stay low," and Tannor and Princess were cozied up against the wall.

"Okay," Ky said. "Ninety-some years have passed on this planet. My body is somewhere around thirty-five, maybe forty of your years. S'hard to know; lost track for a while."

Tom shook his head sympathetically. "Relativity, man."

Ky chuckled and wiped the corner of his mouth. "Relativity."

Tom imagined the possibilities and felt utterly overcome with jealously. Space travel! *Extended* space travel! To multiple populated planets! *In space!*

"Well," Ky said, "back to work." Then he pulled a knife free from his belt and flung it with a slap into the wall next to the princess's head.

•

Relai blinked at the knife. Half the length of her forearm, handle included, and like all of Ky's knives the metal was black and pressed to match the weave of his clothes. She pulled it from the plaster.

"Enough talk," Ky said, sauntering over. "Cut me up."

"What?"

Out of the corner of her eye Relai saw Tannor straighten up off the wall.

"Cut me." Ky dragged his shirt over his head. "You've never killed anyone, and that's going to get us killed when you hesitate." Off went his pants. "Don't hold back. Watching you might teach the others a few things."

The knife rested lightly in her hand as Ky hunched forward, touching his vulnerable points—the tendons behind his ankles, the sides of his knees, the creases of his groin and the dips in the front of his shoulders. "Here, here—we'll start with disabling cuts, then work up to killing."

She watched his bare chest stretch with his breath, bones under muscle under skin, and the grim smile on his face. He'd been nearly as muscular as Milo when they met, but he'd drained himself closer to Goren's build with all the healing. It made him look fragile. It made Relai angry.

"No thanks." She tossed the knife away and it clunked across the carpet behind Tom's couch.

"You think I let just anyone hurt me?" Ky asked. Under the cavalier attitude, his voice took on a dangerous edge. "C'mon. I know you have skill but it's different when you're actually hurting someone. You can't hesitate. If you want to get good at something, the only way is to practice. Now *pick up the knife and cut me.*"

Relai backed away from him, putting Milo and Goren between them.

"I don't want to be *good* at violence," she said.

•

Goren let out a wail as Milo bent his arm way too far backward and said, "See? Like that." From the wall next to the window he heard Relai say, "I don't want to be good at violence."

Milo rotated his hips and Goren found himself pinned with his face trapped against the dirty carpet. It smelled terrible.

"How easy for you," Milo snapped. Goren elected not to struggle, and luckily Milo let him go and stood.

"Oh, thank gods," Goren moaned. He stayed where he was, panting, one arm folded under his cheek.

"What?" Relai asked.

In the background Ky muttered something unintelligible.

"Relai Orist Aydor," Milo said, still catching his breath. "What happens when we get to Arden?"

Goren eased up onto his elbows. It seemed like time to get onto his feet now.

"You know," Relai answered. "I'll take back control."

"And?"

Goren looked between them nervously; Milo wanted Relai to let Eray split off into its own thing. What would they even call it? A half-planet? It was ridiculous. They used to rule themselves, just after liberation, and obviously it hadn't gone well or they'd still be at it. The coalition wouldn't deal with Eray on its own, anyway.

"Arden's one planet, Milo," Goren said.

Relai said, "Goren, maybe you should go keep watch outside," and Goren threw up his hands in frustration.

"Go away, lack-wit," Milo said. "You're giving everyone a headache."

Goren frowned and waited for Tannor to speak up and defend him, but she didn't.

Milo demanded, "Now, reesh." He was being mean, even more than usual.

"I saved your life, though!" Goren protested, but everyone ignored him as Milo stood up and asked again:

"What happens when we get back to Arden?"

The queen faced him in the center of the room. "Trials. Civil, fair trials."

"And Eray?"

"She has more important stuff to deal with," Goren said. "And I thought most of them were dead now, anyw—"

Out of nowhere, suddenly Milo was shoving him hard and shouting, "Shut up!"

Tannor pushed in and then Ky materialized, too, and somehow Goren ended up on the other side of the apartment from Milo, a new ache from the shove just starting to register in his chest. Then Relai ordered:

"Goren, leave."

"If he wants to tear apart everything our people fought for—"

"Go!" She pointed toward the stairs leading up to the door.

"Fine, I will!" Goren shouted, stumbling to his shoes. He could feel the heat in his cheeks and he didn't want to look at these people anymore, so, *fine*. "Ky? I'm going to go shoot things. Your gun is coming with me."

He snatched up Ky's spit gun and stomped up the stairs. They were going to feel pretty stupid when they finally realized how mature he had to be to put up with them.

Hopefully Relai would put Milo in his place.

"Don't lose my baby!" Ky called after him.

Goren bellowed, "I take better care of her than you do!"

Then he slammed the door behind him.

●

Milo stood shaking, his fists in knots, and searched the window for anything—grass, a tree, the sight of anything to stop the crawl of heat over his skin. Nobody was touching him and he needed it—he felt cold and alone and so, *so* angry. At least with Goren he could fight it out, talk with his whole self instead of just his mouth, he could try to explain and teach the kid, show him—

Most of them were dead now.

Fuck that.

"We're not all dead, Relai," Milo said. A warning and a promise.

"I know—"

He turned and asked a third time: "What happens when we get back to Arden?"

She swallowed. "We'll reform."

Another year and we'll consider it, they'd say. *At next year's council meeting. We'll put it on the agenda.*

Milo drew from the energy still thrumming from his wrestling match, pacing from end to end of this tiny, dank box so he wouldn't loom. "You'll give us our freedom or you'll go from one fight to another."

"Milo," she said, so reasonable, so calm, "no. I'm sorry. I'm so sorry for everything that they did to your people… but we're one planet. And please don't—violence won't solve this. Can't you understand that?"

This was how they kept it up. Word after condescending word.

•

Relai tried to catch Tannor's eye, but she wouldn't meet her.

"You act like we're the ones who started this," Milo said, "Like you're pure, and clean, and we're the dangerous ones." His eyes burned in a way Relai hadn't seen since their first frightening exchange.

"I don't think I'm pure. I just don't want to hurt anyone. It hurts me when I hurt someone."

"You think it doesn't hurt us?" Milo's voice rumbled like the frame of a ship shaking before it crashed.

"No, I—" But that was a lie, and she didn't want to lie to him. "I don't know. Does it?"

Ky shrugged with an ugly, empty smirk. Milo, though, wasn't so flippant.

"To even ask that—*I cannot explain this to you.*" As he spoke Relai saw a shine in his eyes that made her want to go back in time and swallow her words. "You haven't earned the trust required to hear what I would say. We'll kill for you but you won't lift a hand for yourself? For us?"

"There's no point in even starting this conversation right now," Tannor said loudly. "Wait until—"

"No," Milo barked. "What happens now matters, so we need to talk about it now. We're killing for her, and she's gonna arrive back home crying and she's gonna hold up clean hands. The crown depends on us accepting what we're given, and what they give us with their clean hands is *violence*. They kick it down so they don't have to live it, Tannor, while we're living it every day."

He said *we* like he meant Tannor, too. He sounded… delusional. The Aydor monarchy didn't hurt their own people. Their planet wasn't a dictatorship. The bombing of Eray—that was the False Relai. An enemy they all shared.

They were on the same side.

"And how will shouting at her change any of that?" Tannor snapped. "What if she doesn't understand? Will you shove her like you just shoved Goren? What if that's not enough, either?"

Relai dropped her eyes.

"No," Milo said.

"Eray isn't dangerous," Relai said. She found her courage and raised her chin. "They say it's dangerous, but that's a myth. Xiong told me and he *knows*. There wasn't any more violence in your life than anyone else's—I mean, up until—"

"Our lives are violence," Milo ground out. "Our lives are silence, and rivers, and no salt for bread. You don't even understand the words I'm using, and you think you have anything to say to me?"

He was right. She didn't understand, but—

"Why wouldn't I have anything to say to you?" she exclaimed. "You think I'm silly and—and stupid, because I grew up greater class, and I can't possibly have any insight?"

Milo leaned forward until he took up most of her field of vision. "We don't want your insight, Mora. We want you to shut your mouth and listen."

Shut made her flinch, and she opened her mouth but Milo didn't give her the chance to speak. "You think everything you do is justified, and if we fight back we're barbaric. You're fine with anything that benefits you, as long as it costs us and not you. You don't hate our illnesses or our—"

"Illness isn't violence, and you think I don't know illness?"

"—suffering, and no, you don't. Every hurt is healed for you, with devices powered by the poison *we mine*."

"I never asked for that! You think I wanted every bump and scrape healed? Because I didn't! That's just one more thing they took away from me—"

"And yet again, everything turns to you, *you* and *your* hurts and *your* thoughts. *You aren't listening.*"

"*FINE!*" she shouted, the loudest she'd raised her voice so far, and everyone stilled.

•

Milo watched her pull her shoulders back, close her lips over those snarling teeth, and settle her feet shoulder-width apart. Then she deliberately turned her head to the right, keeping eye contact, and lifted the edge of her jaw.

Milo waited to see if this was real. The gesture was a way of ceding the floor in a debate, a High Council way of respecting the speaker.

He sucked in a breath.

"So. Did you know that the most common impairment in Eray is the loss of a limb? If someone touches metalock we chop what we can to save them." Relai stared, eyes wide.

"I thought metalock killed instantly," she said quietly.

Milo went to Bry in his mind, because it was the worst, even though Bry never made it to the mines because of his lungs.

"It's supposed to be instantaneous, but it's not. I don't know if that's just a reesh myth made up to excuse our mortality rate, or if it's the dust or the water or something stranger, but we can live up to eighteen hours after touching it."

A green-black stain had crept under the skin of Bry's fingers, traced up through his veins, and in Milo's head had rung the sort of incredible, painful bells that made him want to tear down mountains, and it was his best friend. He had to do it.

"There should be time to call a scanner to you, then," Relai said.

"Metalock poisoning is considered a *choice illness*. Scanners, powered by the thing killing us, are locked against healing it. You see? *That's violence.*"

Mouth not so open, now. He watched her swallow.

"Milo," she said, pained, "that doesn't make any sense."

"*I KNOW!*" he roared.

She stumbled back, a hand at her ribs where he knew she carried that knife.

He didn't stop. "Did you know they cut our rations of salt and flour if we don't meet mining quotas? And when our bakers can't make bread, the grain giants from Vilutta set up shop and bleed out our businesses, and they do it over and over again in every way they can? And that we risk being imprisoned if our debts aren't squared?"

She didn't try to speak.

"Did you know that we're forbidden from performing sacrifices to our god, and if we're caught slaughtering an animal they take the offering, plus a fine?"

At that, Relai blinked. "I didn't know you followed any—"

"My god and I haven't spoken in a while," he snapped. "If you even look at a guard wrong and you're letting our hair grow, they shave it off. They force us on our knees and shave our heads and it's humiliating."

"That's not—"

"You don't know anything!" Milo clenched his fists and stood over her at his full height, and he saw Relai tense reflexively. For the briefest of moments, real fear flashed across her face.

Milo tried to breathe evenly. This wasn't what he wanted from his time with the queen. He wanted empathy, compassion, regret—anything but reasonable, reproachful scolding. And anything but fear.

He thought he'd been reaching her, but how could he? What would words matter, if all she remembered was the way they'd met?

•

Someone needed to stop this.

Tannor deliberately put herself between Milo and Relai and said, "Milo Hemm, *sit down.*"

Milo tore his eyes away from Relai to look down at Tannor with a sort of desperation bordering on madness. "What do you want from me?"

"I want you to *sit.*"

"He's not an animal," Ky growled.

Tannor ignored him. "We can debate the best way to change our planet all you want, Milo, but you don't get to hold the threat of violence over our heads. *No.*"

Milo rubbed his hands over his face and stalked away, muttering, "That's not—"

"Did we all lay down weapons before we walked in this room?" Ky exclaimed, throwing his arms open wide. "We will not turn meek and proper to make you comfortable!"

Tannor tissed at him; he was so used to pain, he didn't see it as a threat. Probably saw anyone who feared pain as weak and scorned Relai for her delicacy. He probably *liked it.*

"You don't see a difference between revolutionary acts and just lashing out in anger?" Tannor disregarded Ky and aimed herself at Milo. "You don't see how that'll weigh on you differently? How every conversation will stink with the rot of your threat, and she won't be able to speak freely, or trust you, ever ag—"

"Tannor, stop," Relai said quietly.

Tannor spun. "What?"

Relai wasn't looking at anyone. "We're past that point, and you don't speak for me."

"What do you mean, you're past that point?"

Milo was silent, his eyes wide.

"At Haadam," Relai said.

"At Haadam, *what?*" Tannor said. "He saved you from the guards trying to kill you. He brought you to me to heal."

"I shot her," Milo croaked, "to bring her down."

Tannor froze.

"I sat on her to keep her still. I used my hands on her throat... I tried to wring the life out of her. I don't remember a lot of it. It was dark and my head was a fog. I. I hurt her. I only barely stopped myself from killing her."

"Milo..." Relai began, but she didn't seem to have any words to offer beyond that.

Tannor looked at him in shock.

Why is he helping her?

He's not.

Milo let his shoulders drop as he stared at Tannor in bare anguish. It certainly looked like he felt bad. Men always felt bad, after.

I don't know you, she thought. There had been moments where she had felt...but, no. She was stupid to trust him so quickly. Tannor was never this stupid.

"Oh, shut up," Ky snarled, even though no one was talking. "He wasn't clear in the head then. It wasn't his fault."

•

Tannor's face held a sort of horror Milo had never seen before, but Relai's was worse. She was staring at the floor like she had no reason to expect any more from him, and he couldn't stand it.

"What can I do?" Milo clenched his fists at his sides. If he could just touch her, he thought, maybe Relai would be able to tell he wasn't going to hurt her. He just wanted her to hear him.

He felt utterly lost.

"I've already vowed not to hurt you again." His voice felt thick in his throat. "I'm doing everything I can to protect you. What will make me safe enough? Should I kneel?" He dropped to his knees where he stood, there next to a claw-shredded couch and an overturned lamp, sweating in the shadowed heat of the day.

Ky paced away, cursing loudly. Relai stood speechless.

"Do you want a show of blood? You already took my family, you have my blood, your high court lives are built on our blood and I'm not going to stop." He didn't even try to stem the emotion welling up in his own face. "What will satisfy you?"

He heard a crack.

It was Ky's fist through plaster.

•

"I'm sorry," Relai said. She was crying, too. "I'm sorry they hurt you."

"They?" Ky spat. The white dust on his hand clumped black with his blood as the shredded skin closed. *"You."*

Relai expected something from Tannor, but she was only staring at Milo, aghast.

"You think you're better than us," Ky hissed, and Relai reeled back from the disgust in his face. "You don't deserve to bow at his—*look at him*—to bow at at his feet, and you think you're superior to him."

"Ky," Tannor said, but he ignored her as he stalked toward Relai. In the corner of her eye, she saw Milo rise. Still, Ky didn't pause.

"You pity us? You *need us.* You judge us? You should be *thanking us.*"

Something about the change of light on his face, maybe the tilt of his head, made the shadows deeper around his eyes and his skin seem gray. His voice shook. His eyes caught a flash of light.

This was going to get ugly if she didn't do something.

So she said, "You're right."

Relai swallowed and stepped forward. When he didn't move, she tentatively extended her hands.

Oeylan, she thought. *Oeylan for thank you . . .*

She put her hands on his neck and pulled gently until he lowered his forehead enough for her to press hers to his. She maintained eye contact, watching as the shadows faded, and pulled away when she finally heard him take a breath.

Ky leaned back, his jaw slack, then he flashed a stilted glance at Milo. He blinked a few times, turned, and walked up the stairs and out the door.

Milo looked between Relai and Tannor, his face a twisted mess of confusion and pain, and took a deliberate step backward. "We won't go far."

And then before Relai could speak the proper words, thank him with her voice because she wouldn't dare touch him, not now, he was gone.

Relai spun and fixed her glare on Tannor. "Who do you think you are?"

Tannor looked ill. "I thought we could trust him—"

"I'm not more afraid of him than any other man," Relai said in a low voice. "I'm not a child, Tannor. How dare you?"

Tannor stared at her, her eyes growing more resolved in their horror moment by moment.

Relai shook her head. Out of the corner of her eye, she noticed Tom emerge from the bathroom.

"I'm going to shower," Relai muttered.

She fled to the bathroom, Tannor said nothing, and Relai shut the door behind her.

○○●○○

iii.

Milo found Ky just outside, balanced on one hand in the center of a plot of grass, his body drawing a straight line from ground to sky. The day was quiet, calm, and the only sound came from motors passing by and Ky's measured breathing. Milo said nothing as he hoisted up on one hand next to him.

Ky did not lose his temper. Ky did not lose control. Ky's voice did not *shake*.

Not once during the last eight months—even through the screaming and the burning and re-growing the muscles needed to stand after they crashed here on this alforsaken planet, when Ky had given him nothing but an unending litany of scorn (*"After all I've done for you, this is how you die on me, you asshole?"*)—not for a moment had he sounded angry.

At least, not genuinely. He could sob or whine or cower better than the best (or the worst, depending on how much one valued sincerity), but Milo always recognized the real Ky when he saw him. He thought he saw more of him, now.

Ky switched from one hand to another and Milo followed. His fingers spread and clutched at the grass as he strained to balance, threading deep enough to find cool dirt under soft blade. He couldn't keep this up as long as Ky, but he'd try.

"She's not going to let Eray secede," Ky said.

"I know."

"You see how she looks at you. Use it. You could have her begging—"

"*Stop.*"

Milo dropped to his feet, breathing deep, focusing on the burn in his muscles to keep himself from lashing out. Ky wanted Milo angry, he realized. Was this all a distraction? Milo brushed blades of green and clumps of dirt from his hands. Such a privilege, this dirt.

Ky finally let his feet down. He shook out his arms.

"Up on the roof," Ky said, "when she put her hands under mine to heal you. Was that the first time she's touched you?"

Milo swallowed.

"Yes."

Ky nodded without turning back, and then he pointed out four corners of an imaginary boundary. They'd keep the blood on the grass.

"First to five."

"Ten," Milo said, and then he attacked.

∘∘●∘∘

iv.

What sorts of colossal, embarrassing idiots used coalition technology on all of their doors with no analog failsafe? Fass nearly shot the door in frustration, but he didn't want to waste the bullet.

The idiots would be cleaned out in the uprising.

As he himself was no fool, Ed Fass understood what had really happened here: an all-tech lockdown. Nothing, from lighting to generator guns to med scanners, would change its state until an all-clear order flowed through the base. The doors had locked in place—everything open would stay open and refuse to lock, and everyone trapped in disgusting workshops full of oil and bright lights and grouchy underlings would stay trapped until the one who ordered the freeze relaxed it.

Fass huffed and turned to Horten. "How are the bombs coming?"

Horten scratched a quartet of red lines up and down the side of his bare head and sat back from his table. "I have two. We planned for ten. I need another—"

"You have three hours."

"—Six hours, at least! And another hour to make up for—"

"We need to use one of these to blow a hole in the wall."

"—The bomb we use to blast our way out of here." Horten sighed. Fass swelled with the urge to punish him, but looking at the soldier reminded him of his partner.

"And where is Lilya?"

Horten looked up warily. "I don't know. I've been focusing on the bombs."

Lilya was tall and thin, with long black hair and rich, perfect skin. She'd done as she was told for the past year at Haadam, flouncing and sunning and leaving traces of a royal presence just begging to be noticed, and she'd serve her purpose now. Just as Horten would. Just as all of these soldiers would.

Fass spun to snatch the attention of the room. *"Find Lilya, now."*

∘∘●∘∘

Ososi lingered in a distant corner of the mechanics workshop, kneeling toward the wall and bowing to the floor periodically.

Keep Lilya sick enough to stay put, she prayed. It had only taken a few drops of hydrometagen leaked into the swallows of water Lilya had taken during the flight here. Ososi had timed it perfectly. Lilya hadn't been able to walk when the assault began, and inshallah, she would remain back in the jumper this entire time.

But not too sick to recover, she went on.

Stop her from figuring out the communications system in the jumper.

Stop her from hurting anyone here.

Upon A'lah we have relied. Decide in truth, and You are the best of those who decide.

○○●○○

313

v.

Relai scrubbed Tom's foul-smelling shampoo into her hair, submerging her head in the hot spray, breathing in steam.

What could she do now, *right now*, to alleviate Milo's pain?

Offer to open communication on Arden.

(Might give Unity free reign to organize.)

Offer to declare the owners of those pins dead.

(Might terrorize those remaining. Might trigger an all-out war.)

Send an open relay asking for Titus to intervene on Arden.

(Tantamount to ceding power?)

Offer to give Milo a rank—in the guard? In the greater class? A spot on the High Council?

Maybe that would work.

She fumbled with the plumbing controls, briefly scalding herself before she managed to turn the shower off. She dried herself with the bathroom's lone, musty towel, and ran fingers through her hair.

"Soooo... Can I ask some questions now?" Tom said through the door.

"Okay." Relai opened it a tiny crack, angling her body so he couldn't see her. "Do you have some clothes I could wear? No white, no black... long sleeves?"

"Way ahead of you," he replied, and shoved a stack of cloth against the crack. She moved her foot and accepted the offer. "Now as I was saying—"

Relai shook out the things he offered and discovered several unexpected items. The shirt might have been his, but the bra and underwear? "Tom," she interrupted, "these are not your clothes."

"Yeah, the tenants upstairs are mostly dead-eyed harbingers of societal apocalypse, but there's a nice one. I just told her my friends were visiting from Turkey and the airline lost your bags, so she lent you this stuff. You look about the same size except you're at least three inches taller. Sorry."

She smiled. "Thank you. Okay, ask—"

"Alien abductions. Yes or no?"

Relai stepped out of the bathroom properly clothed. "No."

"Build any... pyramids or ancient cities on Earth?"

"No! At least, I don't think so... Now, will you help me set a table? I need to mend some things."

"Yeah, yeah. Speaking of mending, I eavesdropped on your fight and I think I got the gist of it. What are you gonna do? Give Milo a title or something? Level up his power so he holds his own with the other upper crusters?"

Relai stared at him, startled, feeling heat in her cheeks.

Tom slapped an obnoxious beat on the wall and sang in her face: "Second verse, same as the first, a little bit richer and a little bit worse!"

"What does that mean?"

"It means that's not gonna work! It means BURN IT DOWN!"

"We can't!" she cried. "It's in my blood, *literally*."

Tom screwed his face up to argue, but Relai rushed on.

"My blood is the only blood that controls our most powerful technology—our travel blocks and our ships, infrastructure, communication—"

"Whoa, hold on, hold on, hold on!" Tom flipped open his binder of notes and plucked a pen out of a mug full of them, throwing the pen across the room when it refused to write and grabbing another. "Your *blood* controls technology?"

"Well, my... heredity? What is it called? Genetics. Anything we inherited from the Sevati."

"Ah, right, the alien race that colonized the four planets long ago using humans harvested from Earth as labor," Tom nodded, flipping wildly through his notebook. "Sevati. Evil alien overlords. They were from another galaxy but they were able to... cross-breed? That seems highly unlikely."

Relai gritted her teeth. "Well, it happened."

"I bet they scienced it. Whatever. Go on!"

"Um. Okay. That means the ships, vehicles, communications, water systems, med scanners, blocks—"

"Blocks? Ky didn't explain those nearly enough."

"They're, uh, gateways through space. A ship passing through them instantly comes out light years away at the block it is connected to. It's the only practical way to travel between the Coalition planets."

"How? Worm holes? Quantum entanglement?"

"Um. I don't know. There are technicians who understand more or less how they work, in theory—enough to keep them running—but we've never been able to build a new one. Can I finish what I was saying?"

"Sorry, sorry!"

"All of the Sevati tech can only be used under the authority of my family line."

"Well, there's gotta be a line of succession, right? Someone else inherits it if you bite the dust."

Relai winced. "The, um. The thing is... we don't know how to change who is in charge."

"*Sure* you don't."

"No, really. Arden broke free four hundred years ago because the daughter of the Sevati king mutinied for humanity. She transferred power to the first human king and then she died before she could show us how she did it. Since then we brought freedom to all four Sevati worlds, but the tech remains in Aydor control. We've never been able to alter the system. I'm *literally* the only one left who can rule."

"Yeesh." Tom looked up from his furious scribbling. "So that's why everyone's after you?"

Relai nodded. "We only have one Aydor child per generation, so there is no one else. No one else can take control, and the only one who can assign control or take it away is me."

The rest of the Coalition thought that the next in the line of succession—Relai's cousin, Sana—would inherit the power over the tech along with the title. It was a carefully guarded High Council secret that only Aydor blood would work. The Sevati had assigned a complicated line of succession, and none of that had changed when the first Aydor became king. If Relai died, the power would go back to the Sevati. And there were no more Sevati left in this galaxy.

If she died, there might be a shusa descendant of the old line of succession out there. Waiting.

Relai's throat constricted involuntarily.

"Whether I like it or not, *I have this power*. Now that my father, the king, is dead... I'm the only one this powerful in the entire galaxy."

Tom chewed on his thumbnail.

"Jeez," he said. "Pressure."

Relai laughed weakly, and then the apartment door opened.

•

Milo descended from blister-bright heat to the shadows of the house with all the hearty good ache and burn of the sparring match humming through him. He'd cleaned off with cold water from a green hose they'd found outside, lying coiled like a wild snake waiting to slither free of this planet's version of civilization. The shirt stuck to his damp skin and he flicked drops of water out of his hair. He took a moment to let his eyes adjust to the new lack of light and the change in sound, wide and open to muffled and dull.

Ky was still hosing himself off with the outside water, but he'd be right behind in his own time. Milo didn't need anyone by his side for this.

He cleaned a smudge of blood from his lip and favored his aching right foot and felt *here* and *known*. He felt ready to talk.

Relai was standing tall and still behind a table she must have dragged from the kitchen into the meager space between the central room seating and the kitchen's half wall. Tannor should have been placed at Relai's right shoulder, but apparently she didn't see herself as a second to Relai here, either. Instead she was off at Tom's work table with her back to the room, focused on the sad little toy engine parts while Tom sat on the counter and judged them all. Tannor didn't even turn when Milo arrived.

Relai swept her hand over the table, stiff like a stranger, and said, "Milo Hemm. Will you sit and talk with me? Please?"

Milo looked at that bare surface, straw-colored wood showing through wounds in the dull brown stain, and considered the path he wanted to follow.

He wanted to lead. He didn't want to terrify her, but he couldn't do this on Kilani terms.

So he said, "In Eray, we don't start with talk. We start with food."

Milo waited for her to nod, hey eyes wide and nervous, then he turned and moved into the kitchen.

Relai's eyes roamed over the relaxation in Milo's shoulders, the confidence, the drape of the cloth over his back, completely baffled. Then Ky stomped down the stairs.

"Uh-oh," he declared. "Don't let Milo into the kitchen." Overt denial that anything happened—Relai's native tongue.

He tromped down the last step and, as he passed, he threw an arm around her and pulled her along with him.

"Milo's shit in a kitchen. He's terrible. You think you're getting food out of this deal? Nope. You have to eat it, though, or you'll insult him."

He didn't skimp on the contact, and she looked down at his hand on her arm she saw it was open, his palm pressed to her skin.

"Can I touch the food?" she asked.

He just squinted at her. "If you don't touch the food, I'm going to throw it at you."

She grinned. "Okay."

"And then I'll eat it, so we don't waste."

"*Ky.*"

Relai waited until everyone was standing at a chair before she tried sitting, feeling desperately awkward and sure she was offending someone with every move.

Everyone else sat, and then Milo started in on the dishes of steaming meat mixed with vegetables first.

"In Eray," Milo began, "if you want to eat the food, you help make the food. Everyone helps, everyone eats, everyone cleans."

"What if you're really, remarkably bad at cooking?" Ky inquired.

"Then you listen to someone who knows what they're doing."

Ky took a piece of bread and used it to scoop up a handful of the stew-like mix. "I say, whoever cooks eats, and the rest of you can figure yourselves out." He folded it all together and took a huge bite, no utensils in sight, then looked to Relai expectantly. Relai realized it was her turn.

"Oh. Uh. The most honored eats first, we don't—we don't eat with the people who cook for us... and you never eat all the food on your plate."

"Why?" Milo asked, so neutral it came off as kind. It sounded stupid now, but it was how she was raised. She never knew any other way—except, while she was on Earth, meals alone.

Tannor answered when Relai stalled. "To show excess of wealth, probably. Or keep her thin."

"Abundance, yeah. And... yeah." Relai followed Ky's lead with the bread and gathered a huge scoop. "What about you, Tannor?"

"Hmm," Tannor considered. "The cook gets served and doesn't have to clean. The youngest always helps the oldest. The leader—Mom, usually—sets aside a portion of her food to offer to the ground for next year."

"Every meal?" Milo asked. "We only do it on the day of rest."

"Well, meals can vary when you're harvesting, and we—"

Then Tom burst out of his room carrying an open laptop with the sound of a video running. "Guys! Are zombies an alien thing? You need to keep me appraised of these things, damn it!"

·

"What is a—"

Milo didn't finish because Ky moved like a shot toward the computer in Tom's arms and Milo could only follow. It was a local news report.

"—in Minneapolis today. Police are searching for a woman who escaped from the Hennepin County Medical Center morgue just a few hours ago." The visual in the video window showed a simple, distorted drawing of a woman—the one who should have been dead in that stairwell, who definitely should have died from the fall off a building. Milo had killed her. Goren had killed her again.

"The woman was initially brought into the morgue as a deceased person, but—here's where the story gets weird, folks—she woke up before the autopsy could begin. Three employees and a security guard are dead, witnesses say by this woman's hand—"

"She's like me," Ky breathed. "She's better than me."

"What do we do?" Milo asked, checking the windows one by one. He signaled, strong and certain, and they followed his direction to the center of the apartment. Tannor tapped wildly at her tablet as she moved.

"Knock her out before you kill her," Ky said. "Healing's not automatic, we have to think it."

"No sign of new ex-terr tech within a thousand yards," Tannor said, eyes on her tablet. "Safest point is there—" she pointed to the wall next to the bathroom.

"She'll need time to heal, won't she?" Relai asked. She put her back to the wall. "She won't come after us until she's better."

Ky slapped a palm on Tom's chest, nearly knocking the laptop out of his arms, and steered him backwards next to Relai. "She's better."

Milo hovered close on one side, Tom and Ky on the other, Tannor between them. Relai listened.

Listened.

"How could she find us?" she whispered. "Tannor, we're hidden, right?"

"Every way I know how, yes. But—but she flew the jumper we took from that roof before we did. She might have put a tracker in it that I didn't sense to silence. She might have made a draw for it—those are passive. She might have tech to hide herself so she can get close—"

The jumper sat in the barren yard of a foreclosed home three lots down across the alley.

"Let's go now," Relai declared. "Now, now—"

Tannor cursed. "Where's Goren?"

They heard sirens.

∘∘●∘∘

Goren tromped back toward the safe house, sweaty and gross and the most relaxed he'd been since he crawled into bed two nights ago blissfully ignorant. This part of the globe seemed so scattered, so loose, at first he couldn't stand it. None of the buildings matched! Different colors, different materials, different plants creeping everywhere like the place was at constant war with itself and the planet underneath it. The buildings were even different *ages*. Was no one in charge of things here?

It was madness, and yet Goren welcomed the experience. It would result in personal growth, he assumed.

He'd found a park a few blocks over with a decent wooded area, climbed a tree, and spent a few hours sniping leaves five hundred yards away. Ky's spit gun had proved surprisingly reliable over longer distances—Ky might have cobbled her together from all manner of stolen parts, but she shot like a proper weapon. He'd even picked up some tiny pebbles for ammunition to practice adjusting for irregular shapes.

Goren felt better knowing exactly how he needed to hold her to hit a six-inch square from a quarter mile away (though he'd need a scope if he really

320

wanted to make a shot like that). Tannor could probably build him one from the crap lying around Tom's place.

He recognized a landmark: blue house, red door, five houses from Tom's. (The lack of uniformity made the place easier to navigate, at least.) He skipped left across an empty thoroughfare to the shadier side of the street, flapping the shirt around his torso to simulate wind. There was someone up ahead moving in the same direction.

Goren used to entertain his little sisters by peeking in their rooms, giving them time to change just one thing, then peeking back again. His mind wandered, sure, but Goren Dray payed attention when he needed to. He noticed things. He didn't always understand what he noticed, but right now, with the sun blazing and the air dead-still, he knew a mark from a neutral.

Boots of interlocking black and brown leather. Titian utility pants. Unsteady gait, massive shoulders, eyes locked on the tech in her hand. Different jacket. Blood.

How—?

Goren flushed hot and cold, then hot again and he pulled out the spit gun and fired before his terror stopped him—*one—two*—the woman stumbled—*three—four*—and someone on a plot of grass nearby screamed.

The bounty hunter drew a gun but Goren shot her in the hand and she dropped it and barreled toward him.

Goren should have run the other way, he really should have, but the hunter was never going to stop coming for Relai, so Goren couldn't run. There was never any choice. Good thing, too, because if he had a choice he was pretty sure he'd act a coward.

He never learned to fight like the smaller one in the match. His training commander picked every opponent and not one had ever been taller or bulkier than Goren. They must've seen his height and his hands and it was obvious he was going to end up looking like his dad, given two or three years, so they trained him to fight that way. Like the bigger one.

The hunter was the bigger one here.

If you don't stay low—

The hunter jumped as she reached Goren, elbow high and fist poised to put the whole weight of her body behind the punch, but Goren went down before she could. He fell backwards and the blow glanced across his crown and he rolled and kicked and sent the hunter crashing and tumbling right over him. Goren scrambled to his knees to find the spit gun but the hunter rolled onto her feet and snarled and Goren thought he should probably run, now, after all.

He managed to throw himself backward to avoid a kick to the face. He didn't know how to kill someone that could survive falling off a damned building, so—so if he could just hurt her enough to buy the others a little more time, that would have to—

Go with the motion and deflect—

The hunter kicked again and this time Goren went with it, let her connect with his shoulder so he could grab that foot and pull with his hands, maybe he could go for the eyes or the neck, something, but the hunter came down on top of him, elbow to sternum, and Goren couldn't breathe.

He thought he heard sirens wailing.

The hunter bashed the flat of her palm into Goren's nose. *Crack.*

The hunter flipped him on his stomach on a gray sidewalk square and stomped one boot on Goren's wrist and the other on the back of his head—

.

Runn hated this alforsaken planet. Especially this country. Everyone fucking armed all the time.

Didn't have time to kill this guard come out of nowhere—marching a perimeter around the jumper, probably. Police showed up, wasted more time.

Two officers. Two problems.

She let go of the runt.

Lunged.

One got off one shot right in Runn's gut. Runn grabbed, seized the weapon—twisted the arm—snapped the neck. One: solved.

The second fired. Bullets lodged in the first.

Runn fired. Two: solved.

She ran. Hobbled, more like. She was past the limit. *Way* past. Couldn't take more.

She held out her hand and followed the pull of the metal fibers embedded in her skin. They dragged her across a yard, through an open gate, into an alley. More sirens bit at her ears. Almost there.

There. She woke her jumper—Applica's jumper—climbed inside, and set it to take her to Curragh. Enough chasing; she needed a drink. There had to be a doctor in that market able to work on her implant, and then she'd be full up for a fight.

The jumper lifted away.

She'd rest and wait. Eventually they'd come to her.

○○●○○

EPISODE IX:

RESCUE

GOT HIM, GOT him, found him, here!"

Relai threw herself in front of the computer screen, nearly crushing Tom in the process. "How? Where? Is he okay?"

Tom flailed his hands in her face until she backed away. "They took him to HCMC!"

"Where?!"

"Hennepin County Medical Center. It's a hospital, calm down!"

"How is he? What happened?"

"Um, um—"

"Let me—"

"Off, harpy! OW! Listen: he's white and adorable so the po-po won't harass him, and since they won't be able to find an interpreter they won't know what to do with him. No drugs or alcohol in his system, right? Cool your space jets! He'll be fine."

Relai shook her head. "We have to go get him."

Tom gave a dismissive snort. "We show up and they'll realize you guys could translate—" ("Interpret.") "—whatever, and then we'll have to go through the whole legal process thing and do you really have time for that?"

"No, Tom, we don't. I don't think we have time for his photo to crop up in the Coalition search for me, either."

"Nah, *they* already know you're here, don't they? Whoever *they* are."

"The bruise and swelling will throw off image searches, right?" Relai asked Tannor.

"It doesn't matter." Tannor was busy tearing apart Tom's electronics setup. "Jumper in a lake, dead Titians, those stunned Regent Service guards, and a guy survives falling off a building? Earth Monitoring's—"

Ky finished with her: "Already here."

He stepped towards them. "Is the kid worth delaying our progress for?"

Relai said, "I can't believe you're even asking that question!"

"Neither can I. Milo," he said, "this is your call."

•

Milo blinked.

Goren was an adult. He wasn't their responsibility. Also, he was *just a kid*.

"We move on," he said. "He was in more danger when he was with us." Before Relai could even start, Ky looked sideways and admitted, "Won't be long before someone gets to him. They'll hurt him." His jaw muscle clenched. "Still your call."

Milo took a deep breath and steeled himself against Relai's desperate expression. "Everyone around her is going to get hurt. It's unavoidable. We move on."

"No!" Relai exclaimed. "Milo! *That cannot be your answer!*"

"It's not an answer, it's a fact. Do you think he didn't know what he was getting himself into?"

"He only entered service, what?—" ("Three months," Tannor supplied.) "—three months ago! No, he did *not* know what he was getting himself into, not that it matters."

"You heard him earlier—he has no respect for the lesser class, no respect for my people. Why would you want someone like that with you?"

"It's not about *him*," Relai exclaimed, "it's about the kind of person I'm trying to be! I won't leave him to be tortured, if I have to ditch you all and get him myself!"

"I could stop you," Milo snarled.

"*Try.*"

"All right!" Ky laughed, "this could go on until the stars burn out. Would it make a difference if I said we could get him out quick and easy? Just need to move fast."

Milo recalled the last time they'd been joined by a third; it had been a man at Essex, the block port just outside the atmosphere of Gastred. The man had asked Ky about his sleeping habits and then cleared a security path for them through the coalition transportation administration building. It was thanks to him that they tracked down the last known location of Relai's travel pod—the one that supposedly left Earth just after her father died, but instead only hopped continents. It was how they'd found her. Milo had barely made it back onto their stolen spaceship before Ky kicked off, and their third hadn't made it at all.

Milo never asked him his name.

(He remembered the man's face, though: dark blue eyes, blue-black hair, shorter than he and Ky and split right between their ages. Milo remembered him saying, "Live well, not long," and then, "We're not all—" before they cut him down. Milo would have preferred not to remember, but there were other things, worse things, to silence inside his head.)

Goren would've voted to leave himself behind. The one time his presence would've been useful, and he wasn't there.

"The one time," Milo muttered, and backed down.

•

Ky was already stripping out of his space clothes. "We need to hurry."

"I thought that's what we were doing," Relai snapped as she cleaned and charged the gen-guns just like he'd shown her.

Shirtless and promptly pantless, Ky shook his head and tore open Tom's closet. He still couldn't believe they were actually doing this. He couldn't believe he didn't mind.

"What are you going to do?" Relai demanded. Ky ignored her. "You're going to tell me to trust you and then later I'm going to feel like shooting you, aren't I?"

Milo smirked. "You get used to it."

Ky slipped on Tom's plain, worn Earthan clothes, and Milo followed with the clothes they'd bought for him. Ky attached his knife belt and Milo took up a gen-gun.

"What are we facing?" Milo murmured.

"Local police, maybe local anti-terrorism. Earth Monitoring and whatever Earthan forces those guys can pull. All armed." Ky looked Milo up and down, nudging back the gen-gun just a bit and handing him a mid-sized blade to conceal. Milo straightened Ky's collar. "Shoot our way in, grab Goren, shoot our way out."

"That is the *worst plan—*"

"No!" Tannor shouted. "You're not thugs, you're not assassins, and I was giving you too much credit when I thought you weren't *complete imbeciles*."

Ky snorted. "Saved Princess, here, didn't we?"

Tannor responded by throwing a hand out and clenching her fingers into claws. The gen-guns under their clothes popped and sizzled, and Ky let out a wordless snarl.

Milo cut in between them. "It's not safe for you, Relai Mora Aydor, to walk into an Earthan military facility, and we do nothing alone, remember? The Ardenian guards we stunned might recognize Tannor on sight. Ky and I know how to work together. You stay here."

It was cute, Ky thought, how Milo assumed Ky would've left those guards merely stunned. By now the kid should know how he felt about loose ends.

"First of all," Relai railed, "this hospital isn't military. Second, they all carry guns with real bullets!"

Ky wiggled his fingers.

"You can't heal everyone all the time!"

Ky looked at Tannor instead of Relai and snapped back, "Fix our gen-guns and we can stun them before they shoot us."

"Get this drug tick of my body! *Oh, wait—*" Tannor slapped a hand to her neck, her eyelashes fluttered, and she pulled it off herself. *"I don't need you!"*

"Are you going to drive over there in a stolen car?" Tom threw in, watching them argue as he typed and clicked. "Because that's a pretty stupid idea if you ask me."

"Ha! He's right," Relai said. "Now slow down and let's *think* about this."

She breathed in and out through her nose.

"Okay... I think I have a plan."

○○●○○

ii.

It was official. Goren Dray *hated* Earth.

The first time he woke he could barely open his eyes, mouth so dry he wanted to cry. He couldn't cry, though—he couldn't even breathe without vicious pain clawing through the whole right side of his chest, but he had to breathe so he had to feel it. Nothing made sense, nothing there was real, except the pain and the fog in his head.

He'd torn out everything stuck in his body, including *the thing up his penis, what?,* rolled out of the strange bed he found himself in, and huddled in a corner in teeth-chattering terror. Too many people had rushed in and crowded around him—three in blue, one in white, and three armed guards. He didn't know what was happening, where they'd taken him, or how long he'd been unconscious. Was this a prison? Gods, everything hurt so much.

That was hours ago… maybe days. Everything still hurt, and now they kept him bound to the bed by the wrist. It seemed this was prison. At least his organs remained (so far).

He couldn't read anything and he couldn't understand anyone because his comm wasn't working. They shouted in his face or spoke quietly and kindly, but he couldn't understand them either way. After a while they started throwing different languages at him, but he just scowled and wondered if anyone would ever come and rescue him.

Probably not.

Goren wasn't a complete idiot, whatever Milo might say. He could tell he was in trouble. His face hurt and the wrist restraint was rubbing his skin raw. At least they hadn't bound the wrist covered by a white molded case— that one hurt enough already. He wondered if it was broken. (His face was definitely broken.)

He was going to die in here.

The light outside was shining a painful mid-day bright when a blue lady came to take Goren to the bathroom. She and an Earthan guard, the lurky shadow always just outside, followed him to the bathroom door and wouldn't let him close it. Goren hunched sideways and tried not to look at himself in the mirror. He didn't want to do this anymore. He just wanted to go home.

The blue lady said something in a soothing tone as he peed with his ass hanging out for everyone to see.

"Your water smells weird," he replied, "and these ceilings are too short. This planet is embarrassing."

The guard didn't try to restrain him again as Goren shuffled back to the bed. When Goren realized he was just standing there with his wrist out like an idiot, his heart started to pound. Were they done with him?

The blue lady sat him down and offered him another little paper cup of beads.

He asked dully, "Are they gonna teach me English?" and pushed them away.

She just sighed and poked around his body and shined her little light. She had skin like Milo, sort of, or maybe more like Niko Yansa of Titus, and she seemed young. He could see hairs on her arms but he couldn't seem to muster the proper disgust.

"Tannor won't leave me here to die, right?" he asked.

She smiled and he could see pity in her eyes.

"Yeah," he sighed. "She knows Relai's more important. And Milo and Ky don't care about me." No one would come for him. Why would they? The queen was probably off-planet by now. His sisters would miss him, at least. They were so little.

The blue lady pointed to the door and spoke her nonsense slowly and clearly. He winced. "It's kind of a boring color. Does no one paint around here?"

She patted his uninjured arm. The door opened.

In walked a tall woman with dark, shiny hair and a light gray suit. No one else so far had been gray. Another Earthan guard and a man in a brown jacket followed her in, but the new woman was the only one who made eye contact with him. She was in charge.

She sat at the small table next to the cell's window, set out a large tablet, and beckoned him to sit in the opposite chair. Goren checked the Earthan guard; he didn't look angry.

He hoped he was understanding this right.

Goren eased himself off the bed, watching for any sign of violence along the way, and just barely made it over to the chair without exposing himself.

The woman started talking. Since she was a quieter sort than the others who had badgered him, he just stared apathetically at her tablet. Hadn't they told her that he didn't speak her language?

She held her hands to her chest and repeated something. Again and again, she said it slowly and intentionally.

"*Hope.*"

He glared at her.

"What am I, a pet? I get it, your name is *Hope*. I'm tired."

She rattled on in Earthan some more, then pointed at him. He sighed and rubbed the crook of the elbow on his broken arm. What was the harm in telling her his name?

He pointed at himself. "Go. Ren. Goren."

"*Goren!*" she cried with her thick accent. It was sort of sweet, actually. He could see a gun under her jacket but she wasn't wearing one of those uniforms—maybe she was a sort of communications expert or something. Maybe she was just trying to help.

He pulled in a shallow breath and pushed himself to his feet. The guard and brown coat guy perked up so he curled his chin tight against his chest, deferential, and clapped his injured right arm across his chest to cover his rank tattoo with his hand.

Hope jumped to her feet and mirrored him. It looked ridiculous. Goren just sucked in air and looked at the bland speckled ceiling until she stopped.

They sat back down.

Hope pulled a picture out of a fold of paper and flipped it in front of him. It was the bounty hunter, gross and broken and dead-looking on a silver metal sheet.

"Ew," he said. "I really thought I killed her. I mean, she fell off a building. I freaked out about it. I *yelled* at Relai." He shook his head. "I can't believe she survived that fall."

Hope asked a question, intense and quick.

Goren could only slump a little further forward. "You probably don't need to worry about her. She wants Relai, not me. Relai's gone by now."

Then Hope glanced furtively at the two Earthan guards, creaked her chair closer to him around the table, and pointed up at the ceiling.

"Yeah, I agree," he said. "Way too low."

She tapped firmly on the bounty hunters face and then pointed. *Up. UP.*

He frowned. "I don't think she's in the ceiling."

Hope huffed and gave up on the bounty hunter. She moved to her tablet, instead, and opened it like a book—it was an Earthan computer. He'd never used one, but they'd seen one in the Earth intro class. You could actually pop off the little keys; they were *pieces* instead of a state of the material.

She tapped away and then spun it around to show him the visual. She hit a key. The image moved.

He recognized Captain Fass, the utter bastard, looking sweaty and rugged and dashing, held unbound in a cell much darker and more menacing than this one holding Goren. Soldiers questioned him in Italian and Fass said nothing at all until someone adjusted the video feed and he noticed he was being recorded. Then he looked straight at the camera and said:

"The Queen is here. Kill her. Strength to Unity."

Goren's mouth opened a little. He looked at Hope, trying to find any sign that she understood the words. No. She was only watching to see if he reacted.

He swallowed. "That's not good."

•

The boy, Goren, absolutely recognized the survivor from the Gallinara crash, and Hope didn't need to speak his language to understand. Whatever the crash survivor had said, it scared him.

She'd seen the report: Goren had suffered a concussion, a broken wrist, and three broken ribs. Witnesses said he shot an unarmed woman four or five times without provocation, and then the shooting victim assaulted him and went on to snap a responding officer's neck and shoot another with her own gun before she escaped. The local PD, with Detective Dan Rooney in the lead, didn't see Goren as a threat—but they weren't going to let him go without answers, either.

She wanted to take him home, feed him, and give him a comfortable bed to sleep in until all his bruises disappeared. The doctor had estimated his age to be between sixteen and seventeen years old; if it weren't for the gun and the language thing, the Hennepin County PD would have thrown him to the child services wolves by now.

The gun. She'd collected it from the station on her way to the hospital. Detective Rooney, Hope's new best friend, had met her when she picked it up. He thought she'd left it in the trunk of her car. It was currently in her ankle holster.

The boy pointed at the survivor on the computer screen and did a funny little head shake, repeating a word over and over again.

She tried to repeat: "Sock vier eh? Shock vee ra?"

He grimaced again and seemed to accept her butchering of his language. Just to confirm, she put her hand on her chest and said, "Hope," a finger nearly touching the boy's chest, "Goren," and tapped the screen, "Sok Vira?"

He frowned and said, "*Neh! Sak fass!*" He tapped again, harder, and emphasized it like a name: "*Fass! Sa kvi rah.*"

Okay, that was something. Hope pulled her notepad from under the laptop and a pen from her pocket. On the pad she wrote:

"neh = no"

It was a start.

Then Goren pounced on her pen and paper. Hope waved the jumpy police officer away and leaned forward to watch.

He drew a fair caricature of the survivor from the video, sneering as he added an overly square jaw and a crooked grin. He pointed at both the drawing and the screen. "Fass."

Then Goren scribbled out the man's face, nearly tearing the paper, making a gagging noise of disgust as he went. "*Rah.*"

Hope smiled. "So he's bad. Fass is bad?" She made sure to match a glowering, nasty facial expression with the key word to get her point across.

"*Rah!*" Goren grinned. If she were a few years older she could be his mother. (What a depressing thought that was. The last thing Hope wanted was children (to the shock and disappointment of her entire extended family, including three tias in Mexico who had built a whole altar to San Gerardo for prayer on the issue); she had enough to worry about.)

Goren pointed at himself: "*Tov.*" At the survivor, with an exaggerated frown and a gravely voice: "*Rah.*" Back at himself, smiling: "*Neha rah. Tov.*"

"Good. You are good, *tov.* He's bad, *rah.*" She mimicked his change in countenance to show she understood.

Goren laughed and nodded. Hope clapped her hands in satisfaction, proud she was finally getting somewhere. Instinctively, she clasped hold of his unbroken arm. "Goren. It's okay. We're going to figure everything out."

But then the nurse came back carrying a folded pair of hospital scrubs and a white cotton t-shirt, followed by Detective Rooney and a man in a dark suit. Hope pulled away from Goren, squared and alert.

Rooney looked pissed.

This new man was tall and muscular and handsome, with intensely black skin and a serious face, and he was armed. Hope stood up.

"Bad news," Rooney said. "It's a done deal and I couldn't do anything to stop it."

As he spoke, a sharp motion brought Hope's attention back toward the door—the man lifted his right hand like a chop, palm flat and fingers lined up tight, to his right shoulder. It was quick and fluid and he wasn't trying to hide it. Goren pushed away from the table and stumbled backward. He stopped just short of cowering in the corner, breathing shallowly and wincing.

Goren cringed and swayed like he was about to faint, then he brought his feet together, straightened his back, and put his injured hand to the opposite shoulder. The same thing he'd done for Hope. *A salute?*

"What does that sign mean?" Hope demanded.

The nurse shook the scrub pants loose as the man ignored her question and held out his hand. "Colonel Terrance Iverson, State Department." His voice could've melted butter.

Hope took his hand and tried to match the strength of his grip. "Agent Hope Valdez, Homeland Security. You can't have him."

Rooney groaned and rubbed his temple. "I know, Valdez, believe me, but he's legitimate. Like I said, it's done."

Iverson only raised his eyebrows. "We're leaving as soon as he's dressed."

This guy was so tall, *damn*. It was the first time in her life Hope had ever wished she were wearing heels.

The nurse had convinced Goren to sit back down, but the boy couldn't bend forward far enough to get his feet into the pants so she had to crouch beside him and help.

"Look," Hope said, "he can *barely move*."

"That isn't your concern anymore," Colonel Iverson replied. Goren stood and pulled the pants up to his waist, cinched a knot in the drawstrings, and then turned his back to them and shook off the hospital gown.

Hope stared hard at the massive boot print swollen purple-green across his skinny back, then at the dip in the ridge of his shoulder where his tattoo began—a tattoo which, Hope realized, was exactly where he'd placed his hand when they did their weird salute-thing. The mark didn't take up too much space, extending a few inches down his chest from the distal end of his collarbone, simple and dark. They'd photographed both bruise and tattoo when the kid first came in. The tattoo pic file kept going corrupt.

"The doc put his age at maybe sixteen," she said, lowballing. "He's a minor."

"War on Terror," Iverson replied. "They like to recruit young."

She scoffed. "He's a witness, not a suspect. The weapon they brought in might not even be his."

Iverson barely moved, so infuriatingly calm. "My investigation supersedes yours."

With the nurse's help Goren finally got both arms into the t-shirt, and when the fabric shifted down and covered the ugly bruising on his back and ribs Hope let out a breath of relief.

She angled herself between Iverson and Goren. "We haven't identified his language yet. The doctor won't discharge him before he understands how to take care of his injuries."

Iverson's thin smile left her cold. "That won't be a problem."

Detective Rooney had to grab her arm to stop her from doing something rash, so Hope used her mouth instead. "Those police officers that died," she demanded, "do their lives mean nothing to you? You can't just disappear with the only witness who knows who killed them."

Behind them Goren just stood there like a tired toy soldier, still barefoot, listening to people argue over him in a language he couldn't understand.

Iverson paused. Every blink and twitch of his lip seemed calculated to intimidate. "The killer you're referring to is one target of my investigation. Believe me," he chewed each word before he spat them out at her, "I am more equipped and more motivated to catch her than anyone here."

"Then work with us," Hope threw back, mimicking his tone, "and maybe we'll catch her even faster."

Before Iverson could respond, the door burst open and the nurse rushed back in. Hope hadn't even noticed her leave.

She stopped short before the crowd of people in the tiny room, then picked out Hope to address. "There's a man coming," she said, breathless, "he says he's the patient's father."

Hope glanced sharply at Rooney. "Did he give the patient's name?"

"No, he described him, tattoo and everything. His English isn't good— we couldn't get him to fill out any forms. He looks worried sick and he keeps muttering to himself in their language."

"Where is he?"

"The waiting room at the end of the hall."

"Great!" Hope swept her arms out. "Let's go meet Dad!"

"No," Iverson said, and she wanted to punch him in the mustache. He was examining the room, checking the windows and the bathroom. "Bring him here. Have your talk. I'll be across the hall until you're done."

Then he walked out.

"What the hell?" Rooney said.

"Five bucks says he's gonna arrest whoever comes through that door," Hope replied. Then she turned to Goren, who'd sunk back into his chair in obvious relief as soon as Iverson left. "Your dad's here, maybe?"

Dad, boss, superior officer? Handler?

Hope had a sneaking suspicion that she wasn't going to get much time with the man, but she wanted to look him over before he got to Goren.

They met him at the door.

The man was medium height, black hair, with darker skin than Goren and vaguely Asian (or Pacific Islander?) features; the two definitely didn't appear related. It looked like he'd cobbled his outfit together from bins in a second-hand store and she could tell he was holding himself so he looked smaller than he was.

"My son, my son," the man was saying. Thick, inscrutable accent. "Where?"

Hope smiled. Rooney stuck out his hand and introduced himself.

The man only stared at the hand with a confused expression and didn't say a word.

"Yeah, sure," Hope said. "My name is Agent Valdez, Homeland Security. Not ICE, don't worry. What is your name?"

He shook his head resolutely. "You show me my son."

Iverson had disappeared completely. They traded side glances, and then Detective Rooney grunted. "We show him his son."

Hope stepped backward into the room. Inside, Goren looked up from his seat at the table.

○○●○○

iii.

Relai checked for movement through each of the car windows in turn.
Nothing so far.

Across the street sat the sprawling concrete and glass hospital, glowing
warmly in the setting sun and the incandescent streetlights that had just
turned on. Eight stories tall and covering five large city blocks, the complex
was nearly the size of the Kilani bazaar. Despite her years on Earth, Relai had
difficulty imagining the need for a facility of this size devoted solely to the
healing of the sick and wounded. (During her travels, Relai had always had a
med scanner nearby, and, of course, nothing remotely similar existed on
Arden. Medical scanners couldn't solve every malady, but the greater class
had doctors come to them. The lesser class had clinics, but she'd never been
in one.) Fortunately, Tom had been able to find some floor plans on the
internet to help them navigate its labyrinthine corridors.

She'd parked a new stolen vehicle across from the doors where Milo, Ky,
Tom and Goren would exit. Once they reached the ground floor she'd pull
around and pick them up just outside the entrance. There'd be no pursuit on
foot because Tannor would lock the doors, and they could ditch the car after
they cleared downtown Minneapolis. Simple.

Beside her, Tannor was silent. When the others left, she'd closed her eyes
and claimed she could pick out everyone's comms except Goren; his must've
broken during his run-in with the bounty hunter. Relai watched the
movement of her eyes under their lids and the flinching of her eyelashes, then
Tannor unbuckled her seatbelt and leaned forward far enough to rest her
head on the glove compartment. Her curls swarmed around her face so Relai
couldn't see her anymore.

"How are you?" Relai asked.

"It's a lot…" Tannor mumbled. "I keep getting dizzy."

"Is this going to work?"

Tannor rubbed her temples. "I'll make it work." She sounded more
stubborn than confident.

Relai chewed the inside of her lip until it bled. She spoke through her
comm.

"Ky: update?"

•

The problem with stealing an Earthan medical uniform, of course, was that very few doctors stood 76 inches tall. Milo saw Earthan workers in the periphery of his vision as he clipped down a long, sterile hallway, but he ignored them all. Tom Wood stomped ahead of him, driving away anyone hoping to catch Milo's eye.

"You're not going to make it ten feet looking like that," Relai had said. "Someone will stop you, and what are you going to say?"

Looking like that. So matter-of-fact.

Milo knew how people perceived him. He'd seen enough narratives with a hulking, silent, predatory Erayd character, always the villain or the silent stack of muscles, to feel sick in his belly when he played that role himself. But Ardenians recognized the beast, and he needed people to fear him.

Either one must remain terrified or become terrifying.

It worked. He could terrify.

But right now, he needed to do the opposite: he needed to blend in, and so he'd allowed Ky to cut off most of his hair and trim his beard. He hardly recognized the person in the mirror afterward, but there wasn't time to ponder. It didn't matter, anyway.

Judging by the other doctors' attire, this coat was supposed to fit more loosely, but they moved fast and made no eye contact. Plenty of people stared as they passed, but no one stopped them to question their presence.

They turned left. Tom was rambling on and on, "—So then I said to her, get off my back, *sssssss*! But not in a mean way, like, in a respectful way—"

Relai: *Ky: update?*

Ky: *Getting close.*

"Uh, we're inside the building somewhere, going deeper into the building," was Tom's reply. "Anyway, then she punched me and that's how I got a liver bleed, and *sssss ssss sssss*, I know you didn't see this one coming: that's how I met Marisa! She's—"

Milo heard a low whistle from behind, coming from among a group of middle-aged women. Though Tom was the one making all the noise, Milo was the one drawing eyes. One woman walked into the edge of a door.

He wasn't terrifying anyone, but he certainly wasn't blending in.

He cursed Ky for giving him that haircut.

Not that Milo was a stranger to this reaction. Every stereotype came in multiple varieties—and just as often, people saw in him their fantasies: the brute of cheap commons erotic fic, untamed and irresistible, unconcerned with greater class propriety. After eight months of performing, the truth had wormed its way into his head: what people feared, they also wanted—to be possessed by or to possess, to be dominated by or to dominate.

They wanted. Milo didn't. Milo could kill, he could stalk and loom and snarl like the best disgustingly simple caricature, but he couldn't smolder and cant his hips and *lie*. (He wasn't Ky.)

(*How can you think that way? He's saved your skin so many times.*)

They reached the first set of locked doors. He saw exactly what Tannor had told him to look for: a thick metal bar at the top of the door, clamped to another in the door sill; a black square on the wall beside the door. An electromagnetic lock and its control panel. As instructed, he pushed one of Tannor's little 'door ticks'—a clever improvisation consisting of one of Ky's drug ticks, some wire, and a single paper-thin gen-gun cell—under the control panel.

"Okay, first tick's in."

"Now, stay sharp people!" Tom said with flair. "I always wanted to say stuff like that. Like we're spies or *sssssss* or something, and we get to say, 'Code Grey Duck, *sssssssss*, the Fox is the in the Hen House. Repeat: the Fox is in—"

Milo turned off the interpreter function on his comm. He couldn't respond to any questions from hospital staff or security (Tom would step in as a mockery of an interpreter if needed) and there was no point in understanding Tom right now. All Milo needed to do was appear annoyed.

Which was not hard.

He placed the next tick, Tannor did her thing, and he pushed against the horizontal metal bar. Tom followed close behind.

Tom tried to turn left at an intersection, but Milo had memorized their route so he grabbed the back of Tom's thin blue shirt and steered him back the opposite way. One more door tick and then Tannor could create an exit path for Ky and Goren.

Another tick, through a door to a stairwell. Up.

Relai's voice cut through Tom's: "How close are we?"

"I'm on his floor," Ky said. "Just say go."

"Ten seconds," Milo whispered.

He placed the last tick and stopped without opening the door. Tom leaned against the concrete wall of the stairwell and tried to catch his breath.

Milo knew Tom's comm could translate for him, so he switched his own translator back on and said, "Well done," as he dug into the pack of clothes for Goren.

Tom bent himself in a strange way and stayed there far too long. "Thanks, friend."

Milo sighed. "What are you doing?"

"Yoga! It's for my anxiety."

"We're ready," Milo said.

·

Relai swallowed and looked through the window at the hospital entrance. "Can you control the ticks?" she asked Tannor.

Tannor breathed deeply, in and out.

"I can't—" Tannor gasped. In again, out again. "They're too far away, there are too many electronics in the building." She sat back, hands on her temples. "I can't control them. Shit."

Relai sucked in a breath and nodded. "Okay." She pulled Tannor's left arm down and forced her to look.

"It's okay. Do you have your gen-gen? We're going inside."

"No—we can't go inside, what if someone—"

Relai got out of the car and Tannor had to follow, tucking her jacket around her gun as she hurried after. "It'll be okay," Relai said. "In and out. You can open and close those doors so no one can follow us. We can stun anyone who gives us trouble."

Relai swept through the sliding glass doors and started down a hallway. She tapped her comm back on. "How close are we, guys?"

Ky: *I'm on his floor. Just say go.*

Milo: *Ten seconds.*

The hallway became a bridge of sorts into the next building, crossing over the street below. Large windows revealed the glass towers of the city, lit up for the night. One in particular caught Relai's eye...

The tower.

Milo: *We're ready.*

"Just give us a minute."

Milo: *Relai, what is it?*

·

Instead of answering Milo's question, Relai said: *Tom?*

Her voice was urgent, breathless. Milo looked to Tom, confused.

Relai: *The building the hunter fell off of yesterday—I can see it.*

"Yeah," Tom said, "it's like six blocks away. So?"

Relai: *Are there any other hospitals even closer to it than this one?*

"No. Why?"

Milo glanced down the stairs, muscles tensing. "What, Relai?"

There came a long pause.

Relai: *Nothing. Keep to the plan.*

He stared at the bland tan door, then turned and paced to the opposite wall. He remembered every word Relai had ever spoken to him and he knew her face, but her face wasn't here, and it didn't matter because he knew her voice. She was lying.

He caught Tom's eye and the guy shrugged. Milo shook his head. "We're coming to you now."

He nearly missed Relai's next words beneath the thudding of his feet as he descended the stairs and Tom's protests behind him.

Relai: *No! Stop, okay? We're already inside the hospital.*

Milo halted on the next level down. Tom peered over the railing at him and Milo gritted his teeth. "Why?"

Relai didn't answer. She must have been talking to Tannor with her comm off.

Tannor: *Ky. We need you to find Olin Batar and tell us where he is.*

Ky: *Who? Why should I know?*

Relai: *The Applica agent you healed on the roof. You didn't heal him fully so he might be here.*

Ky: *Why would you care? I don't know where he—*

Relai: *He told me, Ky. An Applica agent was already attending me and it's not Tannor so it has to be you. Your agents can find each other no matter where you are, can't you? So where is he?*

Milo stopped.

"What is going on?" Tom said. Milo barely heard him.

344

Ky cursed and said Milo's name. He cursed again, and that's when Milo realized it was true.

He had been an assignment.

("Gastred's boring," Ky had said. The groundship had just barely escaped the atmosphere and Milo could feel his own intestines slipping under the press of his hands. "Now watch this. You're not dying. Just watch. It'll hurt but it's worth it, I promise—")

Not even an assignment... the path to an assignment.

Nothing.

"Uh, guys?" Tom broke in, "Why does Milo look like someone just died?"

Ky: *It's not what it sounds like—*

Relai: *Throw your punches later, guys. I need to know where Batar is right now.*

Ky: *Look, I'm retired from Applica, I can't—*

Milo turned his comm off.

.

"None of these signs make sense," Relai whispered. She held Tannor's hand, fingers laced, and led her deeper into the hospital.

"You okay?" she asked under her breath. She smiled at a security guard but he missed it, too busy staring at Tannor's chest.

Tannor's eyes fluttered half-closed, but she managed to point to a sign that read 'Trauma Center'. They crossed the lobby and then Tannor jerked at her hand.

"Stop, I have to..." she pulled her hand free and rubbed at her eyes. "I need everyone to stop moving around."

Relai turned toward the wall and snapped, "Everyone stop. Just stay where you are."

Tom's voice crackled in.

Tom: *I think Milo turned his thingy off.*

"Make him stay in one spot, then!"

Tom: *What am I gonna go, latch onto his leg? He's THREE OF ME. Hey, Relai says stop, man. Tannor needs you to stop.*

No one paid them any attention at all.

Tom: *Wow, it worked. Cool.*

Relai watched Tannor carefully. She still wasn't focusing on anything around them, but she didn't look in pain.

"Okay," Tannor finally breathed. "I know where everyone is. I'm okay."

"Ready?" Relai asked.

Tannor closed her eyes and found Relai's hand. "Let's go."

They pushed through the doors to the Trauma Center. Relai saw two, three nurses going about their business. No doctors, no emergencies. It was peaceful.

"They'd take him to the Trauma Center and we're there. Ky. Tell us where to go."

Ky: *Tannor, turn his comm back on.*

Relai hissed through her teeth at him. "Leave him alone, asshole. You're a liar and he needs a minute. Find Olin Batar for me now."

An orderly walked past and Relai ducked her head and clasped her hands to her lips while Tannor just stood planted, eyes closed. Usually people here were pretty good about leaving supplicants alone while they were talking to their gods.

Ky: *Listen to me. I can't find him for you. I cannot. I only told them I had you to keep a team off our backs and it didn't work. Tannor, just look in their system and track him down by his time of admission and injuries.*

"Okay, okay," Relai said. She clutched Tannor's arm and pulled her along until she saw a dark, unattended computer on a rolling cart.

•

"Milo," Ky tried again, even though Milo wasn't listening, "Applica has nothing to do with you. I called them the moment a team grabbed Relai and they wouldn't tell me anything because *I'm retired.*" Relai could hear him. Tannor, too. And Tom. All of them could hear him.

He checked himself over in the reflection of the glass waiting room window. Distraught, messy, and older than his years. He might even manage to muster some tears.

Relai: *Just go get Goren. No one cares.*

Yeah, no one who mattered.

The nurse waved from the door of the waiting room and said, "You can see him now."

Ky hopped to his feet and clasped his hands. "My son?" he said in English, rolling the words like ball bearings around his tongue. "Thank!"

Six doors to the left, six right. Third one down, door cracked. Three at the nurse's station. Hallway clear. They'd retrace his steps but turn right at the station just before the waiting room, then left, down the hall and through Milo's door. Tannor would lock it and any pursuit would end there. They'd get Goren dressed. Down four floors, through another door, lock it behind, and then they'd walk out to the car like normal people, no pursuit.

He switched back to Ardi and whispered as he walked. "If he's not in running shape it'll take another ten or fifteen seconds. Milo... Tom, make sure Milo's ready in the stairwell."

Tom: *He's ready! We have the pants all set to go. Goren can just stick his feet out and jump through the air and slide into them without stopping. It'll be awesome. We're good.*

"Good," Ky muttered. They came to Goren's room—"My son! My son!"—and a dark-haired woman stepped out.

○○●○○

iv.

"*There.*"

Relai followed the line of sight Tannor created with a jerk of their intertwined hands.

No guard at the door.

"We don't have time for this," Tannor whispered.

"We'll make time," Relai said. She tapped her comm on so Ky could hear her. "Ky. We found Olin Batar. Can you stall for... three minutes?"

Ky: *How about thirty seconds?*

"Three. Minutes."

Fine, he spat back.

There were too many people around for them to get into the room unnoticed. Relai turned to Tannor. "Can you make an alarm go off or something? What about the lights above the doors? Set one off."

Tannor opened her eyes. The shadows under her eyes seemed to be getting darker. "I've been practicing. My fingers. It's like—I don't know. Look."

She brought up her left hand and pointed at the door light furthest from them. Relai watched her fingers as she jabbed and then pinched with her finger and thumb. Her eyes went vague, the tips of her fingers turned white from pinching, then she flicked them open and the door flashed red. The alarm emitted a piercing *squawk! squawk! squawk!*

The nurses turned heads in unison like a flock of birds.

Relai dragged Tannor inside the hospital room and eased the door shut.

"That was great," Relai whispered into the silence of the dimly lit room. "So great. You're amazing."

Tannor shook her head, but Relai found a figure in the hospital bed and lost track of the rest of her words.

He was lying asleep, half-reclined, with a blanket up to his waist. An orange halo of light glowed around the shades covering the window, just bright enough for her to see the details of his face when she came close.

His brow was smooth. The whole hour she'd known him, she'd never seen his face relaxed like this. His ears stuck out the same and he looked pale, but he was alive. Now that they weren't being chased by anyone, she took a moment to look. Beauty helped, after all.

Relai leaned into the bed, her hands hovering over his shoulder, his arm, finally reaching past the cloth of his sleeve to the bare skin of his wrist. She gripped it firmly.

"Olin Batar," she said, "I need you to wake up. Wake up, Olin." He didn't respond, so Relai squeezed his wrist harder and said, "*Wake up.*"

His breathing changed.

"No," he sighed.

Relai laughed, and the sound of it startled her. "Tannor, can you get him some water?"

Tannor moved off. Relai didn't turn.

"Olin, look at me," she said.

He opened his eyes. His brow wrinkled and then he smiled. "You made it."

"You died for me," she replied. "Thank you."

He tried to shrug and cringed. The hospital gown around his chest split up the front and tied just below his collar bone, and underneath it she could see white gauze with strips of tape holding it in place on his chest.

"Only mostly. Raphe pulled me through."

Tannor came with water. Olin bent his elbows and pushed himself up to sitting. Relai helped with a hand on his back and when he settled she didn't remove it. He was pleasantly warm and the fabric was thin so she could feel muscles moving as he shifted.

"I'm so sorry," she said, and she felt it in her eyes. "I'm sorry you had to go through that. Thank you."

He rested on his arms, breathing delicately, and smiled with just the corner of his mouth. "It was my choice."

"I know. You don't have to do what I'm about to ask you to do, either. You can say no."

Olin shifted subtly into an Applica agent, square and capable, stupid ears and all. Relai put a little distance between them. She wanted him to put his hands on her shoulders again so she could pretend she was somewhere safe, but that wasn't going to happen.

She heard him in her head:

What do you need?

○○●○○

Ky stepped through the doorway and tried to look stern and distant so maybe Goren wouldn't react. He failed; the kid saw him, gasped, and knocked over his chair as he scrambled toward Ky. So much for keeping this professional.

"I'm glad you don't weigh very much," Ky laughed, but it was drowned out by Goren's wail of pain as they collided in the center of the room. Stupid kid. Ky rested one arm gingerly around Goren's back and the other on his neck so he could get at the skin. He closed his eyes and dove in, seeking out the most serious injuries first. Head, then ribs.

"I thought I was going to die in here!" Goren mumbled into Ky's shoulder. His fingers wrinkled the canvas of Ky's shoddy stolen jacket as his body wrenched through healing. "They barely fed me, ow, oww, and Hope is the only one who tried to understand me—ah, I can breathe, thanks!—and I swear she's nice and I think she'll help us, except you're here now so you're going to get me out of here, right?"

"Stop talking," Ky replied, and let him go.

Goren pulled back and scrubbed his uninjured hand through his lack of hair. "I thought it would involve more explosions, actually, but this is better. You should rescue people for a living!"

Goren's smile alone could have lit the room. Ky put a hand to his shoulder and looked him over, head to toe. He was paler than normal, his face nearly unrecognizable with the giant purpling bruise across his eye and cheekbone. No shoes. These police officers hadn't harmed him, Ky supposed, but he hadn't expected that sort of thing this early anyway.

The right department hadn't gotten to him yet.

Agent Valdez cut in. "Can you interpret for us?"

Ky spared an English, "No," for the agent, then Goren started rattling again.

"There's a Titian out there! He's dressed like a—I don't know what, maybe a really important guard? Oh, hells, so many hells, I thought I was gonna be tortured to death with something even worse than all the crap they did to me here, which was not fun at all."

A Titian. Earth Monitoring.

The best-case scenario had already evaporated. On to the second plan, then.

"I see I'm too late," he said in English, dropping the sad excuse for an accent as he turned to Agent Valdez. "Are you the highest authority associated with my son's case so far?"

The other guy, the detective, scratched behind his ear and said, "Great. Okay. I'm just gonna watch because he's not mine anymore."

Valdez smirked at him and then went and sat at the table. She crossed her legs and relaxed back. "You're not Goren's father. You answer questions, not me."

Ky clenched his jaw and glared at Goren. "You told her your name?"

Goren winced. "She's nice?"

Ky took the seat across from Agent Valdez; there weren't enough chairs so Goren just hovered awkwardly over his shoulder. Valdez looked Ky's age, maybe a little older, or maybe she aged well. Ky noticed her give a soft glance back at Goren—it seemed she was already responding to his wide-eyed youth. Stupid kid with his eyelashes and his earnest face. Ky marked Valdez in their camp if this came down to a fight.

No, *when.* Two minutes from now, probably.

"Who else is here for him?" he asked.

Agent Valdez didn't react except to slide a photo of his spit gun across the table.

He kept his face perfectly still. She smirked, probably a bluff, but it didn't matter. Ky wanted his baby back.

"Someone is here," he said. "You don't know him and he wants Goren."

She didn't disagree.

Goren looked between them apprehensively. "Ky? Oh, should I not say your name? Sorry, sorry! She doesn't understand anything, though. She thought Fass's name was Bad when I was telling her he was bad—"

Ky snapped his head around. "What were you telling her about Fass? *Why would you*—"

"Oh, they have a video feed of him being interrogated by some Earthan military guys, and he said, 'The queen is here. Kill her. Strength to Unity.' They wanted to see if I knew him and of course I do, sorry, but there was no hiding it, and I really think she's trying to help us. The Titian guy was terrifying compared to her! Don't kill her, please?"

Ky took a slow breath and stopped Goren with a tight grip on his forearm. "Shut up."

An inkling was growing deep in his mind. A terrifying Titian in Earth Monitoring...

Could Ky *know this guy?*

If he did, it meant—

He leaned forward and reached out across the table. "I never shook your hand."

Valdez peered at him suspiciously, but in the end she shifted and pressed her palm firmly into his.

Ky's eyelids fluttered as he concentrated and yeah, he found it, poison working its way into her system. Her body knew it was there and it was trying to fight it, but it was losing. He inched forward out of his seat without letting go and murmured across the table very quietly:

"Are you feeling ill? The man who wants Goren—he's cleaning up loose ends."

She jerked her hand away and leaned back in alarm.

"Explain."

Ninety seconds.

"I'd leave immediately," he said, settling back into his chair, "but I feel a little bad about leaving you and... by the end, probably most of these people, I think, to die."

"*What?*" the other man exclaimed.

"Who are you?" Valdez hissed.

Ky stared at the door. "Nobody important," he said.

"I think my head hurts," the detective said.

"I'm sure my friend is listening," Ky said. "Why don't I just address him directly?" He stood up. He spoke in Ardi.

"It's hardly fair that you can hear me and I can't see you."

Behind him Goren choked out, "Ky?"

Ky shook his head. "I know you're there. Coward."

The door burst open.

Oh, he was *really* going to get shot for this.

.

Relai glanced at Tannor. She'd moved back against the door and now she was resting against it with her eyes closed. Focused on everyone else, probably. Good.

"Olin, Unity is trying to take over Daat Base," Relai explained. "I locked it down using my authority, and I need you and your team to go—your team is coming to get you, right?"

"They already tried," Olin said, pointing at a small vase of purple flowers with no card. Then he threw his legs over the edge of the bed. She saw his feet angle and stretch. She closed her eyes, then looked back at his face. "I was in the middle of surgery. A bullet lodged in the lining next to my heart and they couldn't leave it there, even with my wounds six weeks healed." He smiled softly. "Half-healed and covered in new blood. Lots of people want to talk to me."

He shifted and Relai held up her hands to stop him from standing up. "You just had heart surgery? No. I can't ask you to go into battle now."

He tilted his head. *Applica agents aren't soldiers, Relai. We don't go into battle.* "Besides," he said out loud, leaning into her space and sliding off the bed to his feet, "a new jumper should be coming for us from headquarters tomorrow. It'll have a scanner."

"Why haven't you left the hospital, then?" she asked.

He scratched his shoulder. "I was tired."

Then the heart monitor started beeping and it jolted them all. Olin put one hand over the gauze on his chest and sat back onto the bed, eyes closed, breathing through his nose. "I don't think I'm ready to stand yet, actually."

"Yeah, I see that." She helped him lie back down and when he settled she touched his temple again. "Rest for now."

"I could use a few shots of vodka," he mumbled.

Relai smiled. "Scandalous."

Damn if she didn't want to crawl onto the bed next to him and forget the rest of this life. She'd never wanted to do that before, ever, with anyone.

She was never going to feel safe enough, ever, with anyone.

Suddenly she couldn't breathe, couldn't stay in that room a moment longer. She was so stupid, so stupid—

No, you're not. You're scared. I'm sorry I can't help you more.

You've already done more than enough, she thought back. *It's my job to take care of everyone. And that means you have to go to Daat.*

He opened his eyes. *No rest for the weary?*

I'm sorry, she thought. *We can't let Unity gain a foothold on Earth. We can't let the coalition take Earth over with the excuse of protecting her, either.*

The brow furrow returned. *What are you saying?*

Before she could even think, Tannor's voice cut through the dim room. "Ky? Do you need me to come?"

Relai spun away from Olin Batar. "What?"

She reeled at the fury on Tannor's face.

"You turned your comm off. Damn it, Relai, there's a Titian here for Goren and now he's got Ky, too."

•

The Titian roared into the room and Goren reached for a weapon that wasn't there as the man bore down on Ky with an Earthan gun raised.

"Iverson!" Ky exclaimed. "Nice suit."

"I WILL SHOOT YOU!" Iverson shouted, and Goren realized that everyone in the room had also drawn their weapons. Hope, the nice officer, the other guy—everyone was armed except Goren. Since hiding wasn't an option, he shuffled sideways until he stood between Hope and the crazy Titian waving the gun.

"Eight years, Jack?" Iverson snarled. "You show up after *eight years? Whose body did we identify in Yemen?*"

The others were shouting at him, probably telling him to put away his gun. That's what Goren would have been shouting.

"As far as Earth is concerned," Ky said, far more gently than Goren expected, "I *am* dead." He put his palms out. "I'm not armed, Terrence."

Terrence Iverson breathed slow and loud and deep, and then he put away his gun. His face (which was sort of grizzled and handsomely aged, the kind of face Goren hoped to have when he was his father's age) faded from fury into a more normal level of anger. He said something in English and everyone else stood down. Goren nearly fell over in relief.

"So is he gonna help us now?" he asked. "My feet are cold."

"Twenty seconds, kiddo," Ky replied.

Goren groaned and steadied himself to run. Of course they were outnumbered and unarmed and they were about to die. He'd hoped too soon. This was pretty much the worse rescue ever.

•

Ky needed another twenty seconds without cuffs or bullet wounds, so he smirked and said:

"That mustache makes you look Earthan."

Perfect.

Ky narrowly avoided the swing of Terrence Iverson's fist and landed a halfhearted blow to the stomach in return. Iverson had always been built like a mountain, and it felt like punching stone. Ky didn't put much effort into it; Iverson needed to understand that he wasn't trying to hurt him.

Iverson's other fist caught his jaw next and Ky snagged the lapel of his suit just in time to stop from pitching backward. He jerked himself in close, connected forehead to nose. They were both still as fast as eight years ago, the last time they sparred, and now Ky could tell Iverson wasn't moving to kill him. Finally at the same port on that one.

They managed three hits, one and a half seconds, before the others pulled them apart. Valdez on him, Goren's police guard on Iverson.

"There's a bounty on her head and you know it," Ky shouted over the struggle. "I'm working *with her*."

Terrence shook himself free and brushed his clothes straight, glaring at the officers who'd dragged him back.

"You can't keep her safe, Jack," he spat.

"Likewise."

They stared each other down.

"I'll kill you if I have to," Iverson said.

Ky smiled. "Likewise."

Iverson sighed and his shoulders shifted to a less aggressive tilt.

"The SEAL team threw you a funeral, you know."

"Shame," Ky replied. "I like to attend all of my funerals."

•

Hope tried to fit this new information into her understanding of the events: Colonel Iverson had not only understood their language, but could speak it and had taken the man's words personally enough to burst through the door and point a gun at his head.

Then the guy had smirked and it turned into a fistfight instead. Hope had the pleasure of dragging the mystery guy backwards, feeling his strength and getting a sense of how he balanced. She could take him in a fight, she thought.

"Explain, or I'm arresting you both," Hope demanded as the men straightened themselves out.

Iverson spat, "Previous acquaintance."

"Didn't end well, I take it?" Hope said.

Iverson glared. "You don't have the security clearance for me to answer that."

Great. Aliens with security clearance.

Iverson looked from Hope to Detective Rooney. "You—Valdez, Rooney—cuff him. These men are terrorists. They are both under arrest— and you can drop the accent, Jack, it's not fooling us."

Hmm. Jack West sure sounded like a fake name.

•

Ky hated working with his hands bound.

"Wait!" He threw out his arms and everyone flinched. Good.

He switched to Ardi.

"What are you going to do with the kid?"

Iverson looked between them, softening just slightly. "If he tells us everything he knows about the missing queen he can ride along when we deliver her to Arden."

"And if he doesn't talk?"

Iverson's upper lip twitched. "You won't, but he will."

This guy always was an asshole.

"Fine." Ky put his hands up. Back to English. "I surrender. I'll go with you. Just let Goren walk out the door, and I'll tell you whatever you want to know."

"What did you say?" Goren asked.

Ky craned his neck and whispered, "Left, right, through the double doors, right, through the stairwell door."

"What?" Goren squawked. "No, you're staying with me—I mean, coming with me, right? You can't rescue me and then just—just give up!"

Ky sighed; there was no point in pretending he didn't know. "Our Titian friend has poisoned these people, and I want my gun back."

"Don't make messes if you don't like how I clean them up," Iverson interjected.

"Never said I didn't like it," Ky replied. "Goren, leave now."

"He's not important to you," Iverson mused. "Mora Aydor took him with her when she escaped the rebellion at Haadam Base. He must belong to her."

"What?!" Goren exclaimed. "What does that even mean?"

Ky could see Iverson thinking and he couldn't let that go on, so he switched to English:

"I surrender myself in exchange for the kid's freedom. The offer only stands for another ten seconds, then things are going to get ugly."

"Cuff him," Iverson ordered. "Nobody follow the boy."

"He can barely walk!" Hope exclaimed.

"Goren, *now*," Ky repeated. He wasn't afraid, but he needed Goren to be. He needed him to run. If he didn't run Milo would come, and Iverson was a good man. If he saw a wanted terrorist, he wouldn't hesitate.

Goren looked from him to Agent Valdez anxiously, then said: "Don't let her die, okay? She can't die just because she met me. Please."

Ky nodded once and Goren finally disappeared out the door.

Agent Valdez grabbed the metal handcuffs out of the police officer's hand and went straight for Ky. She reached up and rotated one of Ky's raised arms down and behind his back, then the other.

Ky felt metal snick around his wrist, tight and painful, then heard another click. Nothing tightened on his other wrist, though—he looked down in disbelief. Agent Valdez had cuffed herself to him.

He gaped at her. "What the hell?"

"You said I'm dying anyway," she said. "Good luck getting out of here attached to a dead body."

Iverson registered at the link between their wrists and sighed. He always thought too fast for Ky's liking.

No one had a chance to react before Iverson pulled out his gun and shot Ky neatly in the knee. The bullet lodged behind his kneecap near the center of the joint, painfully solid and real. A shock of electricity pulsed through his whole body like a powerful gen-gun blast.

Ky collapsed sideways against Goren's messy hospital bed with Valdez half on top of him. Rooney shouted, "Whoa, wait a..." and then he wavered on his feet and toppled over.

"Rooney!" Valdez shouted, reaching as far as she could while still cuffed Ky.

"You burned me out," Ky groaned through gritted teeth. His comm, the control pad in his palm, controls in his teeth—all of them were dead. "We're not friends anymore."

"Deal with him," Iverson ordered, pointing to the uniformed cop, and then he disappeared out the door.

Seven hells if Ky was going to let Terrence Iverson take Goren and Milo without a fight.

Ky snarled in clear English: "There's a bomb in the hospital."

The cop's head snapped up, his skin already pale and sweaty, and Ky nodded at him. "That's right. Bomb's on a timer, no way to turn it off. You have eight minutes. Get everyone out *now*."

The cop scrambled out the door.

Agent Valdez muttered, "You dick," and then clutched her head.

Ky gritted his jaw and *healed*.

·

Tannor put her hand on her gen-gun as an emergency light started flashing.

"Blue alert—blue alert—" a disembodied female voice stated.

"Milo? Tom?" Relai tapped her ear frantically, finally turning away from the sexy guy she'd decided to flirt with instead of focusing on surviving this shit. "Tannor, what did Ky do?"

Tannor closed her eyes and searched out, further, until she found the plans for—

"Bomb threat. There's a bomb in the hospital." She opened her eyes. "Damn it, Ky."

Milo: *Someone just grabbed Goren. I'm going after him.*

Tom: *Hey guys. Sooo…Milo ran off. What should I do?*

Tannor grabbed Relai by the arm and dragged her into the bathroom. She sucked air through her teeth to hiss, "They'll be coming for Batar."

Tom: *Hello? Guys? There are alarms going off…*

"Ky claimed there's a bomb in the hospital. Just stay alert, shut up, and try not to get arrested," Tannor snapped.

Tom: *A 'please' would be nice.*

She pulled the door shut. Tannor just managed to drag Relai into the tub and slide the plastic curtain closed when someone slammed into the room.

They both froze, silent, staring at the shower curtain. Tannor expanded her comm space to include the planetary emergency channel. She heard Iverson order: "*No.* You're going to tell me where she is."

•

Goren didn't run, exactly, because he didn't want anyone to notice him. He walked as fast as he could, though.

What did Ky say? Left, yeah. He went left down the hall. He took the next possible right, then pushed through double doors and then right again, trying not to let his bare footsteps make too much noise. He didn't hear the door shut behind him.

He saw the stairs where Milo must be at the end of the long hallway and picked up his pace, and then Goren found himself being pushed forward, gripped in giant hands, and shoved left through the wrong door and into another hallway. Iverson had a strong arm under Goren's as he half-carried him deeper into the hospital.

Goren yelped in pain and cursed his stature (because Iverson was huge, like, *Milo*-huge, with another twenty years of taking no shit from anyone (except Ky, apparently)). A few hospital staff and a crowd of people who didn't look like they belonged here noticed them, and a couple of them even called out. Iverson answered in English with his perfect, determined authority, and instead of helping him the people bolted away.

"Thanks a lot!" Goren shouted after them.

Iverson held up something to a door which beeped, then shoved Goren through into a dark hall. They pushed through a barrier of plastic sheets, which didn't at all match with the rest of the decor. This area had no workers—everything was half-built and covered in dust, sparsely lit by a few bare bulbs. Goren managed to twist and wrench his arm painfully free, stumbling as he dove to put distance between them, but Iverson just went with the motion and directed him so he fell backward through a doorway onto a dusty, raw grey surface and landed pathetically on his ass.

A bright light on the wall started flashing and an automated voice blared, "*Blualurt—blualurt—blualurt—*"

Goren wondered what those words meant.

Iverson hooked a foot under his knee and flipped him over on his stomach and Goren shouted from the bruises Ky hadn't healed. Iverson reached under Goren's belly and dragged the hem of his new white t-shirt up and over his head, and when Goren's head popped free he cracked his cheekbone against the floor, which was just perfect, *thanks*. Iverson pulled the shirt down so Goren's arms tangled up at the elbows and then heaved him back into a sitting position.

"Ow!" He put in a decent attempt to wriggle free, but Iverson just said, "*No.*"

Goren couldn't help but follow the order; he slumped and looked up at Iverson resentfully.

"You're going to tell me where she is," Iverson glanced his guard tattoo, "Private. Was she keeping you at Haadam Base? Are you Unity?"

"What? No! No way—" Goren tried, and failed, to get his arms free. "This restraint is awesome, you gotta show me how to—"

"Did you and Jack kill those Applica agents?"

"No! That was a bounty hunter! She's still out there, so go chase her! We're keeping Relai safe, okay?" He couldn't get to his feet, not with Iverson standing over him like this.

"Where is she now?"

"Probably trying to rescue me because she's nice!" Goren kicked himself further away, sliding through dust piles on the rough grey floor, but Iverson just followed.

"Were you taking her to Daat?"

Goren shook his head, then winced in embarrassment. He probably shouldn't be telling Iverson anything, even though he was pretty sure the man was on his queen's side (if not on Ky's). Then again, maybe he should tell this man everything and then Relai would have a proper Titian escort home.

"You're not Unity," Iverson concluded. "That's good. Did Jack join up with Unity or the Quiet? Both?"

Goren took in a deep breath. Communication was important, but not getting shot again was also important. Relai was important.

He didn't know what to do.

"Look, Private, you can run a truth drill on me if you need to. I have a med scanner in my jumper; all I have to do it call it and it'll be here in five minutes. *I aim to keep your queen safe. I will* get her back to Arden unharmed. We can get her to Buzou base in three hours and off-planet in nine. You care about her? Help me."

See? This was the kind of guy Goren wanted leading their group. Titians were jerks, but you definitely wanted them on your side. The firepower alone would make the difference between success and failure once they'd entered space, so one good Titian leader would be all they'd need.

But before Goren could answer *yes, of course,* Milo attacked.

•

Tannor heard Iverson grunt, and then with a thud and a hiss, Milo's comm went out. Tannor stared at Relai without blinking.

They heard shuffling and concerned voices outside the bathroom door.

They're moving me, Olin Batar's voice whispered in her head. *I can't whisper to you more than a few feet away but I'll call for my team; they should be in the building right now, and the guy from Earth Monitoring is—*

His voice faded to nothing.

Tannor tried to slow her breathing in the silence.

If everyone knew the queen was in custody, the rebellion would halt.

At least, all the reasonable actors would pause. They'd wait for the outcome of the inevitable trial.

The reasonable ones would tamp down the extremists. (Milo was an extremist.)

Relai would get her fair chance to prove her story.

Tannor searched Relai's eyes, the tension stretched through the planes of her face, trying to understand what sort of person could show such raw emotion one second and turn terrifyingly void the next. How could Tannor go on with this doubt?

"What happened to Milo?" Relai asked. "I can't hear Ky, either, but—"

She'd never know for sure.

"Tannor?"

She shut her eyes and *thought,* activating the drug tick she'd placed gently on Relai's neck after she'd released it from her own skin with her tech ability back at Tom's house.

Relai dropped, heavy and limp, and she would have cracked her head on the metal sink if Tannor hadn't clutched at her arms and pulled her sideways.

Tannor dipped and lifted her over her shoulder, grunting, then moved to the door. Everyone on this floor had already cleared out.

She found an empty gurney.

○○●○○

v.

Milo crept deeper into the half-built area, leading with his gun, and focused on the sight of a stranger looming over Goren. The kid was bruised black across the face, his arms restrained at the elbows so his skinny, bare torso curved in a sullen arc, already splotched purple and green. Milo's world went silent and red before he could think any further than that sight.

He didn't give this guy the courtesy of a gen-gun blast, no. Milo lifted his gun and brought it down on the back of the man's head, snatching the gun bulging under his coat on the pullback as he sent him stumbling over Goren.

The man didn't fall. He was only a few inches shorter than Milo. Strong.

The Titian found his footing and spun to attack. Milo pulled off one shot but it skewed high when the man dove in close and they tore into each other by hand. Milo usually had the advantage of height and bulk over any opponent, but not now. His reach surpassed the Titian's and that was it.

Goren shouted, a dull noise in the periphery of grunts and thudding flesh, and then Milo's head snapped sideways from a blow behind his ear. One of the first rules of dirty combat: take out your opponent's comm. No one had managed to pull that move on Milo until now.

One of them was going to kill the other.

Milo roared.

•

"Colonel Iverson," Tannor said. She closed her eyes and pressed the heels of her palms firmly into her eye sockets. This Titian, Iverson, was the only one who could hear her over comms now, and she was the only one who could hear him. "You're looking for Mora Aydor. I have her."

She heard a grunt and a snarl.

"You'll transport her—both of us—safely and immediately to Arden. You'll know it's her as soon as you run a scan and you'll keep her safe and when she gets there everything will stabilize."

Iverson panted out, "I don't... deal... with terrorists."

Tannor heard a painful thud and labored breathing. She rose her voice nearly to a shout, far too loud for the fragile quiet of her hiding place: "I'm not a terrorist, I'm just a guard! I'll bring her to you. Just—just leave everyone else alone. Tell me where to go and I'll meet you now."

At the end of her bellowing the transmissions went quiet. She heard heavy breathing and then a deep and dangerous voice sounded in her ear: "Deal."

•

Oh, gods and monsters, seven hells—

And Goren had thought Milo was being rough with him.

Their wrestling match had been—they'd been *playing*, Goren realized, like Goren tousled with his little sisters. Milo wasn't playing now.

He hardly seemed human, cutting and tearing and clawing, precise like no one so angry should ever be. Iverson threw his bulk behind his blows, used it to absorb Milo's, but after a single string of parries Milo adjusted, feinting and jabbing at softer spots, keeping tight, forcing Iverson to react.

Goren wasn't stupid; he looked for Iverson's gun, but it had disappeared in the scuffle. He scrambled on his knees to the wall, narrowly avoiding the men wreaking havoc on the unfinished hospital room. He needed an edge, any sort of protrusion, he needed—*yes*, he snagged his t-shirt on a board protruding from a stack along the wall and stood up to drag it down and free himself. He wasn't getting in the middle of this unless it looked like Iverson might beat Milo… but that wasn't going to happen.

Milo might be too far gone into the violence to stop himself from killing Iverson with his bare hands.

"He has a jumper!" Goren nearly shrieked. He wasn't sure Milo could hear anything but he tried anyway. "He can call it and it'll be here in five minutes! Milo, don't kill him!"

Miraculously, Milo did seem to hear. He delivered a particularly vicious blow to Iverson's face and then pulled back.

"Call your jumper," he ordered.

Iverson dove at Milo and brought him crashing to the ground, tearing down a floor-to-ceiling tarp as they went.

"I don't," Iverson growled, lashing out with a fist, "deal," he landed a sounding blow to Milo's chest, "with terrorists."

Goren wished like hell that his comm would work. That Ky would snake his way out of there like he always did and find them. That everyone could just get along.

Milo did a crazy thing with his legs, flipped Iverson on his stomach, and bent one arm right to the edge of snapping two different joints.

The frenzy stopped.

Milo's face scaled down, breath by breath, from crazed and terrifying to a more normal level of focus. Goren slumped in relief and climbed back into his t-shirt.

"I," Milo said, spitting blood, "am not a terrorist."

"Just call your jumper," Goren begged. "We can tell Relai about it and she'll take your offer. She will!"

Iverson jerked. Failed. Went silent in pain, sweat sliding down his brow. Goren found Milo's gun lodged in the corner behind the leg of a chair. He yanked it free and trained it on Iverson.

Finally, Iverson relaxed. "Deal."

Goren nodded.

Milo released Iverson, stood up carefully, and took three measured steps back toward Goren. Without even asking, he took the gen-gun out of Goren's hands.

Iverson eased to his knees and then had to paw at a shelf to pull himself to his feet. He leaned on the shelf and caught his breath. Then he raised both hands and stepped backward.

"I'll call my jumper when I see the queen herself," Iverson said.

Goren exchanged a nervous glance with Milo. "We, um…"

"Call it now," Milo demanded. He closed the distance between them.

Iverson sneered. He moved one hand slowly inside his suit jacket. "I'm taking out my tablet."

Milo tensed. *"Slow."*

Goren watched with knitted brow as Iverson's hand emerged, ever so slowly, holding a dull grey rectangle. He brought it out and extended his arm so the screen hung in the air level with his head. His thumb moved across the surface.

Milo inched closer to look at the screen when, out of nowhere, before Goren could so much as lunge forward, Iverson's other fist connected with Milo's face and laid him flat.

Goren cried out, "Milo!" and Iverson bolted. All Goren heard after that was a beep and the slam of a door.

·

Hope retched, vaguely aware that someone was pressing firm fingers into her head to keep it bent sideways, stopping her from vomiting all over herself. Her stomach muscles clenched furiously again and the reflex tried to split her head in half at the jaw and her mouth burned and her teeth rubbed raw against each other, and then it was over. The fingers withdrew, patted her crown, and she heard Jack West say,

"Wow, lucky you threw up that poison. Weird how that happened spontaneously with no help from anyone."

She opened her eyes and lifted her chin, inching away from the puddle of sick, to see the guy who definitely wasn't Goren's father, who definitely wasn't named Jack West, who *wasn't human*, reaching out across the blood-slick floor.

It was all his blood—alien blood. Iverson had shot him. They were still handcuffed together, ha-*fucking*-ha, so he dragged her along as he put a hand on Detective Rooney's face. She watched him roll Rooney's head back and forth, peel one eyelid open, and then slump back next to her. She spit out traces of acid and sat up.

"Too late," Jack concluded. Hope gagged out another mouthful of bile.

Iverson killed Rooney. Iverson tried to kill her.

Jack looked awful, sick and pale like the bullet had hit something worse than his knee. She wondered if Iverson had somehow managed to poison him, too—he'd punched him, right? Poisoned knuckles? Hope laughed.

She might not be okay, actually.

Jack eyed her, then shook his head. "You wanna go catch the guy who poisoned you?"

"You wanna tell me what the hell is going on?" She spun the cuff around her wrist so she could get up on her knees. "Let's start with what planet you're from."

"It's called Oeyla," he said without hesitation. "Lately from Gastred, though. Now, don't let me down: where's my gun?"

She shook her head and cleaned the corners of her mouth on her sleeve. "I want to know everything."

"Help me up, then. We're going after Goren."

oo●oo

EPISODE X:

WHOLE

AGENT SURAI SUGRIVA closed his eyes and tried to see. He reached out, *out*, grasping for the threads of space that could draw him through time… All he got was an elbow in the ribs from Kish and the sound of old leather creaking underneath him.

"Let them go," a deep and authoritative voice ordered, snapping him back to the present moment. He looked out the police cruiser window. It was the same man who'd helped them clean up the bodies of Rugo and Cem— the Earth Monitoring guy, now flanked by Olin and Linnet and looking murderous.

"Agent Dad looks pissed," Kish muttered next to him. "Guess I have to keep these cuffs on for now, huh?"

Surai knew Kish had only let herself be thrown in the squad car because they'd gotten Surai first and his English wasn't great. He was miserable; Applica shouldn't have hired the him for the Earth team—it had made no sense at all, until the thing with the search dogs in Luxembourg when their comms went out and Olin directed them all via his voice in their heads. They'd realized pretty quickly that they weren't a normal Applica team.

They were something special.

Iverson was speaking too quietly for them to hear. Surai rested in the silence as the officers argued. Amid shouts and the ruckus of constant radio chatter, another flock of wailing ambulances arrived to transport patients to safety.

"—With obviously fake IDs, sneaking around in the middle of a bomb threat!" The police officer who'd detained him had risen to shouting. The man planted himself right outside the car door; Surai could watch Iverson fume if he tucked his head to the fetid seat and leaned his forehead against the window. Olin and Linnet were now wearing matching blue jackets which must have come from Iverson's jumper; Linnet's looked two sizes too big, Olin's three inches too short for his torso. When Linnet turned sideways, Surai saw tall yellow letters on her back.

F.B.I.

"You want to explain to me, sir," Iverson growled, "why out of a team of four F.B.I. agents, those two are in handcuffs while the two behind me were treated like victims?"

"It's not my job to take chances with bomb threats," the officer retorted.

Iverson held up his phone to the officer's badge. "A lot of things won't be your job, this time tomorrow."

"Are you threatening me?" Next to Surai's face, the officer's hand went to his gun. Kish flickered in and out of visible next to him, so Surai nudged her knee and shook his head, no.

Iverson met the man's hostile stare and replied with slow and clear and vicious promise: "I'm *seeing* you."

Surai blinked through another set of flashing police car lights and caught Olin ducking away from a team of familiar nurses.

They'd just barely gotten Olin dressed and healed with their reloaded med scanner, tucked like rodents in a tiny closet with *blue alert-blue alert* blaring over their grumbles and whispers, when Iverson had barged into their comm space and demanded back-up. That was the downside of mandatory military service: you never really got to retire.

Relai Mora Aydor had actually been in Olin's room—as close to safe as she'd get on this planet—and then everything must have gone to hell and now a murderous terrorist called the Monster of Eray had her.

Relai Aydor might be a tyrant, might not, but Kish was only breathing because of her.

"Now, either my team is going in *unobstructed* to find and defuse the bomb," Iverson said, "or you can waste time locking up the brown ones and let it all blow."

"Don't be an idiot," another officer cut in, shoving the men apart as she tossed a ring of keys to Iverson. "How can we help?"

Iverson handed the keys to Olin and shouted over the growl of a departing ambulance, "Is the hospital empty?"

"No," she replied. "The critical care units are still—"

Their voices faded.

Surai eased back and closed his eyes, allowing himself just one brief crackle of relief as the door opened.

"Remind me why we like this planet," Olin muttered as he helped Surai out of the back of the squad car. None of them knew what Iverson was getting them into, but at least Olin had survived the roof. Surai hadn't seen that far.

"Karaoke," Surai replied. His hands clicked free and he stretched his shoulders self-consciously. "And that time you ate fried cheese and threw up on Linnet."

"Free money," Kish added, kicking the car door shut with enough force to leave a dent. "That's always nice."

Olin tugged at the hem of his jacket and directed them to follow Iverson. "Their economy's going to notice eventually."

Linnet brushed a finger down her chin to let them know the perimeter was set. "Yeah, well. It's coming one way or another."

"What?" Surai asked. Linnet's words felt like one of his visions turned solid, but not solid—audible—

"Wake up time," she said.

Iverson led them inside the emergency room entrance. As soon as the glass doors slid shut with the promise of no interference from the locals in this ward of the hospital, Linnet opened her jacket and distributed gen-guns designed to look like Earthan weapons at a glance.

Surai took one and held it like it might bite him. The downward turn of Olin's mouth spelled worry.

They reached the elevators.

•

Milo woke like a crack of thunder, gasping and swinging wildly as he rolled to his feet and his brain caught up with the sight before him. Iverson was gone. The room was quiet, empty but for Goren frantically shaking his shoulder.

Milo fell for a stupid, simple misdirect?

"Is your comm working?" Goren demanded. All Milo heard was *I thought most of them were dead, anyway.*

Milo winced to his feet, head swimming in the too-bright light. They retraced their steps to a door with a black panel just like the ones Milo had placed ticks on—it was locked tight. No ticks left. No Tannor to control them.

"Iverson beeped something and got the door to open," Goren said.

"Get out of the way," Milo replied. He squared off facing the door and shook out his shoulders. Hopped on the balls of his feet.

"Just tell me Relai's safe, at least!" Goren said.

Milo targeted a swift kick next to the seam opposite the hinges and the door thudded but didn't break. He felt the impact as a throb in his head. "Can't," he said, sucking air through his teeth. "And so that we're clear: I wanted to leave you behind."

"Good!" Goren exclaimed. "Too bad nobody listens to you, huh?" He tried to line up alongside Milo, but the bare feet and the broken arm and the marks on his chest added up to more liability than help. Milo pushed him away by a spot on his shoulder with no bruises.

"Too bad," Milo agreed, and then he reared up and kicked the door again.

○○●○○

ii.

Tannor eased Relai's gurney to a halt at a bank of three elevators, just as Iverson had instructed. As soon as they'd cut out the blue alert and footsteps had tapered off, she'd set out through deserted hallways. Ceiling lights still flashed. The drug tick seeped a steady stream of sleep into Relai's neck.

He was coming; she only had to wait. She peered left, right, then behind them down long, menacing hallways. Nothing.

She palmed the control panel, closed her eyes, and found the lift and felt it rising. *Not too far. Keep coming, keep coming...*

It seemed the Earthans had evacuated the hospital—or, at least, this section of it—with fantastic efficiency. Surely local law enforcement was arriving, assessing the situation. Iverson must be keeping this whole floor clear of emergency crews so they could meet up. She might actually pull this off—no more running, no more bounty hunters. Safety. Tannor adjusted her grip on the gurney and didn't look again down those hallways.

Hurry. *Hurry.*

She was doing her best in a bad situation. She was never going to be able to know if Relai really—

The lift stalled. She lost track of her place in the hospital for a moment as she tried to find it, wrap her mind around it better, get it moving again. She couldn't sense any of the others besides Relai, not anymore. Goren's comm had never been present and then, one by one, Ky and Milo had disappeared from her mind. She felt woozy.

A crash jolted her back to the tangible. A doorway only a few yards away burst open and Tannor scrambled around to get between Relai and whoever was coming—two people, one helping the other stumble through—and then she recognized Ky.

"There you are, damn," he exclaimed in a strange, shaky voice. One of his legs swung unbending as he hobbled along with an arm looped around the neck of a tall, dark-haired woman. Tannor saw blood on both of them and they were holding hands, his right to her left, and then Tannor made out metal hand restraints.

"Ky? How—?"

He stumbled up to lean against Relai's gurney, looked from Tannor to the unconscious queen, and let his head drop forward.

"No pin deflector," he groaned. "So this is what we're doing now? Okay."

The woman rested alongside him and spat out English words. After a second's delay, Tannor's comm regurgitated: "Who is this?"

"Nobody special," Ky replied in English, and then he leaned toward Tannor and said in Ardi, "I need bolt cutters or an ax."

Tannor sucked in a heavy breath. "I have my tech pen," she said, instead of *what?!*

Ky grinned.

The elevator pinged—finally—and after a beat the doors slid open.

Instead of an empty lift, they saw Milo and Goren.

"Tannor!" Goren cried, going as bright as a kid could with a face bruised unrecognizable. "You made it…"

Tannor had already drawn her gen-gun. Milo looked from her to Relai and she panicked and raised it. Behind the gurney, *oh, no*, Ky pulled an Earthan gun and aimed at Milo.

Milo bristled into his nastier form and pulled his own gen-gun.

Goren just stood there looking confused.

The doors began to slide quietly shut again, but Milo slapped out his giant hand and held them open.

•

Hope held her breath at the sight of this new guy who showed up with poor Goren. *Bad guy.*

Jack West whispered, "You. Sit on the floor and keep quiet and maybe you won't get shot."

Hope sneered but did as she was told. He'd snatched her service pistol the moment that elevator dinged and she wasn't going to fight him for it in a standoff.

"What if *you* get shot?" she whispered. "Again?"

He shrugged. "Good luck getting out of here attached to a dead body."

Hope settled into a crouch on the opposite side of the gurney from the new people, as low as she could get while still cuffed to Jack West, who remained standing.

The moment he looked away, she slipped her hand under the cuff of her pants.

•

"Just listen, please!" Tannor pleaded. *Iverson was coming.*

"Put your gun down, Tannor," Milo ordered.

The curves of Relai's body glowed in the flashes from the emergency lights. Nose, chin, fingertips, all soft and still. Her hair covered her eyes.

There was nothing still about Tannor's hands, but she kept her gun raised and pointed at Milo.

"Just let me explain—"

Goren stepped out of the elevator, barefoot on a cold floor. Tannor reeled backward.

"I don't understand," Goren said. Milo followed behind him, his footsteps careful and deliberate like Tannor was really a threat.

Goren almost came within reach of Relai, but Ky ordered, "*Stop,*" with an edge of death in his voice that he'd never aimed at any of them before. Goren stopped.

"Listen," Tannor tried again. "There's a chance she's been lying—"

"So much for being on my side, huh, Kyro?" Milo spat, aiming at him across the queen's body. Tannor couldn't see the look on Ky's face. When he answered his voice sounded steady, but she didn't believe it for a second.

"This *is* me being on your side. Tannor says we can't trust her, so we can't trust her."

"Tannor's wrong," Milo said.

"Yeah," Goren said. "What are you thinking, Tannor? It's Relai! You know her!" He held his hands up. One bore a plaster cast.

Tannor bit back tears. "I don't know if I do."

"Finally going to fulfill your Applica contract, Ky?" Milo snarled, and Ky groaned.

"I told you, I'm retired—"

"I never could figure out why you latched on to me," Milo went on as though he hadn't heard. "I'm the most wanted man in the galaxy. Did Applica assign you to help me catch her? Or was I just an easy cover for the trip? Monster of Eray—no one cares who you are when they can aim their guns at me—"

"No," Ky said. He sank another six inches against the gurney. His aim didn't waver from Milo's head. "This has nothing to do with Applica."

"Then why? *Why?*"

Ky's face twisted but he didn't answer. The woman handcuffed to him had enough sense to keep her mouth shut.

Tannor wanted to vomit, or sit down, or at the very least throw her arms around Goren, but it was too late now.

She had to make them see.

"Relai could have been ruling the whole time," she said. Ky and Milo looked to her without changing the lines of their weapons. "She could be using us, lying every second, so when we get back she can take her throne and look innocent and wronged and everyone will bow to her and think she deserves it. I can't tell if the records in my head have been faked, but I did her medical scans and I know they're real and there's something—I found something. Something bad."

"What?" Goren didn't show a hint of doubt, only concern. Milo's face was stone.

Tannor shook her head. "If she doesn't know—if this is something they did to her, I—I don't know how to tell her—" she had to swallow past the lump in her throat. "I think it's better if we keep her asleep."

"No." Milo's voice crackled with fury. "We're not doing that to her. That's what they did to her."

Relai's finger twitched and Tannor jumped.

"You wanted to take her back, too—"

"By her choice!" Milo shouted, and then the second elevator dinged.

•

Iverson focused on the elevator doors. He spoke to the four people behind him without turning. "I've given orders to local law enforcement to keep to the lower levels, but I'm not sure how long they'll hold before finding some way to muck this up. We need to be fast. If you see Milo Hemm, go after him. Don't kill the teenage boy if you don't need to. Kill Milo Hemm."

"We don't kill people," Agent Palia said at the same time that Kish retorted, "We're not your drones, asshat."

Iverson clenched his jaw. He'd already established a shared space for their comms earlier that day when he stopped by HCMC to collect the two Applica agents who'd been hospitalized during the time it took to clean up the dead bodies in the IDS Tower. Agent Batar had been five hours into a six-hour surgery, and Agent Palia was in-patient for internal concussion injuries from the explosion on the roof. Iverson had been able to extract and heal her immediately, but she'd had no idea how she survived the fall off the building.

"Kill him or he kills you." Iverson took out his gun. "And Mora Aydor."

"We shoot to disable," Agent Batar said. "If you're hit, stay down. No one is dying here."

"Not if Titus here has anything to say about it," Kish muttered.

"Any thoughts, Surai?" Batar asked. The lanky barata kid, Agent Sugriva, hadn't said a word since Iverson put out his Earth Critical emergency call. When Sugriva replied, his voice came soft and hesitant.

"I think we're on the wrong side."

The doors slid open.

.

In the time between the sound and the doors opening Milo saw Ky push Relai's gurney toward the empty nurse's station and shout, "Go!"

Milo swept his free arm back, too quick to care if Goren kept his footing or not, and drove them both laterally away from the elevators and through a set of clear automatic folding doors. They came too fast for the automation and broke one panel off its hinges, then another panel cracked from a gen-gun blast.

Milo got off three shots before his view of the people creeping out of the elevator slipped away. He counted four. Might not have seen them all.

The first one out was the Titian.

Goren yelped at the gunfire as he slipped and sprawled across the floor, then scrambled up and followed with his broken arm tucked to his chest. Milo picked a door with an obvious through-line to multiple rooms, potential to circle back toward the others, and barreled in. He pulled a couple of tiny snap grenades out of his sleeve and threw them, one after another, through the door. One made it all the way into the hallway before *bang*.

Milo tore a tray from a stand and used the metal rod of the base to bar the door. "I counted four," he said. "You?"

"Um... uh, five, I think?" Goren groaned. "Who are they?"

Five. Goren couldn't fight with that broken arm, Milo thought. He was useless here.

"Probably Earthan guards. Don't kill 'em if you don't have to."

Milo needed to talk to Tannor *now*.

The bounty hunter had trashed Goren's comm, probably the same way the Titian had broken Milo's: brute force. The hardware itself was resilient enough to withstand quite a beating (more so than a human brain), but a strong enough blow could've dislodged the alternator plate that fixed energy from the body to power the comm.

They were in a room full of medical supplies. Milo couldn't fix himself, but he'd fixed Ky's a dozen times.

He started tearing through the room, pulling out clanging steel drawers and scattering plastic-covered tools. "Help me find a blade," he said

"What? Why?" Goren did as he was told but his voice tipped toward panic.

Milo raised an instrument and spun it in the light to check the sliver-thin blade.

"Lean over that table. I'm gonna fix your comm."

·

Tannor took the first doors with electronic locks, pushing Relai through feet-first, and locked them. Another set, another lock. Milo would have to keep himself alive, and he'd protect Goren, too. They would be fine.

If anyone pursued her they wouldn't be able to pass through those doors, and she checked every angle to make sure bullets couldn't reach them from outer hallways on either side of this room. She'd keep Relai safe until Ky and Iverson cleared out whatever local police or bounty hunters or mercenaries might be out there.

She brushed a section of hair from Relai's face and said, "Iverson, is this you? It it the police?"

No answer.

·

Goren let out a yelp after the first quick, deep cut and Milo had to pull away from the accompanying jerk.

"Stay *still*," he growled.

"What is that sound?" Goren wailed.

"It's you whining, like always," Milo replied, then he felt the edge of the comm and made the second cut.

The movable light they'd found helped Milo see silver under all the blood. He dug the scalpel under the corner of skin he'd created, pinched it, and put down the blade.

As he peeled the skin away, he pressed Goren's head down to keep him from squirming. "Another ten seconds. Stay still, okay? *Ten.*"

Milo went back to the scalpel, *nine,* gave the cover plate a quarter twist, *eight,* and popped it free, *seven.*

Clean scalpel, *six,* pulled out the alternator plate, *five, four,* pressed Goren's head down, said, "Still," *three,* dropped the plate back in, *two,* cover back on. Twist. *One.* He released the flap of skin.

"That was longer than ten seconds!" Goren gasped. He rested on his elbows and pressed white fingers around his ear as Milo rubbed across his shoulders and up and down the knobs of his spine with the clean back of his wrist.

"You're gonna have to tap it," Milo said as he tucked a fold of gauze under Goren's fingers.

Goren pushed himself up, pressed the gauze down, and ground out, "Yeah," through his teeth. Milo pulled off a strip of white cloth tape to stretch over the wound, then stood back to look the kid over. Blood smeared down his neck, shoulder, and arm, and every movement spread it further. Goren sniffled.

Milo saw shadows moving in the smoke through the tall, bare windows. Plain glass. Time to move.

He pulled back to the supply room and steered Goren into the darkness.

"I need you to convince Tannor to wake up Relai. You're our line to her." Milo backed Goren into a recess beside the shelving and pressed his hand to the boy's chest, fixing him against the wall. "I need you to do this."

Goren swallowed. "I will."

Milo let him go. Goren tapped behind his ear, cringing, and said, "Tannor."

Milo backed away and took up his position at the door again. No one was firing yet.

•

When Tannor didn't respond, Goren raised his voice even though it terrified him.

"Tannor, listen: we've been in this together. You watched her, same as I did. You know she's not lying, so—so that must mean that whatever you figured out is really bad."

No answer. Goren could only hope the comm was working right.

"Tannor, I saw you. I heard you. You looked more scared that the bad thing is gonna hurt her than worried she's lying. You didn't want her to be hurt and—and you screwed up. Tannor!"

Milo glanced back at him from the door. Goren lowered his voice.

"Fix this. Wake her up."

Silence.

"Tannor, you railed on Ky for the drug ticks."

"Goren," Tannor whispered.

"Yes!" he said, squeezing his eyes shut. "I'm here."

"What if it breaks her?"

"We won't let her break," Goren said. "We won't let her."

Goren pressed viciously against his bleeding head and wished he were there with her. If he could just touch her, he was sure it would remind her that she wasn't alone. She could lean on them. She could.

Tannor cursed, sniffled, and then said, "Okay."

His head swam with a cold blazing rush of relief, or maybe it was the blood loss. Goren pushed off the wall and said, "She did it."

Milo clapped Goren on the shoulder and shook him. "Good. Stay here. The blood is good—"

"Wait, what?"

"—And if you hear anyone coming, just lay down and pretend you're dead."

"Like seven hells I will!" Goren exclaimed. "I'm in this!"

Milo exhaled, all calm and focused, and checked lines of sight. "You're not armed."

Goren shoved past him and stomped across the room with his blood on the floor to wrench the metal rod out of the loop of the door handles. "Yeah, I am."

Milo raised a brow. Goren tried to seem bigger, more intimidating, like Milo always did. He wiggled his toes and adjusted his grip on the rod. He could punch people with the case on his arm if he needed to, damn it.

"Will you follow me?" Milo asked.

"If you lead me to Relai, yeah."

Milo nodded. Goren nodded back.

Then a series of shots shattered the glass all around Goren.

.

Relai heard heavy breathing. Light flashed beyond her eyelids and the surface beneath her compressed under the pressure of her shoulder and her heels. She opened her eyes.

Tannor was standing next to her... this bed was so high—no, not a bed, a hospital gurney. She felt no pain anywhere in her body. The look on Tannor's face meant something had gone horribly wrong.

Relai sat up and threw her legs over the edge. Tannor jerked back when Relai tried to touch her.

"What happened? Are you okay?"

"I knocked you out," Tannor stammered. "I offered you to Iverson."

Relai stopped. Tannor's eyes shone at the edges and her cheeks were splotchy red. Relai couldn't see any blood, but that didn't mean Tannor wasn't hurting somewhere.

"To save the others?" Relai asked.

Tannor shook her head.

Relai breathed through it, swallowed around it, like she could draw it into her chest and then cough and destroy it. It didn't matter. She wasn't sleeping anymore.

She used her breath to say, "Okay. Are you okay?"

Tannor pushed her hair back with both hands and clutched her head. "No, you don't—I don't know how to know, and he said he'd take a truth scan—I told him to leave Milo and Goren alone but I, I don't know— " her voice cracked, "I locked the door and he's out there and Ky wasn't healing when he told me to hide—"

"Oh, Tannor," Relai said, "It's okay."

Tannor's voice dropped low like a groan. "It's not okay. He's telling me to come out now. He has Ky."

Relai swallowed again, nodding to herself. "You don't believe me. You're the smartest person I've ever known and you don't believe me."

She should have expected this. She'd left; why would anyone believe in her when she tried to return? This was nothing more than she deserved.

Tannor clenched her hands at her sides. "There's a reason. I—"

"I'll go with him." Relai sucked in a deeper breath and walked to the door. "I'll stand trial and the council can decide. Open the door."

Tannor's face crumpled. "Wait. Relai, I found something—"

"Now, Tannor. Open the door."

Tannor flicked out her fingers. Relai turned and almost pushed through, but then she paused.

"How did you knock me out?"

•

They fired as they came out of the elevator, but Hope wasn't hit because she dropped like a sack of potatoes and screamed, "Don't shoot!"

Jack still had her gun and she heard him take two hits as she dragged him down with her, then his weapon skittered off as footsteps gathered all around them.

She shoved Jack away as best she could while still handcuffed to him (stupidest idea she'd ever had, but in her defense, she'd been poisoned at the time). Iverson loomed over them. In her periphery, she noticed three or four others head after the tall guy and Goren.

Hope rolled up to sitting and realized that Jack had been bleeding all over her. This wasn't just the knee—Iverson got him good this time.

Jack didn't try to rise. He just lay there and groaned out, "Leave with her. I know you're not gonna sell her. Just go. Leave the rest of—"

Hope pulled the weird alien gun from the backup holster strapped to her shin and aimed it at Colonel Iverson. "Put the gun down."

"My baby!" Jack exclaimed, his voice weak.

She sneered at him. "Give me a reason not to shoot you, too," she said.

"Eh... you don't know how to fire it?"

Hope kicked out her heel and ground it into the sticky red spreading across Jack's belly. He shouted and rolled away from her on his side.

"I'll dislocate your shoulder next," she hissed. "Shut up."

Iverson strode forward, weapon pointed at Jack and not Hope. "Jack West is a terrorist, remember?"

"What about Goren?"

"Goren should surrender if he doesn't want to be shot," Iverson said. "He's choosing his side."

Hope bent Jack's arm back so she could reach the round knob on the side of the alien gun. She couldn't tell which direction meant *on*. She took a guess. "That other guy dragged him away. What if it's not a choice?"

"You should be aiming that thing at Jack West," Iverson replied. "He'll kill you. I suggest you shoot him first."

"YOU tried to kill me."

"No," Iverson snapped. "You're supposed to forget and you didn't. Do I need to shoot you now, or are you ready to do your job?"

Hope wavered. Next to her, Jack West started coughing. She saw blood splatter from his mouth onto the floor.

"Rooney—the detective—he's okay?"

Iverson arched an eyebrow at her. "He's just unconscious."

She spun back to Jack West. "You told me he died!"

Jack West coughed. "I think I left it open to interpretation…" Then he rested his head on the floor.

"And Darcia!" Hope demanded. "Dr. Darcia Rowan, the Hennepin County chief medical examiner. What about her?"

"Chief medical examiner…" Iverson mused. "I collected seven bodies from her. My people. She'll wake up tomorrow morning with a terrible headache and no memory of any of this. Why would I kill the people I'm sworn to protect?"

She could only pray that he was telling the truth. Hope prayed maybe five times a year, and this nonsense had already used up three of them.

"I don't have time for this," Iverson grumbled. He tapped behind his ear and walked right past Hope and she didn't try to stop him. She heard him say something in another language.

Hope turned the alien gun on Jack West.

•

ii.

Grenade smoke wafted in from the hallway to the left, and two bodies lay crumpled near the head of the doorway as Relai walked through. Under the flashing emergency lights one man stood, watching and waiting.

"Colonel Iverson," Relai called. "I'm here."

"Mora Aydor," he said. His voice was deep and even.

"I'm here. I'll go with you."

He didn't lower his weapon. "When Nikotus of Titus proposed to you, what did you reply?"

Relai frowned at him. No one knew the answer to that but her and Niko.

Ky lay on his side on the floor, curled away so she couldn't see his front. His chest expanded and contracted. Beside him, the Earthan woman was aiming a gun at him—Ky's own spit gun, by the look of that purple charge string.

"Ky," she said, "do I answer?"

Ky lifted his head and tried to look at her. "Iverson's Goren, only smart," he answered, barely audible. When he moved she saw blood smeared on the floor next to him.

"*No*," Iverson ordered when she stepped in Ky's direction. "Answer the question."

Relai rubbed her brow. "I didn't say anything. I kicked him in the leg and walked away."

Iverson nodded and holstered his gun. "Mora."

"Call your jumper," she said.

Iverson glared. "Nice try, but Jack West has survived worse injuries than these and I don't want him within a thousand yards of my jumper."

Then a familiar voice called from the smoking hallway, "We're coming out."

Iverson recognized the voice too, apparently, and didn't treat it like a threat. He never let more than a few seconds pass without glancing at Ky.

Through the smoke two figures stumbled out. Goren, and—

Goren's face was a mess of blood and snot and tears as Olin Batar shoved him forward by the arm. Batar was wearing plain clothing under a jacket declaring the letters *F.B.I.*, not a hospital robe, and had a gen-gun shoved between Goren's shoulder blades. It didn't make any sense.

It didn't make any sense.

"Get your hands off of him," Relai exclaimed.

Batar obeyed even as he kept his face completely blank. "Milo Hemm is dead," he said. In her head Relai heard Olin say: *This isn't how it looks, I wasn't lying*—

"They're all dead," Goren howled, drowning out the whisper in her mind. "Milo killed them and then—and then he killed Milo."

Relai stood absolutely still. She refused to believe it.

Then Goren wiped snot from under his nose and muttered, "When he died he sounded just like those people at Jaya Point."

Relai covered her face with both hands and let her shoulders shake as she grinned.

·

Tannor didn't catch the mumble that came after Goren told them Milo was dead.

She barely stayed on her feet.

She watched Relai cry into her hands and she saw the perfunctory nod from Iverson, then Tannor spoke through the thickness in her throat. "I told you to leave him alone."

Iverson didn't even look at her; he nodded approvingly at the woman handcuffed to Ky and then replied, "Mora Aydor can't pardon him on behalf of other planets. He met a just end."

"Screw you," she exclaimed. Relai turned and grabbed Tannor's wrist and the warmth of it took all the fight out of her.

"We should go now," Relai said.

Iverson nodded. Then Relai's grip clenched tight and she pushed Tannor back.

"You can't come," Relai said. She released Tannor's wrist.

"No, absolutely not. You need me." Tannor stepped closer. "He's not safe."

Iverson pressed the elevator button and looked between them coolly.

"*You're* not safe," Relai said.

Tannor felt her face tremble. Relai wiped her hands on her thighs and went on, loud and clear for everyone to hear, "No—I mean, if he's honest, he'll arrest you. If he's false, you're nothing but dead weight dragging us down."

Iverson raised his eyebrows. "That is true."

Relai blocked his line of sight to Tannor. "We'll leave now."

Iverson nodded. Tannor just shook her head in despair.

•

Relai took a few steps in Goren's direction but Iverson blocked her way. "I have to escort you," he said with an edge of menace. "I don't have to like it."

She saw disgust burning in his face. He reached out to grab her arm and she carefully put her hand over his wrist, looked him in the eye, and pushed it away. The drug tick stuck to his skin without a hitch.

Then she placed herself in front of the elevators.

Behind her she heard Iverson say, "Batar, handle the bodies. Agent Valdez, arrest and charge Jack West if he lives. I'll direct the State Department to collect him from you as soon as possible." The woman handcuffed to Ky looked at Iverson with contempt and seemed about to snap, but instead she replied: "What if he doesn't make it?" She gestured to the growing pool of blood. "He doesn't look too good."

"Then we both have one less problem. And Goren Dray..." Iverson tilted his head. "You're free."

Relai glanced over her shoulder. Goren frowned, but he seemed too distracted by all the blood around Ky to respond.

Relai crossed her arms in front of her and touched the spot on the back of her neck where Tannor had pulled off the drug tick. The elevator doors opened without a sound. She tapped the spot, *tap, tap, tap.*

Then she and Iverson went into the elevator and the doors shut behind her.

•

"Would you rule Earth if you could?" Relai asked as they rose through the building.

Iverson glared down at her. "I don't make deals with dictators."

Relai examined the blurry sheen of the elevator interior wall. "I hope you keep it that way," she said.

Ding.

•

Hope Valdez considered possible responses to her situation, none of which seemed terribly constructive, most of which involved shooting someone with this alien gun.

"Whoa, whoa," she said, aiming said gun back and forth between the two remaining people. The guy with the big ears had disappeared down a hallway and another man, really tall, had rushed into the second elevator while rattling through a quick, *alien* conversation with the blond woman and then the lift had carried him away.

It was just Goren and the blond woman now.

"What the hell just happened?" Hope demanded.

The blond woman told Goren something, gesturing at the gun, then pinched her fingers and flicked them open and—

Hope shouted, "Oww!" and dropped the gun as a sudden electric charge emanated from it, pulsing through her body like a taser.

Goren, who had apparently expected this, picked up the gun and went through the motion of shoving it in a hip holster (obvious military training), but he was only wearing scrub pants so it didn't work. He frowned and handed it to the blond woman instead. They moved quickly. The blond one held out some kind of device that looked like a fancy pen. As Hope watched, she pressed the glowing tip to the handcuff chain, melting it clean through.

"What the actual fuck is happening?" she said.

Goren spared her a pitying look, but he was clearly more concerned with Jack West, who'd stopped moving altogether. The man probably needed surgery if he wasn't already dead. Goren and the blond shook him, trying to get him to wake up, to stand up, but he was completely limp.

"I'm supposed to arrest him," Hope said.

Goren looked at her, desperation all over his bruised face.

Damn it.

•

As Relai exited the elevator, the muffled captive sounds of a building interior swelled into the great open air. A portion of the exterior wall was missing, the floor jagged with metal and concrete and chalky white dust. A plastic sheet snapped in the wind.

Iverson scanned the area intently and then tapped his palm. The plastic sheet rattled and shook and then a large shadow overtook one section. Without a sound, the entry ramp of Iverson's jumper eased down and settled to a stop. He'd pulled it up alongside the building. Salvation.

"Your jumper is finally here," she observed.

Behind them, the second elevator opened without a sound.

Milo.

Because of the silence and the wind Iverson didn't turn until Milo had advanced within arm's reach of Relai. She put herself between Iverson and a clean shot and said, "You won't deal with dictators. Will you deal with an outlaw, instead?"

Iverson spun, gun tight in his hand, finger on the trigger. When he saw her careful stance and recognized Milo, his face tipped into rage.

Before he could fire, Milo said, "Wait." Relai glanced back to see him raise up a finger and thumb pinched together to show a tiny object. Neither of them reacted at first. Milo held it up just a little higher than his gun and waited.

Relai recognized it. She gasped, "Oh, Milo, don't—"

"Condensing seed," Milo said. "I set this one to a long delay, but you'll want to stand down and talk fast."

"Mora Aydor, move away from it, now!" Iverson ordered.

Relai said, "No."

Iverson peered between them, viciously focused, and then put his gun away. Relai moved sideways to let them see each other.

"She's not what you think, and neither am I," Milo said.

"I don't care what you think you are," Iverson answered.

Milo asked: "Is there metalock on Earth?"

Iverson's startled face sent a spark of hope through Relai.

"What?"

Relai held out her hands, placating, and asked, "What resource does Earth have that our greater galaxy would want?"

Iverson looked from Relai to Milo, back and forth. "Why?"

"One of the soldiers on the squad from Buzou Base was carrying that condensing seed," she said.

Iverson's scowl deepened. "The squad you murdered."

Milo ignored the accusation, even as it made Relai cringe. "We use condensing seeds in Eray to transport metalock," he said. "Why did he have that condensing seed?"

"Why?" Relai echoed.

Iverson shook his head once. "We're not mining anything on Earth."

"When you discover you're wrong," Relai said, "will you defend the sovereignty of Earth or the crimes of Titus?"

"You defend a *terrorist*," Iverson said flatly.

"My people are dying," Milo snarled. "Call us what you want now; when we circle as coalition peers you'll use different words."

Iverson's nostrils flared. "Your tantrums distract from the legitimacy of every other fight for freedom."

Milo curled the hand with the seed into a fist and squeezed, veins bulging, skin straining, and shook it at Iverson. "Aren't you tired? Aren't you *here*? How can you point that gun at me and condescend to our anger when you live *here*? I don't know much of Earth, but I know Titians don't come here, and if they do they don't stay. How do you live on a planet with a knife in your back?"

Relai didn't know what Milo was talking about. She didn't understand—Titians didn't tend to stay on Earth, true, but that was just because Titus was so much better. Niko had visited when Relai was completing her practical diplomacy, and he'd never complained. The worst thing he'd mentioned was the dryness of the air.

"Here and *here* are very different places." Iverson's voice came out so low and rumbling, Relai couldn't be sure she wasn't feeling it instead of hearing it. "You know less than you think. Titus is soft and easy and she does not understand where she came from. Earth is our family, our brothers and sisters, and Earth needs me more than it hates me."

"I don't understand," Relai said.

"This isn't for you, Mora," Iverson snapped. "Earth doesn't blink at the wailing of mothers or the starvation or the blood that builds her systems. Neither do you."

She wanted to argue, but she recognized what was happening here: *shut your mouth and listen*. It wasn't for her to argue, whether he was wrong or not. This was for Milo.

But instead of screaming back at Iverson, Milo eased. With each quiet word, he lowered his weapon further. At last he said, "I left the smoking remains of my life to come here. Someone calling themselves Aydor is destroying Eray. My family and my people... they're dead. I came here to find her. I hunted her and I found her imprisoned at Haadam. Relai *Orist*, not Mora." Relai felt that word, her own name, like gentle fingers on the nape of her neck. Milo put his gun away as he finished, "She's my only hope of finding justice."

Iverson finally stood back. He looked between them with a stunned sort of intensity. "The relay from yesterday was legitimate?" he said. "You're not his, he's not yours, and you weren't at Hadaam by choice?"

"I wasn't there by choice," she agreed, "and I told Arden I'd be home soon."

Iverson eyed Relai. "You're working *with* him?"

Relai nodded.

"We're not mining anything," Iverson said finally. He dipped his chin at Relai. "I did not approve it. I wasn't consulted... but I knew it was happening." Admission. Like guilt, but Iverson didn't look guilty. "No one is mining Earth. We're receiving."

"Receiving what?"

"Metalock."

Relai lifted on the balls of her feet in shock.

"From where?" Milo asked.

Metalock could only be mined from one place in the galaxy.

"The same people who have always mined it."

There was no way the Aydor monarchy would allow such a thing—and that meant—

Milo whispered, "Titus treats with my people?"

Iverson finally lowered his weapon. "Not officially, but yes. I don't know any details."

Relai fought to stop herself from grinning as the two men stared at one another. She could feel the joy emanating off of Milo. Some of his people had survived—and not just survived. They were mining in secret.

After a long pause, Iverson tilted his head. "She's not angry."

"I'm not a lot of the things you think I am, Colonel Iverson," she said, finally allowing herself to grin. "Now put away your gun, please."

Iverson finally did as instructed. From beyond the barrier of plastic they heard a swell of shouts and sirens down on the ground level.

"Thank you," Relai concluded. "Now, we're taking your jumper. We're not traveling through your base."

Iverson's eyes widened and he held out a hand, open and empty. "I will deliver you to Arden unharmed."

"I decline," she replied. "We're using a black market dock that's trafficking Earthan people and we'll send you the coordinates as we leave. The *second* we're off-planet you are going to shut that dock down. And then you're going to help Earth wake up."

Relai couldn't quite read the emotions frothing below the surface of Iverson's face—confusion? Fury? Shock? Relief? But what he said was, "Yes, Mora."

She stood alongside him, knowing he'd follow, and led him around Milo and back to the elevator they'd risen in. "Tannor, I'm sending Iverson down. We're parting with respect."

Iverson stared at her in astonishment. "He'll get you killed."

Relai swept out a hand and directed Iverson inside the open carriage. "I wish you all the luck, the strength, and the blessings of the seven stars. I'm depending on you to stay and help Earth. Now, please. Go."

The doors clamped closed.

They both sagged. Relai had nothing to lean on, so she paced a few steps and wiped her face on her shirt as Milo swiftly pulled out an egg-shaped case and placed the condensing seed safely inside.

"You didn't knock him out," Milo said after a moment. "Tannor said you were going to knock him out."

"I had to try," Relai said. She didn't touch him, however badly she wanted to. "The Applica team?"

"I stunned them all and then their leader, the man you saved, spoke to me in my head." Milo tilted his head. "You seem to inspire a lot of loyalty. If I didn't know better, I'd say you're dangerous."

"They're not just alive, Milo, *they're mining*." Relai rocked toward him. "You have something to go home to."

The corner of his mouth curled up. "I always had something to go home to."

Then the other lift finally arrived with everyone else.

It was Goren and Tannor and Olin Batar and Ky—no Earthan woman—and they were trying to get Ky to his feet but he wouldn't rise.

He looked dead.

Milo made it to them before the doors even finished opening, with Relai right on his heels.

"Why isn't he healing?" Relai demanded.

"He's not answering," Batar groaned just as Goren lost his grip and Ky slipped down, his shirt dragging up in Goren's fist so they could all see the wounds still open and seeping on his chest and belly.

Milo scooped up Ky's legs and picked him up like nothing, pushing Goren and Olin away. "Into the jumper, we'll figure it out in there."

Relai nodded as he stomped away with Goren and Tannor just behind. Relai held back.

She touched Olin Batar's forearm. "Your team is fine, right?"

The corners of his eyes crinkled with his smile. "Your warrior only stunned them."

"*RELAI*," Milo bellowed from inside the jumper. A gentle breeze rustled through the hallway.

"He kept thinking your name," Batar said. "I listened to his thoughts as he took down my team. *Relai, we have to get to Relai*, over and over again. Not Orist. Not Aydor. *Relai*."

His eyes were soft. She nodded and stared at the red smudges on his shoulder to remind herself.

"Contact Xiong on Oliver Station," she said. "Work with him. He wants to wake Earth. He built a groundship and he probably has more. Work with Iverson. Buzou might defect to Earth. Make her strong. And don't—don't let the Earthans hurt our ex-terrs when she wakes, okay? I want Earth to be an equal member of the coalition, not an enemy."

His eyes traced over her face, open and honest and more heated than the touch of fingers, his mouth slightly open.

"You'd let that happen?" he asked.

Relai cupped the elbow of his opposite hand and squeezed. He shook her arm in return.

"It's the only way." She held his forearm like that could satisfy every need she'd ever felt, relished the muscle and bone under her grip.

Olin Batar wrapped his other arm around her and pulled her to him, their arms crushed between them.

"I won't fail you, our Glory."

As much as she hated to, she drew back. "Ugh, don't call me that."

"Our Glory, our Honor, our Light…" he teased. Relai had to turn and walk away, dropping her feelings in the press of her feet on the rough concrete floor. They were well and gone by the time she passed through the jumper door.

•

iv.

Hope's phone trilled. She looked at the caller ID, scowled, and slumped back against the wall where they'd dragged some chairs as she answered. She wasn't in bad enough shape to need a stretcher, not that it mattered in this chaos.

"Hope! Are you here?"

"Define *here,* jackass."

"Oh, right. HCMC!"

"THOMAS."

"Aw, you sound like my mom! Are you okay?"

"I'm not okay," Hope snarled, jerking her wrist away from the nurse who was dabbing at the blood around it, "I was poisoned."

"Nooo, Hope! What do I do?"

"Don't worry, an *alien* used his *alien healing powers* to *heal me.* In an *alien manner.* How are you? No, don't answer that, fucker. I'm on the eighth floor in front of the main elevator bank. Find a cop to escort you—give them my name."

"Yeah, okay, I'll be right there!"

Someone finally found handcuff keys so Hope didn't have to gnaw off her thumb to get out of the cuff. It was just embarrassing at this point; the alien gun was gone, the aliens were gone, and her head felt like a boulder rolling down a mountain slope that never ended.

Tom finally burst through the doors at the far end of the hallway. The cops were busy swarming the people—F.B.I. agents, maybe?—they'd found unconscious throughout the surgery wing, so Hope decided to deal with her idiot first.

Tom was wearing a set of scrubs (obviously a disguise, and he was going to get himself arrested) and he'd actually showered and shaved. He somehow looked even worse this way; she knew and loved the greasy, rumpled Tom Wood. This guy was a weirdly normal stranger, even as he did a classic broomball slide on his knees to come to a stop next to her.

"I was third back-up to drive the getaway car," Tom said breathlessly.

Hope leaned forward with her forearms on her knees. "There are many layers wrong with that statement."

"Okay, okay, jeez, I was here to interp—okay, to pretend to interpret in case anyone started interrogating Milo. He doesn't speak English so it woulda been really awkward if—"

"Milo," she repeated flatly.

"The tall, sexy one. Did you *see* him? Legs up to here and a beard that just won't quit?"

"Ah. Of course. Go on."

"The whole point was that there's this *zombie bounty hunter*—sorry, I can't believe myself, either—who was stalking the space princess, and Goren—"

"GOREN."

"Yeah, sweet kid. Kinda dumb, but whaddya gonna do? Anyway, he got zombie-smashed and they took him here before we could do anything about it, so we came to save him before mysterious suits absconded with him!"

Hope forced herself to pause before she committed her first murder.

"You get a choice..." she hissed through her teeth, "between exposing the presence of aliens on Earth, or hiding them... *and you hide them?*"

"Well first of all, they threatened to kill me a little bit. I mean, it was implied. But there are layers within layers, Hope Valdez, and I'm still not completely sure we're not getting colonized no matter what happens. It seems to be a choice between nice aliens or scary ones, so I picked the nice ones!"

She rubbed her eyes. "I can't believe you. And now they're all gone!"

"Yeah," Tom sighed. "Milo ran off and then all the doors locked so I couldn't follow him. But what am I, an idiot? I knew you'd be here so I ran to the other stairwell and maybe it was the bomb threat but those were all open. What do you need? What can I do? Who poisoned you?"

Hope stood up, wobbled, and steadied herself on Tom.

"*The Smoking Man,* Tom! The Cigarette Smoking Man poisoned me! I need some painkillers and a shot of tequila, and I need you to tell me everything you know *right now*. Let's start with the phrase 'space princess' and go from there."

"Counter-proposal: you explain to me what all this alien healing powers nonsense is, because all of my aliens are human aliens."

"Human aliens. *Human aliens?*"

"Yeah! And the bad ones aren't human... I think."

Hope stared at nothing, thinking wildly. Human aliens. They couldn't have cropped up on other planets simultaneously... so they must belong on Earth as much as anyone.

The guy who healed her wasn't human. He looked it, but he wasn't.

He was the real enemy. And Iverson, probably.

"No," Hope snarled. "*No*. We can't just let them get away. Do you know how long before the invasion starts? What kind of technology we're up against? *Anything* relevant?"

An elevator opened.

"Er, is a really tall black guy who looks about a thousand percent done with today relevant?"

Hope reached for a gun that wasn't there, not since the alien took it from her, lost it, and then she lost him, *shit*—

"He's one of them," Hope hissed, "He's our Smoking Man." Tom clutched her arm so wildly that she almost fell over.

"You," Colonel Iverson barked directly at Hope, "Homeland Security, right?"

"...Yeah?"

He walked right past her, talking like he expected her to follow. "You're now a liaison for Earth Relations."

Hope followed, dragging Tom along with her. "What the hell does that mean?"

"We're waking Earth to the presence of galactic life outside this planet. You need to contact your superiors and start identifying key officials who can ensure this process moves smoothly and without chaos."

"Are you asking us to *take you to our leader?*" Tom started laughing in an unhinged manner; Hope patted his back so maybe he'd rein it in before she had to slap him.

"I'm going after the rightful queen of our galaxy. She's still in danger."

Hope muttered, "Space princess?" out of the side of her mouth, and Tom replied, "Yup."

They came to a stop in front of to the recovering FBI agents and the nurses tending to them. Hope counted five people, various states of dress, inscrutable ages and races. The young man with prominent ears waved off a nurse as he checked the others one by one. Hope wouldn't have pegged him for more than thirty, but his eyes seemed ancient and tired.

"Who are these—" Hope tried, but Iverson barked over her:

"Agent Batar! Do you a jumper in range?"

Hope jolted at that word, *jumper*. Agent Batar took a stance like he was shielding the others from Iverson.

"No. Our other jumper was in China and it's on the way. Six hours."

"Not fast enough," Iverson muttered.

Hope decided she wanted to be something more than a shitty pawn for this guy. She wasn't afraid of him, and if anyone was going to keep Earth Relations in line, it would be her.

She shoved right between Iverson and Batar and interjected, "I know where you can get a jumper *now*."

"How do you even know what a jumper is?" Tom hissed.

She put her palm in Tom's face.

"Who are you?" Agent Batar asked. Behind him, the other agents whispered feverishly in the same language all the rest of the aliens had spoken. More aliens.

Human aliens, or bad ones?

Hope narrowed her eyes at him. "Homeland Security. Who are you?"

Agent Batar took a shocked step backward and looked to Iverson without responding.

"We've been ordered to wake Earth, and I'm doing it," Iverson said. "Valdez, tell me what you know."

While Batar turned and huddled up with his own crew, Hope pushed off of Tom and got right in Iverson's face. "Are you human?"

Iverson's head tilted and his face took on a sort of approval. "I was right to pick you," he said.

"That's not an answer."

"Yes, I'm human."

Hope judged the steely assurance on his face and came away satisfied. Then Iverson turned to the group of agents. *"Batar!"*

Agent Batar glared from his spot without moving closer and said, "You're not in charge of us anymore. We're under Mora Aydor's orders. She's sending us to Daat to free them from a freeze against Unity."

"She's in serious danger," Iverson said. "Do you know where she's going?"

Batar rolled his eyes. "Why don't you track your own jumper? The one they just stole from you?"

"They have Tannor Mellick," Iverson said, as though that was all the answer anyone needed. "*Do you know?*"

"No!" Agent Batar clenched his teeth. His head tilted like he was listening to an earpiece, then Batar gestured towards Tom and said: "This man—he knows."

Everyone looked at Tom, who grinned like an asshole. "I totally know."

"How—" Hope began.

"They gave me an earpiece that translates," Tom explained reasonably, and Iverson pinched the bridge of his nose. "I bet they'll give you one, too! Hey, man, how did you know that I know, though?"

Batar paused. "They told me before they left."

Well, that was clear and present *bullshit*.

"There are rumors," Iverson said, a dangerous edge creeping into his voice, "that Applica hires *shusa*. Sevati half-breeds that look human but aren't. Is that true?"

Agent Batar's face hardened. "We're all human."

Hope's head ached with the strain of looking back and forth between them. Half-human, did he mean? This job had better come with a pay increase.

Iverson narrowed his eyes and loomed. "You don't belong on this planet if you're not."

Agent Batar didn't flinch, even when Iverson crossed in front of Hope and came within a breath of him.

"We don't have time for this," Batar said through gritted teeth.

Iverson stared too long and then sneered. "You do as your queen ordered."

Agent Batar scoffed, turned, and stalked away with his team filing behind him.

"You," Iverson pointed at Tom. "Tell us what you know. Now."

Tom crossed his arms. "I want to come."

"No. Where are they going?"

"I will take this secret to my grave if you don't—Hope!" Tom shrieked and ducked behind her when Iverson moved for him.

"Wow, you're an asshole," Hope exclaimed. "You really think we have time to argue with him? Let's go. We'll leave him in the jumper when we go save the space princess."

"Yeah!" Tom added.

Iverson looked between them and scowled.

○○●○○

v.

"Goren, put your hand on that wound and lean on it—"

"Are we masked?"

"*Harder!* Milo, get over here."

"Yes, and on the way out I reached into Iverson's tech and—"

"I need to fly. You work on him."

"—Buzou won't be able to track or remotely control this jumper anymore."

"He needs you, Milo," Relai insisted. She shifted to fit her knee between Ky's leg and the bench so she could put more pressure on two of the bullet wounds. "Tannor can fly."

Milo snorted from the helm. "Neither of those are true."

"Don't be an asshole," Tannor snapped, but Relai jerked her head to quiet her. Tannor was busy rooting through the jumper's systems, anyway.

"Goren," Relai said, her head just a few inches away from his, "did Iverson do anything weird to him?"

Goren leaned on the third bullet wound and blinked rapidly; his neck was a mess of smeared, flaking blood but his eyes looked alert. "Besides punch him and shoot him? Maybe he poisoned him? This jumper has a med scanner somewhere. Tannor, find it!"

"Scanner won' work on me," Ky slurred out. "No pin."

"Found it," Tannor said. A hole opened up in the wall next to her. "Here. I know it's regulation but I can hack it so the pin won't matter—"

"No!" Ky's grimace turned desperate. "Don't. It'll hurt me."

Goren checked his allotted wound and grimaced. "Okay, well, can you do the thing? The life-energy-transfer healing thing?"

"Bring back your injuries if I do," Ky mumbled. "Hasn't been long enough."

His skin looked gray. Relai rubbed his shoulder. "Milo, I really think you should get over here."

"Flying," he called without turning around.

"Tannor will fly it with her brain if she has to," Relai growled. "*Your friend is dying.*"

Milo slammed and banged unnecessarily as he rolled out of his seat and crouched at Ky's head. "He's never dying. He's probably just hungry."

Ky half-smiled, blood outlining his teeth. "M'mad at you, too, buddy."

Tannor had closed her eyes and put a hand to the wall to control the jumper when Milo left the pilot seat. "We're almost to Tom's—wait, I can—oh!" With that exclamation as the only warning, the benches receded into the walls and a table grew up in the center aisle, lifting Ky smoothly as they all scrambled to their feet. "Metamercurial interior. I can mold it with my mind. Cool."

Milo rested his hands on either side of Ky's head without touching him. He'd shed the white doctor's coat as they left the hospital and he'd pushed the sleeves of that same old black shirt up around his elbows so Relai could see the tension in the muscles in his forearms. He swallowed and his voice came out flat:

"How much of this trip was an assignment to you?"

"None," Ky said.

"You pointed a gun at my head," Milo said. "And *you*," he glared at Tannor, "knocked Relai out."

Before Tannor could respond Ky went into a coughing fit, speckling the table and floor with more blood. Tannor rolled him sideways and patted his back as she glared at everyone.

"We weren't violent," Tannor said, like it might somehow let her drop the guilt from her face. "Not like you."

Milo's hands turned to fists pressed into the table. "I didn't know her then. You know her now, how could you—"

"Just stop it, all of you!" Relai exclaimed. "What—do you think of me as something they tried to steal from you?" She stepped around the table, forcing Milo back. "Is that how you see me, Milo Hemm? Am I a *thing* they tried to steal from you?"

"No," Milo breathed, the anger gone out of him. The skin around his eyes shone in the light.

"No," she agreed. "They'll answer to me for this. And I don't need an answer."

Milo searched her face, then finally blinked away. "Well, I do," he said.

He stared down at Ky. By now the man's blood could have coated the whole table, except that the surface was repelling and directing it down in patterned rivulets until it disappeared. Titians didn't like blood in their vehicles, either, it seemed.

"How can I trust anything you say?" Milo asked.

"You want someone loyal," Ky groaned, "or someone obedient? M'only good for one."

Then Tannor stood.

"We're landed," she said ("Masked?" "Yes."), and then she leaned on the edge of the new table and hovered her fingers over Ky. "Something's wrong in his body. He feels weird to me—not," she coughed, "I mean, my sense of tech is—"

"What?" Relai asked.

Tannor closed her eyes and moved her hands up and down his limbs until she reached Ky's right knee.

"Here. There's something here. It's sending out electricity. I think it's stopping him from healing."

Relai felt Ky's pants and found a bullet hole at the knee, stiff and sticky and red. She pinched the material on either side and tore the pant leg off.

"Goren," she ordered, "take a gun, go inside, and grab everything you can—food, tech, extra clothes—grab some of Tom's clothes and shoes, too, the grosser the better—and blankets—"

"No one goes anywhere alone," Milo said. "I'll go with him."

"Are you sure Ky doesn't need me?" Goren asked as Tannor waved a hand and split a seam down the rear wall of the jumper.

"My son," Ky mumbled. Then he laughed, his whole face pinched and waxy, and a tear slid down his temple into his hair.

"Go, now," Relai said.

Goren darted suddenly to Tannor, threw his arms around her, and said, "I love you, you know?"

Tannor hid her face as she hugged him back, and then they went.

Relai pushed the fabric up Ky's thigh and down his calf and Tannor helped her lift his leg to see from all angles. Beneath caked blood they found a half-healed circle of angry, raw skin. When Relai tried to bend the joint, Ky cried out and opened his eyes for a second.

"Okay," she concluded. "We have to get it out."

She peered at the wound, the complicated angles and wells of clammy flesh, and Tannor twisted to show the correct angle. "It's right here, about two inches in."

Relai took her thumb knife from her side and put it to his skin.

Ky's brow tightened. "I was seven," he whispered.

"You're going to do this now?" Tannor said. "Milo's not even here."

"I noticed." Ky tried to smirk at her, but when she touched his shoulder his face failed.

"Tannor, keep him steady," Relai said, and then she cut. The thin blade pressed deep and precise, just central from the bullet, then she twisted and sliced out laterally. Ky didn't flinch. She squelched back in with the knife and a finger and she felt slippery bone and heat, and then finally metal.

Out.

The bullet stung her fingers with a tight, terrifying power. She threw it on the floor and shook her hand, hissing, as his body relaxed. Relai felt Tannor's eyes on her but she only watched the wound.

The blood wouldn't stop.

Milo and Goren bounded back in with packs and arms full, ninety seconds and no trouble, then Tannor shut the door and took over piloting with a hand buried in the shiny surface of the jumper wall. Milo clunked down Ky's clean boots and a pack full of supplies, and he wasn't fooling Relai for a second; she saw how his gaze stalled at the bright, fresh blood, then darted away, then checked Ky's face, then retreated again.

Goren, meanwhile, freed himself from all the supplies he'd dragged in and clambered over to Ky's side again.

"It's out? You got it out? Was that bullet the reason he can't heal?"

"The electricity is gone," Tannor said as the jumper floor opened up and swallowed the bullet. "Damn, that thing is powerful. It should have knocked him unconscious, I think, but he didn't give up—he's been fighting the whole time."

"I was seven," Ky said again. Milo froze. "When the war ended on Oeyla. Lost everything. I can't go through another war. We can't let our planets slaughter each other. Everyone on top's gonna use the people at the bottom like chum. There has to be another way." Ky's breathing evened out, still too shallow. His eyes met Milo's. "You're it."

Relai watched Milo's mouth fall slack.

"Ky, you're going to bleed out," Relai said. "Pull your body together."

"M'fine," Ky whispered. "Never get to rest."

Silence settled in the jumper. Ky hadn't shrunk as thin and pale as on the rooftop, but his face bore something worse this time.

Relai stopped watching for signs of healing and tied a clean cloth around his knee joint, knot right over the cut. Goren covered the other three wounds and then settled on holding Ky's forearm. Next to Relai, Tannor rested two fingers in the crook of Ky elbow.

"Such a baby," Milo said quietly. Ky jolted.

Milo shifted down the table around Goren and went to work on Ky's shoelaces. "We can dump these for trash; they're soaked in blood, anyway. Tannor, does this jumper have water?"

"Yes. I'll route it."

Relai watched Milo pull off one shoe, then another. Ky might have been asleep but for the tension in his brow.

She wondered how many bullets he'd pulled out of himself, alone, while Milo slept.

"I can help!" Goren said. "You smell terrible."

Ky muttered, "Like father, like son."

A trough dipped in the metal and the water swirled in. Milo swept it up Ky's calf, flushing away thickening gobs of blood. Relai just barely heard him scoff.

.

Goren kept contact with Ky's skin just in case he needed to absorb some life energy. Broken ribs weren't much compared to bullet wounds (probably?), and he wouldn't want Tannor or Relai to give themselves up. Milo really should have been the one to give, considering he had the most self of any of them to start with, and there'd be ample opportunity as he cleaned Ky up.

Still. Just in case.

Relai took her time shifting past Tannor and around the foot of the table so she could pull Goren carefully into her arms (which he appreciated, because Ky had healed his breaks but not his bruises). Goren momentarily forgot about being miserable and hugged her back.

"You look horrible," she told his shoulder, and then drew back. She'd gotten blood from his ear on her cheek.

"I'm fine," he mumbled. "I'm a really good actor, right? I didn't know I could fake crying like that."

She kept up that fond sort of serious look, too real and too close, and he couldn't stand it for more than a moment before dropping his eyes.

Seconds crawled by, suns rose and set, cities crumbled and at least ten babies were born, and still she didn't say a word. He watched the table clean itself of every little skittering drop of blood, then drain the dirty water as Milo methodically scrubbed Ky clean from toe to head.

"You really shouldn't have come back for me," he finally mumbled.

"Sorry," Relai replied, and she kissed the cheek next to his black eye.

"Ow," he said.

•

Tannor waited until the Ky and Goren were truly asleep, cradled in wells of metamercury she'd crafted with her mind, and Milo was busy piloting, before she moved. As she sat she spread the bench to accommodate her, then tucked up her feet and hugged her knees. Next to her, Relai's legs stretched out, the soles of her feet pressed into Goren's arm.

After a time, Relai asked:

"Are you going to let us go on?"

She'd dimmed the lights, but Tannor could still see the crests of Relai's face lit with gentle sea-green light. Relai didn't seem upset, but Tannor's heart still fell at the words. "I—I'm not going to try to stop you again."

"No," Relai whispered. "Me and you. Will you go on… traveling with me? Or can it be better than it was before, now that I know I still need to prove myself to you?"

"Relai…" Tannor couldn't stop herself from shaking her head. She'd made the wrong choice. Even if, even *if* Relai had been lying to them this whole time, she still deserved a face-to-face confron-tation. Tannor owed her that.

And she *still wasn't sure.*

She said so out loud.

Relai bumped their shoulders to fit hers just behind Tannor's, slid her arm underneath, and slipped their hands together.

"It's okay."

Tannor kept her hand limp.

"I don't understand. *Be angry with me.*"

Relai shrugged and Tannor felt it through her whole body.

"I do understand, though. I'm not angry."

The warmth of their breaths mixed between them. Tannor tightened her fingers. "I hurt you. I thought Milo died. Ky almost *did* die."

Relai clicked her tongue. "If you're going to make a move, you have to accept what comes with it."

"How can you accept anything when you don't know—when you don't know what's real?"

Half of Tannor felt chilled, the other half burned where Relai pressed up against her. Relai took a long time before answering.

"There will never be enough evidence to erase all your doubt, Tannor. You're too smart. You're never going to eliminate that tiny chance that you're wrong. For now, can you accept that I forgive you? Just accept it?"

Tannor closed her eyes. "I need to tell you what I found in the data I downloaded."

"Is it going to stop me from going home to Arden to regain my crown?"

Tannor thought through the possible reactions Relai might have. She couldn't be sure, but... "Maybe."

Then she felt Relai bump her head gently. When Tannor opened her eyes, Relai wasn't looking at her—she was watching Milo's back as he flew. Tannor had been cruel, trying to distract Relai from her betrayal with the memory of Milo's attack. She shivered in shame.

Relai said, "Tell Milo. He'll know the right time to tell me, and you won't be the only one who has to carry the secret. I don't want to know until all of this is resolved. I don't need any extra despair right now."

"Okay," Tannor said, lost again at the inexplicable trust Relai seemed to show in all of them, when none of them deserved it. Trust Tannor didn't think she was capable of.

She could try, though.

•

Milo Hemm knew what he believed. It consumed him, head to foot and breath to breath. He believed in justice and fairness and consequences for wrong. It came not just from the teachings of his god, but from the depths of his stomach.

He knew what he believed: Tannor Mellick should meet the same fate as Milo himself—to work for redemption until the fight killed her, as it should, because she deserved it.

And yet.

Never, since hands around an innocent neck, had Milo believed himself to be any better than the worst. He *was* the monster, like it or not. All he could do was use his last days of breath to claw up through the pit he'd dug for himself, even though he knew he'd never rise high enough to stand on solid ground again.

And yet.

Relai said she didn't need an answer. Relai didn't see a pit—no—she saw it, and she threw down her hand and said *climb up.*

Maybe he could look at Tannor and see the monster he hated in himself and, instead of despising her, he could stand alongside her. Maybe they wouldn't get what they deserved.

He swept them up into the quiet heights of the lower atmosphere.

○○●○○

vi.

Tannor was supposed to be awake, but that didn't mean she couldn't rest her head for just a few minutes. Goren lay on his back with his arms crossed behind his head, his body stretched out away from her, and his arm looked more comfortable than a wad of Tom's smelly clothing. When she lowered her head onto the crook of Goren's elbow he shifted, his head lolling to one side, making room.

She closed her eyes.

Tannor saw a thousand tiny lights in her mind, all connected by spindly fibers and thrumming with energy below them. They were beautiful as they slid past the shivering light of their aircraft. At the edge of her mind a heavy, dark expanse crept closer; she supposed it was the ocean between this continent and their goal, quietly spotted with little muffled lights of its own. The water itself held its own light, broad and sweeping and muted in contrast to the sharp sparks of electricity on land. She breathed slowly, in and out.

Then she heard a thud and opened her eyes.

She saw a rumpled figure standing in the shadows. By the long, black hair she recognized Relai, but she wasn't moving the way she normally did. After a moment Relai shuffled over the blanket that had fallen off of her as she rose, and Tannor realized that everything about her looked drastically *wrong*. Her head bent sideways, neck limp, hair covering her face. One hand dug through her clothes, twitching, and Tannor recognized the shape of Relai's little thumb knife against the dim ambient light. She croaked out a half-formed whimper as Relai uncurled a hand and sliced her left palm open.

"What are you doing?" Tannor hissed. Ky jerked up, abruptly healed and reaching for a weapon that wasn't there.

"Tannor, what—"

She only pointed, flicking every light in the jumper bright with a thought, as Relai shuffled back to the rear wall and dipped her opposite fingers in the blood streaming from her hand.

"She cut herself, I don't know—" Tannor didn't know whether to touch her or not, whether she was sleepwalking or—or— *"Ky."*

Milo woke. He leaped up and reached out a long arm to grab her, but Ky snagged his jacket and jerked him back. Against all sanity, Ky breathed, *"Wait."*

Relai raised her fingers up above her head to the metamercury wall and began to write. This whole time, her head never lifted. It rolled back, then sideways, and as her hair parted Tannor could see her eyes were half-open, her mouth slack. She wrote,

the brother

Milo growled, "She's bleeding."

"She'll be fine," Ky said. "We need to see the whole message."

the brother
befriends

Tannor watched in confusion and horror as Relai finished scrawling out, using her own blood,

the brother
befriends
the king

Next to her, Goren sat up and leaned forward. Tannor flashed a glance at him, worried that he'd do something rash, but it was the same horror all over again: everything about his face, his countenance, looked *wrong*. He was pursing his lips in disdain and he scoffed as he pushed Tannor aside and stood.

"So, this sad feint is how you choose to speak? Though far in form, I'm near enough to cringe."

The voice was his, but the accent and intonation were utterly strange.

"Goren?" Tannor demanded.

This person who was not Goren ignored her. Not-Relai's head snapped to a proper position and she turned with a huge, spitting huff and glared at him with one hand cocked on her hip.

"I was attempting to," she hissed, "create a bit of weighty atmosphere, you *wretch*. 'The mists of prophecy so tinged with doom—demand you honor ere you heed the song.'"

"All that—"

409

"*All that* demands you show respect for your last living relative, old hag!"

Not-Goren scoffed. "Respect? A concept lost on you, dear child, and one I won't endeavor to employ."

But Not-Relai laughed sharply in his face. "You are too weak to keep that body, cuz. Go sleep your tragic final days away, and leave me meddling in this little play."

Not-Goren simply stood there, sneering. "*You* are telling lies. I cannot let them pass."

"No!" Not-Relai snapped back. "This is the truth. I've seen it—mark me, every word is true!"

She pointed to Ky with her bleeding hand, imploring, and Not-Goren snarled. The sound sent Not-Relai reeling back, and then she looked furious to be caught afraid.

"You cannot harm from where you are, Macha. Do try—we'll desolate your hold once more. Try and *try and try*—"

"*Who are you?*" Ky roared. "What do those lines mean?"

"The final word correctly written: *queen*," Not-Goren answered. He looked Ky over with a judging eye, and said with great disdain, "You changed your face."

Now Tannor saw stark terror in Ky's eyes. "I'm not who you think I am. Who are *you?*"

"We are the last of ours, she's last of hers."

The echo came, Relai but not Relai:

"We are the last of ours, she's last of hers."

"And don't the words fit well? *She is the End.*" Not-Goren took one step closer to Ky. "We, Kyro, I promise you, are *not.*"

Then Not-Relai drew out the knife again. "Or I could kill him now, in front of you."

Not-Goren's lips drew tight into a sneer.

"Entertain me, then," he spat, unmoved. "He'll end that body 'fore you leave a mark."

The hand with the knife swayed slightly toward Ky and Milo lashed out and twisted it from Not-Relai's hand. The specter didn't put up a fight and Milo didn't maintain a hold on Relai's body; it just huffed and crossed Relai's arms instead. The wound on her hand smeared red across her bicep.

"You've gone so boring in this human age. You see what happens when you wait for death? So meet it now—I'll help, I promise you." Not-Relai's shoulders were languid, rolling with the small movements of her hips and the arch of her back, creating an effect so unlike the normal Relai that it soured Tannor's stomach.

Not-Goren glared, a foreign entity barely restrained in Goren's skin, molding a bizarrely cold and cunning look on the poor kid's face. "Oh, I remember promises, Annan."

Not-Relai only smirked, then turned to Milo.

"*King*," she swore. "Her kin befriends the king. Remember it."

"Whose brother?" Milo demanded.

"Orist."

"The word is *queen*," Not-Goren said, "and don't believe a single word this liar says." He spoke next just to Ky, his voice bent low. "Turn off their ears. I have some thoughts for you."

"Yeah," Ky drawled, "that's not something I can do."

The thing huffed through Goren's nose. "You chose the coward's side, forgot too much."

Behind them, Not-Relai cackled again.

Not-Goren just ignored her and went on, "Remember that which you forgot, my spark. You'll have to, if you want him to prevail. And when you do," Not-Goren flashed a sneer, "you'll leave the woman and join us. You *will.*"

"Okay," Ky said, "you had me up until your shoddy recruitment pitch. Try harder next time, witch." Then he shoved his palm into Goren's forehead and pushed. The kid flopped helplessly on his back. Whoever was controlling Relai tossed her hair and laughed.

"She sees the stuff she hopes," the phantom said. "I'll see you next on Oeyla, Warrior... *if* you last the time it takes 'til then."

Relai wavered where she stood and Milo sprang to her, his hands hovering over her arms, but she steadied herself. They all watched nervously as Goren groaned and rolled onto his hands and knees.

After a moment he said, "Who. Who was just in my head? What was that?"

Tannor pulled him to his feet.

Relai blinked a few times, her eyes hazy as they traveled high enough to find Milo's face. He didn't step back until she nodded, and then Relai grimaced and wiped her bloody hand on her pants. "Gross."

"Witches," Ky spat, and then he stewed in silence until Milo demanded that he explain.

Apparently the Sevati were not so extinct as previously assumed.

·

Relai kept still through the searing splash of pain while Ky muttered about tiny wounds and whiny royals as he closed the gash on her hand. Then he explained that, yes, those two voices were Sevati aliens somewhere in their galaxy.

Sevati.

Goren slapped his own cheek in awe. "I got possessed by a witch? A *MAGICAL witch? A magical SEVATI WITCH?!*"

"Not magic, Goren," Ky said. "*Witch* is just the best derogatory term for those two."

"Awful lot of witches and prophecies floating around for *not magic,*" Milo muttered.

Relai ignored him and demanded to Ky, "You know them?"

"I know *of* them. I was hoping they'd be dead by now, but you never how long a Sevati is going to live. Some of them were a few thousand years old when the war started. They must think I'm someone else."

Relai shivered as she stretched out the hem of her shirt and used it to scrub at the blood flaking on her fingers. *They called you by name, you liar,* she thought. But out loud she said, "If they can take over people's bodies and live forever, how did they lose the damned war?"

"Not all of them could do that," Ky said. "It's exhausting, especially over long distances. If they're on other planets right now we should be safe for a while. I don't know how long." Ky bit into the foil of a candy bar while Goren unzipped Relai's pack and pulled out a different shirt for her.

"No," Ky interjected. "The blood'll fit in once we get to the dock."

Relai tried to muster a comforting look, for Goren's sake.

"Why were they trying to help us?" Milo asked. He'd been doing an awful lot of absent-minded touching, she'd noticed—Goren's head, Tannor's shoulder, Relai's wrist where he'd grabbed her to make the Sevati drop the knife—and Relai wasn't sure that he was even aware of it. He settled shoulder to shoulder with Ky, closer than the space required.

"Depends on which we decide to believe," Ky sighed. "Depends on what the brother wants. Depends on who's the king."

Relai shook her head. "I know one thing: I don't have a brother."

"Yeah," Ky snapped. "Apparently you do."

She shook her head again, at a loss. She *did not* have a brother. This point was extremely important for the Aydor line: one heir per generation. Only one. No child of the Aydor line ever had brothers or sisters.

Never.

"Maybe—maybe my father secretly allowed another child after he heard the prophecy. 'She is the End,' right? If there's another heir, I'm not the End. I'm not the Defiant."

"What if you're not?" Tannor whispered. She looked almost afraid.

Relai didn't know how to answer that question.

"Or the brother isn't your father's," Milo said quietly.

It would be… best to pretend she didn't hear that. Milo settled back against the cold metal of the wall, his arm stretched behind Ky.

"They said," she coughed, cleared her throat, looked to the wall, "they said 'the brother befriends the king,' or 'the brother befriends the queen.' One or the other. Like that's the key, as far as they're concerned. Like help from this 'brother' determines who… wins."

"Sevati are shipshit," Ky muttered. "They'd say anything to ruin humanity now."

Relai looked at Goren, all earnest and concerned, and Tannor, who couldn't seem to take her eyes off of Ky. Ky, trying to hide the shiny edge of vulnerability in his eyes. And Milo.

Milo.

She smiled weakly and said, "It'd help if we knew the King."

Milo met her eyes and didn't look away.

I hope it's not you, she thought.

"It's probably me," Goren said, and Relai laughed.

"We're not going to listen to either of them," she declared. "We go on as planned. Like they never came."

One by one, some quicker than others, they nodded.

○○●○○

413

vii.

Relai stood over Milo's shoulder and peered out into the passing clouds. He'd taken over piloting, which meant they must be getting close.

"How far are we from the coordinates?"

"Maybe twenty minutes," he replied.

"It's about time to, uh…" She tugged vaguely at a lock of her hair.

Milo gave a low, thoughtful hum as he tweaked a gauge. "We can cut your hair after we land."

"I think I figured something out," she said, before she lost her nerve.

Milo asked with his eyebrows, *what?*

She watched the clouds. "Before, when I asked if it hurt you to hurt someone, I didn't realize then… you're always in pain. All this—everything you're doing is to try to stop it. What you said to Iverson: 'aren't you tired?' You're tired of always being in pain."

Milo took a quick breath and she looked at him, terrified that she'd made things even worse. His face showed the same intensity he always wore in a fight, but now without any anger.

He searched her face, his brow knit, then turned back to the flying.

"You were raised to be selfish, so that's all you see."

Relai went cold. "That's not—"

"I wasn't tearing you down, just helping you understand. I'm here for more than stopping the pain," he said. "Stop it, yeah… then heal it… grow… and make sure it never happens to anyone else again."

Relai, for the first time, pulled back far enough from the plot of land she called her mind to look at him and realize how little she understood. How she might not be able to understand. Milo had never seemed so foreign as he did now, here. Close to her, leaning closer.

"I go numb," she breathed. "All the time. It's fine when it's for myself, but I can't do that when it comes to someone else's pain. It'd be too easy to—"

To turn into my father.

The jumper dipped below the cloud line and Relai saw a vast, blue-grey expanse of snow and shadows.

"Then don't," Milo said.

She felt the jumper slow, and then Milo set them to coast and turned his whole seat to face her fully. He rested his hands on his knees and said, "Relai."

The tone of his voice sent an unreasonable swell of fear through her. Serious, like an ultimatum, or a declaration, or another useless plea for sovereignty.

"Milo, I—"

"I don't think," he began, as the green light from the screens painted dew around his eyes, "that I went more than a few hours without touching another person, not in my whole life, until they razed Elik. We Erayd, we don't—we don't live life alone. We don't isolate ourselves. Voices are one thing, but touch is…" Milo winced and finally met her eyes. "Important. I'm not used to keeping myself from everyone around me. We knock hands and shove shoulders and wrestle, and friends, parents, brothers and sisters, we kiss when we meet. It was the beating of my heart. It's how I knew I wasn't alone."

The jumper rocked in a gust of wind and Milo went on. "This life, after Elik—except for—"

He stopped.

•

Relai saw the wet in his eyes. She kept very still.

On one level (the detached, diplomatic level) she found this whole concept fascinating; in Kilani, all physical contact depended on familiarity, intimacy, and hierarchy. People simply didn't touch, not without a mutual agreement beforehand. Never.

(Her father had been a true scientist in his dissection of her.)

On every other level, Relai wanted to dive into Milo until not an inch of his skin remained untouched and he never felt alone again.

It was terrifying.

She buried it.

Think, Relai, think… he mentioned family to explain this to her. He saw her as a sister? No. That felt wrong.

A friend?

He hates everything you represent, she reminded herself. *When the False Relai falls, he'll tear you down next.*

They only shared a common enemy.

Allies. Milo considered her an ally. That word felt right, at least. He wasn't alone in this struggle and he felt alone because he couldn't touch her.

Finally, a problem she could solve.

•

"It took a while," Milo forced himself to go on, "even with Ky." He couldn't help but glance at the man himself (who gave no sign he'd heard anything, the liar). "But your rules are different. I... first, I hurt you."

"I'm not—"

"You're not afraid of me, I know," he smiled.

Her hand moved and his stomach jumped, but then she wavered and retreated. She wouldn't, Milo knew. Not without clarity.

"I'm telling you this because I need you to know that I'm... if you need to keep that distance, that's fine. I respect it. But if—if you—" Milo stuttered into silence.

He couldn't do this. There was no way to say it without sounding predatory. And it wasn't just for her, it would be for him—he needed it—he needed her to talk to him without talking, the way his people taught him how to talk, not as enemies, not as strangers—but only if she *wanted* to—

It would've helped if they were friends.

Milo didn't want to be friends.

He dropped his head and scrubbed his hands over his face.

"Milo," Relai said. He felt the soft pads of two fingers run across his knuckles.

He looked up.

"You can hold my hand if you want to," she said.

He unfurled his fingers and, gently, hers found their way between his. Her grip was warm and strong, and for a moment Milo forgot what breathing felt like.

Then Tannor cried, "Hey! Everyone!" and they snapped apart.

•

Tannor sat up and uncrossed her legs. "I caught a message from Ed Fass. One of his team's Quiet, I don't know who."

"Who's receiving?" Milo asked from the pilot's seat as Relai said, "What does it say?"

Tannor just muttered, "Who are you talking to, you slimy bastard..." as she concentrated on the screen open in front of her.

Ky pulled out his tablet and started tapping. As he relaxed backward, she pulled up the interior of the jumper to cradle his back and leave room for his head. "How about a footstool?"

"It hit a transmitter halfway to Oliver—" Tannor muttered, her toe twitching to prompt a small block of metal out of the floor under Ky's crossed feet.

"Here, let me chase it," Ky said, and Tannor flicked her hand from her screen to his, imagining the relay data flying to his device. "Now, what does it say?"

Tannor read aloud: "'*The bird is dead. Your fleet may retrieve the scraps. Buzou still functions. I will stand on Earthan legs. By your leave, ever faithful, Fix.*'"

Relai scoffed. "I'm already dead? He's very confident."

Ky set his tablet in his lap and looked at everyone. "Recipient is... a faceless nobody on Oliver Station. An intermediary."

"Someone on Titus," Tannor guessed. "I bet the mention of Buzou was an update on friendly weapons."

"Sounds like I need to freeze Buzou, too," Relai said.

"In case I die," Tannor agreed, nodding as she set up the interface.

Relai gave her hand for approval as she said, "Iverson said Buzou is neutral because Titus is neutral, but *he's* not. Earth Monitoring exists to keep Earth safe, and I think I trust him to do it. He's the highest ranking Titian officer on Earth now. I'll give him back Buzou once we get off-world safely."

Tannor watched Relai's face tilt into that distant look that meant she was formulating a plan.

"Fass wants to kill me before we leave," Relai mused. "He must know where we're going. He must have a plan to catch me, right?" She looked from person to person, her eyes settling on Tannor. "Let's catch him first."

"Stun him on sight," Milo said.

"I can snipe him from a distance," Goren offered.

"No," Relai said. "He'll be a martyr for Unity and they'll just get worse here on Earth. It might even get more people to join. No... the people who have joined up are fighting the False Relai, and I need to give them a reason to lose faith in Unity. I might never convince them to trust in me, but I can make them doubt him."

"He'll talk to me," Tannor said. "He's always been… creepily interested. And I have reason enough to come to him. I can approach him representing the Quiet, asking to deal so they stop hurting and killing people."

Relai tried to keep her voice neutral. "I think Fass would believe that you'd betray me."

Tannor smirked bitterly as she spun toward the wall. "Yeah."

She opened a vidcomm as a paper-thin sheet of metalock rose up between her and the rest of the jumper. Just before it closed her off completely, she said, "Don't listen in," as if she'd give them a choice.

oo●oo

viii.

"Incoming hail," the Titian pilot announced, and Ed Fass perked up. The jumper was swimming before his eyes, his limbs loose like his bones had gone floppy, and he felt invincible. This could be a report from one of the Unity factions across Earth—perhaps by now they'd gained a country or two. If they weren't completely useless, they should have made some progress by now.

"Name?" Fass drawled, joining the Titian at the front and absent-mindedly laying a hand at the back of her neck.

"Tannor Mellick."

The bile in his stomach roiled at that name, but his mind tripped its way into the most logical explanation after only a small delay. Tannor Mellick hated him; she wouldn't call unless something had gone wrong. Very wrong, for her to be willing to try this.

She was ready to bargain.

Fass shoved the Titian out of the pilot's seat and engaged the hail with a confident smile.

Tannor appeared in a window before him; her hair was disastrous and her normal droll expression had been replaced by desperation. She was wearing trash-worthy Earthan clothing in drab colors, and behind her Fass could only make out a blank grey wall. The window framed her face so he couldn't see her breasts.

"Ed," she greeted him shortly.

"Tannor," he replied.

She grimaced and her eyes flashed left, as though she was worried someone might be listening. Her voice was muted over the link so that only Fass could hear her.

"So. *Strength to Unity*, huh?" She didn't try to hide her disdain.

"Tyranny can only continue for so long before someone stands up to it," he said. He sounded powerful, he thought.

Tannor tightened her gorgeous lips. "Well... look, I will never join Unity, but I went over the medical scans of Mora Aydor we did on the groundship when we left, and I found something about her body... I think you know what I mean."

Fass hummed in pleasure. Of course she'd found it. And she was ready to deal because her precious queen had let her down.

"I do," he said with a smile. "Disappointing, hmm? But why are you contacting me?"

"Because I joined the Quiet a long time ago, and I think we can make a deal that will save a lot of lives."

Ah, the Quiet. Of course she had joined them; there was no way they would've posed more than an annoyance for Unity without someone like her involved.

"Oh?" Fass asked coyly.

Tannor swallowed, and it was a beautiful sight. "I'm with her now. I can bring her to you, if you'll agree not to kill her. Listen, Unity's all about freeing Arden, aren't you? You don't need Earth if you have Mora Aydor. And if you keep her alive to stand before a court of all Arden, the Quiet will work with you. You just… you have to let me come with you to guarantee her safety."

"Oh," Fass said, keeping his glee entirely internal, "oh, yes. That will work nicely. Beautifully, in fact. Where can we meet?"

○○●○○

EPISODE XI:

DOCK

L EMME TELL YOU a story," Ky began. "It's an old one."

Relai closed her eyes, grateful for the distraction. They'd landed the jumper and Milo had ventured out into a frigid snowstorm to deal with the workers come to process them. She couldn't delay this any longer.

Ky grabbed a handful of Relai's hair and put it to the sizzling end of Tannor's tech pen. "There was a beautiful young woman, a human, named Emsa," the tip hissed down through her hair, "and one of the Sevati Lords named Hos saw her, loved her for her beauty," a huge splash of hair hit the floor, "and took her without asking."

Relai tried to keep still but he wasn't being gentle. It went fast; her head felt lighter after only a few words. She lowered her eyes to the fists in her lap.

Ky continued: "So Emsa was ruined, virtue gone—that's how these stories go—and then to top it off Hos's wife, the Sevati Lord Ixta, tracked her down. She scarred Emsa's face to make her ugly and cut out the girl's eyes."

"This is a great story," Relai muttered.

"Thanks! So, eyes out, and in their place Ixta put two stones inlaid with metalock. Emsa saw out of these new eyes and after that, anyone who looked at her was poisoned and died as though they'd touched the metalock themselves."

"You're so weird," Goren said through the muffled barrier of his arms.

"At least I'm not short," Ky replied. He finished with the sides and back and went to work on the top, his knees knocking against Relai's as he traveled around her.

"Okay, good story, thank you," Relai grumbled. "Are you trying to scare me?"

"Nope," he said. She detected just a bit of disappointment in that quickly clipped word. "What do you think, though? What did Emsa do next?"

"Paid Hos a visit, I hope."

Ky brushed his palms over her scalp, her shoulders, and she felt the sting of cold on the nearly-bare skin of her head.

"The eye thing didn't work on Sevati Lords. Immortal, you know."

"Yeah? What are they up to these days?"

He clicked his tongue. "It's just a story. Now, look."

He tapped her cheek to get her to open her eyes.

Oh, it was *bad*. Perfect, in fact—she looked like a boy.

A cowering, terrified, unimposing fourteen-year-old boy.

"Am I handsome?" she asked without thinking.

Ky rolled his eyes. "I teach! You learn nothing!"

Goren hovered in her periphery, grinning like an idiot. "You're a very attractive young man!"

"Nothing!" Ky repeated. "Tannor?"

"She was probably vilified and exiled because people are stupid and people are the ones who write these stories," Tannor answered. She'd taken one of Ky's black Gastredi shirts and it somehow suited her perfectly; she looked ready to kill anyone who glanced at her wrong. "And maybe she thanked Ixta for saving her from a ruined life. At least everyone probably left her alone after all that."

"Until they cut off her head," Ky agreed. "Okay, we're ready to go."

No more mirror. Walk out that door and Relai would be male. A boy. Angular and graceless and hard and everything her father mocked her for being.

Maybe she'd be more herself now.

"She could've just blinded herself again," Relai said. "Better than killing everyone you lay eyes on."

For once, the smile on Ky's mouth leaned curious instead of bitter. "We'll see."

Then Tannor waved the entrance open and Milo burst in, fresh and snow-dusted. They huddled away from the blast of icy wind that he brought with him, then he shook off his coat in a puff of snow as he raced through an update.

"I got local clothing for the hike in. The ones buying and selling sounded Earthan except for one—they called him a blade, or blaird, something like that. Comm couldn't tell what language it was." Milo sliced open a sealed plastic pack, shook a pile of sweaters and coats onto the floor, and then tugged a thick green sweater over this head. "Jumper got us sixteen thousand credits each, which means nothing good. Are they buying up coalition tech? The ex-terr told me no Earth weapons allowed, so we're gonna trade those guns at the entrance…"

Then he saw Relai and said, "Oh."

His mouth opened with the sound and stayed open. He looked impossible—stupidly soft and competent and solid and strong—

Relai clutched desperately at the ends of the sleeves of Tom's ratty old shirt and shrugged.

Beauty was power, until it wasn't. Beauty was a weapon, except when you were talking about someone's ability to hold you down.

(She'd broken the minister's jaw with the leg of a chair.)

(Why was she thinking of that now? *Not now.*)

Tannor was beautiful and pale and soft and small; she didn't get it. Emsa wasn't safe when she was ugly. No one was ever safe.

And where did that leave people like Relai? Twenty-two years old and untouched because she'd *fought it*, and she still felt like fighting now any time a man came near her, and even though Milo made her mouth water she worried she'd still flinch if he laid his hands on her with intent and *no one would ever want anything like her so stop thinking about it.*

This was a new kind of ugly feeling, worse than the one she'd thought she left behind so long ago, and she killed and buried it with angry digs of a tired shovel blade. Left it to rot.

She relaxed her hands and looked Milo straight in the eye. "We're ready to go."

.

Milo studied Relai with approval; she'd pass for a teenage boy. She was damned brave to try it, and he'd be by her side the whole time.

He would keep her safe.

425

He told her so, the way she'd asked him to: he reached out and grasped her wrist and squeezed, lightly. The strength in her gaze was stunning. She nodded.

•

Goren put on the last coat left over after everyone else took their pick. He and Relai were both wearing Tom's clothes, and the similar haircuts paired with their different builds made him look older than her (which was just weird). He felt better all bundled into warm obscurity.

"Do I get to be armed?" he asked as Milo tied up his hands.

"Slaves don't get weapons," Milo answered, shoving three fingers under the binding cord to ensure Goren could wiggle out if he needed to, "but if things go bad you grab this," he turned and lifted his shirt, revealing a gen-gun tucked into a band along the back of his pants, "or this," the knife strapped to his outer thigh. "Same on Ky and Tannor. We scavenge everything we can, so stay behind me and you gather weapons from anyone I down. Clear?"

Goren blinked. "Yes, sir."

"And keep your mouth shut," Tannor added. "I know it's hard, but you're supposed to be Earthan. We're not your friends now."

Goren only scowled for half a second before he realized— "Wait, we were friends?"

•

"Comms, guns, food—everyone should carry food, in case Ky needs it…" Tannor muttered to herself. "Milo! Is your comm still crackling?"

They'd fixed comms and healed up using the jumper's med scanner, but if Milo's went out at the wrong time they might all be screwed.

"Not anymore," Milo answered. He held out a full hand and Tannor found herself a new grenade carrier. "Concussion, flash, snap, shriek."

"That's a good idea," she said, more to herself than to him. "Shrieking. I can make people's comms shriek if we need to stop someone. Might even fry their auditory nerves."

Milo raised his eyebrows. "Scary. I'll remember that."

"And I realized I can get a sense of things that contain and conduct electricity, too—the size and shape. I knew Xiong's ship was there before we could see it."

"Tannor, you are so magical," Goren said as Milo helped him wrap a massive scarf around his head.

"Shut up," Milo said, tucking in the end of the scarf and giving the top of Goren's head a little shake. "Ky will take the rear. I'll handle Goren and Relai. Tannor, don't fall back. I want you next to me the whole time."

Tannor stared at him.

"Actually," he amended slowly, "you could take the lead? I'll be your second."

After what she'd done and all that she knew of Milo, Tannor couldn't understand. For a moment she even wondered if this was some sort of trap, but she quickly discarded that thought and shook her head. "I want to keep my head open to the tech around us. I can see how they're scanning us and if they identify us, I'll know. I need my mind free."

"Well. Equals, then?"

An ache rippled through her, and she looked over at Relai talking to Ky. Tannor swallowed and nodded.

.

Be young, be male, be scared, Relai thought. She and Goren would be the captured kids; Tannor, Milo, and Ky, the captors.

Ky caught her by the shoulders and she went pliant in his hands as he bound her wrists in front of her. It wouldn't be difficult to slide into tensed muscles and overwhelmed eyes once they walked out the door, but first Ky tugged at her chin with one finger and peered at her hair and face, evaluating. She met his eyes and let confidence and trust show through. It didn't mean she wasn't scared.

She said, "You can hit me if you need to."

His face hardened. "It'll look wrong if I'm not rough with you, but I won't enjoy this."

Pick up the knife and cut me, she thought. "Not many chances to be gentle these days, huh?"

He grimaced, she smiled wryly, and then Ky grabbed her head in his hands and kissed the bridge of her nose.

Relai was too surprised to move. He pulled back and found her eyes, nervous, checking her reaction.

Oeylan, she reminded herself. Sana had kissed her that way, in a kind of sympathy, after Relai turned Niko Yansa away. Relai had never seen Ky nervous before.

She nodded.

Then Goren laughed, Relai looked his way, and Ky punched her in the face.

○○●○○

ii.

Tom decided flying in an alien shuttlecraft ranked as the coolest thing to happen today, even beating out the revelation that MMN was apparently crawling with a bunch of nice human aliens. It was turning out to be a pretty remarkable day, in general.

After a brief pit stop at Tom's place to get the laptop that actually contained the location of the secret dock (because of course this guy Iverson refused to just believe him; Tom had set up a program to passively log everything the aliens did on his devices, and that was proof enough), plus a few other things for the trip, Tom snuggled in next to Hope on an uncomfortable sideways bench. Their Cigarette-Smoking-Man-in-Black had to fly the jumper, but they were under no illusions that he couldn't hear every word.

Another two hours, Iverson had said. He'd fit Hope with an earpiece of her own and explained the basic premise of galactic politics vis-à-vis historical human enslavement by aliens, the alien tech that supported a human monarchy, the subsequent uprising, et cetera, and exactly how messy this whole situation really was. Apparently the leaders of Titus had declared total neutrality after Unity kidnapped a princess from one of the other planets and started threatening all the other royal children, so not everyone from the Titus-owned base was willing to help them out. A few would be enough, Iverson seemed sure.

It was chilly in the jumper and Hope's nose was running; she kept sniffling and trying to hide it.

"So," Tom said. "Aliens, huh?"

Hope gave him one of her *looks*. She'd only been a little poisoned at the hospital, and frankly Tom would've traded places with her to experience alien healing powers. She seemed fine now. Tom did not feel bad for her.

He tried again. "You think everything is going to be okay?"

Hope peered at the wall and then glanced at Iverson. "I'm not going to let us be colonized."

"Yeah, good luck with that," Tom snorted. "People will be scared, and fear unifies. Let it get out of hand and we'll be the ones colonizing them in a few years. If we haven't killed 'em all first."

Hope scowled. "I don't want to kill humans."

Tom kicked her ankle, scandalized. "You don't want to kill anyone! Right?"

"Not if I don't have to!" Hope leaned forward and rubbed her temples. "We're not ready for this. I don't know what's going to happen."

Tom shrugged. "People are people. You know how it'll go."

She levied him a sideways glance. "Someone is going to think violence is the easiest way to deal with them."

"*Safest*, Hope. They always say safest."

Hope hummed but didn't reply.

Tom scratched at his receding hairline. "Okay, let's set a goal: no world wars. How does that sound?"

Hope rolled her eyes. "I'll do my best. I have no idea how much power I have right now. I thought it would be a straightforward fight, you know? If we ever actually came face to face with real aliens."

Tom tapped his lip with his thumb. "Mmmm… I say give it a few weeks. It sounded like ships from Gastred are on the way."

Hope delivered the most beautifully deadpan glare and said, "Looks like you have a lot to tell me before we get to Russia."

"We're setting down in Nigeria in five," Iverson announced from up front. "We're picking up soldiers and supplies from Ife Base. Over maximum capacity for this jumper, but we'll make it."

"Wait a second," Tom said, whipping out his notebook. "They didn't mention anything about a base with that name. Is that another name for… whassit… Buzou?"

Iverson grinned in a manner that made Tom shiver. "Ife is the independent Titian base on Earth. The people you met know nothing about it."

"So we're stocked if we have to go to war with them," Hope concluded. "Excellent."

"What did I *just say*, Valdez? No war!"

She shrugged. "Mutually assured destruction only works if one side can't obliterate the other with a single thought, you know."

Iverson turned back to the helm. "No one is obliterating anyone. We'll be able to stop any major threats before they reach Curragh. Nothing's getting past us."

"And I get a better gun," Hope added.

Iverson didn't even pause before answering. "And you get a better gun."

Tom shivered in excitement. *This was really happening.*

He clutched the objects hidden in his coat—an eighteen-year-old bottle of fine, single-malt peat-smoked Scotch, and a tablet, the one Tannor had left behind at his house—just a little more tightly to his chest.

iii.

"This planet is—what do you call it?—bullshit!"

"You can still just say shipshit, Goren."

"I'm *adapting* to Earth."

"We have bulls in Reyet, you know. That's what we call the males on our farm."

"Really? Is their poop shaped like this planet and FREEZING COLD?"

Milo tromped along, feeling muscles in his ankles work that hadn't been challenged since that mudslide last year. Snow battered them from all sides, turning their whole world white; a violent gust of wind followed the rumble of a passing military vehicle and they all huddled closer. These soldiers kept the airfield surface remarkably clean for the weather, but ridges of rough ice still clawed up here and there, ready to trip them when they got careless. If a local soldier—he was Earthan, not ex-terr, dressed all in white to fit the environment—hadn't been leading them, they wouldn't have made it down the straight line from jumper to hangar. The blizzard and their gear prevented voices from carrying, but they were all on comms now and the conversation flowed like murmurs in a still room.

"I can barely see you under all your covering, chaff," Milo said. He jerked the cord leading to Goren's hands, making sure not to pull too hard.

Tannor knocked her way between them. She'd taken on the persona of a heartless slave trader already; she wouldn't look at Goren or Relai and when Goren tripped she didn't even pause. "I'm the smallest here and I'm not cold at all. We get wind and snow like this in Reyet, plus another fifteen feet."

"You have many nice layers of fat," Goren countered, "and I am nothing but bones and bruises and bad luck."

"And smell, don't forget that part," Milo added as Tannor replied, "True," and then Milo threw his arm around Tannor to shove Goren's head sideways.

"Act your parts, children," Ky growled from up ahead. "We don't know who might be watching. Goren, fall back with—do we have a new name for you yet?"

Goren mumbled, "No one can see us through this snow," as he dropped back a few feet.

The scrawny kid trailing behind them coughed into bound hands. "You're stealing me. Do you care what my name is?"

"Not really," Ky said. Milo heard the apathy in Ky's voice and tried to settle himself against a swell of revulsion. How could they talk about stealing and selling human beings so carelessly?

Then Ky added, "...but I think you'd care. Just for yourself."

Their guide led them into a cold, ancient-looking gray building. They were out of the elements, but somehow it didn't feel any warmer. The storm had hid their surroundings but Milo knew from the topography map displayed in the jumper as they landed that this small building stood alone in the airfield. The dock would be underground, of course; the terrain dropped off into vicious serrated cliffs not too far away, which meant the launch tunnel probably opened on the side of the mountain.

"So?" Milo asked as they shuffled through creaking metal doors and shook the snow off of their bodies. "What's your new name?"

Relai wiped her red-tipped nose and thought a moment before catching his eye. "Slavers don't get to know."

He tucked his grin into his coat and said:

"You don't know my name."

Relai froze in a shower of snowflakes. He stared back, sure and full of promise, and watched a glint of challenge grow in her eyes.

Then Ky grumbled and tugged Relai away by the cord around her hands.

•

Milo calculated.

Three between them and the entrance, one in the lock, two at a panel with faces lit by a soft orange glow. All armed with Earthan or coalition retrofit guns. The native Earthan soldiers stayed on their end of the room, separate from the blaid. The low ceiling and dark corners reminded him of Gastred, but both walls of the lock were a loose-knit metal fence woven so widely he could see through both, fifteen feet apart, into the dim area beyond. The area between gates was crowded with two seated figures—travelers, by looks—and another moving methodically through the shadows. Probably a health check, maybe some sort of decontamination. They'd need it before they left the planet.

A stocky man with a round head and a beautiful pair of Gastredi work boots—apparently the boss here—stepped up to Milo and said in Ardi, "Ten bits metalock *pob*."

"We have fifty thousand credits on this key," Milo replied, raising two bare fingers next to his chin with the key poking up between them.

Boss Blaid smirked; the rest looked bored. One threw a gesture past Milo's group, probably meant for one of the Earthan soldiers, and then laughed at whatever response he received.

"Don't take credits," Boss Blaid said. "Earth is tricky. Credits might mean nothing here in a week's time. We take solid wealth or you go back out that door. Luck finding the nearest town... in eight thou *milli*."

Ten bits of metalock might as well have been ten million for the lack of it on this planet. To his right, Ky picked his teeth; to his left, Tannor sniffled through a runny nose. Milo stood completely still.

"We can barter guns."

On cue, Tannor dropped her pack between them and opened it to show the guns they'd collected over the past three days—ten in all.

The blaid parried with a laugh. "Oh, these Earth guns? Not allowed inside, *frind*. Cost of the favor of disposal is another bit of metalock for every single one. You're up to... sixty, looks."

Oh, hells—*pob* meant *each*. Milo heard Tannor click her tongue, updating her comm to re-translate with the new information, and then she tucked her head behind his back and whispered, "Wolf. Blaid means wolf."

Milo stepped forward with his hands relaxed at his sides. "I'm betting our *frind* here has a suggestion for how we pay."

Boss Wolf raised an eyebrow. "Smart man! We take a costrel of blood, knock down the price by half, if you rather."

He motioned to the lock behind him, where Milo realized the seated travelers were reclined, arms out, needles in. Those benches sat in front of carts with tubing, and through the grey of the shadows he picked out hanging reservoirs of fluid the size of his open hand.

One of the wolves at the screen wasn't aiming his gun at anyone—he was whispering in the ear of the woman next to him, his sharp eyes on Milo.

He was tall and rough, with ruddy skin, cropped hair and thick beard. Same clothes as all the wolves. As he spoke the woman's head snapped up. She peered at Milo in bare shock and tapped into her screen.

The sharp-eyed wolf had recognized him.

Milo turned to Tannor. Her eyes had faded, brow furrowed, the way they did whenever she was reaching out with her ability. "It's okay," she murmured. "No outgoing relays, no alarms. And yes, they're just taking blood. I don't know why."

Ky growled, "Can't be good."

Milo let his shoulders drop.

Nine.

If the soldiers behind intervened, that nine would turn into twenty. More from ahead, as well. They'd never get off planet if they started a battle here.

Then Goren doubled over in a coughing fit behind them and Relai whispered into her comm, "Give them the med scanner. I packed it after you sold the jumper. It's in Ky's bag."

Milo repressed a smile as he dug into his pack and found the device.

"We're carrying something more valuable than blood or metalock," he declared. He held up the scanner.

The wolves' reaction told him all he needed to know—these people wanted a med scanner. They needed it. They'd take it.

"Eh," Boss Wolf blustered, "that covers your fifty. Still need our ten bits meta. Or blood from one of you, plus one of your catches? Not the sick one."

Tannor replied without missing a beat: "Scanner's still reg."

Boss Wolf froze.

Tannor went on, "Needs to read a pin before it'll heal."

The wolves around them all shifted and scoffed and one spat on the ground. Boss threw up both hands.

"Then it's trash, *asty*."

"Let us through and I'll hack it for you," Tannor replied.

Boss's eyes turned cunning. "Can't."

Tannor stared him down without blinking.

Then the sharp-eyed wolf broke off from his computer terminal and strode over to Boss Wolf. He crossed behind the man to speak to him, and when he turned his head Milo saw the sharp-eyed wolf's left ear.

Ten feet away, a dull silver bar spanned a notch cut in his ear. Milo froze.

The man eyed Milo sideways, purposeful and clear in his display. As he whispered, he gave Milo a tiny nod.

Milo squared his shoulders.

Boss Wolf snorted and waved a blithe hand through the air. "Fine! Fine. I see the logic. Hack the scanner for entry, *frind.*"

Tannor went to work on the scanner, clearly taking longer than necessary, and then Milo took it from her and met the sharp-eyed wolf in the center of the room. Behind him, Tannor roughed Goren back onto his feet. Relai made so little noise, kept her face down so well, Milo could've forgotten she was there.

(But for the pull in his stomach, of course.)

"Brother?" he murmured in Erayd. *Not Monster, not Monster, not to this man—*

"Tinder," the man answered. Milo had no idea what that meant, but from the man's demeanor it seemed he should. The line of the wolf's brow looked familiar, though Milo had little hope of knowing his family personally. Still.

"Tell me your hail."

"Shunna, lacking ten years, from the waters of Tanith and Prichella and Kawla. My name is Ithail Sur."

"Shunna," Milo breathed. He loved the bread in Shunna. They didn't skimp on salt.

Milo tasted it on his tongue in a flash of memory and he was forced, against the last crumbling shreds of his will, to realize how utterly *alone* he'd felt for the last eight months. He could only see it now that he stood face to face with one of his own. A brother.

Ithail prodded at the med scanner, making sure it turned on and the fuel cells were full. "Da," he called, then he tossed it to Boss Wolf who wandered away, poking at it like a child with a new toy. Ithail jerked his chin to get Milo to follow. "I'll take you through."

He led them past the blood-letting and through another gate. Only once they left the sight of the entrance and reached a massive spiraling set of stairs did any of them speak.

"We need to leave on one of the next ships," Milo said.

"Yeah, you do," Ithail replied. The rich tones of confidence and eagerness and something else in his voice almost made Milo stumble.

He hadn't dared to check the commons since he left Arden; he couldn't stomach the wailing pain of all the messages begging for news about those missing or dead, and the authorities were always seconds away from the moment of access, anyway. He'd declared himself fiercely alive and promised justice, then disappeared from commons life. He knew from glimpses of public telay and overheard conversations that they called him Monster, but nothing more.

So he asked, "What do you know about me?"

Ithail cocked an eyebrow. "You're the Flint. You got out of Elik, *peace where they rest,* and screw what Tower calls you, all of us Erayd know—you're bent on trapping her. They say you found her hiding and she seduced you, brought you low, but I never believed it. You're bringing her back."

Milo nodded grimly. "I'm bringing her back."

The rest of the group lined up behind him as they reached another fence. Ithail shoved a solid metal key into a block to unlock the gate and the woman he'd whispered to earlier appeared.

"The Flint, himself, alive before me!" she chirped. She stood nearly as short as Tannor, with badly-dyed silver hair and brown skin. Her ear wasn't notched, but she looked too young for it anyway—maybe younger that Relai, even. Erayd sounded strange with her Earthan accent. "I'm Elur Maat. Justice comes as Flint strikes Steel! I knew they were wrong about her relay—"

"Hush, El!" Ithail hissed.

"She hasn't tamed you, has she?" Elur cackled as she slapped Milo hard on the shoulder. "*You* cowed *her!* I knew it!"

Then she peered over Relai and Goren, nodded in satisfaction, and spit on Relai.

"Tsh," Ky exclaimed, "keep yourself to yourself over this one. She's ours."

"She's his, fishface, and that means she's *ours,* justice come! He's the Flint, we're the Tinder, and what are you?"

"Holding the cord that's dragging her along," Ky replied, acidic-sweet.

How could Milo explain all of it to them? There was no time—but just as quickly, Elur Maat switched over to regard Tannor. "Tannor Mellick! I know you. Techie. Thorn between our toes."

"And I never knew a thing about all this," Tannor said. "I didn't realize I had competition on Earth."

Ithail threw his head back and laughed and—the sound of it, the sight— it hit Milo in his chest like *home.* "I like her," Ithail said.

"You should," Elur sneered. "She's a genius."

"You need to move fast if you want to find a seat," Ithail warned. Milo swallowed his words and agreed by taking the first step into the abyss.

The sound of their boots on the metal walkway echoed down through the central column of shadowy open space.

·

Relai found a rhythm in the gentle tug of the cord and the thud of her feet on the stairs and retreated into her mind. At the very top of the stairs Relai had noticed an inscription scrawled on the concrete wall: *May the stars be your light, the gods be your protection, and your journey end in blessing.* It was some ancient Ardenian saying, and she'd seen it carved at the entrance to every spaceport and dock she'd ever set foot in. In fact, it was so commonplace she'd never before given it thought. Clearly, it was an inscription that only applied to some of the people crossing through this threshold. Not to those brought through as property.

As they descended into a seemingly bottomless concrete shaft lit only by intermittent sickly-green lights, her mind drifted to another inscription, one she had read in a piece of of Earthan literature back when she was trying to understand Earth by reading its books. She hadn't made it very far into this particular book, but one scene was etched in her mind: the book's protagonist, entering some dismal subterranean Earthan version of the afterlife, passing an inscription.

Abandon hope, all ye who enter here.

She collected the burning in her chest into one central spot just below her sternum and then gave it a name: anger.

More than anger. *Fury.*

These people, these wolves from Eray and everywhere else—they'd just waved Relai's group onward. No questions. No concern.

They were allowing it. Profiting from it.

Human slavery.

If she were anyone else with hands bound and face bruised, she would be a young man of Earth. She'd be tied up and led along, terrified at the lack of control and the vicious voices speaking unknown languages, and she'd be packed and logged and then sold.

Not a person. A thing.

These people, her people, people of her coalition, led by the Aydors—they were enslaving people of Earth—Relai bit down so hard her teeth ached, the pain a neat distraction from her throbbing face. It was no different from how the Sevati had taken Earthans like beasts, her own ancestors, nothing changed, no one—

"*No different,*" Relai growled out without intending to.

"What did you say?" Tannor asked, just a step below her.

Relai flexed her wrists, judging the looseness of her bindings. She was such a farce. Her whole self—this whole lie—riches built on the losses of others. She brought her fists to her face and dug her knuckles into the place where Ky had hit her until her eyes teared up.

"It doesn't matter what I said." Relai sniffled and swallowed around the dank stickiness invading her mouth as they descended further and further into the depths of this horrible place. "What am I going to *do?*"

•

They reached the bottom of the stairs, at least twenty flights spiraling upward at right angles above them.

"Tell me," Milo said, "security, scans, currency."

"You're safe from scans; I told El to ruin everything and she's good at that. We guard ourselves, but this place is packed tin up with desperate so you can blend in. As for currency," Ithail opened another gate at the base of the stairs, "this will cover all your people and you." He shoved a handful of credit keys into Milo's hand, then craned his neck. "Hey, El, throw me one of the back-ups, yeah?"

He caught a tiny thing El lobbed from a rack of supplies and poked at it with a grimy black-painted fingernail. "Use this if you need to talk to me. It's only me on the other end and it's secure."

Milo nodded, slipping the comm in his ear. "Tell your wolves not to bother us unless we call for help."

"You won't be stopped, I swear it. And El's sending you tech details of the dock so you don't get snagged."

Ithail held out his arms, one hand for the ribs and one for the neck, as they always did it in Eray. Milo nearly stumbled meeting the embrace—the first real presence of home in eight long, miserable months.

"We coming with you?" Ithail asked. It was almost an insult, even asking, but Milo knew the question came from longing and not doubt.

He closed his eyes. "I want my family with me, always. I'll contact you once we find seats and you can meet us at the ship."

"*Yes,*" Ithail growled.

Then Relai cleared her throat.

Milo stood back from his brother and watched her rise to her feet, slowly and deliberately, with a stiffness in her movements that hadn't been there earlier. She squared her stance, straightened her back, and by the time she'd finished she held the full attention of everyone present. She seemed taller, somehow.

She fixed her gaze on Milo and said, "That's it?"

The anger in her voice was clear, and Milo felt a grinding in his chest.

"Relai... they're family."

"What about Earthan families that are losing their children? You forget about justice when it's someone you care about that did the harm?"

"Hey, hey," Ithail said, "we didn't put out the calls, didn't do any catching, don't do any buying. We just work here."

Relai's face matched the acid in Milo's stomach at that defense. No, not even a defense—a weak-willed deflection unfit for a man of Eray. Milo let himself feel the loss and collected it into grim resolve.

Climb up, he thought.

He turned to the wolves.

"You were exiled from Arden, were you not?"

"Me, her parents, more, yeah." Ithail squinted and scratched his beard. "We're in all the dirty cracks of this planet."

"Have you found a home here?"

Ithail paused. "You call, we answer."

"You helped ex-terrs steal children from this planet and ship them off to be slaves, or worse," Milo said. "So here's my call: stay here, work with Earth Monitoring. Unity's trying to take over Earth and you can help stop them."

Ithail barked out a laugh. "What, brother?"

"Earth *Fucking* Monitoring, are you wit-sick?" Elur Maat scoffed. "They'll kill us as soon as look at us!"

"Then you'll die," Milo said, "and it's nothing more than you deserve. You know our law."

"We have no quivers about breaking laws to get us free, Flint."

Milo flashed a glance at Relai to steady his voice. "We will do it without rotting from the inside out."

He heard movement behind him, probably Ky and Tannor gearing up for a fight in case these shifty wolves decided Milo wasn't the hero they thought he was, but Milo simply stared Ithail down.

Finally, the man spat and then grinned. "Never got a good feeling from those Unity guys, anyway."

Elur Maat rolled her eyes. "We gonna bow to Earth Monitoring now?"

"You owe Earth a debt," Milo said. "Not Earth Monitoring. Keep that sorted or you're free to follow me."

"Sounds kinda nice, actually," Elur mused. "A proper job. What if we don't feel so... punished?"

"You're always free to choose execution if you prefer to feel more *punished*," Milo replied. "This isn't about your feelings. Give your life for Earth, in labor or not."

Ithail moved closer. "You sure you don't want me to come with you, at least?"

Milo grimaced. "I want you with me. But you owe a debt, and I can't leave Earth to a Titian alone. Make her strong."

Ithtail stared a long moment, nodded once, then straightened up, all business. "That bruise isn't going to be enough to get her off-world," he said, tapping his own eye with his knuckles and pointing to Relai. He shoved two grimy sacks at Milo. "Cover their heads until you find a cove."

Milo gripped the rough cloth with the pads of his fingers, tugging to be sure the fibers would let air through, then folded them inside out to check for blood and crust. "A cove?"

"Places for travelers to hunker until next exit window. Stick to north center to draw the least attention. We'll notify you by comm if trouble decides to show."

He grabbed Milo's elbow and pulled in close. "Tinder for Flint," Ithail said.

Then he kissed Milo roughly on the side of his face. Milo returned it, and then they parted ways: Ithail Sur and Elur Maat back up the stairs to the surface; Milo and his crew, through the final tunnel leading to the dock.

•

Tannor glanced pointedly at the cloth head sacks, then up at Milo.

He answered by asking, "You rot their facial recognition program?"

She nodded. A real person might recognize Relai, but only if they recognized Milo first and realized the importance of anyone with him. Otherwise, who would look at this scrawny, dirty, bruised boy and think of Their Glory, Their Light, Their Hope?

He tucked the sacks into his jacket. "I'm not blinding two of my people."

Tannor looked up at him in surprise. He smiled, just briefly, and glowing light from the caged fixtures above caught in the green of his eyes.

oo●oo

iv.

They pushed through a pair of thick, heavy doors guarded by two bored, unfamiliar wolves, into a rush of warmer air and muffled sound. Relai followed Milo and Tannor by the pull of the cord between her hands, with Goren and Ky behind her, and they gathered on a landing that stood just one short flight of stairs above the main floor of a giant marketplace.

Whether it once held machinery or tables of scientific experiments or aircraft parts or weapons, Relai couldn't imagine; what the room held now was the ground floor of a haphazardly-grown Ardenian cityscape. Jagged edges of walls stretched out like a maze across the massive expanse. The original Earthan roof, carved out of the mountain itself, hung high enough that it might have held five floors if only the builden had grown into actual buildings instead of open-topped cubes; the structurally-responsive mold must have needed a chemical in the air of Arden, or different air pressure, or different water. Stalks of the mold's skeleton jutted slightly higher than the rest here and there, like the beginnings of an industrial forest spiking above an unnatural system of canyons. Hoverlights scattered at different heights cast a blue-tinged glow through the place.

From their vantage point, Relai could just see inside some of the shops and rooms comprising the makeshift town, and she could trace a pattern of pathways running through the space. She counted dozens of people visible, imagined hundreds milling through the marketplace. A hazy distance away, she saw brighter lights rising from a gathering area against the far wall. She looked left the same moment Milo did—north, where Milo's wolf had said they would find the coves that weren't rotting. Relai saw a row of recesses in the builden running along the wall, just as Ithail Sur had said there would be. Some were lit by hoverlights, others by flickering fire, and a few sat dark.

"This is a nightmare," she heard Goren mumble. "I'm in a nightmare of crime."

"Let's move," Milo said.

They descended one last flight of steps to a concrete floor pocked with failed builden buds, and Ky skirted forward.

"This is more my song, so I'll take the lead."

Milo nodded curtly and took up a place at the back.

Only a few steps into the outside ring of shops, and the rich smells of home began to make Relai's mouth water. People were cooking Vadan food here—hestia-spiced sambusas and sweet vinegar meat, five-leaf tea and clawbean soup. When was the last time she'd eaten? She couldn't remember. They'd be on a ship soon, though, and she wasn't foolish enough to fill her stomach now. They hadn't eaten recently but they also hadn't fasted, so Relai didn't know how they were going to deal with *that* problem… but she suspected the sounds of glopping fluid and groaning behind one room marked 'System Cleanse' held the answer. Ky didn't even glance that way, though, so maybe each slave ship captain monitored the travel pod preparation for captured people?

"Why are so many people trying to get off-planet?" Relai whispered into Ky's back. She stared as they passed a family of Oeylans trying to corral a (very illegal) pet pig as they bought edible plastic packets of food.

"Because this idiot planet has nuclear weapons, and there are at least five different reasons they might use them in the next few weeks," Ky replied.

If only there was someone trustworthy in control of all of their tech, Relai thought in a dark part of her mind. She didn't say it aloud.

"Haberfish! Five for three!" a vendor shouted. "I got the Arctic Monkey's latest, too, half off. And dick socks, 'cause they don't care if your junk freezes off in transit but you sure do!"

"What?" Relai whispered, to which Milo rasped, "Just keep moving; you don't want to know."

Ky marched forward without acknowledging the cacophony. A spinning shop sign declared TATTOO REMOVAL and Relai tugged at the cord binding her to Ky.

"We could use—"

"Yeah," Tannor agreed. "Just Goren and I."

"Aw," Goren grumbled, "I've only had mine three months."

Milo snorted. "You have to get naked for the travel pod, you know that, right?"

Goren screwed his face up to argue, but Ky cut in before he could reply. "We'll be your owners, full circle. No one else is going to see you naked. You never know who might catch a glimpse of what, though, so go."

"Oh… okay," Goren said grouchily.

Tannor unclipped him from his bindings they split off to the stall without any more arguments.

Relai remained bound to Ky, wondering if it would be better to wait here or find a cove without them, and then they heard:

"Problems with death on the way to the market? Struggle no more!"

Ky halted, arching his neck to locate the source of the words as Relai bumped into him and then peered around his shoulder. It was an older sanda man wearing a long worn white and gold coat with plush fur lining that might have been from Titus fifty years ago. The merchant realized he'd caught someone's ear and laid on the charm.

"Buy a travel trunk today! Make your next foray more profitable, I promise you, my dear friends!" He slid forward and spread his arms. Behind him, stretchy tubes of light formed a makeshift halo around a tall stack of black and blue ribbed trunks. "What is the loss to transport for child merchandise?"

Ky's shoulder jerked. "Maybe three for every ten?"

"Four! Four out of every ten die in transit from catch to port! Too wide a margin of loss, you must agree! And of course the smaller they are, the more economical the transport costs—but too small and the survival rate is quite dismal. So the ideal subject would be..."

"Eight-year-old male," Ky answered.

Relai hunched away from Ky, her back pressing into Milo. He answered so easily, so business-like. He wasn't guessing.

"You know your merchandise! Excellent show! So you must know that younger children and females are also in *high* demand. What can be the solution?" The man appealed to a surrounding crowd that wasn't there, and found no answer. "We can do better. With my travel trunks, merchants have reported losses of only one for every ten! One! My trunks can fit cargo as small as thirty pounds or as heavy as eighty, and every model improves upon the drug and oxygen systems so you can expect to lose even less product *if* you remain a loyal customer and take advantage of our exclusive future discounts." He grinned encouragingly.

Ky shook his head, his face blank. "I only transport one at a time. Delicate work. No losses."

That brought the man to inspect Relai more closely. "This one is too big for Borey's compartments, you know. That's right, my friend, I know all the right people. Izer Borez is the only one docked right now who smuggles slaves and he'll never let you cross his shipstep. Plus, I happen to know he's full up. Twelve compartments, no vacancies. I could take him—"

"This is a contract. *Step back.*"

The man swallowed, laughed nervously, and then dared to glance one more time. Relai clenched her eyes shut—he was going to recognize her, in a moment he'd—

Ky surged forward with one hand sliding out of his coat and the man grunted. Ky pushed him back and down into his stall until he was hidden, surrounded by his travel trunks. He stayed there, just where Ky put him, still and staring.

Relai had just enough time to recognize the stream of blood oozing from under his jaw before Milo pulled away after Ky and, hands jolting forward, she had to follow.

"Future discounts," she heard Ky mutter.

Milo's hand found its way to her elbow and he squeezed it as they shuffled along. She hoped it was supposed to be comforting, because that's how she decided to take it.

oo●oo

"I don't want to do this," Goren mumbled to the floor.

The tech pulled down a bench on a hinge from the wall and patted it with a smarmy grin in Tannor's direction. "Shirt off, darling."

Tannor sneered at the guy, sat herself on the edge of the seat, and stretched her collar sideways.

"It's illegal to erase your guard tattoo," Goren went on, fidgeting. This place hardly had enough lighting for any sort of—*procedure*. The filaments would just dissolve with the application of a certain sound wave frequency, but still. "You'll never be a tech sergeant again."

"Colonel," Tannor corrected. "Show some respect."

Their host laughed and keyed up a cylinder the size of Goren's forearm on the end of a cord connected to a power source. Goren knew some guys back home who were really into this Earth-nouveau interpretation of energy and technology, and these types of cords seemed to be a big part of the aesthetic. It was all vaguely prenatal and weird.

Goren crossed his arms as the cylinder thing finally whirred to life. "This place is gross, *Colonel.*"

Tannor smirked and shook her head. She leaned back and the tech put the nose of the cylinder to the peak of her tattoo. (That thing didn't look clean. It wasn't supposed to cut into her skin, but what if this guy didn't know what he was doing?)

Goren almost opened his mouth in protest, but Tannor cut him off.

"I don't need it," she told him. "I know who I am."

The whirring kicked up and Goren had to resist plugging his ears. The black of her tattoo went fuzzy, then grey, then dissolved into nothing. Ten seconds and her skin was clean and perfect. Goren looked away as she stood up and adjusted her shirt.

"Pretty white skin," the tech said, pleased. "Now you, pretty too."

Goren copied Tannor and refused to undress in front of this creep.

"I know who I am," he echoed. He sat, looking at the picture someone had stuck to the ceiling without really seeing, and felt the tap of Tannor's boot against the bottom of his shoe.

Ten seconds and clean.

"Still know who you are?" Tannor asked.

Goren let himself glance down and see his bare, dull, naked skin. No rank, no recognition, no respect... So, pretty much normal.

He smiled for half a second, then frowned and looked back up at the ceiling.

"Is that an onion?"

Tannor shoved his shoulder and hustled him out the door.

○○●○○

They claimed an empty inlet along the outer circle of the massive central room where travelers could settle and wait for their ships without bother. Relai watched as Tannor confirmed the reach of the tech jammer; she'd be able to tell if coalition guards came anywhere near.

One person on guard would be enough. Relai looked to the ceiling and read the departure clock listing times for each docked ship: the soonest was -12 minutes, the latest, -47. The name Borez sat beside a ship called *Vimana*, departure -42 minutes. (*Full up.* He'd meant full of children. Stolen Earthan children, packed in one of the ships, *right now. Twelve compartments, no vacancies.*) They didn't have time for this conversation.

Relai cleared her throat. "Ky. Back there..."

His eyebrow twitched up as he heaved his pack to the floor.

"How do you know so much about slave trafficking?"

His gaze settled on the floor, and he sighed.

Milo, impatient as ever, asked again:

"Ky. How do you know slave trafficking?"

Ky clacked his teeth together. Relai listened to them and watched his mouth twist.

"Experience," he said finally. He refused to look at any of them as he pulled out pieces of tech for the trap for Fass, and Relai had seen enough of him to know his range of shoulder expressions by now. This wasn't an aggressive reaction. This was shame.

Relai felt bile rise in her stomach and spikes of alarm shot across her chest. He—he—

Now. Think about *now*.

"Okay," she said, catching Milo's devastated eyes in the dim hope he'd follow her lead, "we know you now. What you do now matters. What you've done matters, too, but you're here now. With us. Right?"

Ky waved in dismissal. "I mean, from the merchandise side of things."

He focused on the carbon mesh in his hands, tugging and spreading the fibers, and Relai just caught herself before she gasped.

"Ky," Milo said in a throaty voice.

Relai grabbed a gun from Milo and started searching her own layers of clothing to hide it somewhere. "Forget Fass. We're rescuing those kids."

Ky slapped the mesh into Tannor's hands so hard she stumbled backward as he said, "No. We're not."

Relai gaped at him. "What do you mean, *no?*"

Ky stood stubbornly in the middle of the cove. "We take out Fass and we buy seats on a groundship and the escape window closes in... forty-one minutes. We don't have time to waste."

"Waste? *Waste?*"

Tannor broke through Relai's horror. "Relai, I'm sorry... but we don't have time. Not if we want Fass."

"Tannor, please," Relai exclaimed. "How is Fass more important than these children?"

Tannor's jaw clenched and her head wavered back and forth. "We need to capture Fass. He knows something you need to know if you—if we—"

"What happens if we collect those kids and then Fass finds us halfway to safety?" Milo cut in. "And what safety, anyway? Are we giving up on leaving now?"

"No," Ky snarled. "We leave. That's it."

Relai took one long look at his face. (Ky cooking eggs for everyone at Tom's house. Ky with bare feet.)

She could handle this.

So she said, "Tannor. Go tell Milo what you need to tell him. Go now."

Tannor's eyes flashed between the two of them, and then she grabbed Milo by the arm and dragged him away.

Goren said, "I guess I'll... keep watch?" and disappeared after them.

Then Relai faced Ky in the dim light and said gently, "We're saving those kids."

"This shit is gonna strand us here, you *stupid little girl.*"

She couldn't see his eyes.

"We're saving those kids, Ky," she repeated.

He wasn't storming past her. He should have been storming past her by now—he never waited for her to catch up, to agree. But he just stood there, stiff as death.

"There is no saving," he said. "All we get it rot."

"Ky—"

"They grab kids without anyone to miss them, Relai. Are you gonna stick around and find 'em happy Earthan families? Are you gonna stop people paying for the use of them?"

"So—so slavery is better? *From experience*, you're saying it's better?"

"No," Ky said savagely, "We just don't know that it's *worse.* And who deserves better than the shit we live through, anyway? All we get is rot because all we are is rotten, all of us, and anyone who gets time without suffering deserves the shock that comes when the muck finally gets them. There is no good in life, Relai. Only bad or ignorant."

He turned, but Relai followed around to find his eyes. "You don't really think that."

He swiped a hand across his mouth. "Yeah, I do."

"Milo," she said. A quiet declaration so the man himself wouldn't hear.

Ky's eyes flew to her. He shook his head.

"You love him."

"I'll die for him," Ky said. "That's more than love."

That's the best kind, she thought, but she didn't say it.

Instead she said, "You don't actually believe any of that 'everyone's rotten' stuff. Maybe you did once, but you don't believe it anymore."

Ky was silent.

"He loves you, too," she offered.

He clenched his jaw. "He doesn't trust me now. He never should've."

"No," she said. "He'd die for you, too."

"He won't."

"You know that?"

"Well enough."

"Ky," she said carefully, "who is the Sacrifice?"

He met her eyes, desperate.

"I don't know."

This stupid prophecy was messing with their heads, and Relai had had enough of it. She could try to make them fit with each of those words— Defiant, King, Warrior, Lover, Prophet, Guide, and Sacrifice—or she could focus on the situation before her. She couldn't do both.

She stared back at Ky for a moment, thinking hard. They were saving these children, but he was right about having no time. She could do what she needed to do, be what she needed to be, but she needed to act before she missed her chance.

This moment might be her last chance. She pulled out her thumb knife and dragged up the hems of her shirt and sweater.

"I wasn't ready before, but I am now. I want you to cut out my pin."

∘∘●∘∘

Tannor chewed on her lip.

"Milo," she began. He broke off from glaring at the cove to glare at her instead.

He would take care of Relai, she told herself. He would know the right time to tell her.

"I need to tell you what I found." She cleared her throat. "In the data in my head."

The anger on his face eased into concern.

"From the download," he prompted when her throat closed up.

Tannor nodded. "It's medical information, treatment and procedure history, and it's true. It's real."

"What is it?" He knocked his knuckles against her forearm. "Just tell me."

Tannor shook her head and looked him in the eye.

"Relai gave birth. She had a baby."

Before he could think far enough to ask, she supplied, "Three months ago."

"Three months."

"Three months."

He stared at her, unblinking.

Tannor went on, "*That's why*, Milo. If she'd gotten herself pregnant and wanted to hide it, this whole thing could have been a lie. People must think she was hiding herself, waiting it out. But if—but if it's not a lie—"

"They put her to sleep a year ago. More than a year ago."

Tannor swayed on her feet. "Yes."

Milo shook his head, stared blankly at a spot on the wall, shook it again. The word that came next was almost inaudible. "No."

Tannor agreed, really, but no amount of that word would change the truth.

ᴏᴏ●ᴏᴏ

Relai called out, "We're done."

Milo stormed back into the cove, a furious shadow of the man who'd sat across from her and swept his fingers through salt and asked her to set his people free. He came to a rigid stop before her.

Tannor had just told him the secret, Relai remembered. She'd forgotten about it for a second.

"Not now, okay?" she told him. "We have to get out of here first."

"Let me kill him," Milo answered. "Let me kill Fass."

She almost rolled her eyes, but he looked so angry—Ky would have laughed with her, but he was busy cleaning the knife from his latest murder and avoiding eye contact.

So Relai diverted herself by touching Milo's jaw, instead. He'd asked her to touch him, hadn't he?

"What was your sister's name?"

He closed his eyes and leaned into it. "Shayla."

"Shayla. Okay. Think if someone could have saved her, if they just took the time."

Milo let out a shuddering breath.

"We can't let Fass go, and we can't leave those kids to be stolen," Relai said. She turned to the rest of the group. "So... we'll fix both."

"We don't have time—" Tannor began, but then she and Goren both jolted and clapped a hand over their left ears. They looked at each other and then at Relai in mirrored alarm.

"It's Iverson, he's here already!" Goren cried as Tannor shook her head wordlessly. How had he followed so quickly?

"I'll deal with him," Relai said, and in the blink of an eye Tannor brought her into the Earth Monitoring comm space.

Iverson: —*in place to secure the base immediately, but your Earthan contact has already entered without my knowledge and against my explicit instructions.*

"Wait, what? Who?" Relai asked.

Tom! an angry female voice answered in English. *Tom Wood! The poor, stupid man you put in serious danger when you took over his apartment!*

"Hope?!" Goren broke in. "Are you here?"

Relai mouthed at him, *Who?*

"The Earthan woman who tried to help me at the hospital!" Goren supplied.

Iverson: *She's Earth Relations now, and we're coming inside.*

Relai looked frantically to Milo. "Tom is here, too?"

Iverson had no access to Milo or Ky's comms, so neither of them could hear a word of any of this. Milo's face just screwed up with incredulous impatience, and Ky didn't bother to react at all.

Iverson: *We traced the messages sent by the tablet he must have gotten from you; he's meeting with an ex-terr contact here. They're set to meet at the bar and he's planning to jump the planet.*

Relai repeated all of this for the vigilantes of the group and then groaned. "He's gonna get himself killed."

"Don't come inside," Tannor snapped. "You're going to tip off Fass and we'll lose him."

Relai put up a hand to silence her. "Come in, but not geared up for an assault on the place. Just get into position *quietly* so you're ready to move when we take off. You can help us with Fass."

Iverson: *Agreed.*

Relai signaled Tannor and, another blink, she was out of that comm space. "Goren, you keep in touch with Iverson and Hope for us. Milo's our contact with the wolves. We stay in our shared comm space, just us, unless something changes. Good?"

Everyone nodded.

"I'll grab Tom when I buy us seats on a ship at the bar," Ky said as he pulled on his jacket and double-checked his spit gun. "Stun him, throw him in a supply tunnel. Iverson and Dodge can get him after all the ships have left."

"No one goes anywhere alone," Milo said. "We all agreed."

Relai shrugged. "We don't have time to stick together."

He glowered at her. "It's not safe."

"Yeah," Relai said, "and that's the only thing that matters if *we're* the only ones who matter, but we're not. Milo and Goren, you'll have to get the kids out."

Tannor went into motion immediately, separating out packs so each group had the supplies they'd need. "Fass is expecting me and Relai, and that's who he's going to get."

Ky nodded. "I'll come in late to back you two up on Fass. Sun's setting, and if we don't leave by the end of that countdown, there's no leaving at all. Earthan military'll see us and shoot us down."

Relai turned to Tannor. "Are you ready?"

Tannor's mouth took on a dangerous smirk. "Do I need to explain to you how much I hate this guy?"

Relai smiled. "I don't like him much, either."

Tannor nodded, then Relai looked from face to face. Four people.

Her people.

"Okay," she said, "Ky, get us seats. Milo and Goren, free the kids. Tannor and I get Fass. We meet up as soon as we can, then we head to the ship."

•

Milo couldn't understand how Ky wasn't storming out to save those children, but he knew enough now not to press… Then Ky called out, "Don't expect me sober when we meet back here. I'm a slaver now. Gotta get in character before I find us a ride," and Milo understood. Ky wouldn't be buying them seats on a ship.

He was going to kill his way to one, and Milo couldn't find it in himself to mind.

"Put your hood up," Tannor called after Ky as she tugged the end of the scarf over her nose.

Relai held out her hand to Milo. He took it and squeezed.

"May we meet again improved," Milo said, then he turned and signaled Goren.

•

Tannor heard Ky's parting words and caught his pointed glance as he walked away.

Well. That was one way to get them a ship.

She woke her tablet, wormed into the dock's transit system, and pulled visuals of each traveler cleared for the ship belonging to Izer Borez. Four faces.

She wrapped them up in a neat data package and flicked them toward Ky, and as he disappeared into the crowd she saw him pull a phone out of his pocket.

"Put your hood up," she called. Rising to her feet, she navigated the tablet to the *Vimana*'s secure details and then tossed the tablet to Goren.

•

Relai waited as Tannor collected the tech pen she'd stuck into the wall and lit up for illumination in their cove, one finger tapping the thumb knife still stored against her ribs. The ghost of pain from the pin removal and healing still lingered, but it withered to nothing in comparison with the unbelievable lightness of *no pin.*

She watched Milo and Goren until they disappeared into the market; a few seconds that felt like an eternity.

Then Tannor drew by her side and handed Relai one of the spare tablets from the jumper's stock as they set off into the market.

"This is a current map of the dock I got from Elur Maat," Tannor explained. "See the dots?" Five little yellow points stood out over the green and blue lines marking the original Russian structure and the Vadan adaptations. "That's us."

Relai could tell which two were hers and Tannor's based on which direction they'd left the cove, and she assumed Ky's was the solo dot quickly approaching the bar. Still, it might get confusing if anything went wrong... "Names, instead?"

Tannor's eyes went heavy-lidded for a moment, then the dots became names. "I'll add Iverson as soon as he enters the dock. We're heading here," she pointed to a room tucked deep in the base through a series of tunnels, "to meet with Fass. Best place for a trap, according to the wolves. Metafuel tanks on all sides, so no one's gonna risk shooting up the place."

Relai nodded her thanks and then announced, "Thirty-six minutes. I want to hear your voices in my head, everyone, okay?"

Ky: *Whatever you say, Princess.*

Goren: *Okay, except Milo already told me to shut up twice.*

Milo: *You don't have to say everything that goes through your head.*

Goren: *I can't do the hand signals if you're not looking at me!*

Milo: *I'm always looking, I just know how to be subtle.*

Ky: *[snort]*

Milo: *I heard that.*

Tannor's jaw twitched, and then Relai heard her through the air but not over comms. "Do we really have to listen to these idiots the whole time? My brain has plenty to do, you know."

She tucked a curl of hair back under her scarf and her eyes looked like glowing amber in this light. Her brow showed that little dent of annoyance it always got when people tested her nerves, but her mouth was soft.

Relai smiled. "Just keep me in your head. I'll watch over everyone else."

○○●○○

v.

Tom should be leader of this planet, he was so good at bullshit.

(This was turning into a Frodo-at-Mount-Doom thing, wasn't it? Destroy the One Ring of Bullshit! Where was Gollum when you needed him? Hope was probably Gollum in this scenario.)

Hope was back in the aircraft with the Boss Man in Black himself waiting dutifully for the princess of the galaxy to give the go-ahead to storm this place, which gave Tom around 45 minutes to sneak inside, find Gecko, hop on a spaceship, and wave adios to this sad excuse for a progenitor of human life.

He'd ducked out the ship's rear door and scampered as fast as his broomball-conditioned muscles could carry him across the wide, treacherous land of Siberia wearing a blanket like a hat-scarf-balaclava-shawl. True to Gecko's promise, the eyes of the gate guards had nearly popped when they'd laid eyes on his bottle of Scotch (though Gecko hadn't mentioned he'd also need to give blood). They'd let him through.

Escape the planet?

What, like it's *hard?*

He wandered through the bizarre gnome-land these guys had grown inside the defunct Soviet nuclear bunker or whatever it was. It reminded him of those dystopian Amazon shipping centers crossed with the cliff dwellings at Mesa Verde, except if the cliff dwellings were built out of spray insulation foam that puffed into geometric patterns instead of round ones. So far, he hadn't seen any alien critters, but there were definitely lots of nouveau-soviet clothes, accents, and strange merchandise on display. Tom sent off one last text to Gecko as he headed for the big cave on one end where sounds of hustle and bustle and drinking and negotiating floated out over the market stalls.

almost there, where are you?

His phone buzzed just as he was trading his blanket with a ten-year-old for a bottle of slavic orange soda. Good stuff.

hiding

Tom frowned.

tell me what to do buddy, i'm here for you

*when you come in, see the scary lady
at the end of the bar with the black
jacket? distract her so i can get out*

got it

The bar turned out to be in a large shack covered in corrugated tin sheets, one of the few structures not made of the strange coral/foam/whatever-it-was. Inside, hanging fluorescents lit a space that was unmistakably a bar, despite the fact that the bar, tables, and chairs were cobbled together from Cold War-era shipping containers and electronics consoles. The whole vibe was more *Ice Station Zebra* than *Star Wars* cantina, but Tom supposed he could live with that.

He sauntered along casually, looking for a black jacket and someone Gecko might consider scary.

Bingo.

The woman in question looked like she could kill Tom with a well-aimed sneeze, so this was going to take a little strategy.

Alas, Tom didn't have time for strategy, so he just kicked up against the bar, smoldered his eyes a bit, and said, "Hey, stranger. Buy me a drink?"

And, as the very fabric of the universe itself suffered a heart attack, the stranger turned and looked at Tom...

It was the ZOMBIE.

HE ASKED A ZOMBIE ALIEN TO BUY HIM A DRINK.

But all the lady did was sneer like burning and turn her back on Tom.

She probably didn't speak English, after all, but everybody who was anybody had a comm with an interpreter, right?

The lady didn't need a com to understand when Tom breathed out, "Fffffffuuuuuuuuu—" and then ran away.

Somebody grabbed him by the sleeve and dragged him into a little corner inlet thing where people probably had sex, and Tom screamed in what he considered to be a manly fashion until they clamped a hand over his mouth.

"Shut up!" his assailant hissed. "You hit on her? That's the most dangerous killer on this planet, man!"

Tom matched this guy's cramped slouch, knees askew and ass hanging off the seat so no one would see their faces if they glanced inside, and looked him over. His luxuriantly cushy physique didn't fit in the space between the table and the seats, so he was sitting more sideways than straight; he had a decent few day of dark stubble on his face, an impressively asymmetrical afro, and dark blue eyes.

Gecko! In the flesh!

"Dude," Tom exclaimed, "you're super-handsome! Why didn't you tell me!"

Gecko's face crunched up in an incredulous glare, then he shook his head so the 'fro bounced against the seat back. "You're lucky you're alive."

"You said distract, I distracted! She wasn't all up on this business, okay, and for that I can't blame her. Why didn't you run, anyway?"

"Not enough time. I couldn't chance it."

"Why's she looking for you?"

Gecko shoved a lump of knitted maroon material into Tom's hands—a cap—and started wrapping a long strap of cloth around his head to condense his hair. "Her implant ran out and she needed an ex-terr doc to refill it. She must've found someone else to do it, but she'll still roast me for turning her down if she sees me." Tom tried to put the cap on, but Gecko smacked it off his head. "That's for me!"

"What? Implant? What—"

"A med scanner. It's in her spine and it heals her shit. That's why she's so dangerous—she's pretty much unkillable."

"Oh, snap!" Tom eased up and snuck a look at the zombie bounty hunter, who was now talking with a new guy. Clean-cut, same haircut and posture as Goren. A soldier. "You think this new guy is a doctor, like you?"

Gecko scoffed as he tied off the scrap of cloth and yanked the cap onto his head low over his eyes. "Who cares, he's distracting. Let's go—"

"Wait!" Tom hunkered down and fussed with his earpiece. "I was with— and they might want to know—just wait, okay?"

He managed to turn the thing back on, only to hear a running rant from Hope.

Hope: —*swear to God I will murder you myself if you're not already dead. ANSWER ME.*

"Hey, Hope! Yeah, hi. The zombie is here, and she's not a zombie! You were right, those aren't a thing! It was just their alien technology—she has a healing implant thing built into her spine. Just thought you should know, since she put Goren in the hospital and if you meet up with Goren and she sees you together she'll probably kill you, too. Don't die, Hope!"

Hope: *Come hide with me so I can put YOU in a hospital!*

"Let's call that Plan B, 'kay, love-you-bye!"

And with that, Tom switched off his receiver.

"So!" He clapped his hands and angled his neck to look at Gecko properly without accidentally biting his shoulder. "To space?"

Gecko nodded intrepidly, and one after another they slithered to the sticky, pock-marked floor and crawled out of the bar.

•

Ednar Fass sipped his liquor and glanced at the bounty hunter, Runn. Runn didn't touch her drink.

Fass knew every line of the short list of willing and capable hunters on this planet, and each of them offered a unique set of skills. Only one of them could draw memories from the mind of a mark, and it wasn't a piece of shusa scum with brain-melding ability. It was this woman and her mind probe.

Fass forced the hand hanging loose at his side, inches from his sliver gun, not to twitch.

"Where is my merchandise?" he inquired.

The hunter picked at her teeth with a dirty fingernail. There was a spoon lying on the bar next to her, which Fass found incredibly disconcerting.

"Just landed."

"Then why," Fass ground out, "are you sitting here?"

The smallest obscure shift in the hunter's stance, the change in angle of her shoulders, sent an unreasoned chill through Fass. No reason to let the woman think Fass would be foolish enough to come there alone, he decided—he lifted a finger in the air and Reddig appeared behind him.

"Yes, sir?"

"Is everything ready?"

"Yes, sir."

Fass smiled and turned to Runn. "I'm expanding our deal. I'll pay equal bounty for every other member of the group traveling with Mora Aydor." He held out a tablet with three faces and a grey circle. "Goren Dray, the Monster of Eray himself, Milo Hemm, and a man named Bevn Kyro. No pictures exist of the last one, but—"

"Seen him," Runn cut in. "Oeylan. Friends with the Erayd."

Fass flinched; he didn't like being interrupted, but these were extenuating circumstances. "Yes, well—"

"This one," Runn interrupted again, tapping the face of Private Dray. "You the superior officer?"

Fass sneered. "Yes."

"You get me his guard roster code and comm administrative access." Runn took out a narrow tablet the length of her hand; Fass had never seen anything like it.

"They've been under a transmission blocker; you won't be able to tap into their conversations," Fass warned.

Runn leaned slowly, deliberately in Fass's face. "Will if I get past their blocker," she said. Fass shuddered at the smell coming off of her and cleared his throat.

"So. Do we have a deal?"

Runn grabbed Fass's glass and downed the liquid that remained. She swallowed with flourish and grinned as she slammed the vessel down. Then she pocketed the spoon.

"You want just their heads, or whole bodies?"

oo●oo

EPISODE XII:

WAKE

-33:00 minutes until departure

THROUGH THE MARKET, past the rowdy bar, under the childish shape of a groundship painted in green over a large tunnel, Goren and Milo reached the ship bay without being stopped once. There were enough people milling about, hurrying through departure procedures, that they only had to walk with purpose and no one gave them a second glance.

Tannor's map led them well; Goren saw two open tunnels (the one they'd just used, then a smaller second one at the far left end of the same wall) and a series of connected doors that must have been for fuel and storage. Three exits.

The far right wall bore the closed groundship exit, and it was unlike anything Goren had ever seen before. He could just barely make out massive red-stained lifting mechanisms on either side of the dull grey slabs of metal. This was no coalition design—it must have been Earthan. It struck him as lazy, not to build a new higher-quality door, but Goren supposed these were criminals. They weren't concerned with quality.

The map was wrong about one thing, though: this room was supposed to be much smaller and more narrow. The ceiling stretched high and the opposite wall arched out like a misshapen belly. Goren spied a tiny Oeylan commuter ship, all closed up tight and ready to go; three standard Ardenian shipping vessels (pretty damning); and one Gastredi military vessel (very damning). Five groundships fit in here, when not one would have fit on the map.

"This way," Milo muttered.

Descending time markers hovering above each ship flicked through the seconds until departure, alongside a name—they slipped between loads of cargo to the open ramp of the Ardenian shipping vessel *Vimana*.

No guards; they must be inside.

"What do you think we—"

"Find the kids; I'll keep watch at the ramp," Milo ordered, peering around the edge of a tall metallic crate.

Goren nodded.

They raced across the open space and into a halo of light surrounding the sort of military ship Goren might be working on if he hadn't been placed on Earth. Milo stayed at the entrance hatch while Goren crept inside.

He guessed a path based on his knowledge of the ship's design, passing floor-to-ceiling rows of cargo containers through a doorway into a smaller room—

Little kids.

Goren's heart went crazy in his chest. In front of a row of open travel pods stood a line of terrified, silent children with bands around their necks—bands that must be stopping their voices because otherwise they'd be screaming, and who wouldn't, because they were being *stolen for slavery*.

He couldn't help but scan the faces and find the ones close enough in age to his sisters to slow his heart with rage. He wanted to murder everyone who ever touched these kids with wrong intent.

But Milo was watching the door, so Goren took the tablet Tannor gave him and turned it on and sent it to eat into the ship's system. It found the kids' control bands and Goren was just trying to figure out how to release them when his body went tense.

He couldn't move. His skin sizzled with a structured force, every muscle frozen.

The ship. It had paused him.

He could move his eyes and he could breathe, so he tried to look far enough left to see Milo—that dark, still shape must be him. They were both frozen.

Someone entered the hold, huffing and grumbling. A foot tapped the red circle glowing next to his feet and Goren felt the change like tripping into control of himself. He spun to face a massive woman with frazzled grey hair and an Earthan gun on her hip.

"Muck-scavenger scum!" she roared at him. "Trying to steal my cargo!"

She'd woken him because he was smaller, probably. Or maybe because he had a tablet in his hand with her private cargo listed.

He had the list… and Milo could definitely be his guard. Goren wasn't dressed right, but he knew how to stand.

He thought about his Uncle Toff and his dislike for the green parts of boiled egg yolks, and of his mother and the strain of choosing a new hair color for each planet.

Goren brushed a fleck of dirt from his chest. "No need to yell." Then he opened his jacket, found a credit key Ky had slipped him on their way in, and held it out. "Here. We didn't pay you enough to carry these."

The woman opened her jaw wide and stared at the key. She snatched it up and ran her finger across it to transfer the funds, then said, "What? You're not the catcher."

"Ew. Obviously. But the men who caught these are gone and now I have to deal with them myself. You see, my bodyguard," Goren tilted his head at Milo, "and I were on a short tour of this planet and we noticed these children. I want them and my father won't pay for them. He said," Goren huffed, "if I want new staff I have to get them home myself."

A dangerous glint of suspicion shone in the master's eyes. "You picked these all out yourself?"

Goren put seventeen years of greater class poise into not fidgeting and said, "Yes."

She leaned her grime-creased face into his, and when she spoke he watched her nose hairs twitch. "You gonna pay Djurot in full when you get there, no mind to naught?"

Now, *that* implication genuinely irked him. Goren tilted his head with the sort of condescension that only a true member of the greater class could achieve. "You think they will cost more than my mother spends on hair colors in a month? Please. The forced company is a far greater price to pay."

Another grunt. "And what happened to your ship?"

"My father left with it, of course. Are you completely stupid? He came in by an Ardenian port so he had to leave from there. And now Haadam's gone and Daat is worthless, and this is all so annoying I cannot believe it."

The master's watery eyes peered into him, all the suspicion replaced with calculating hunger. "Need to check the sets, make sure you don't owe more. What'd'ya do wrong?"

"*I* did nothing wrong," Goren corrected. "If you must know, days pass differently on this planet and *someone* did not understand. Several of these are infected with minor viruses and, due to an error by my staff, not me, we need to recalibrate the correct sleeping parameters. This will cover the difference in cooling—"

"WHAT?" the woman shrieked.

"I know, I know, he's fired," Goren assured her.

"Ardenian scum! You try to slip exotic disease past me?" She tried to smack him with the butt of her gun but he jumped backward, yelping. "Get your cargo out of my hold! Waste of my time… and I'll take the full credits to cover disinfection!"

"What?! How dare you!"

"OUT!" the master screamed. Then she slapped the wall and released all the children at once. The bands around their necks snapped free and they huddled and rubbed their sore skin.

Goren shouted all sorts of abuse at the master as he tried to gather the children and usher them out. Convincing them to leave the ship took no effort at all, and when the last kid hurried out the master released Milo and slapped his ass out the door.

oo●oo

-30:00 min

Ky ran his lower lip along the glass of blue vodka, catching a stray drop with the edge of his tongue.

Needed vinegar.

Travelers crowded from one end to another, far too many for the number of ships on that departure board, blustering and high with the anxiety of the times. Most of them wouldn't be finding a seat, but some were trying their damnedest.

He could turn a human body into one massive blister. Fill a layer under the skin with sticky yellow blood plasma until the outer shell sloughed off at the slightest touch.

He could dissolve all connective tissue. Watch them slop to the ground in a bag of blood and bones, unable to breathe or cry out as they died.

He could fire all muscle cells at once. Watch them clench to death in tremendous pain.

Or reverse their livers so their own bodies poisoned them.

Or light up the nervous system in pain until they died of the overwhelming horror of it.

Ky imagined these things as he watched the slavers from his bar stool. Then he finished his drink, nodded thanks to the bartender, and rose.

He slipped and slithered across the bar and came to their private little inlet, gaining permission to enter with the pleasant, silent promise in the flash and downturn of his eyes. He sat.

This inlet hid them in shadows to discourage curiosity, but the walls were thin and there was no curtain.

"Bevn Kyro," he said. "I hear you have a ship."

"We full up," the first slaver replied.

He needed three seconds before the first died to finish shaking hands with the third, so brain aneurysms would have to do.

"Hear me out," Ky said. "I might have something you want."

Then the second slaver leaned across the table, squinting. "You have any other names?"

Ky smiled. "One or two."

"Tell."

Ky thought about blisters and muscles and poison. He thought about the bone in his chest, the left clavicle, that his slavers had replaced with metasteel so he couldn't break it and escape when they hooked and leashed him.

He eased forward and murmured, "*Odene.*"

Proper fear took over their features, and Ky savored that fear because it was all the satisfaction he was going to get (besides their ship). One tried to draw on him, one tried to duck, and the third tried to run. He planted a foot across the entrance of the inlet to keep it contained and then he killed them, first touch, one-two-three.

No outcry. Just a bit of rustling.

Then he dove into their pockets.

oo●oo

-29:00 min

Goren led the way with an air of inconvenienced fury, just in case the angle of his nose was the only thing standing between them and a firefight; they'd made it thirty yards from the groundship and already they were getting suspicious stares. If everything went right, Hope Valdez would meet them at the end of a supply tunnel next to the main staircase to collect these kids and then, after Tannor and Relai and Iverson took down Fass, they'd lock down the dock without a single shot fired.

"That was good," Milo muttered as they huddled the children through a washroom and into the smaller side tunnel leading back to the market. "The reesh thing."

"Thanks," Goren said. The word still stung a little, but Goren just sighed. "It felt vile, but I guess I know the part well enough."

"Same," Milo said, signaling all-clear to proceed. "It's exhausting."

Goren looked at him again, frowning, then realized he wasn't talking about acting like a reesh. He meant—he meant *Milo*. The Monster of Eray.

Goren realized he might have been drastically wrong about a lot of things.

"I'm sorry I called you dirty hill trash," Goren said. "And all that other stuff, too."

Milo gave him a wry smile. "Mountain trash," he replied, then they reached the market.

oo●oo

-29:00 min

Tannor glanced back for the thousandth time; no one had followed them to this corridor. She looked with her ability, too. Nothing.

Only the wolves were supposed to use these tunnels, and the map and notations from Elur Maat gave Tannor a perfect foundation for planning their trap.

"Iverson," Relai said to the air as they ducked into a recess around the corner and one long corridor away from the entrance to the back-up fuel tank room where they'd meet Fass. "We're almost there. Where are you?"

Tannor had no interest in letting that man into her head again, so she couldn't hear his response. After a moment, Relai told her, "He'll be here in three minutes. He stopped to check for Tom but he's not in the bar."

"Fass will be here in five," Tannor confirmed, eyes on her tablet.

Relai grimaced at as she laid out the sheets of mesh framework that they'd stripped from the Titian jumper in a rough border around herself.

"Are we going to be ready?"

Tannor opened her bag and took out the dense lump of metamercury she'd cleaved from the Titian jumper. Her mouth curled into a smile as she laid it over the mesh. "Worst comes, I can just make his head explode."

Relai stared at her for a moment, and then she laughed.

○○●○○

-28:00 min

One of the children was crying.

It was a little boy, maybe five years old, wearing a sleeveless green and yellow striped tank and muddy shorts. An older girl wrapped an arm around his shoulder to keep him moving through the erratic stalls and half-grown camps, but Milo listened past Relai and Tannor's chatter and he could hear the boy's whimpers and unintelligible words over the thrum of the market. Milo couldn't speak any of their languages and even a steady string of nonsense in a comforting tone would have called attention to their group, so he kept quiet.

He noticed something flash past the end of the aisle parallel to their path. The reason it caught in his mind didn't register right away.

The children were all wearing their own Earthan clothes, clearly, but since they'd been collared and loaded onto the ship they must've gone through system cleanse. That meant they were hungrier than Milo was, with the bonus strain of a child's metabolism and the panic of being stolen.

"I'll be after you in ten steps," he whispered to Goren over comms. "Don't stop."

Milo saw Goren's eyes flicker back, then he slipped through the entrance of a strangely deserted food stall. He grabbed a paper sack of bland gray-brown bars—heavier than bread, more like cakes, smelling of scented fruit—and swiftly caught up to the group. He tapped the older girl on the shoulder and shoved the bag into her side. She let go of the little boy to look.

"Eat," Milo said, checking aisles and the walkways over their heads for unwelcome notice. She frowned up at him as they moved, but then the little boy gave up on walking, plopped down, and started wailing with all his might. Milo was surprised it hadn't happened sooner, considering the circumstances, and he didn't waste time before scooping the kid up and holding him close. They were almost to the exit.

Another flash of movement down another aisle. It could have been anything... but Milo had a bad feeling about it.

"Something's wrong," he said.

Up ahead, he saw Goren draw his gun.

Goren: *What?*

"I don't know. Ky, do we have seats?"

No answer.

"Ky?"

Relai: *He probably just turned his comm off for a second. He's bartering and he doesn't want us to distract him.*

Then Ky's voice returned to their comm space.

Ky: *Shit. Those kids weren't random. The catchers were taking blood samples and they only took kids who tested positive for something.*

Milo peered at the little boy in his arms, who was holding his fruit bar and sniffling but not eating. He didn't look sick or strange. He was just a little boy.

"What?" he whispered.

Ky: *I don't know... but I'm really glad we didn't buy our way in here with blood.*

Relai: *What is going on? What are they looking for on Earth?*

Ky: *We need to find out who was going to buy these kids on the other side of the trip.*

"Same people buying blood from the wolves?" Milo said.

"The shipmaster said it was someone named Djurot," Goren said.

Milo waited to hear if anyone recognized the name. Nothing.

Tannor: *You think they're looking for shusa?*

Relai: *How many shusa can there possibly be on Earth?*

"Ky," Milo hissed, "do we have seats or not?"

No answer.

Milo reached into his jacket to draw his gen-gun but his knuckles hit something unexpected. He unzipped an inner pocket and felt inside.

Goren: *Left or right?*

Milo looked up to say, "Right," as he pulled the thing out.

It was his calfskin pouch. The pins of his people.

Ky was supposed to—

"Ky, what the hell are you thinking?"

Across their shared comm space no one spoke. He fought through two, three, ten steps, and no one replied.

Then came Tannor's voice.

Tannor: *He disappeared. He's not showing up on my map anymore. I can't find his comm.*

Goren flashed back a look of alarm.

Milo straightened his back and craned his neck—they were almost to the supply tunnel. He touched the pad of his middle finger to the nail of his pointer finger and rotated his hand until he felt the draw—back, into the market—

Then he heard a new voice.

Killed you once, I'll kill you again.

It was the voice of the bounty hunter.

In Milo's head.

∘∘●∘∘

ii.

-28:00

"We need to find out who was going to buy these kids on the other side of the trip," Ky said as he shoved the slaver's tablet into his coat and began sorting all the stolen creds from the slavers onto one key.

Then he heard a hiss and felt a heavy fog.

He registered light more than dark only a few seconds later—if he hadn't lost time, *crap*, what if the others had already left—

"Scanner implant? I knew it," Iverson growled. "You recover too quickly."

Ky pushed his body to clear his head and figure out where Iverson had dragged him. They were inside an empty stall on the edge of the market; art screens blinked on the walls and he recognized the tubing and set-up for system clean. A woven metaplastene door covered the entrance from prying eyes.

Ky saw glass and metal and a shelf within reach. Weapons everywhere; he just needed to be able to lift his hands—

Iverson shot him with the tranquilizer again.

When his head cleared this time, Iverson had secured his wrists in a pair of ugly blue custody hovercuffs.

"Jack West," Iverson said, "alias Seung Li. You are under arrest by the authority of Earth Relations and the U.S. Department of State."

A pair of little orange lights blinked on and the shackles hummed tight and then rose up into the air, the flexible ribbing against Ky's skin rotating as his wrists turned, stretching him out and leaving his whole body vulnerable. The restraint stopped just before the balls of his feet lifted off the ground.

Ky cursed and announced to the group, "Iverson's arresting me."

Iverson tapped behind his ear and checked lines of sight through the cracked open shop door. "They can't hear you; the shackles are blocking your transmissions." He prodded the keypad in his palm. "Valdez. I have West and I'm going to collect Fass now."

Ky rested all his weight on one wrist, then the other, and the restraint held. Didn't even tilt. Ky couldn't angle his fingers to reach it, and if he tried anything with his teeth Iverson would just trank him again.

They'd had fun together on the joint task force. One time Ky had saved Iverson from a nest of radical nationalists (whom Ky had also been supplying with firearms) just because Ky liked him better than the other guys.

The problem was, his life-for-a-life credit burned up with the bomb Ky planted in the British Embassy in 2007, plus another twenty-seven lives, and Iverson wasn't one to let a debt go unpaid.

"Look, I know what I've done," Ky tried, putting something like sincerity into his voice, "but I'm a little busy for squaring debts."

"Not anymore," Iverson replied.

Ky tried to kick.

Iverson tranked him again.

When he came to, they were traveling down an echoing concrete hallway toward a chain link fence. The hovercuffs were dragging Ky along with his boots scraping the floor and his shoulders aching like hell until he stumbled up to support himself.

"No one called you out on this, huh?" Ky mumbled. He couldn't bring in enough air with his arms so high.

"No one cares about you," Iverson replied.

Ky pulled hard and useless on the restraints. "Terrence! You know I'm with Mora Aydor. Let me down so we can both go help her."

Iverson wouldn't look at him. Ky heard him say in a low voice, "Delayed. I'll be there in three minutes. Wait for me before you approach Fass."

They walked in silence for a dozen steps, then Iverson finally replied:

"I'm going to cut the med scanner out of you. I thought you'd keep at least a few of the scars from our time together, but you didn't care enough to carry any of it with you, did you?"

"I'm not sure my body *can* scar," Ky muttered.

Iverson halted. He turned around at looked at Ky with piercing realization. Then he took out his tablet and held up his hand to scan.

"Terrence…" Ky began. He'd never thought about Iverson's opinions on shusa.

"No med scanner," Iverson concluded, his face full of disgust. "*You're not human, are you?* You're shusasevati. That's how you're doing it."

Ky pulled against his restraints. "I'm human."

Iverson spun around and charged onward. Without looking back, he said, "I'm going to ask you about every crime you've ever committed on this planet, and you're going to answer me. Then, once I'm done with you, Fordev will want you."

Fordev.

No, no—

The others were on their way. They'd take care of Fass and those children. They'd leave Earth, stop at Oliver Station or maybe Ligost, then pass through Oliver Block. Milo would charge Relai, soft heart and all, and he'd win. She was the End.

Ky looked up at the brick of metal holding him captive, then down the length of his body to the floor. He could stop his own heart if he needed to.

Then they rounded a corner and a twitchy man in an Ardenian guard uniform shot Iverson in the chest.

iii.

-27:00 min

Closer and more intimate than the stench of the breath in her face in that skyscraper stairwell, the bounty hunter's voice rumbled in Relai's head:

Killed you once, I'll kill you again.

Frantically she checked back and forth down the muffled corridor where they'd set up for their trap. She saw no movement anywhere, heard no hint of breathing or footsteps just beyond a corner. Was the hunter talking about Ky? Was she the reason Ky's comm disappeared from Tannor's map? Relai looked to Tannor in horror.

With a twitch of her jaw, Tannor's voice left their comm space and came to Relai only through open air.

"Well, that's a complication," she said.

"How did she get into our comm space?" Relai hissed.

Not you, Queen, the hunter said. *Gonna deal with the monster first. I'll find you next.*

Milo: *Where are you?*

Nice kids. You want 'em to watch you die?

Goren: *Oh, gods.*

Relai dropped out of the space for just a second to demand, "Get her out of our heads, Tannor!"

But Tannor was focused on her tablet, fingers flying. "Why? This is good."

Relai jumped back in the comm space. "The kids have nothing to do with this," she insisted as she stared, waiting for an explanation from Tannor.

Relax, I don't kill kids, the hunter replied.

Tannor's eyes had drifted closed, one hand spread over her tablet, and then the corner of her mouth curled up. "Look: with transmissions jumping between all of us, I can map an exact location for her. She wants in our ears, she tells us where she is."

Tannor held up the tablet—a new blazing red circle was hovering a short distance from the names *Milo* and *Goren*.

Relai nodded breathlessly. She didn't need to tell Tannor to share the image on her screen with the tablet she'd given Goren. She hoped they didn't need to tell Milo and Goren, either.

"We're out of time," Tannor said. She stood and looked toward the fuel room with fierce resolve on her face.

Relai closed her own eyes and took a deep breath. "Milo," she whispered, "get back to us safe."

When she opened her eyes, Tannor was gone.

oo●oo

-25:00 min

"I see the door," Goren whispered, his back pressed against the corner of the last wall of the market. He'd left the comm space where the bounty hunter was lurking for the one dedicated to Earth Monitoring, but he still felt the hunter's menace like a cloud all around them.

Hope: *We're here, but I can't open it.*

The builden cityscape ended with a wide open margin—a dangerous amount of space—between them and safety. They huddled the children against the wall and searched for any sign of the bounty hunter.

Milo touched his ear—that guy had given him a disposable comm, Goren remembered. "Flint," he said, "I need a way to open the door along the setward wall of the market."

Barely a moment passed before Milo relayed the response:

"Keypad to the right. The code is zero five two six one zero. We run for it. Fast as we can."

"I'll go first and cover from that direction," Goren said.

Milo nodded. "Go."

Goren went.

The only people he saw were hundreds of feet away, silhouettes framed by an orange glow as they ran in the opposite direction. Goren reached the door. He muttered the number sequence over and over again as he typed it in, then he grabbed hold of a thick metal bar the length of his arm and wrenched it in a downward arc. The door swung open toward him, and there stood Hope and six others.

Goren grinned at her and said, "Hi!" in English, like he'd practiced.

"Don't say 'hi' to me like you're not a space alien!" Hope snapped, the comm in Goren's ear translating her irritated tone along with the words. She stepped through the doorway and took one hand off of her little Earthan gun to wave at Milo and the children.

The children didn't need much direction; they were scared and lost and they moved like a flock of deer. One, five, ten—all twelve little heads bobbed across the open space.

Goren covered the open space to his left, Hope covered to the right, and creeping backwards from the rear was Milo.

Just a few more seconds.

•

Hey, Monster.

•

Milo felt his back hit the cold metal of the door to their escape as he swept his gun back, waiting for the first shot to hit him, and then the hunter stepped into the light.

Fifty feet away in the same market path Milo had just left, she stood clean and healthy and ready. Milo fired the moment he saw her, hitting her squarely in the chest. The hunter just peered down at the point of impact—Milo couldn't see any blood, she hadn't even wavered—and then looked back up at him, grinning like a corpse.

Then she held something up next to her head in the light of a hanging lamp for Milo to see.

Thanks for clearing a ride for me, the hunter said. *Ship master was a charm, eh? Now I'll collect my cargo and go.*

Milo squinted and realized what the hunter was holding up in the light, fresh and wet: an eyeball. It must have been from the grizzled old woman Milo and Goren had met in the ship, whose hand and eye could pilot that groundship.

The hunter withdrew a spoon, shiny silver glinting yellow and blue in the lights of the market, and slid it into the inside corner of her right eye—the one with wrecked skin around it—and popped her eyeball out. It dropped and bounced as it hit the floor. Then she rolled her fingers and squelched the new eye, the ship master's eye, into the empty socket. She grimaced and blinked out a few drops of blood before the eye straightened and—and *looked right at Milo,* a new shocking blue iris alongside her other brown one.

The hunter nodded once, then stepped back like a shadow into the chaos of the market.

"Come on, Milo!" Goren called through the exit.

Milo put his hand on the door and pushed. It swung closed, safe and final and locked, without him on the other side. Then he shot out the keypad to keep it that way.

"Help the kids," he ordered. "I'm going hunting."

•

Goren gaped in disbelief as the door slammed shut.

Hope and the soldiers who must have been Iverson's Earth Monitoring lot rounded up the children into a huddle along the tunnel wall.

"MILO!" Goren shouted. No answer. "HOW AM I SUPPOSED TO HELP RELAI FROM OUT HERE?"

Small hands tugged at his coat, the pockets of his pants, and two of the kids were standing on his feet. He picked one up without thinking, and a tiny face breathed into his neck.

Milo: *Help the kids.*

I'm getting paid for every one of you, boy, the hunter said. *Come back inside.*

The memory of a boot stomping on his back flashed vividly through him.

"Get them out of here," Goren said to Hope. The Earth Monitoring guys started checking the children, trying out languages and looking for injuries, but Hope kept peering behind them down the hallway and she didn't put away her gun.

"Is that blood?" Hope demanded. "Is anyone hurt?"

He rubbed the child's back; the sharpness of her tiny shoulder blades pained his heart.

"I don't—I don't think so. I have to get back in there."

He pushed the little girl away from his chest and into Hope's, and the girl transferred to her clinging like kids did when they were cold or sleepy or hurt or scared.

Hope grimaced as she took the weight of the child. "You're dumping them on me? That's bullshit. You have a concussion! You're going to get shot!"

"Yeah," he said, pulling out the tablet to look desperately for any way in.

He saw tiny names spread across the grid of green and blue lines: *Relai* and *Tannor* off in the maze of corridors and storage rooms, *Milo* nearing the center of the market, *Goren* on the other side of a long set of parallel lines marking the northern border of the market… and a bright red dot that hadn't been there before. *Milo* seemed to be following it.

Was that—

It had to be the hunter. Tannor Mellick was an *alforsaken genius*. Too bad Goren had the map and not Milo, though it didn't seem like the hunter had any interest in evading Milo. She'd even let them get the children to safety before she showed her face, and now she was leading Milo somewhere.

The map showed that this tunnel ended here, halfway down the length of the market, and didn't connect with the maze of other tunnels where Relai and Tannor were meeting Fass. He'd have to backtrack all the way around to the main entrance to get inside, then cross the market all over again.

Then he noticed a very faint map of orange lines underneath the green and blue. A sub-level? Goren saw a line of colored dots along the margin of the map and toggled to the orange one. The blue and green map faded to the background and the orange lines lit up.

This new map was bare compared to the complicated detail of the previous one; the main elements were two tracks running along the length of the inside of the market along opposite walls, and then squares spread throughout the facility that must have been the stairwells and elevator shafts. Right next to his position on the map, a yellow bracket crossed the wall and led to one of the tracks.

"What are you looking at?" Hope asked, peering with him at the tablet. "Is that the layout of the base?"

Goren nodded, searching the wall and floor for anything that might correspond to that bracket. "I'll share it with you, just get… a tablet…"

A ladder.

There—the ladder led to a metal grate landing in front of another door in the wall. The set of pipes running along the ceiling surely required maintenance and they'd built walkways, ones that ran the length of the giant room on the other side and connected here.

"Wait!" Hope grabbed his wrist. "What about Tom? Did anyone find him?"

Goren had completely forgotten about him. "I don't know."

One of the Earth Monitoring guys held out a tablet and Goren flung the data transfer to him as Hope spoke.

"Listen, Tom contacted me to tell me the woman who escaped from the morgue in Minneapolis is here. She has... I don't know, technology inside her body that helps her heal fast."

Goren reeled. Medical scanners couldn't be internal. They *couldn't*. And even if they could— "But she *fell off a building*."

Hope shrugged. "Really fast? I don't know how your bizarre alien crap works!"

Milo wasn't going to be able to kill the hunter, Goren realized. None of them could... except Tannor.

"Okay." He twisted his arm to grip her hand and squeezed tight for a second. "Thank you."

She looked at him with a frantic sort of anger, clenched her teeth, and nodded.

Then he scrambled up the ladder.

·

Goren: *Relai! Milo! This bounty hunter—it's tech. She's got a med scanner inside her!*

Yeah, I do, the hunter said. *You want to come watch me take the head off the queen?*

Relai: *Fass is here, I can't—*

Milo: *Everyone off comms.* Now.

∘∘●∘∘

480

iv.

-22:00 min

Ky's calves burned. He leaned on one leg to stretch and flex the other; his hips could only tilt so far and he didn't want to dislocate his shoulders in front of these men.

Fucking Unity.

They'd kept Ky in the hovercuffs and dragged him and Iverson, who was wounded but not dead, inside the freezing cold supply room where Fass's horde of lackeys seemed to be hiding. They'd bound Iverson by the elbows and feet and thrown him in a corner, then realized that a tablet inside the man's jacket was linked to Ky's shackles and with it they could drag him anywhere.

Ky gave it another two minutes before Tannor laid eyes on him, the hover restraint popped off, and he could start killing people. Six more minutes of this.

"Hey, I know you," one of them said suddenly. He stomped up and shoved a finger in Ky's face. "You're that mucker from the Haadam groundship. You took my pants!"

Ky peered at him. He... had a face, that was certain. "If you say so, Pants."

The guy kicked Ky hard in the knee. "I had to walk nine miles in my underwear, soaking wet! Fass wants you alive for now, or I'd kill you."

Ky couldn't shrug with his arms over his head like this, so his eyebrows had to do all the work. "Pretty serious threat from a guy named Pants."

"I have a name! It's—"

"*Pants.*" Ky jerked against the force on his wrists and the guy flinched backward. "It's always going to be Pants. You're never gonna be more than that word."

"You—you don't—merc scum, you're nothing—" The guy stomped away and back with his hand on his gun as the rest of his crew watched in interest. Ky still didn't recognize him. "I can't kill you, but you know what? I'm taking your pants! *I'm taking everything!*"

He flew at Ky, fumbling with his belt and cursing. Ky kneed him in the groin, laughed, and received a gen-gun jolt to the head.

When everything cleared and he stopped shaking, he took stock of his body: the soldier had managed to drag off his boots, socks, and pants. Then the guy dug his grimy little fingers under the band of Ky's underwear and yanked.

Yes, this was what Ky needed right now.

"M'hands are bound, buddy," Ky coughed. "Good luck getting my shirt off."

Pants skittered away from the lash of Ky's leg and reached into his jacket. "I've got a knife and slippery hands, mucker."

Ky gritted his teeth.

∘∘●∘∘

-22:00 min

Milo would've kept to the south wall, the quietest part of the market, but the hunter chose the center lane and Milo couldn't let her out of his sight.

He might not be free to talk to his team, but they weren't the only ones around. Milo tapped the disposable comm in his ear canal.

"Tinder," he breathed.

Ithail: *Flint, what do you need?*

"Chasing a killer who's after all of us. We can't kill her; I need help steering her to someone who can."

Ithail: *Where are you? What do you mean, we can't kill her? I'll kill you anyone, just point her out.*

Milo snorted softly. "Scanner built in, stops her from dying. We need to get her to Mellick."

Ithail: *I'm on my way.*

"Move fast and be well, brother."

Ithail: *And peace when you lay down to rest, yeah.*

∘∘●∘∘

Goren hid behind a giant vertical pipe and studied the map. Milo had disappeared after the hunter through a set of doors on the far side of the market alongside the same wall as the bar, and Goren just needed to figure out how to get down to that level. Relai and Tannor shouldn't have to deal with Fass alone.

He couldn't acknowledge how the hunter had been whispering in his ear; the concept was too horrifying. Later.

"Crap, crap, how do I get down?" he muttered to himself. He couldn't just go back the way he came—he might not be able to get back into the main room. The opposite end of the walkway likely had another door, right? He checked the map: *yes*.

Milo ordered him to stay off comms… but he didn't know what to do.

"Relai," he said desperately, "what do you want me to do?"

Relai: *I want you to sit down, safe, and make sure those kids find some moments of peace.*

The whole inside of his chest felt like it dropped through his feet, and then she finished:

…But I need you to get to me. Fast as you can.

"Okay," he breathed, and took off running.

○○●○○

v.

-21:0 min

Ososi Tena entered the place of the final meeting—a fuel storage room between the market and the dock—first. Fass had run a scan of the room and found two occupants, one with vital signs indicating unconsciousness, and not a single weapon, and so he sent her through the door.

Ososi did not believe that scan.

She held her hands out from her sides with fingers splayed wide in a clear attempt to show her lack of threat. Close to the far wall stood a woman wrapped in warm local garb, hair covered and chin tucked into swooping folds of a scarf. This must be the woman who contacted Fass: Tannor Mellick. *Colonel* Mellick. Behind her lay the still body of a woman dressed in white, whose long black hair splayed out across the floor but left her face uncovered: the queen of the galaxy herself, Mora Aydor. Betrayed.

Ososi knew full well that in this moment she appeared to be just another one of Fass's fanatical Unity thugs. She wanted to shout, *I'm not one of his!*, but it would do no good. Fass would hear her and end her life, or this would end up a trap and she'd fall another way. All she could do was look with her eyes and see, up to the last moment.

"Who are you?" Tannor Mellick asked.

"First to die, if this is a trap," Ososi answered.

"Are you here to speak for Ednar Fass?"

She shook her head.

They simply stared at one another for a moment, and then Ososi ventured a question.

"Is Mora Aydor dead?"

A hint of concern crossed Tannor Mellick's face. "No. Where is Captain Fass?"

"Just wait."

Fass had ordered her to watch closely as he ran his scans a second time, to see if Tannor Mellick was using any obvious technology to disguise weapons or people or anything else. All Ososi saw now was a slight flutter of the woman's eyelashes.

Even if she had seen something, her report would have been the same: "Nothing."

Captain Ednar Fass entered the room, followed by two more soldiers.

His face wore a mixture of smug pride and wariness, but he didn't unclasp his hands from behind his back as he came to stand in an area with particularly dramatic lighting.

"Keep watch for the other three fugitives," Fass warned his men. He wasn't speaking to Ososi.

She faded back into the shadows, and the others hung back, too, as Fass sauntered forward. Ososi watched how Tannor Mellick didn't move but for the tracking of her eyes as he approached.

"Tannor," Captain Fass said, and he tipped his chin.

•

Because she couldn't spit in his face, Tannor chose instead to say:

"I can't believe you joined Unity."

Loud enough for the others to hear, Fass replied, "The queen was too vile; I had to take action."

Tannor scowled and kept her voice quiet—but not too quiet for the recording her comm was making. "I understand that, it's just—*Unity?* They're a bunch of brainless, violent children. You're not brainless. You have to know there's no way they'll actually gain control of this planet. It's nonsense."

Tannor's disdain was completely genuine, and it worked. A flash of anger crossed Fass's face and then he took a step closer and lowered his voice to an intimate level. "It *is* nonsense. You and I know better. This uprising will last a few weeks, at the most, before the coalition stops it thanks to those of us… uniquely positioned to provide counter-efforts at exactly the right moment."

It was all Tannor could do to raise her eyebrows in feigned surprised. "So you'll turn on Unity when the coalition arrives."

"And I'll be rewarded," Fass said. "You can be rewarded, too, Tannor. By my side."

Tannor stared at Captain Fass's perfectly proportioned face, revulsion swelling inside her, and then she switched on the transmission jammer.

The vid screen went blank, the comm in her ear fell silent, and Relai distantly felt concrete meet her back.

"Tannor? Can you hear me?"

The darkness in every shadow around her seemed to deepen. The sound and video had cut out—did that mean the projection of Relai had disappeared in the room, too? The projection of a proper, long-haired Relai Aydor was only supposed to lay unconscious on the floor, but if needed the image could awake and interact with Fass. The eyes of the projection could follow the movement of Relai's eyes; the mouth would speak as she spoke. The projection modules Tannor had built in the jumper would even convey her voice, indistinguishable from her real presence. Relai only had to stand here in the shell of metalloy Tannor had suspended over the mesh framework from the jumper, ready to perform for the cameras Tannor had built. Relai was free to switch comm spaces to coordinate with everyone else... but Milo and Goren had gone silent in pursuit of the bounty hunter, and both Iverson and Ky seemed to have vanished entirely.

And when Tannor's voice disappeared, so did all of the markers on the map in Relai's hand.

"Milo? Goren?" she tried again, switching from space to space. "...Ky? ...Iverson?"

Goren might have just switched off when Milo ordered everyone to, or he might be dead. Maybe had Ky decided he was done with all of this and caught his own ride off.

What if Tannor was going through with this plan sincerely? What if she was giving Relai up to Fass?

"...Is anyone there? Anyone?"

Never allow yourself to become desperate. If you are desperate, never show—

Relai might really be alone.

The plan had made so much sense when they were plotting, but now Relai felt like a fool. She'd chosen the coward's position, huddled against concrete at the end of a cold, pointless path while everyone she cared about faced danger without her, the *coward*, and she'd get what she deserved now: silence.

Maintain authority. Nothing matters more—

Maybe she should run.

You are my greatest disappointment—
Shut up, Relai thought. *I trust them.*
She pushed away from the wall.

•

Tannor allowed herself to lean closer to Ednar Fass and his mud-mucked smile than her sanity recommended.

"You know the only reason I contacted you," she said in a low voice.

"Yes. You discovered her… little secret."

Tannor asked in a whisper tinged with bile: "Are you the father?"

"What?" Fass snapped.

"Are you the father of Relai's child?"

His face widened in surprise and he let out a laugh, but his words stayed disgustingly intimate between them. "Me? The father of the next ruler of our galaxy?" He gave a pitying smile and tilted his head. "No. You understand so little. I serve in my own small way, and I will follow the child when it grows old enough to rule. As will you, and everyone on every planet in this galaxy."

Tannor tried to find a lie, a gleam of pleasure at the thought of fathering such power—nothing. She actually believed him.

"Where is the baby? Is it safe?"

He laughed at her again and muttered, "Women."

Tannor was ready to blow the comm inside his head at this point, but she needed him to tell her where the baby was. (And why would he find it so easy to follow the next Aydor? Who was the father? If not Fass, then it must be whoever Fass was working for. Tannor needed more time, she needed Fass to tell her—)

The door to the room burst open and two, three, four more soldiers filed inside. Fass didn't react, so he must have instructed them to come after waiting a certain amount of time. Tannor took the opportunity of the disruption to reach out with her mind and disable all of the gen-guns in the room. Then she lifted the transmission jam and said, for Relai to hear, "I didn't contact you so you could kill her."

"These events will make sense to you someday," he replied. Tannor barely managed not to snarl.

Then one of the new soldiers called out, "Sir! Look what we found!"

He handed a weapon to Fass, who took it by the grip. It looked like an Earthan gun, not a gen-gun.

"We stunned the man carrying it and took his prisoner." Behind him drifted the body of a man hanging by his wrists from floating hovercuffs.

His arms were twisted in a painful stretch so that every joint and muscle looked wrong, pulled too thin underneath angry skin, and his head rested in the dark shadow between his biceps. Black hair. His upper body was marred with shallow slashes and trickles of blood, and as Tannor's eyes took in the sight of him she realized the man was completely naked. Her mouth dropped open in horror.

"Odd," Fass said.

The man engaged his muscles, found his feet, and pushed himself up enough to take the pressure off of his shoulders and ease his head upward into the light.

Ky.

Tannor didn't see Fass's next move before she felt and heard the result. Pain tore into her foot, then a moment later she recognized the sound of a gunshot. Her whole body clenched against a massive, mind-eating buzz of electricity burning up from the wound, and she screamed as she begged, demanded, *ordered* the pain to stop—

And it stopped.

She recognized the burn. The bullet in Ky's knee—it was one of those bullets. Fass had shot her with Iverson's gun.

"You'll be fine," Fass said mildly. "I don't like the way you look at him."

"You asshole," Tannor hissed from her position on the floor.

Fass ignored her to address his team. "Any sign of the others?"

"We caught an Applica relay that says they killed the other one, Milo Hemm, in Northus earlier today. We can't confirm."

"Hmm. Goren Dray is nothing, but Milo Hemm can still cause problems if he's alive. Keep looking."

Ky wrenched ineffectually at the hovering cuffs, glaring at her like he expected her to fix this. Tannor tried to reach out and free him—

Nothing.

Fass had blown out all of her internal tech with that bullet, and with the death of her comm Tannor realized the world around her had slipped away.

Like losing sight of just one color, or the ability to feel a certain temperature. Like numb spots fogging up her head.

It was gone.

Her reach was gone.

·

Relai was already halfway to the fuel room when she heard new soldiers enter and then, out of nowhere, the sound of a gunshot. She never wanted to hear Tannor cry out like that ever again.

The final stretch of corridor was blessedly empty as she approached, and then Relai wrenched the heavy bar handle of the door and threw herself inside, shouting, "Don't hurt her!" with her hands high in the air.

Tannor was curled up on the floor just beyond Fass with her hands wrapped around one ankle, her movements smearing a small splash of blood across the floor. Her boots and pants were dark so Relai couldn't see well, but it looked like only the ankle or foot had been hit. Relai tried to circle wide around Fass to reach her, but she only made it halfway before Fass chose to aim the gun at Tannor's head.

Relai stopped.

She prayed Tannor would sense the grenades lining her pockets and prepare herself. Relai didn't know how to protect Ky, not while he was bound this way, but he'd survive anything Relai tried. Why hadn't Tannor freed him yet? Why hadn't she set off the snap grenades tucked strategically around the room—the ones Tannor had masked during Fass's scan as she mimicked the presence of two people instead of one?

Fass glanced back to where the projection of Relai's unconscious form used to lay, where now there was nothing at all, and laughed. "That anyone thought you could rule..." he said, shaking his head.

"Take me. Let them go," Relai said.

Fass signaled his men, and she found herself grabbed and kicked to her knees, the jacket torn off her shoulders and her pockets emptied.

"You are nothing, Relai Aydor. Less than nothing," he said.

"She's the one who beats you," Tannor said, her voice tight with pain, "so if she's nothing, you must not be much."

Fass sneered. "I'm in control, here. You lost. The entire galaxy was at stake, and it's already over. When you see—"

Relai tried to listen, but as Fass launched into a string of vile speechifying the tiny soldier in Titian whites threw herself at Ky and slapped him in the face, and she got distracted.

·

"You!" the Titian exclaimed in a whisper.

"Do you mind?" Ky hissed. He wasn't exactly enjoying himself, and getting slapped added nothing to the experience. "I'm trying to listen."

"They had families," she choked out. "They were *loved*, they *mattered*, and you just killed them."

He gave her more than a cursory glance this time, and realized: this was the Titian from the other side of the field at MMN. The one he would have preferred to kill, but Relai had stopped him.

Ky's eyes went hard.

·

"...Chaos and conflict in every corner, and greater suffering than anywhere else in the galaxy! We have a responsibility to help this planet," Fass droned on, "and we will..."

·

"I had no choice," Ky said. "I don't expect forgiveness."

The Titian slapped his bare chest. "Expect justice!"

"Who are you to demand anything from me?" Ky pitched forward, jerking to the limits of his binding, and the Titian stumbled back. "We brought weapons that stun and your team brought Earthan guns. You think we don't know what that means?"

"You shot first—"

"So they wouldn't," Ky exclaimed, voice rising, "and don't tell me first shot wasn't the only power I had in that situation."

Blood flushed high in the skin of her cheeks. "Anyone can kill! That's not power—it's *laziness*! You took a cowardly way out when you could have done anything, anything—"

Ky leaned back and rested on his shoulder joints.

·

"You're lucky I ever looked your way, Tannor Mellick," Fass went on. "You'd be dead now if I didn't want you with me."

Tannor rolled her eyes.

·

The Titian girl could have been Goren's age, maybe a few years older, and when Relai heard her voice it was Relai's own voice, younger and frightened and braver than Relai had ever been.

Ky went slack under the hover restraint and Relai almost couldn't look at his body now, the splashes of light along his lengthened torso, the heavy stretch of his muscles and the sharp points of bone—

Fass was going on about submission or something when he finally noticed no one was listening to him. He stopped and turned toward the conversation on his left.

·

"Look," Ky whispered, "I'm sor—"

A snap and splatter halted him and he realized, blinking, that Captain Fass had shot the Titian through the back. Her eyes stood out like cries in silence, then she fell on her face in front of him.

Ky slumped, his eyes wide and his hands swelling purple past the stricture of the restraint.

"I was talking," Fass said.

The Titian's head lay next to his bare foot.

·

Tannor watched it happen in horror.

"Now," Fass drawled, so proud and satisfied, "as I was saying—"

Heal her, Ky, heal her, Tannor thought fervently.

·

Ednar Fass paused, debating whether to just kill the queen now or take the time to set up the public execution like he'd planned. It never paid to be lazy.

Motivate through fear, Lady Redas always told him.

Tears streamed down Tannor Mellick's face as the queen cried out beautifully, and then they both went still in terrified submission. Fass had never noticed anything appealing about Relai Aydor, but this—he could see beauty in her sad little shocked face.

He should have woken her early.

Then a thrumming noise like an avalanche engulfed the room, and Ednar Fass clutched at his chest.

•

It was a storm, somehow.

A storm inside the base.

Relai couldn't understand what was happening around her, but she covered her head with her arms and crouched and ran for Tannor. She couldn't see Fass; someone must have set off a grenade, but not a normal grenade—no smoke, no heat, in fact it was getting colder and colder, the roaring louder and louder—the hover restraint flew over their heads in pieces—

Relai threw herself on top of Tannor, squinting up through the sweat in her eyes to see a metal walkway high above them begin to shake. It shook and then it bent up like—like the metal was in pain.

Was this Tannor? Tannor couldn't bend metal with her mind—

Ky.

Ky hung there unbound, arms free from the restraint, still the shape of a man but unseeable because his body neither gave off nor reflected light, like he was taking every bit of it into his body. The space around him skewed in, too, distorted and uncanny, and Relai had to look away as her stomach turned.

She decided maybe she just wasn't seeing things right.

Every conscious soldier there with a brain and a sense of self-preservation scrambled toward the door, but Fass...

Fass stumbled backward. He dropped his gun. He clutched his chest and turned red, then purple, his neck bulging around his collar. Sounds came from his mouth like an animal being crushed.

Relai didn't have time for this.

She let go of Tannor and pitched herself up toward Ky, into the void, grabbing for whatever might be in there that hands could still touch.

She shouted an exasperated, "Ky!" and her fingers found flesh in the whipping wind.

Her hands crawled up his bare skin to his shoulders and she pulled him down and cracked his forehead against hers and said, *"Stop."*

And it stopped.

∘∘●∘∘

vi.

-20:00 min

Hope snapped her fingers in one guy's face, motioning for him to give up his damned jacket for one of these poor freezing kids, as she hissed into the communicator that Iverson had connected to her cell phone so it would work even down here.

"Use GPS to track my phone, moron. See where I am? That's right, the frozen left testicle of Siberia! I'm in a secret military base where a bunch of Unity terrorists—you know Unity by now, right? They tried to assassinate the prime minister of Malaysia—"

"Are you talking about Hong Kong?"

"You know what I mean! Hong Kong, reddit, I think they even tried to pull shit at Google Headquarters, didn't they? Well, they're trying to take over this secret base, and I'm not gonna make the mistake of assuming this place doesn't have super-weapons shoved in a corner somewhere."

"You can't be serious, Valdez," her supervisor tried wearily. "You know what needs to happen before we can even—"

"—NO. Make the call, pull the lever, hit the button, enter the code. Commandeer a TV station and talk directly to Vladimir Putin's face. Do whatever the hell you have to do to get us some international attention before Unity takes over, or even worse: Russia comes in and sneaks off with all the alien technology before we can keep a lid on it!"

"I'm not sure I can—"

Hope nearly screamed, but she kept it to a gravelly shout for the sake of the kids. "We will lock this place down until there's a decent UN resolution or whatever, but until then we are trapped. Call up the State Department and—you!" Hope waved at the other guy covering the kids. He was one of the men they'd picked up in Nigeria. "Is there a code word or something that the U.S. State Department would understand? Something Iverson might tell them?"

The man blinked, breathing heavily as he crouched next to her and listened to his comm interpret her words. "I believe Colonel Iverson already sent it," he replied. "The state circles have begun the process of waking. The cascade begins with... *fox thirty-one green eleven twenty-two twelve.*"

"Ha! *Fox thirty-one green eleven twenty-two twelve!*"

"I'll try it, Agent Valdez," her supervisor said. "…Whatever you're doing in Siberia, I hope it's worth losing your job over."

Hope snorted. "I don't work for Homeland Security anymore. I'm Earth Relations."

∘∘●∘∘

vii.

-18:00 min

Tannor dug her fingernails into her ankle and sucked in air through her teeth as the twist in her vision snapped back into normal sight. Something impossible had happened, and her ability to reach out and sense the energy of it had gone numb after that gunshot.

The forms of Unity soldiers lay strewn through the room and just outside the door, twitching and letting out faint wheezes. Not a single one was conscious. Relai had collapsed backward with Ky strewn across her legs in an unresponsive heap, and Tannor had to crawl past the Titian woman's body to get to them.

"What... the hell... was that," Tannor breathed as she tried to get a grip on Ky's skin through the sweat and blood. He'd already healed all of the small cuts, and just touching him now, while he was still unconscious, she could feel her foot begin to heal.

Relai shook herself free, touched Tannor's ankle gently, and then scrambled away.

Tannor had no idea how to deal with this, but they needed Ky to be able to stand.

"Wake up, Ky, come on." She tapped his cheek. Nothing. She looked up and saw Relai pushing Fass onto his back.

"What the hell?" Tannor exclaimed. "Leave him!"

Relai ignored her, listened to Fass' chest, and then sat back on her heels. "Ky stopped his heart."

"Nice." Tannor wedged her thigh under Ky's head and peeled open one of his eyelids. "Hey. Wake up. What did they do with your clothes? You're going to miss those boots, aren't you?"

Relai began grunting methodically. Out of the corner of her eye Tannor saw her leaning over Fass and pressing her hands into his chest.

"What are you doing?"

Ky started to rouse.

"Do we—need him—or not?" Relai huffed.

Ky opened his eyes and looked up at Tannor with bleary focus. The corner of his mouth tilted up.

"If this is death," he mumbled, "I don't know why I was worried."

"Ha, ha," she said.

Ky sat up blearily and Tannor eased forward to support him. "I sure am naked," he said. "What happened?"

"You—" Tannor grabbed his face with one hand and looked in his eyes for any sign of shadows. Nothing. "You stopped his heart with your mind."

Ky looked around in a daze. "No, I can't do that…"

"Ky," Tannor said, "what are we?"

He blinked through drips of sweat.

"I told you before," he said. "We're human."

She saw no bitterness, no cunning in his eyes. Nothing she was used to seeing. Only relief, confusion, and a tiny bit of fear.

"Okay," she said.

"You're human, I'm human, we're all human," Relai panted. "Great."

"I changed my mind," Tannor said. "We don't need Fass! Let him die!"

Then the Titian woman moved.

•

Ososi Tena sucked in an enormous rattling breath and dragged her arms inward against her chest. She lifted her cheek from the painfully cold surface of the floor, forcing her eyes to open and focus on something through the residual pain.

She had been shot in the back.

She blinked and swayed her head to find any sight that would add sense to this nightmare, but before she found any hope she registered the small warning message in the corner of her Seer, the tech in her eye.

Restart? it read.

She lay there, stunned, and realized the recordings of the last few days, all manner of damning evidence against Captain Fass, her accusation of the man who killed her team… they'd been sent. They would reach Buzou in less than a second, Oliver within minutes, and Titus in only an hour more.

She'd died.

And yet here she was, alive.

What was life, then? Had she left and returned? Was any of this real?

The pain in her chest was real.

(Or was it?)

John Paul would have had something wry to say about resurrection, but his continued lack of it spoke loudly enough.

She heard voices.

"...Her with your foot," Ososi heard a woman say in Ardi a few feet away. In the voice she heard awe. Wonder.

"No," a weak male voice responded. "I tried, but she was dead. She was *dead*."

"I was dead," Ososi agreed raspily. She used some unknown strength to lift her chest from the ground and lean back into a sitting position. Next to her was the wretched Oeylan killer... cradled by the woman Fass had come to meet, Tannor Mellick. Ososi finally connected the image of this woman she'd seen on the jumper screen with the blond woman the Oeylan had shot in the head in that MMN testing field.

The dead were being raised every day now, it seemed.

"Who are you?" Tannor Mellick asked.

Ososi declined to answer; instead she turned her head at the sound of grunting from the opposite direction. There knelt the queen of the galaxy herself, Relai Mora Aydor (with all of her long black hair shaved off, so unlike the unconscious figure on the floor earlier), pumping the chest of Captain Fass's vile body.

"Is he dead?" Ososi asked.

Mora Aydor stopped to lean down and listen to Fass's heart. "Maybe," she said, breathless. Then she looked right at Ososi, "Should I let him go?"

Ososi felt fire inside of her, a welling spring of dozens of lives lost and crying out in frustration, and she found the wits to kick a stray gen-gun across the floor to the queen. "Turn the shock to six and strike him just to the right of his heart. I want justice."

A grim smile split across the queen's face, and she did exactly as Ososi said.

•

Fass's body jolted once, then again with a second shock. He coughed, loud and long, like the groaning of the last strands of cord holding a beast nearly escaped.

Then Goren burst into the room.

"Hey!" he said. "Oh, Fass is down, great job everyone! Why is Ky naked?"

Relai let out a slow, deep breath.

.

They'd pooled and redistributed Tannor and Goren's guard-issued restraints before they left the jumper, and Relai watched Goren get right to work securing Fass and his goons one by one while Relai sat next to the Titian soldier and tried to give her a moment to collect herself before they started digging for answers. Or, at the very least, her name.

Meanwhile, Ky peered over the scattered soldiers, narrowed in on one slumped in the doorway, grinned back at her, and said, "Pants!"

The soldier flopped in anger as Tannor ripped open his pack and dumped out Ky's clothing, a slashed-up shirt included but no boots in sight. Ky grumbled as he pulled on just the pants and clipped the waist closed.

"I like your hair now," the Titian said suddenly.

Relai blinked, then glanced at the girl's own nearly-shaved head and laughed.

Then the Pants soldier arched so he could see Relai and gasped out, "You're going to lose."

Relai pondered the ugliness on his face.

"I know," she said.

"Not yet, you're not," Tannor snapped, then she grabbed her tablet and glared at Relai. "Have you heard anything more from Milo?"

Relai shook her head, thrown by the jolt of fear inside her chest. "The wolves are helping him with the bounty hunter, but I lost the map when your comm went out back there."

She jumped to her feet to look at the map over Tannor's shoulder. Milo and the red dot were faded behind the green and blue market lines, moving not far from one another in Relai's direction.

"Maintenance and vertical," Tannor muttered, and the screen flipped to show a brighter overlay of orange lines instead. Now Milo and the hunter shone bright. "They're a level above us. Outside the market, moving this way."

"He went off comms, can you—"

"Mine's destroyed, but here—" Tannor twisted to press urgent fingers behind Relai's ear. After a moment, Relai heard a click and labored breathing.

She demanded, "Milo? Are you there?"

Milo: *Please... She killed the wolf. I'm hurt—I tried—I'm sorry—*

They heard the hunter in their heads next:

Yeah, everyone come help.

Milo: *Don't—*

He cried out in pain.

"Stay here," Relai demanded as she slid a gen-gun to the Titian woman. "Guard them until someone—"

The sound of Milo's breathing cut short with a sickening grunt.

Relai took off running, with Ky and Goren and Tannor close behind.

○○●○○

viii.

-16:00 min

Milo dove behind a pillar of pipes and tried to zip his jacket shut, a weak attempt to hold the blood inside his body.

He'd been so sure of himself. The hunter had tried to follow a straight path to Relai but Ithail Sur had blocked her easily, so she'd gone up to another level. They'd followed.

The hunter had killed Ithail.

The others had the map. They could find him. He knew without a hint of doubt which direction the ship bay must be, so he pressed that way with every break in the violence. He'd managed to toss away both of the hunter's guns and a knife, and his own guns seemed to do nothing so it hardly mattered that he'd lost them. They were fighting with whatever they could get their hands on now.

He only had to last until the others reached him. He only—

The hunter nearly crushed his skull with a blood-wet metal bar. Milo dodged and the thing caught his shoulder—*hard*—and he dove in and stayed low but this woman was so *fast* and nothing hurt her. In a moment of clarity Milo feinted left and slapped the hunter's head right, crashing it against a metal pipe so the point of impact hit just behind the ear. Med scanners couldn't heal a broken comm.

Milo saw a stairwell.

•

Relai sprinted from the storage room of Unity bodies through twists and turns to reach the red dot and the word *Milo* where they hovered in an orange square on the map. It was a stairwell in a deep corner of the base.

Or, they made it to the fence preventing them from reaching him, at least.

Ky silenced them all with a few sharp gestures and gentled his bare feet through the last thirty paces. Relai searched the shadows of the stairwell and found Milo high and struggling, hanging by one hand from a walkway thirty feet above the concrete floor. She wanted to tear through the metal fence to get to him.

"I can't get this gate open!" Tannor hissed. "I lost my tech pen and the lock's not tech, it's just a *chain*—"

"Milo!" Relai whispered. Lazy footsteps banged closer.

Milo: *I busted her comm. She got my shoulder...*

He strained through the words and she watched him kick his legs. Useless.

Milo: *I can't climb back up.*

A line of sparks shot up along the handrail, followed by a quick, musical clang-clang-clang drawing closer and closer to Milo. As the sparks progressed around the curve of the stairwell, Relai finally made out a moving shape holding a dull rod—metal, sharp at the tip. The bounty hunter.

She thought she could hear someone chanting. Finally her brain made sense of it.

"Gonna die... gonna die..."

Relai dug her fingers into Tannor's shoulder and whispered, "Can you sense the bounty hunter's tech?"

"No! I can't sense anything!"

Milo: *I'm sorry, Relai—I'm sorry—*

"Time to die..."

Relai's eyes darted from Milo to Tannor in silent demand.

"I didn't realize before—I was using my comm," Tannor answered. "Iverson's burnout bullet, like the one in Ky's knee—it blew out my comm and I can't affect anything beyond what I touch anymore—"

"Okay," Relai whispered, "You can't blow the implant from here. Did we get the gun? Iverson's gun, Fass had it—"

"I got it!" Goren whispered from the tunnel where he was watching their backs. "Here!"

He checked for danger, then pulled out the gun and lobbed it to Ky. Ky slipped open something on the gun, hissed at what he saw, and on the bounty hunter's next stomp Ky raised the gun and pulled the trigger.

Nothing.

"It's out."

"No. *No!*"

Tannor spun and whispered, "Ky, stop her heart like you did to Fass."

His face snarled up. "*I don't know how to do that.* It's not like—"

"Shh," Relai whispered.

The hunter was five feet from Milo now, taking her time.

•

Tannor looked at the looping chain and then her own jacket sleeve.

There. The implosion ring she took off of Relai's neck on the roof.

They looked up through the flashing lights at Milo's bloodied body hanging there, meat on a hook, with the hunter laughing only steps away.

She was too close. There was no time.

Tannor watched tears well up in Relai's eyes.

"Milo," Relai said as Tannor unlatched the implosion ring and flung it around the chain holding the fence closed. "Fall."

•

The hunter drew close. Milo knew nothing but the sound of Relai's voice and, with a breath and a glance at the rough gray below, he fell.

ix.

-14:01 min

"I'm sorry I'm sorry," Relai whispered after a crack finished off Milo's transmission and his body lay still.

"Please," she said. "Please."

x.

-14:00 min

Milo's mind screamed red and alive.

Tannor was whispering to him past the shrieks of pain. "You have to draw her closer! Milo, don't give up—"

He could see the tips of her fingers like little white fireflies floating out of the darkness beyond the fence.

"I think my back is broken," he said.

Milo heard, "Nice try, time to die," stomping down the stairs.

He couldn't kill this woman.

"Hunter," Milo groaned. "Who are you?"

"Think I'm Odene?" the hunter called back.

"Odene would have finished us all the first time around."

The hunter laughed. "Yeah."

"My name is Milo Hemm," he said, "and I'm dying."

The hunter stepped from the stairs to the concrete floor. Those beautiful boots made no sound now that she'd left the elevated grating. "I know."

Milo let himself rest, jaw lifted, neck exposed. "Who are you? I want to know the name of the one who kills me."

The hunter laughed. "You're the best I ever fought. ...Well, tallest, at least. Made it fun. My name's Runn."

Milo's head lolled left. He mumbled, "What?"

A heavy boot kicked the upturned sole of Milo's foot. "Runn, I said."

Milo angled his head and looked up. "I'll remember it," he said, and then the hunter cracked forward, eyes bulging, neck arched, throat gurgling, and she fell on her side and lay still. Tannor dropped her hand from the height of the hunter's neck, grimacing, and wiped it on her pants.

"I can't believe she fell for *what*," Tannor said.

•

Through the reeling pain and the floating emptiness below his chest, Milo heard scrambling around him. Relai settled at his head and Ky crouched at his side.

"Those boots are cool. I'm stealing 'em," Ky said, his hands brushing over Milo's face and chest.

"I'd fight you for them," Milo groaned without bothering to open his eyes, "but I can't feel my legs."

"I'm sorry, I'm sorry," Relai chanted as she palmed the crook of his neck.

Ky fit his hands around Milo's torso, one under his back and one on his belly. Milo whimpered as the ache of healing grew, but Relai was warm against him.

"Can you fix this?" she asked.

Ky scoffed. "Tannor, get her shirt too."

Milo rolled his head sideways and saw Tannor stripping the hunter, Runn, of weapons and tech and Ky's new boots and shirt. She huffed and kicked the body and then finally got one sleeve of the jacket free. "And I thought Fass was gross," she said.

"Same difference," Relai said. She'd pressed his hand to her mouth and Milo felt the words pass between his fingers.

He forced himself to breathe. "Hunter waited until we got those kids to safety, at least."

Relai actually managed a laugh. "Oh, I forgive her, then."

Ky buried his forehead against Milo's ribs so his words came out muffled. "You should've let me kill Fass."

"Feeling's back in my legs, *fuck, oh*—"

"Sorry."

Milo gritted his teeth through the pain. "I would've let you kill him."

"Ky *did* kill him," Tannor grumbled, "no hands. Relai's the one who won't let dead stay dead."

"No hands?" Milo asked.

"His wake is death, her wake is life," Ky muttered. Everyone went still, and then Tannor let out an exasperated breath.

"What?" Relai said.

Ky waved a hand vaguely through the air.

Milo shifted around his lingering injuries. Relai's grip on him turned firm to help him pull up to a sitting position. "Ky," he said, "Shut up."

Ky tried to ease away, but Milo grabbed his shoulder.

"Wait," he said. With some effort, he took out his pouch of pins, now stained and scratched right down to the fine inner mesh. "I gave them to you. I don't want them back until I'm standing on the dirt of my people."

Ky twitched. "Figured you might feel better carrying them yourself from now on."

"No," Milo said fiercely. He thrust the pouch into Ky's stomach.

Ky grimaced down at it. "Stupid."

Now it was Milo's turn to shrug.

•

"What's this?" Tannor muttered, tugging a heavy cylinder out of the hunter's jacket pocket. "Tech pen? Not a tech pen…"

She reached inside of it with her ability, exploring, trying to understand what it might do. *Spindly. Dizzy. Sticky, strong, and far away…*

Ky heard her and glanced over. "Oh. Ha. Only seen two of those that worked in my life."

"What is it?" she demanded.

"Mind probe."

Tannor's world seemed to slow. She met his eyes sharply.

A wrinkle on his brow asked, *what?*

She swung a pair of boots and a vintage Earthan jacket in the air and jerked her chin toward Goren. He took one last sweeping look and then jogged down the tunnel to meet them.

"The hangar is just through here," Tannor pointed to a door on the opposite wall of the stairwell. "But first—"

"Wait," Relai said, turning to her. "You brought the camera, right? I want to do it now."

"Last chance," Tannor agreed. Without missing a beat, she suggested, "How about standing next to Fass's bound and writhing body?"

Relai grinned.

○○●○○

xi.

-11:00 min

Back in the fuel room, where they found the Titian woman crouched and apparently meditating alongside all the captured men, it only took a moment for Tannor to bring back the projection of Relai. The real Relai stood to the side and watched as a pristine version of herself appeared, sleek-haired and dressed all in white. She put one hand to her shoulder and watched the projection do the same, perfectly in sync. She hated it, but she couldn't risk anyone recognizing her over the last few tense steps from here to the ship. They'd all be looking for this version of Relai, not the real one.

Fitting, really.

Relai turned and raised her chin, and Tannor nodded for her to begin.

•

"People of Earth," Relai said, and upon every screen in Curragh Dock and, indeed, every screen the message could reach on this planet, spreading like a rolling cloud in Tannor's mind, rose the queenly image of Relai Aydor. This Relai shone in the light, her skin soft and unmarred, her eyes bright, and the simple white of her clothes reminded Tannor of the snow. She spoke in Ardi.

"My name is Relai Aydor. I am the queen of a coalition of four planets in this galaxy. Together, we call ourselves Vada. Hello."

It was like watching... a dream. A queen they could all believe in, instead of the tyrant. Instead of the weak thing Tannor had found in that catacomb a lifetime ago.

"You need to wake up now," Relai said. "You've slept too long. The sun is up now, and you are late. *Wake up*. You give to the economy of our galaxy, and you take from us, though not all of you know it. So *wake up*. You're tired, I think, and you might be afraid, but I've seen bravery here, and love, and so much ingenuity. You have power. Wake up and stand. I can't do it for you."

Tannor bit her lip. There was more coming, she could tell.

"As for the coalition citizens living here..." Relai went on, "you have a choice. Stay hidden, or help Earth stand. Vada cedes all rights to our resources and technology on this planet to Earth entirely. In exchange, we expect to meet with all *peaceful* nations after one year of stabilization. I wish you all the grace and peace of the seven stars."

She smiled, and then added:

"Oh, and as for you, Gandred Xiong: I'm not who you think I am. I'm not who I was. I have a planet to take care of first, and then we'll talk again. In the meantime... you can have your river back."

After a decent pause, Tannor cut the video and let the camera drop.

"Gods in stars, Relai," she breathed. "You ceded—they'll be able to fight off Gastred now. Gastred might not even attack!"

"What river do you mean?" the resurrected Titian asked.

Relai smiled. "It's not really a river; he'll know what I mean. Oliver Block. Fass was using me to control it, but now..." she put a palm to Tannor's tablet to approve the order, "Xiong has full control."

Tannor glanced back Milo and found him staring, stunned.

.

The others left to free Iverson but Tannor hung back, promising she'd be right behind them.

She wasted no time in whipping out the device from the bounty hunter, the mind probe, and crouching over Fass's half-conscious body. They'd bound him securely to a pipe running up the wall, and he groaned as she pushed his head sideways, trying to imagine the best place to stab him.

She decided on the base of the skull.

The prongs of the probe flung open with a twist, and she let her eyes flutter closed in hopes of guiding it by the intuition of her gift. She'd never stuck her hand into a spill of vomit before, but the idea of going into Fass's mind didn't seem far from it.

She jabbed the probe into his neck.

It was like jumping into a cloud of burning acid, except not a feeling on her skin—it was all in her mind. *Burning, cloudy exhaustion, then a swell of fear the exact color of Tannor's hair—the smell of a gen-gun charge like putty*—it was like trying to stand on the underwater side of a capsized boat—

Tannor's mind settled with a sudden onset of pain... she realized she was gripping her own thigh with her fingernails so hard there would probably be bruises. She had to focus. She had information to find.

The baby.

Where is the baby?

Her mind slipped down a slide of feathered nausea and she found a name and saw a face, as clear as if she'd seen it with her own eyes:

Kastroma.

And then: *Who planned all of this? Who is in charge?*

She got her answer, a name padded in sticky-sour love.

Lady Jadice Redas.

oo●oo

-08:00

Weary in bone but steady in step, Ososi followed the queen's group through labyrinthine corridors back to confront the last few soldiers on Captain Fass's Unity crew. The Oeylan led them to a tucked-away room, signaled for caution, and they burst inside, weapons ready, to find Colonel Terrence Iverson of Earth Monitoring—a man Ososi had heard much about but never met—just tightening bindings on the last Unity soldier.

He hardly looked ruffled.

The Oeylan said, "Hi, Terrence," in a strangely smug tone, but Colonel Iverson only gave him a cursory glance before he noticed Ososi.

"You—" Iverson began at the sight of her, then he came closer and went to one knee. He looked at her like she was something precious. "You're the missing soldier from Buzou Base. Are you all right?"

Ososi nodded. "I died," she said, "but I have more to do here. Captain Fass needs accusation, and Mora Aydor isn't staying to accuse him, so I will."

The astonishment on his face made Ososi feel as though her feet had left the ground. She came, she saw, and now she would speak.

"Will you join me to wake Earth?" Iverson asked.

Ososi looked over the serious creases of his face.

"Did you hear what she said?" she asked. "Everything is ceded to Earth. Including Buzou."

His eyes softened as he understood, and then she caught a strange sort of look pass over his face. Evaluating, patient... something.

He said, "You are a free person. Go, if you choose."

Ososi looked back at the queen, Relai, who was speaking rapidly with Tannor Mellick. Could she really call herself free?

Finally, she shook her head. "Earth will have complaints against Captain Fass, too. I just need to know that my mother on Arden is safe, and I'll stay here as long as you need."

Iverson smiled. "I'll introduce you to Ife, then."

Ososi tilted her head, questioning, but the moment was broken by the return of the queen's attention.

"Everything here is secure," Relai Aydor said as Iverson rose to his feet. "Colonel Iverson, work with the wolves who run this dock to clean up any lingering Unity and keep the calm and peace. Try to avoid any planetary wars—"

Tannor Mellick appeared and said, "Relai, we need to go."

"—And let them know that the coalition *will not* deal with any one nation that declares itself the sole representative of Earth. Understand? I lived here, I know that's not how it works. I'll check back with you after I secure my crown."

"Understood," Colonel Iverson replied.

"I wish you life," Ososi told the queen.

Relai Aydor smiled warmly and held out a hand. "I'd wish you the same, but you seem to have that one covered."

Ososi accepted, their arms clasped between their bodies, and with the other arm she pulled the queen into a hug.

Titus might be neutral, but Ososi Tena was not.

○○●○○

xii.

-06:00 min

Kaboom.

xiii.

-05:00 min

Relai couldn't hear anything but ringing for a minute.

They'd been moving as one unit through the final tunnel to the ship bay, and then something had slapped her down flat. Loud, powerful, and shaking, it took her breath and all awareness of the world around her.

Then she sat up, reoriented, and the familiar sounds of arguing reached her ears.

"Blasts might be staggered—"

"We have to get out of here—"

"No, we have to make sure this place doesn't come down—"

"That was Fass, wasn't it? What if he put bombs everywhere again?"

"Get me to a panel, I'll scan for them and halt them—"

"I'm okay, thanks for asking, *nobody!*"

They'd been shielded from the worst of the blast, tucked just far enough into the tunnel to escape unscathed. Relai rested against the wall with her shoulder tucked against Milo's as Ky pulled Tannor into the bay and deposited her against a console. She palmed it and closed her eyes as he went further. He scrambled alongside a stack of packing cages, peered over the damage and then scampered back.

"The explosion took out the pistons," he said. "We'll never get that door up now."

Milo shook his head. "We need to get back to Iverson and help secure this place, *now.*"

Relai gripped Milo's sleeve in desperation. "No! We can't give up on leaving!"

From their spot huddled behind a pile of rubble at the edge of the tunnel to the ship bay, she surveyed the damage and guessed that the bomb had been placed at the top edge of the massive dock door. The ship closest to the exit was partially destroyed, crushed by boulders half its size, and debris from the explosion had struck as far as the opposite wall of the bay. Every ship had been hit by it, but to Relai's desperate, stinging eyes the *Vimana* still looked space-worthy.

Then she saw Tannor relax against the console.

"I got them. There were four more. I got them," she called, breathless.

Relai ran to her. "We need to know if the ship can still fly." She pulled Tannor to her feet and they crept out into the bay to reach the docking station panel next to the *Vimana*. Milo and the rest flocked behind as they cleaned the gray dust and rubble from the console.

It only took Tannor a moment, data flying under her dirty fingers. "The ship is fine. It's... it's weird. It doesn't seem to like me very much. And we only have five minutes before the window closes and no one's leaving until we get a whole lot of stuff sorted out."

Relai shook her head. "I'm sick of this planet."

"We're screwed," Ky said. "That door isn't opening any time soon."

Relai peered through the clouds of smoke and dust; the ventilation system seemed to be clearing it slowly away. Maybe they could set off another explosion and the wall would collapse enough to let them escape? (Or the mountain would come down on them, killing them all.)

Maybe—

"Milo!" Relai called. "Do we still have that condensing seed?"

Milo pulled out the egg-shaped case without hesitation and swept his finger along the bottom of the case to look at the specifications. "Maybe," he muttered. "I could change the load dimensions but it would have to be... how thick is that wall?"

Tannor asked the dock system. "The fallout door is a foot thick. Dock door is on top of that, eight feet."

"Thin enough. But there's no way to get it in the right spot."

They all focused, sharp and desperate, on the smoky, flickering expanse of metal. Goren covered his mouth with his forearm and turned away, coughing wretchedly.

"I see a crack," Relai said, pointing. "Look up along the top edge where the bomb went off. See it? There's a sliver of space."

"That's fifty feet high," Ky said. "We need to get out of here."

"No!" Goren shouted. "I can do this! Where's your spit gun? Ky?"

Ky grabbed Goren's arm. "Don't be ridiculous!"

Relai looked between them. "Milo, would the seed even survive being shot from a gun?"

Milo coughed though a cloud of smoke and shook his head. "You prime the reaction in the case and it will only go off when it's set to go off. But," he rubbed his eyes, "if you crack the coating..."

"The force of being shot from—"

"No," he said. "The heat of it. Heat will crack it."

"We don't have time to recalibrate the gun," Ky said.

Tannor grabbed the spit gun out of his hand. "I can do it. I'll force it."

Milo said, "This is pointless. No one can make that shot—"

"I CAN MAKE THE SHOT!" Goren cried, and then he doubled over in another coughing fit.

Ky held him steady by the arm and swept a hand in wide circles over his back, glaring. "No. We're not going to waste our last chance to clear a way back if the tunnel collapses."

"Done," Tannor said, and handed the gun to Goren.

"It might work through the whole wall even if he misses the crack," Milo said. "He doesn't need to be a perfect shot if he has perfect timing."

Goren nodded, gripping the gun. Dust-grey spittle smeared across his chin. "I can do it. I practiced with rocks at Tom's house. I can do this."

"Oh," Ky exclaimed, "he *practiced with rocks*—"

Tannor rolled her eyes and grabbed Ky's face and kissed him. Hard.

After a moment frozen, Ky brought both hands to her face and deepened it.

Relai put her hand on Goren's forearm and dug her fingers in. "Do it."

•

"Starting... now. One... two..."

Case opened, blinking second by second, seed in hand.

"Three... four... five..."

Seed loaded. Ammunition chamber shut.

"Six... seven... eight..."

Tannor steadied her hand on the docking station, then Goren kneeled behind it and set the body of the gun in her palm.

Breath in. Gun set.

"Everything's good," Tannor said. Breath out. "Ten... eleven..."

He found his sights. The black shadow of the crevice pulled at him.

A breath in. In his periphery, the blinking grew brighter.

"Twelve... thirteen... fourteen..."

Breath out. His head felt clear, Ky's hand firm on his neck, keeping the urge to cough from his throat. He waited for a tickle in his chest, but none came. He let go of that concern.

Everything in his body, the gun, the world, pointed to this sliver of empty space.

"Fifteen... tsk... tsk..."

Tannor switched to clicking her tongue for the last five seconds.

Breath in. Condensing would happen at the end of the twentieth second. As the final flash of light went dark.

"Tsk... tsk..."

Breath out.

"Tsk."

He fired.

oo●oo

-03:00 min

Tom Wood knotted another bandage around a crying old lady and shouted, "You'll probably live, congratulations!"

The explosion had probably killed some people, but he and Gecko had only come across injured. Maybe Tom Luck went down the drain in the opposite direction on other continents, because Tom himself didn't have a scratch on him and the gash on Gecko's brow was movie-star-worthy. The man looked seriously dashing. Tom was jealous.

"I don't see anyone else!" Gecko shouted, jogging back to the crate of supplies they'd busted open to use for triage.

"What do we do now?" Tom asked.

"We get on the damned ship!"

Tom shivered and scratched at the itchy wool sweater rubbing against his neck. "Which ship are we on?"

"That one," Gecko said. "The *Tesla*."

"Well I hope it can blow holes in nuclear explosion-proof doors," Tom replied. The ship in question was small, black, and furthest from the explosion, not that any of it mattered. He couldn't see very well, but it didn't look like the exit would be opening any time soon. "Wait, Tesla—are there science nerds in space?! What am, I saying, of course there—"

Then a flippin' *hole* popped into existence. The ceiling was nothing but smoke, and then—BAM! Snow.

Smoke cleared as Tom stepped out from where he'd jumped behind Gecko. "What the heck just happened?"

"I don't know, but look!"

Tom looked. There was now a straight shot out of the dock through that big, crazy hole.

"Let's make like a tree and—no, no, I can do better." He took a deep breath, stood up with his shoulders back and his head held high, and said: "To infinity and—NO!"

He cleared his throat.

"Is this the real life, or is this just fantasy…"

"TOM!"

"Ride on a spaceship, I'll escape from Earth's gravity…"

"NOW!"

○○●○○

-02:00 min

Tannor got to work prepping the pods the second she reached a workable surface inside the ship, dragging the window with her as she hurried through the halls and into the travel pod bay.

"Time?" Relai called.

"Two minutes," she answered. The ship was a standard Ardenian military patrol vehicle, no stranger to Tannor, but it had been heavily modified by years of seedy criminal use. All of the sophisticated programming seemed to have been trashed in favor of tricky bootleg automated code. If she had another ten minutes she could break it down and rewrite everything…

They reached the travel pod bay and Tannor's fingers left the wall for a few unbearable seconds. She reached out and spread her hands out on the control panel next to the closest travel pod, closing her eyes as she worked.

"The ship doesn't like me," she muttered. "It's like they set it up to stop me. I can't get... underneath the programming... it's so simple..."

She heard Ky kick open the personals bin, followed by two thunks as he yanked off his new boots. "Get naked, Tannor," he snapped.

She raced through what she could find. "Autopilot journey, eight weeks. No supplies for conscious passengers during the trip; we have to sleep. Fifteen passengers down to five—"

Milo, shirtless, leaned out to check on everyone. "Weapons in the personals bin, too. And mark that you didn't go through a system clean so the pod can adjust!"

Goren's moan carried across the room. "Waking up is gonna suck..."

⋅

Tom: *Hope Valdez! Guess where I am?*

"THOMAS WOOD, YOU UTTER BASTARD, WHERE—"

Tom: *I'll say hi to your grandkids, okay? Relativity, you know.*

"Tom?"

Tom: *Hope...*

"Tom. You know I love you like hell, right?"

Tom: *Yeah, yeah. Sun shines out of your ass, Valdez. Take care of Earth, okay? And Eris, too. She needs her flea drops for another week.*

"Oh, jeez, Tom, of all the times to—"

Tom: *Bye, Hope.*

Hope dug the heels of her hands into her eye sockets until she saw only sparks of blue and white and swelling orange.

"Goodbye, Tom."

⋅

They'd barely reached the section of the ship with the travel pods when Tannor, hand on a wall panel, yelped in panic. "*Shit!* No, no—switching to wave drive in thirty seconds, everyone!"

"What?!" Relai exclaimed. "What's the destination?"

"I don't know—"

"Can't you delay it, Tannor?"

"This ship hates me!"

"Get your masks on," Milo bellowed. He arched around the partition, reaching desperately, and Relai lunged to meet his hand. She held it in both of her hands, clutched close, almost touching her lips.

"It's not gonna be another year, right?" she said.

His face softened and he shook his head. He turned his palm sideways and touched her cheek.

"Eight weeks, it'll feel like a second. I'll be here when you wake up."

Relai quirked a smile. "*I'll* be here when *you* wake up."

"If gods will it," he answered.

His thumb swiped her cheekbone.

Then Goren yelped, "Goodbye, Earth!" as Milo disappeared and Relai scrambled for her mask and threw herself on her back in the open pod.

"*Masks on!*" Milo barked again.

Relai called out, "Destination, Tannor?"

"Ah—ah—something called Ligost?"

Ky cursed. "Sweaty armpit of space, okay: the other crew lost this ship in a bet, we sell it as soon as we're out, Tannor, be ready to short everything if we wake to a fight—"

Then the cold hiss of oncoming sleep surrounded Relai, the pod engaged around her body, and a gentle fog overtook her.

Eight weeks, felt like a second.

∘∘●∘∘

IF YOU ENJOYED THIS BOOK, PLEASE LEAVE A REVIEW ON AMAZON, GOODREADS, ETC, AND LET THE AUTHOR KNOW ON TWITTER @ACWESTONWRITES! THANKS!

Our heroes will return in

SHE, THE DEFIANT

*where a wretched hive of scum and villainy holds
our heroes captive in the face of their worst
fears and deepest flaws, a sacrifice is made, and
more is lost than found...*

Find updates on the series, art, cut scenes, and more at
www.sheistheend.com!

Acknowledgements

I owe sincerest thanks to my mother, for those long evening walks listening to endless plotlines; to Michelle and Maëlle, for the initial brainstorming that led to so much more; to Elizabeth, for her inexplicable love and support; to my girls, for the clarity they give when I dream of traveling the stars; to the visionary authors who supported, encouraged, and challenged me, you know who you are; and to my husband, for everything, *everything*.

About the Author

A.C. Weston wrote her first book at the age of seven and hasn't stopped writing since. She grasped onto characters like Meg Murry, Matilda, Princess Leia, and Ellen Ripley at a young age as she learned to navigate the realities of life through the wonder of stories, and lately characters like Furiosa and Rey have also captured her heart. She spends her days supporting the public health of Minnesotans as a data coordinator at the MN Department of Health and her evenings writing and doing freelance art. She is very introverted, which is not the same as being shy. She lives in St. Paul, MN with three brilliant little monster children and one beloved husband.

Made in the USA
San Bernardino, CA
07 March 2018